THE HIGHEST SCIENCE

DOCTOR WHO – THE NEW ADVENTURES

Also available:

THE NEW DOCTOR WHO ADVENTURES

THE HIGHEST SCIENCE

Gareth Roberts

First published in Great Britain in 1993 by
Doctor Who Books
an imprint of Virgin Publishing Ltd
338 Ladbroke Grove
London W10 5AH

Cover illustration by Peter Elson
Typeset by Type Out, Mitcham CR4 2AG
Printed and bound in Great Britain by
Cox & Wyman Ltd, Reading, Berkshire

ISBN 0 426 20377 1

With thanks to Yvonne's cafe and Alan's taxi service.

Contents

Prologue:

My heart stopped as I glanced up from the ruins of the temple of fallen idols. For there above me, etched on to the misty green horizon, towered what I had feared most; the shattered remains of the lost city itself!

There I remained for agonizing hours. Every fibre of my body threw itself back from the sight in horror, but that wretched and deep spirit of discovery that may still signal the end for me at last gained control of my legs and forced me up the mountainside!

What dread secret would I find there? And were it fit to tell, would I remain alive to breathe that awesome truth to any other frail human soul?

An extract from *Being an Account of my Discovery of the Unnamable Secrets of Sakkrat*, Gustaf Urnst.

Published by the Magick Quarterhouse Computer Press, Glastonbury, 2421

1

1:

The Chain is Broken

The planet Vaagon. An isolated Earth colony settled relative year 5665. Its economy is based on the cultivation of large sectors of arable land. It has been invaded by an assault force of Chelonians, a scientifically advanced reptilian race. The remaining colonists have retreated to a large underground shelter. It seems inevitable that the Chelonians will triumph and that the humans will be destroyed.

The planet Evertrin, site of the annual Inner Planets Music Festival, (the latter known colloquially as Ragasteen). The year is 2112. Many hundreds of spectators, mostly youngsters, are massing in convoys on the dusty tracks that lead to the newly constructed stadia. A customized motorspeeder carrying three young men is part of the procession.

The planet Earth. The year is 1993. A passenger train departs from the station that serves as embarkation point for the residents of the suburban settlement known as Chorleywood, in southern England.

These events should have been totally unconnected.

The floor vibrated as motors powered up nearby. The hospital trucks were rolling out.

Jobez was certain that he would be dead within the hour and it would not be an heroic death. The invaders' superiority in battle was proven, and his small band of conscripts was now all that stood between them and the civilian shelters.

Nearby, a former engineer and a former travel agent muttered darkly. Their recriminations matched many of his own. The disarmament paper was passed so easily, and see what happened!

What do these creatures want here? Why won't they talk to us? And, most vehemently, what is the wonderful Ostryn doing for us now?

Jobez glanced back over his shoulder. He saw Ostryn's face, orating soundlessly on the screen that acted as their link to Defence Command. In the stinking hole of the shelters below, how many of the elderly still believed Ostryn's promises? How many of their grandchildren understood that this was to be the end of their unstarted lives? The fine statesman of peacetime had become a fool in time of war. The enemy possessed almighty firepower, strategic genius, and a total lack of mercy. They felt no need to sit around a table with Ostryn. They were able to move in and destroy without compunction.

The alien force had arrived in the Wadii deserts and swept eastward towards the major population centres. The mining townships had fallen first, their final transmissions speaking of unstoppable war machines controlled by non-humanoids. The invaders had not replied to any attempts at contact, friendly or otherwise, but had continued forward on their mission of extermination.

It had taken five days for Defence Command to obtain Ostryn's reluctant approval for a nuclear strike. The blast had destroyed the third largest city on Vaagon — ironically, the capital of the nation Ostryn's own had appeased only months before. The enemy, unscathed, had somehow absorbed the energy released to fuel their continued onslaught.

Evacuation from the capital had begun at dawn. The young men had been ordered to assemble at the shelter's mouth to receive a lecture on the weaponry available. Jobez had watched the civilians struggling with the barrels and bolts, and appreciated the hopelessness of the situation even more acutely.

He waited for the order to engage in the final battle.

First Pilot Jinkwa saw three parasites enter the range of the forward screen. He gave the order to open fire.

The expressions on the faces of humans as they died were ridiculous. How could the dangerous fools of the Respect For Life Brigade seriously protest that such creatures possessed anything but the slightest intelligence? They entered open battle

3

virtually unprotected. Chatter fluttered meaninglessly between them almost constantly. Most stupidly of all, they killed one another — an action that had convinced biologists back on Chelonia that nature had realized her error in creating them, and had thus bred self-destruction into their breeding pattern. Reclamation of feeding lands from this infestation was not only morally justified, it was an evolutionary imperative.

The young soldier situated at the gunport next to Jinkwa alerted him to a flashing red light on the communications panel. The area ahead seemed to be clear of parasites for the moment, so Jinkwa opened up a response channel.

The distinguished features of General Fakrid appeared on the panel. His lively green eyes darted happily from side to side as he munched on a leaf from his personal crop, which sprouted from the soil sample on the panel before him.

'Well met, First Pilot,' he began. 'The sensornet reports that the undercity ahead is the last refuge of the parasites. The operation has been a complete success. Losses nil, damage to potential feeding lands very small. A credit to you, Jinkwa.'

'Many thanks, General,' Jinkwa replied. 'However, I would recommend the deployment of plague pellets to extinguish any stray parasites after the undercity is taken out. I've just picked off three stragglers myself.'

'Naturally, naturally. Standard procedure. For myself, I can't wait to stretch my legs on some decent greenery.' He patted the console before him with affection. 'I'm tied to this old thing as much as the next fellow, but, well, I noticed some tasty looking species growing in the pastures to the west, and I'm keen to be getting down to — assessing them.' He tipped Jinkwa a knowing wink. 'For the official records, of course.'

'Of course, sir,' the First Pilot replied with a smile. 'And with your gestation cycle nearly complete, there'll be another reason for you reaching pastureland soon.'

Jinkwa knew that Fakrid was enormously proud of his record number of pregnancies in action, and a respectful reminder of the latest would appeal. It would certainly, thought Jinkwa, do no harm to his promotion prospects from First Pilot.

'Indeed, indeed,' said the General. 'My egg cylinder is itching for a lay. Another couple of hours, and I shall seek a nice, moist,

4

muddy patch hereabouts.'

'Only a couple of hours, General?' Jinkwa queried, his hopes rising. 'The clean up operation will take at least another half day, surely? And you'll want to take charge of that.'

'Oh, Jinkwa,' said Fakrid, 'I think we both realize that your moment has come. I can safely rely on you to mop up any parasites left over.' He leant forward. 'Your conduct on this mission has been exemplary, and I will have no hesitation in recommending you for promotion on our return to Chelonia.'

Jinkwa felt his heart beat a little faster against his plastron. His back feet danced excitedly where the General could not see them.

'Thank you, sir. I pledge to carry out my duties as a senior officer in the tradition of your grand example.' He straightened. 'The First Division is now fully prepared for a strike on the undercity.'

'Good fortune, Jinkwa. But I don't anticipate a great deal of difficulty,' Fakrid chuckled.

'I'll see you after the battle, sir,' said Jinkwa. He saw the General reaching forward to break the connection. 'Oh — and sir?'

'Yes?'

'May all your hatchings be happy ones!'

The gunner congratulated Jinkwa on his good news as their tank rolled forward on to the plateau, and the entrance to the parasites' undercity, carved into the grassy mountainside above their empty capital, came into view. Jinkwa swelled with pride. To think — the lowly born family colours of his shell daubed with the red stripe of high command!

The order was given. Jobez and his troops ran to a defensive position on the left of the shelter's mouth. The hillside echoed back the buzz of energy weapons as the alien tanks opened fire, trundling forward on thick rubber treads. Their gunports swept from side to side, spitting fire as pink as the sun. The aliens' disintegrators were sophisticated particle dispersal weapons. The force bolt machine rifles of Jobez and his comrades barely scratched the reinforced coating of their opponents' machines.

Jobez knew for sure it was the end of his life. He began to

contemplate concepts of death, God and the afterworld for the first time since leaving school. At least it would be a quick, clean death, only a second of pain.

The first of his troopers to die, the former travel agent, disappeared in a puff of plasma. Jobez aimed his rifle at the vehicle responsible. He squinted through the sights.

The rifle's auto-guidance view finder should have provided him with information as to the molecular structure of the target, his distance from the target, and the target's speed. From this, the user could gauge the best moment to pull the trigger and loose a round of force bolts.

Through the eyepiece, Jobez saw the enemy vehicles twist and blur, as if a heat haze had sprung up from nowhere. Bright blue lights appeared and began to dance eerily around them.

Am I dead, Jobez wondered. I don't feel mad.

His confusion was shared by Jinkwa. Every instrument aboard his tank had scrambled simultaneously. The gunner tried to patch through a call to the General, but the communications panel failed to respond.

Jinkwa scowled as the image of fleeing parasites on the forward screen began to break up. The tank tipped over. Surely the primitive weaponry of the humans could not produce this effect and it was unthinkable that Chelonian technology could malfunction.

'Sir, this should not be happening!' cried the gunner.

'I am fully aware of that!' he retorted.

The tank shook, and Jinkwa felt sharp edges digging and right angles jutting where they were not wanted. An unpleasant tingle crept over his body. All four of his limbs floundered as the outside world faded illogically out. The last thing he was aware of was a bizarre sensation of toppling over and over, as if the tank were falling from a great height.

But that was impossible.

The blue glow that traced the outline of the invaders' tanks was believed by many of the human soldiers to be the manifestation of an ultimate weapon. Fearing that this was the end, some fell to their knees or prostrated themselves in the mud.

A few minutes later they got to their feet, curious to find out why the noise of battle had ceased, and why they were still alive. Most joined Jobez in his openmouthed appreciation of the scene before them.

The enemy had completely disappeared. The blue lights twinkled away, and only gouges in the ground remained to show that the aliens had ever existed.

Jobez walked forward unsteadily. He felt with great certainty the presence of the God he had called for again after so many years. This place would forever be His shrine.

A red light flashed. Pain surged through Jinkwa's bones as he stretched out a foot to answer the call.

The gunner's still face was picked out by the dim lemon wash of the emergency lighting. At a glance, Jinkwa could tell he was dead. An ignoble end for a fine marksman. Jinkwa made a mental promise to falsify the record of decease.

Fakrid appeared on the communications panel. Jinkwa was both astonished and embarrassed to see that the rear left foot of his commanding officer had been jolted from its harness, leaving the old warrior dangling uncertainly on three feet. A crack in his carapace had been patched up with sealing salve and he had to stretch his long, wrinkled neck to reach the monitor lens. Oh, the indignity of it! Jinkwa knew how painful it must be for the General to be seen by lower ranks in such a helpless position. Truly, this shame would be avenged!

'The Goddess be praised you live, Jinkwa,' said the General. 'Any losses on your side?'

'I have but recently, —' Jinkwa selected the distasteful word, 'woken, sir, and I have not had the opportunity to check with the other units of the First Division. However, I report regretfully that my own gunner is dead.'

Jinkwa was alarmed to see Fakrid recoil in shock. It was more the reaction of an infertile cripple than a decorated officer.

'Oblaza, of the line of Talifar?'

'The same, General.'

'For the honour of Talifar and the glory of the Chelonian race, I'll see the originators of this dishonour drowned in the froth of their own bubbling life juices!'

Spurred on by the General's anger — a more appropriate response — Jinkwa carried out a systems check on his own tank. Many instruments had been damaged beyond repair, but the exit port, the traction motors, and most importantly the disintegrator, were all operational.

'This unit prepared for immediate strike on parasite undercity, sir,' he reported. 'Forward screen disabled. Request rely on computer guidance from your own vehicle.'

'Parasite undercity?' Fakrid queried slowly.

Had the General lost his mind along with his dignity? 'The parasites are massed beneath the mountainside, sir. We must strike now and destroy them!'

'No, Jinkwa,' said the General. 'That is not possible.'

'But the honour of the race demands —'

'You tell me that your forward screen is damaged, First Pilot,' the General said evenly. 'I suggest you emerge from your vehicle and then report back to me with a new strategy.' He broke the connection.

What was the General talking about? Jinkwa recalled the falling sensation he had experienced. Some delusion caused by the parasites' pathetic weapon . . .

His rear right foot punched at the harness disengage control. He was lowered from the control deck to the exit port. It flipped open, and Jinkwa shuffled from the harness webbing, engaged his personal motor, and advanced.

A thick cloud of green gas obscured his vision. A chemical attack? He sniffed at the gas with an experienced olfactor. No. The odour was unpleasant, but harmless enough.

The ground was harder and more uneven than he remembered from their survey of the plateau. That was odd because, like Chelonians, parasites usually chose to dwell in moist, fertile zones. It was what made the little blighters such a nuisance. Odder still was that, but for the whisper of atmospheric conditions, there were no sounds. Even the incessant babble of the parasites had stopped.

Jinkwa pulled himself up to the point of a crag. Here the gas was thinner, but he still chose to enhance his ocular range by a couple of spectra.

The verdant mountain had gone. The entrance to the parasites' undercity had gone, along with the warm pink sun and the clear blue sky. This was night in a completely different area, completely unsuited to Chelonian needs, a barely oxygenated barren plain. Uncomfortably low pressure and the rumble of distant rainstorms accounted for the sparse and unappetizing patches of deciduous twigs.

Jinkwa turned. He saw the tanks of the mighty assault force, dispatched to clear the pasturelands of Vaagon from infestation, tossed in a muddled heap below. Soldiers emerged from their tanks and stared about in puzzlement.

Fakrid's red stripe appeared from the command vehicle. Jinkwa slipped down from the crag and crabbed over to the General.

'Some other part of the planet, sir,' he rationalized. 'But how?'

'Not so, Jinkwa,' the General replied, offering him a leaf from the stalk clasped between his teeth. Jinkwa accepted and chewed thoughtfully as Fakrid continued.

'A full sensor sweep of this place is prohibited by the same electrical interference experienced in the attack.' He nodded up at the sky. 'Those rumblesome storms are not enough to confuse the sensornet. Something else is responsible.

'But what we can be certain of is that this is not the planet we were sent to clear. Certainly, no inhospitable areas such as this were charted on the initial flypast.'

The two officers stared into the bleak green wilderness.

'So where is this?' asked Jinkwa. 'And how in Faf were we brought here?'

He watched as Fakrid circled slowly about, dragging on his damaged limb.

'We will discover that when we move out,' the General replied. 'I have already sent out patrols to chart the area. I do not believe this to be the work of laggard vermin. We will find the enemy who brought us to this place and crush them. We will sterilize this lump of rotten rock, reassemble the ship, and return in triumph to Chelonia!'

The Shrine of Holy Deliverance became one of the most popular tourist attractions on Vaagon. Ostryn was swept from power

9

as easily as Jobez was swept into it. A weapons research and development programme of unparallelled scale was initiated, and the capital remained the centre of power, politics, and the new religion.

Several generations later, the Priest King, Jobez's great-great-grandson, stood at the head of a mighty army assembled to confront another alien force that had arrived in the Wadii deserts. The people were confident of another miracle and waited for the return of the blue lights spoken of in their histories.

Nothing happened, and the Chelonian assault force extinguished all parasites on the planet and settled down to some determined grazing.

Undercover agents of the prohibited Respect For Life Brigade were among the settlers. Their excavations at the planet's cities served merely to reinforce the consensus of prejudice against humans. The poor, trusting creatures had foolishly invented a protective deity to explain the mysterious disappearance of the first mission, which offered no protection to them against the second.

The strange events of the original mission lived on in a different way. The story of the fearsome General Fakrid and his men, who disappeared in an instant never to return, blossomed into an oral legend repeated by generations of mothers to their hatchlings.

It had been three nights now. Three nights since their abduction from the convoy.

Sendei returned from more fruitless explorations to find Jab Molassi by the motorspeeder, sharpening the blade of his knife with a flaky green flint. His ugly face and long, dirty yellow hair were outlined in the light of a fire.

'You said there was no matchwood left, Molassi. How come the fire?'

Molassi said nothing, but a spark of resentment appeared in his blank eyes.

'Molassi!'

Still silence.

'Hey, Molassi! How did you make the fire?'

'Wild boy,' drawled Molassi in his faked old time American

accent. 'You're a wild boy . . . '

'Tell me, Molassi,' Sendei continued. 'Tell me what you've thrown on to there!'

'Paper. Plenty of paper.' He smirked. 'Clever, ain't ya, clever boy?'

'What paper? We've nothing left.'

'No paper, no.' He leant forward and spat proudly. 'Nothing but clever boy's books locked away where we can't find 'em.'

'You've been searching my things, you filthy —'

Molassi leapt up and threw himself at Sendei. One hand shook him by the throat. The other held the tip of his knife to the boy's heart.

'I'm clean, boy,' he whispered. 'I'm clean, I'm hiding nothing away. But then, I'm not as clever as you, am I, clever boy?'

'Put the knife away, Molassi,' Sendei pleaded, as calmly as he was able. 'Put it away. I'm sorry.'

'I'll cut your pretty face, clever boy!' Molassi shouted. He kicked Sendei's legs from beneath him.

Molassi returned the knife to its sheath on his belt. 'Don't push it,' he warned.

He strode arrogantly back to the fire, rolled, lit, and dragged on a cigarette, adjusted his headband, and picked up his diamond studded guitar. Painted fingernails strummed aimlessly at the strings. The inbuilt amp howled feedback in protest.

Sendei's sobs echoed around the dustbowl with the storms.

Molassi was interrupted by a whooping cry in the distance.

Rodomonte appeared through the green mists, his arrival betrayed as ever by his jangling chains and bells, emblems of the freakster.

'Trash the singer, trash the song!' he yelled, and took a swig from a pink metal can.

He noticed Sendei lying face down on the rock. 'Hey, what's up with shortie?'

Sendei rolled over. Rodomonte was worse than ever. His eyes were now rimmed black, the characteristic of A aftershock.

'C'mon, spill the beans,' he said.

'Getting too clever,' Molassi growled and began to strum again.

How Sendei wished he could wrap the guitar around Molassi's

neck. Instead, he said, 'Nothing, it's nothing,' and tried to hide his tears.

Rodomonte barely seemed to be aware of him, let alone his distressed condition. 'Listen, boy, grab this and smile, yeah?' he urged, and wrapped Sendei's hand around another can he had pulled from his shoulder bag.

Sendei disliked the taste, but thirst engendered by the dry atmosphere forced him to take a sip. 'Sweet,' he said appreciatively.

'Sweet,' Rodomonte agreed, pulling the ring from another can. 'Sweet and neat. Guess what I saw out there tonight, boys?'

Molassi twanged a disrespectful chord. 'Tell us what you saw, sir.'

Rodomonte started to giggle. Sendei hated his giggling. His heavy jowls would shake and a cowlick of thick black hair would flop down to cover his eyes.

'I saw a ... ' He collapsed with laughter and nearly fell into the fire, as if some invisible being were tickling him. 'I saw a great big tortoise thing!'

'Sure, Rodo,' Sendei scoffed, taking another gulp from the can. 'Sure you did.'

'So guess what I did?' he gasped between spasms.

Malice flashed across Molassi's face. 'Funny man, funny man, tell us what you did, funny man, sir.'

'I threw it down a drink!' Rodomonte snorted. 'And it ate the whole can!'

Molassi began to play and sing loudly to shut out their noise from his private world. The lyrics were not his own. In fact, this was his favourite number from Zagrat's classic concept discod, *Sheer Event Shift:*

> Got me out of reality
> Hounded by wolves of transcendentality
> Sucked out through the door by a flashing blue light
> Struck out at the clever boy who said he was right
>
> Got me in nowhere at the end of the road
> Weirdo in the hat speaking secret code
> By the roadside at the ruin saw a pretty lady crying
> The rocks fall down below hear the cries of the dying

Molassi plucked at the strings with hopeless inadequacy in emulation of the solo that followed the opening stanza. Rodomonte lay convulsed with cheerless laughter on the other side of the fire.

Sendei had spent much of the three days they had been on the planet regretting his decision to drop out from the Seminary and pal up with Rodo and his dumb friend for the journey to Ragasteen '12. Here was his chance to do something about it.

He ran over to the motorspeeder, clambered into the driving position and tried to focus on the dashboard in the darkness. The ignition sequence looked even more complex than usual.

His skull shook. His toes curled and numbed. Cramp surged up his legs and he slumped forward, his nose bumping against the steering wheel. The can fell from his grasp and pink foam fizzed up over the leather seat cover.

Sendei's eyes remained open.

Mr Peploe glanced at his watch again and sighed. The platform clock at Rickmansworth station had stopped some months ago, one unexceptional ten past three.

Mr Peploe considered himself to be the exception to the rule that one gains tolerance with age. For nearly twenty years he had been subjected to the eccentricities of London Regional Transport, yet he still retained the capacity to be enraged, and sometimes even surprised, by new variations on the basic theme of delay and discomfort. His physical reactions ranged from uncomfortable shuffle (points failure), through uncomfortable shuffle, cough and sigh (points failure, signalling problem), to uncomfortable shuffle, cough, sigh and rustle of newspaper (points failure, signalling problem, passenger on the line at Chalfont and Latimer). What made this morning's incompetence all the more irritating was that his in-tray was presently piled high after one of management's periodic brainstorms. Life in the dimmer switch business wasn't all plain sailing.

According to an announcement made by the pottering guard from the strange little room next to the gents, the train had left Chorleywood station over ten minutes ago.

So where is it now, screamed the vengeful demon that lurked behind Mr Peploe's respectable exterior.

From his proprietary perch on the edge of the platform, at the exact spot where the doors of 'his' carriage always opened, Mr Peploe cast his suspicious gaze over the unsavoury specimens about him. Was he getting older, or were newspaper headlines becoming even more ridiculous recently? *Daisy the windsurfing duck goes completely quackers*, *How did those bananas get into my chimney stack asks stunning Stacy*, and *Space aliens turned my daughter into a red pepper* were all on offer this morning. How people had the nerve to read such rubbish in public, and why they always maintained such expressions of solemn composure while doing so, was a constant mystery to Mr Peploe. UFOs, corn circles and inexplicable disappearances had become the daily diet of the tabloids and it seemed to be getting more extreme by the day.

He had just begun to contemplate the slow death of a London Regional Transport employee, his most calming pastime on occasions such as this, when he heard the points shifting on the track.

At last, he thought with a sigh. He waited for the doors to arrive before him.

Oh, they had really done it this time! Several people on the platform, partners in suffering whom Mr Peploe had known for years but had never spoken to, actually went to the extreme lengths of tutting and groaning as just one carriage hauled itself painfully up alongside them.

This was too much for Mr Peploe. Twenty years of simmering resentment finally bubbled over. He stalked stiffly over to the pottering guard, who had emerged from the strange little room next to the gents.

'I think we deserve some sort of explanation,' he blustered.

'Yes, I think we all do, sir,' replied the guard, whose infuriating burr matched the rhythm of his movement.

'Well?' Mr Peploe demanded. 'Well?'

'There's no need to alarm yourself, sir.'

'What is going on?' screeched Mr Peploe. He was aware that two young secretaries were giggling at him. Stupid girls.

'All I know, sir, is what they've rung down from Chorleywood. The driver of this train has arrived here towing one carriage. Ten others are standing on the track back there.'

'So?'

'There are twelve carriages on the semi-fast Aldgate service, sir. One of them has, er, gone.' The guard pottered off to consult the train driver, who had emerged, scratching his head in bewilderment, from his cabin.

Mr Peploe gave a deep sigh. The loss of an entire carriage! New depths of uselessness had been plumbed.

Aware that he was attracting attention, something he had always destested in others, Mr Peploe sank on to a bench and opened his newspaper. More delay, more frustration, on today of all days! How could they possibly lose a carriage on the track? Probably rolled off into a siding somewhere.

The headline on the front page of his *Daily Mail* read:
SHREWSBURY SHOWERED BY SARDINES
Scientists Baffled
Unnoticed by everybody, the platform clock started working again. Its batteries had been recharged by a sudden surge of electricity.

Jinkwa checked the fluctuation registered by the sensornet for the third time. The high level of electrical activity had blotted out many of the machine's more sensitive functions, but there was no mistaking what it had just reported. He asked to be directed to the General. A young officer led him through the dull morning air to Fakrid, who was suspended over a clear plastic hatching bubble broken out from stores when it became apparent that no suitable pasture could be found in the area.

'Sir, important news,' Jinkwa began eagerly.

The General was grunting in pain. 'I'm sorry, sir, I'll return at a more opportune moment —'

'Make your report, First Pilot,' Fakrid snapped irritably. 'Do you think a man of my experience is unaccustomed to labour pains?'

'Forgive me, sir. The sensornet has registered an increase in electrical activity nearby.'

'Excellent, excellent,' the General enthused. He let out a cry as, with one final strain, a cascade of eggs plopped from the flattened rear of his carapace into the mud that lined the bottom of his hatching unit.

Jinkwa started forward. Every one of the eggs was twisted and broken.

Fakrid mistook his reaction. 'The miracle of life, First Pilot,' he cackled. 'Never seen a newly laid egg before?'

He noted Jinkwa's shocked expression and swung himself about to examine the eggs. Through the cracks in the thin white coating tiny, deformed Chelonian embryos sprouted, stillborn.

'My babies!' roared Fakrid. 'My beautiful babies!'

Jinkwa took a step back as Fakrid climbed down from the hatching unit and dropped on to the hard ground. A look he had never seen there before came into Fakrid's eyes.

'Mobilize the Second Division,' he ordered. 'Their mission: to trace the source of the electrical disturbance and neutralize it. The enemy will regret the day they tore the womb of the greatest living warrior of the Chelonian race!'

2:

Behold Sakkrat

The traffic that clustered and clogged the spaceways at the centre of the galaxy, where life was fun and there was money to be made, never turned its attentions to the stars beyond Lasty's Nebula. Like so many of the outlying zones of the spiral, it had been renamed after an obscure scientist who had died in poverty. Lasty had not realized that exploration came a poor second to exploitation in the minds of the decision makers aboard the first colony ships. And there was very little to exploit in the area he had gone to chart.

Over the centuries, the Earth colonists who had swarmed out into the hub of the galaxy stratified into the predictable pattern of the tremendously rich and powerful, the hopelessly poor and worthless, and the great middling mass of citizenship content to pass their lives away in shopping malls and public bars. This distant edge of the galaxy went unnoticed by them all. No intelligent life had ever been found there, so even naturalists had found little to amuse or interest them. Eventually, the scientific and commercial imperatives had led to the abandonment of any attempts to journey past the outer settlements. The peoples of the galaxy turned their backs on this unwanted, uninteresting plot of nothingness. They were not to know that, by doing so, they were passing up the chance to discover the answer to one of the most mysterious of the universe's mysteries.

This being the case, there was nobody about one ordinary day in 2680 to see the tubby but functional shape of a Kezzivot Class F61 transporter carrier ploughing a purposeful course on the far side of Lasty's Nebula. These were the final hours of its long journey to a particular planet among the thousands. The ship had been bolted together many systems away at the centre

17

of industralized space, but its creators at Kezzivot would never have anticipated that an F61 would, or indeed could, be used for interstellar travel. In fact, the engineering tolerance of this particular vehicle had been exceeded on many occasions, and its destruction averted only by the addition of various features that were not part of the original design. One such addition sat as comfortably as it could on the flight deck, contentedly gurgling to itself.

The ridiculously inferior onboard computer chattered back with confirmation of navigational data. It was incapable of original thought and obviously saw the completion of their task in much the same way as any other end of program. By contrast, the Cell quivered with anticipation. The journey was over. Beneath was Sakkrat, the lost planet!

The Cell did not care that its master's whim had been indulged. What mattered was that the task it had been stolen to complete was over and it would surely now be allowed to die. It had long ago abandoned its attempts to correct its mistakes, and the decision to develop senses had been the worst of these. Every time it consulted the computer, the Cell's feeble external organs flinched in agony and its roots quivered with the shock. Most irritating of all, it had never figured out how to scream.

As a navigator, it had more than proved its worth. Sifting through reams of data, it had taken the ship halfway around the galaxy in search of its goal. The stellar conjunctions at Naiad; the crystal quasars of Menolot; the furthest reaches of Harma; all had been investigated in the quest for possible clues. Friendly passers by had been hailed with an automated greeting of goodwill. Aggressors had been blasted away by cunningly concealed cellular disrupters. In short, it had done well and expected to be rewarded for it.

The Cell ordered the computer to initiate the final stages of the program. Full life supporting atmosphere was recycled. Lights flickered on around the ship. The instruction was given to unpack the crew. A brief comparison between the manifest records and an instantaneously supplied medical scan showed that all four unfortunates were in a reasonable enough condition after nearly three hundred years of sleep.

Electrical impulses revived the humans, and tiny nozzles attached to their sleep cabinets sprayed life restoring chemicals over their bodies. The Cell waited impatiently to be disconnected and to know peace.

Sensor pods on the ship's hull swept the surface of the approaching planet. A shifting electrical aura blotted out full details of Sakkrat's topography and geology. The pods reconfigured scan criteria to break the static shroud and were able to pinpoint a momentary surge in one particular area.

The dead were interred with full military honours. White grave markers had been erected and prayers offered up to the Goddess. The stirring strains of the Chelonian anthem echoed mournfully from the bugle of the Third Pilot.

A third of Jinkwa's left eye studied Fakrid. He was staring directly at the patch of ground where the ashes of his broken eggs — cremated, as was the practice for the children of an officer — had been scattered. As part of his training, Jinkwa had been taught of the General's monumental achievements. He had led missions to clear infestations on over forty worlds and it was truly an honour to serve under him. Now both his unblemished service record, and the motherhood that complemented it, had been taken from him. The miscarriage appeared to have transformed Fakrid's good humoured determination into pure rage at his impotence in the face of their unseen enemies.

A warbling call sign interrupted the anthem. Jinkwa stifled it hurriedly and moved a respectful distance away from the other officers to answer it.

'First Pilot speaking. Report.'

'A message from the Second Division, sir. They'd like to speak to an officer. Will you take it, sir?'

'I'll be right over. Jinkwa out.'

Jinkwa whispered his apologies to Fakrid and motored back to the area where the communications equipment had been unloaded. The Second Pilot would hopefully bring news of their opponents and a battle plan could be formulated. Such a development would undoubtedly restore the General's spirits.

Rodomonte stamped on the empty can and cut his foot where the sole of his shoe had worn away. He was too far away to make it back this time. None of the rocks about here looked familiar and his shoulder bag was now empty of supplies. He threw it away impatiently. At least the weird noises in the distance had stopped now.

The others had believed him to be hallucinating about the giant tortoise. Rodomonte had more experience of such things than either Molassi or Sendei, and he could easily tell the difference between a flashback and reality. There were periods, during his worst lows, when Rodomonte tried to convince himself that their mysterious abduction to this planet was but a hallucination, and that when the cramp finally eased and the burning round the back of his neck had stopped, he could get some sleep again and wake up feeling good on the chair outside his uncle's farmhouse. Then his Ma would fix him some breakfast and everything would be all right again.

Despite his tiredness, Rodomonte had not slept for four days now. Not since the night when the 'speeder had been moved on from the drive-in burgerdome. The night before the Ragasteen Festival was due to open. The night before the day when a girl from the next motor back on the convoy had screamed and pointed at them, blue twinkling lights had dazzled them, and they were suddenly elsewhere. Here.

The noises began again.

Seventeen black tanks rolling on thick rubber treads trundled into the valley below him. In their wake came two more giant tortoises, moving at a speed much faster than Rodomonte would have believed possible. Each had four limbs which rowed swiftly and mechanically back and forth to propel them forwards. They were talking to each other, but the words were lost to him in the roar of the tanks' passage.

This was no flashback. Those monsters were for real. Rodomonte closed his eyes. He did not feel afraid, or even surprised. He had not really felt anything since his first sip from the pink cans. Not even when the swamp devil had wrapped its tentacles around his throat.

He started thinking about firecrackers, and couldn't work out why. He opened his eyes. It all seemed so far away.

Metre wide black globules were showering the area, as if the perpetually threatening storm clouds had finally broken. This was not rain. When the black globules struck any surface they broke into colour like the firecrackers people let off on Victory Night. The indiscriminate shower continued until one of them hit a tank. It exploded with the most amazing colours, several of which he didn't even recognize. Rodomonte wondered if Zagrat's renowned lightshow would have compared to this.

He was too far out now. Panic, more than the fragments of shrapnel that blew up from the second globule to reach its target, sent Rodomonte scrambling away again. The cramp returned.

He felt that he had run for miles before he finally collapsed in agony. Black rimmed eyes stared up at the shifting, crackling green clouds. Pink vomit dribbled from his nostrils. A stitch coursed round his stomach.

He dragged himself up and stumbled on.

Rosheen was certain that she had been dead, but the memory of the afterlife had faded like a waking dream. Now she was back to the business of life, of making decisions. She recalled the circulation exercises displayed in the manual stolen along with the sleep system, and was pleased to discover them working as she wiggled her toes and fingers experimentally.

A few minutes later she climbed confidently from the cabinet, still dressed in the light blue chemise and matching trousers she had chosen from the L'Arrange boutique several hundred years before. There was a task to perform.

So this was the end of the journey; a development that raised many questions in itself. As Rosheen left the tiny cabin that had been assigned to her, she wondered if Sheldukher had woken and revived them, or if that thing on the flight deck had miscalculated. She did not for a moment entertain the possibility that the insane ambition of her 'master' had been realized.

Klift opened his eyes. A face was staring down at him. A familiar face. Hard eyes, sharp nose, dark hair tousled out of its stylish cut. It was Rosheen. They were alive again.

To his horror, Klift found that he couldn't move.

'Don't try to move or speak just yet.' Rosheen hoped that

21

she had not looked so fragile on waking. This was the first time she had seen Klift so helpless. She didn't like it.

'I think Postine is dead,' Klift heard her say. Straight to the point as ever.

He struggled to articulate, against her advice. 'How long,' he croaked, 'have we slept?'

'We should be able to find that out from the computer.' She sighed and bit her lip, staring into the past. 'But one of my last orders from Sheldukher was to isolate its response to his fingerprints alone.'

Klift clambered more than a little unsteadily from the cabinet. He still appeared dazed and had difficulty standing alone. To Rosheen he seemed paler and thinner than before.

'Now,' she continued, 'we need only reroute a subcommand channel to free it, but we'll have to wait until he's out of the picture.'

Klift stared blankly at her, then reeled back and clutched at the cabinet for support.

'Get yourself together,' she snapped. 'We've got work to do.'

She turned away and strode from the cabin. She felt considerably more anxious than she looked. The sleep process had changed Klift from the arrogant young man who had defied Sheldukher on their first meeting. If he had been anybody else, she would have abandoned him. Their relationship made this impossible. At least, she thought it did.

She felt vulnerable for the first time in years. In centuries, even.

The Cell heard its first sound apart from the rumble of the ship's drive. It snapped open its eyes. Ah, humans! Killers!

'For a woman like Postine to die like that,' Rosheen sighed. 'Survived seventeen major conflicts on the front line and got trapped in a dodgy sleep cabinet.'

On her way to wake Klift she had checked on the third of Sheldukher's reluctant passengers and seen her battle scarred features twisted by a frozen scream.

'She didn't wake, did she?' Klift queried nervously.

'From the expression on her face, I'd say she had,' Rosheen replied.

22

She noted with irritation that the big screen was shuttered down. Without the computer there was no other way to discover their current whereabouts.

A gurgle issued from the dark corner of the flight deck that housed the navigation console. A look passed between them. Klift edged over cautiously.

He leapt back, sickened by the sight of the creature housed under the clear plastic bubble that had been grafted on to the console. Perversely, Rosheen was glad to see him react with genuine emotion. Perhaps he might recover, after all.

Where once they had watched Sheldukher place a tiny red phial, the spoils from their raid on the gene labs of Checkley's World, a monstrosity had evolved.

Or was it three monstrosities tacked together? On one side, it had obviously attempted to sprout some sort of head but had missed out on vital details like a nose and hair. The other side of its top half was a purple, crystalline structure that jutted up in irregular peaks. Most horrifically, the creature's central body, if it could be called that, was a mass of raw grey brain tissue from which flopped tiny, twisted organs and spreading, bark encrusted roots. As Rosheen approached, the Cell sizzled and crackled like an animated rasher of bacon. It would have given them no consolation to know that it found them equally disgusting.

Klift feared that the creature might somehow smash the dome and spring for their throats. 'Can it see us or hear us, do you think?'

Rosheen felt her throat going dry as she looked into the bubble. 'The gene strain in the phial was encoded to create pure, self supporting intelligence,' she reminded him, as dispassionately as possible. 'Even the scientists on Checkley's World would have killed it. Sheldukher has kept it alive. Maybe for hundreds of years.'

They started in shock as the Cell spoke. Its voice came from the tiny purple slit between its eyes that served as a mouth. Its speech was as unpleasant as its appearance. It was the screech of a fingernail scraped along a blackboard.

'I can ... feel ... everything ... perfectly well ... thank ... you ... ' Good, it thought. I'll die even happier knowing that I managed vocalization on the first attempt.

'Did you complete the program?' Rosheen asked anxiously. Unpleasant though it might be to converse with this abomination, it could provide vital information. Surely Sheldukher could not have anticipated that the Cell would acquire the power of speech?

'I . . . thought about it . . . ' it rasped painfully. 'I . . . grew the . . . way I thought would be best . . . A combination, if you . . . like . . . Extra . . . efficiency . . . I thought . . . ' Its limbs twitched horribly.

'Of course,' said Rosheen. 'Animal, vegetable, mineral.'

'The perfect life form . . . I thought . . . '

'I think you thought wrong.'

'I . . . read the program . . . I . . . went the best way . . . about things . . . I . . . took this ship . . . halfway . . . round the galaxy . . . searching . . . '

It went through all the information Sheldukher entered into the data core, thought Rosheen. It believes in all his Sakkrat nonsense.

The Cell spoke again. 'All possibilities were . . . considered . . . many areas . . . covered . . . program completed!'

The shutters over the screen snapped open. Rosheen and Klift turned at the sharp crack of operational machinery, fearing that Sheldukher had somehow revived ahead of their expectations. But the Cell had opened the shutters through its link to the computer.

The ship was approaching an enormous dull green planet with dense cloud cover. That suggested life.

The Cell croaked two words. 'Behold Sakkrat!'

'Sakkrat!'

Rosheen was alarmed by Klift's reaction. 'It could be anywhere,' she reminded him dismissively. She didn't recognize any of the stellar formations visible behind the planet. It was going to be a long journey back to civilization.

'We must explore it,' Klift replied weakly, 'whatever's down there. We have a ship, we can get back.'

'We won't have a ship if we don't put a move on,' she scolded. 'Another hour and Sheldukher's up.' She was already moving back into the main body of the ship.

Unlike the old sleep cabinets his unwilling crew had slept in, and which had cost Postine her life, Sheldukher had been freeze dried in a cryogenic capsule stored near the drive chamber at the rear of the ship. The environment of the capsule was protected by a separate, inbuilt computer. A computer Rosheen had reprogrammed surreptitiously, shortly after the attack on the gene labs, to delay the revival of its occupant for over an hour after the ship's computer gave the order to defrost him.

Klift was about to follow her from the flight deck when there was a furious movement beneath the bubble. The Cell thrashed wildly from side to side.

'Kill me, killer!' it spat. 'Kill me now . . . Program ended . . . end the Cell . . . It hurts . . . '

Klift was more accustomed to cries for mercy than suicidal bleatings. The Cell's request both sickened and distressed him. He hurried out after Rosheen.

Visual linkage was impossible through the electrical surge that the Second Division had been sent to investigate. Now the voice of the Second Pilot was being drowned out by the wash of atmospherics.

'Report, Second Pilot!' snarled Jinkwa. 'Report!'

' . . . enemy retaliating . . . enemy are retaliating . . . '

'Second Pilot!' Jinkwa shouted into the microphone. 'Report the success of your attack immediately!'

' . . . this division is lost . . . '

Jinkwa knew the Second Pilot well. He was the latest in the line of a noble family whose deeds filled many pages of the military histories. To hear him squawk like a parasite was truly alarming. What was going on?

'Report! Describe enemy forces!'

' . . . division lost . . . eight twelves . . . '

The line went dead. Jinkwa knew that the Second Pilot was gone. Anger filled his heart. He released a coolant chemical into his shell to soothe himself.

'Give me that,' snapped a gruff voice behind him. Unquestioningly, Jinkwa passed the microphone to the General as he shuffled up.

25

'Second Pilot. Fakrid speaking. Report.'

There was no response.

Jinkwa formulated unfamiliar words. 'Second Division lost, sir.'

Fakrid's yellow stare turned full on him. 'A jest,' he said threateningly.

'No, sir,' was all Jinkwa could say.

'No mention will be made of this on our return.' The General spoke calmly but his shell was shaking. 'The Second Wing of the ship will be classified as having been lost in a rockstorm, or somesuch. And our glorious victory over the evil creatures on this planet will become the greatest triumph in our history!'

He altered the setting on the microphone, so as to address every soldier in the assault force. His voice blared from every speaker in every tank.

'Troopers! By the powers invested in me under the military emergencies statutes, I, General Fakrid of the noble lineage of Nazmir, hereby declare war on all inhabitants of this planet. Sterilization will now begin. I will lead the charge on the enemy stronghold. All patrols are recalled! Prepare to mobilize! Fakrid out!'

The General turned back to Jinkwa. Already he could see well trained soldiers making preparations to move out.

'General,' began Jinkwa, 'if these eight twelves can destroy an entire division . . . '

'Yes?' Fakrid demanded.

'To confront them will surely mean . . . ' he stammered, and shook his head. He didn't understand what he was talking about himself.

'We are Chelonians, Jinkwa!' bawled Fakrid. 'We will confront and destroy the eight twelves, and I —' he gasped for breath. 'I will rip this planet apart with my four bare limbs! To your post, First Pilot!'

Properly equipped with a toolkit, Rosheen could have scrambled the codes protecting the cryogenic capsule within minutes. Without one, she had to confuse the input panel sufficiently for it to allow her access to the final details of the environment program, and it was taking time. In the last few hours of her

26

previous existence, Rosheen had taken her one brief opportunity to delay Sheldukher. Now she had the chance to kill him and she wasn't going to let it go. When the mathematical safety standard codes flashed up onto the tiny screen above the panel, she realized this was going to be as much of a challenge as any of the complex stratagems she and Klift had used to devise to amuse one another.

Not that Klift had ever been the complex one, the mind. The reputation that had attracted Sheldukher to recruit him was based on the fraud inspired and, if the truth were known, mostly executed by this woman, his assistant. A woman with no official existence.

To gain a position at McDrone Systems, Rosheen had created a new identity for herself, casually erasing the original with its convictions for minor electronic crimes committed in her careless teens. Her entrance examination score of ninety-four per cent had guaranteed her a place alongside Klift in the research unit, testing out new systems and devising applications for the theories they suggested. Rosheen's outstanding achievements had attracted the commendation of company heads — an irritation, because she had been making deliberate mistakes to allay suspicion. In Klift she had found not only a stimulating scientific mind with operational talents almost equal to her own, but a ruthless passion that made him her ideal partner.

The crime they had committed cost the lives of millions, left to starve after the collapse of the central markets when the first enormous, untraceable sum had been lifted. Inevitably, the police had become interested in the new found wealth of two laboratory technicians at a small systems house, and Rosheen and Klift had been forced to 'emigrate' to the North Gate.

For a couple of years their easy life had continued. They had luxuriated among the richest and most influential people in the galaxy and continued, purely for the principle of scientific advancement, the research that had made them their wealth. The police could not touch them and they had anticipated no trouble from their equally nefarious neighbours.

One evening, the sky over their swimming pool had been blotted out by the huge shadow of a greasy old transporter carrier. It had then touched down just outside their ornamental maze.

Sheldukher had been aboard. The genuine article, not one of the many who impersonated him to lend credence to their own squalid dealings. He had threatened to destroy the next planet along the Gate if they did not surrender themselves to him. That didn't concern Rosheen and Klift, but their rich neighbours had been easily intimidated by Sheldukher, the very man whose name they used to frighten their children to sleep, and they had turned them over at gunpoint after a fierce struggle. Sheldukher had destroyed the next planet anyway, out of irritation at having been kept waiting for an hour and a half.

Rosheen became aware that Klift was standing beside her. To her extreme annoyance he started to talk as she worked, something else he had never done before.

'That thing — on the flight deck —'

'What about it?'

'I think we should kill it.'

Rosheen stopped working for a moment. 'That cell is unique. It's worth millions.'

He laughed nervously. 'We didn't ever need money.'

'We don't know how long we've been out. For all we know, our credit rating could be worthless now, even if we could get back to a system served by the central markets. If the central markets still exist.' Her irritation was growing. The old Klift would have known this, would have thought. She returned to the panel.

A few minutes later the way through the devious tangle of misinformation was all but clear. Soon she would gain access to the environment program and put the maniac out of his misery.

'I still think we ought to kill it,' whinged Klift.

Rosheen was about to order him from the room when a new and unbelievable display presented itself on the screen. It told her that the capsule was empty.

'Klift . . . ' she began.

They heard the soft fall of footsteps from the companionway outside. Sheldukher entered the room.

Despite being the most wanted criminal in the galaxy, Sheldukher's talent for disappearing from the scene of his atrocities was such that no two law enforcement agencies could agree on a description and rumours abounded as to his appearance from system to system. Rosheen's criminal ambitions stretched only to money making, with the occasional necessity of murder, and the notion of somebody who wiped out entire systems for kicks, particularly this little man, seemed risible. Perhaps she had spent too long on the North Gate in the company of flamboyant exiles to understand how the most notorious of felons could be so insignificant looking. Certainly she now realized that somebody so intelligent, resourceful and mad, simply didn't need to mouth threats all the time.

'I anticipated this,' he said softly, without a hint of irony or anger. 'Treachery is something I have considerably more experience of and, dare I say, more aptitude in than yourselves.'

He smiled. 'Congratulations, Rosheen. But I noticed you fiddling with the capsule after we left the gene labs. It wasn't difficult to reverse what you had done. Not up to your usual standards at all. I take it you were rushing?'

Rosheen said nothing.

'No,' he continued, 'as part of the original program I was woken two hours before anybody else. I would have come to greet you earlier, but I've been busy checking the drives. Priorities and all that.'

Rosheen noticed that there was a flat black square clasped in his hand.

'I've no feelings against either of you personally, believe me,' he said. 'When half the inhabited worlds are out to get you, incidents like this are all too common.'

'But,' he went on, almost regretfully, 'I have invested considerable effort and expenditure in this project, and I will not allow its success to be jeopardized by the unreliability of individuals.'

Rosheen deeply resented the fact that she was about to meet her death at the hands of a man who had defeated her on her own ground.

'I was last to sleep, if you recall,' he said. 'That gave me another opportunity to ensure your co-operation. You see, I can't afford to lose you, not just yet. If you'd care to examine your left wrists?'

29

Rosheen did as he asked automatically and found a tiny bump under her skin.

Klift had found the same. 'What have you done to us?'

'I injected all three of you with a small unit. It contains a particular chemical. With this,' he tapped the square, 'I can release amounts of that chemical into your bloodstreams. This will have the effect of reacting against the chemical that has kept you so well preserved over the years.'

He could have been conducting a lecture. 'Fascinating, don't you think? It's my organic variation on an anti-preservative developed by farmers on Tayloe. They were flooded by imports on Tayloe.'

He smiled mischievously. 'I think it had something to do with the collapse of the central markets.'

Rosheen was well enough accquainted with Sheldukher to know that when he spoke so casually he was about to do something unpleasant. She took her chance and leapt at him, planning to grab the square and destroy it.

Sheldukher had anticipated her move. Almost before she sprung forward he had turned the square towards Klift and pressed a tiny sensor pad on its side.

In less than a second, Klift aged forty years. He staggered and collapsed.

Sheldukher turned the square on Rosheen. 'I've work to do,' he said, in exactly the same casual manner as before. 'Unpack Postine, will you?'

'Postine is dead,' Rosheen spat. She crouched to examine Klift.

'Not so,' replied Sheldukher. 'I popped in on the Cell on the way here. He is looking well. The computer says Postine stands a fifty three percent chance of coming round. There may be a little tissue damage, but she lives.'

He left the room.

The Cell saw its master returning to the flight deck. Was it now time for death?

'Kill me, Sheldukher . . . please . . . '

Sheldukher had destroyed so much life that the murder of the Cell would have meant little in itself. But it was as much a part of his team as any of the humans, and their exceptional skills guaranteed them all a continued existence until he could be sure he wouldn't need them again.

'Prepare to receive new program,' he ordered.

The Cell sizzled with agitation. 'No no ... the program is ... ended ... mission accomplished ... Behold Sakkrat ... I found it ... for you ... so ... kill me ... '

Sheldukher had not anticipated that the Cell would develop in such a peculiar way. Whilst the growth of sensory organs was a distinct advantage (no need to route commands through the ship's computer), this obsession with its own demise was already proving an irritation. The answer to the problem was clear, however. Pain.

He had found that it was the answer to most of life's problems. For while murder, in all its delicious varieties, was enjoyable enough, it had always been a bit too ... well, final for his tastes. Pain was more fun. When there was nobody else around and he was feeling bored, Sheldukher liked to slash himself across the chest with his little knife. Yes, it was good that the Cell had developed senses. It would now be so much easier to control.

He shorted the contact points between the bubble and the computer repeatedly. The Cell quivered in torment.

Goodness, how this took him back! Back to the first time he had inflicted pain, when the experience had been so fresh and exciting. He had felt happy walking through the crowds in New Boston city centre the next morning, unusually stimulated for a child written off by his tutors as dull and unimaginative. After his seventh birthday the next week, Sheldukher had never looked back.

The educational psychologists assigned to his case had struggled to isolate the root cause of his perversions, and had failed. A stable background, material security and a loving family were not factors renowned for producing psychopaths. What they had overlooked was the factor of boredom. For Sheldukher had quite simply been bored by the mediocrity of life in shopping malls and public bars.

Following the death of his parents in a tragic accident involving a threshing machine, he had left Earth, never to return.

His long quest for things to relieve the tedium had begun. Painful, violent, explosive, funny, gratifying things. It was a quest he had always known would reach its end down there, on Sakkrat.

The Cell gasped and retched, patches of its fleshy side burnt black.

Sheldukher gave the order. 'Prepare the ship for descent spiral.'

Rosheen cradled Klift's sixty-eight year old head in her arms. Sheldukher had destroyed her wealth, her home, and now Klift's mind.

She whispered a promise to herself. 'I'll kill him.'

3:

What's A Nice Girl

The sign on the wall beside her read, *This bar is a fermentation compressor free zone.*

Professor Bernice Summerfield was glad of that. She swished the ice around at the bottom of her third glass of kronka, a curiously named but exquisitely fiery cocktail of cherry brandy, crème de bananas and pure M3 variant, and waited for the man at the bar to stop staring at her. The staring ended, which was good. But then he started to jostle his way through the crowd towards her table, which was bad.

She drained the glass and set it on the table. 'Here goes,' she sighed to herself. 'As I recall, scenario seventeen from *The Everywoman Guide To Hassle Free Space Travel.*'

He indicated the chair opposite her own. 'Free?'

'Unless the translucent species have pushed out this far, yes.'

He laughed and sat down.

It was going to be worse than she'd anticipated. His lack of the grey uniform worn by most of the other men in the bar marked him out as a free trader, which was bad enough. But the tag sewn on to his breast pocket identified him as Kendrick Funass. It was the kind of weird name found only on Van Winkle worlds, where colonists frozen in the first years of interstellar travel had woken to find themselves overtaken by their descendants. Unfortunately, they still carried with them the social mores of a less enlightened age. While the rest of the galaxy had at least attempted to mature out of sexism, Van Winkle colonists had emerged into the galactic community with an impact that had made them notorious. Bernice was shortly to discover that this situation remained much the same in the twenty seventh century as it had been in her own time.

I wish I had a book or a screen to bury my nose in, she thought, instead of actually having to look at this exceptionally

33

ugly young man. Still, that face was nothing a total prosthetic refit couldn't cure.

He began to speak. Bernice guessed that he was going to be a very dull speaker.

She was not wrong. Kendrick Funass launched into a long and rambling account of his recent journey to the harvests on the planet Mang, the appalling catering on year contract haulage flights, and the bumpy docking he had experienced thanks to the malfunction of the Series 9A on the aft wing (which, of course, had only *just* been serviced).

Bernice's contribution to all of this was minimal. Her social face switched to automatic, giving the occasional nod of encouragement or frown of interest. This freed her active mind to compile a top ten of places she wanted the Doctor to take her to.

She became distantly aware that Funass had finished, at least for the moment. Moreover, he had finished on a question that had quite passed her by as she contemplated an evening with Virginia Woolf. She leant forward, cupping her ear. 'I'm sorry?'

'I said, how do you come to be here, then?' he repeated. 'Tell me about yourself,' he added, with blistering insincerity.

Anybody that had ever known Bernice at all well would have recognized the expression that crept over her face at this point. They would have prepared themselves for her to have some fun at the expense of some inexcusably boring associate. Because Bernice had decided to fight back against the tide of tedium unleashed by Funass by telling him, as the Doctor had often warned her not to, the exact truth.

'I arrived by TARDIS, actually,' she said.

'TARDIS?' he puzzled. 'Oh, you mean one of those customized LX44s.'

'I don't, as it happens,' she continued brightly. 'The TARDIS is the creation of the Time Lords, an almost omnipotent, almost immortal race of scholars who have developed the ability to travel through the space-time continuum.'

Funass laughed, as unpleasantly as he had spoken, 'Are you one of these "Time Lords" then, eh, love?'

Bernice smiled. 'No, but I travel with one. And it was him who brought me here in his TARDIS, about, oh let me . . .

About two hundred and thirty years into my future.'

Funass laughed again. It isn't working, thought Bernice. He thinks I'm stringing him along. He was supposed to think I was mad and lose interest. Then again, perhaps he likes the company of mad women? Come to think of it, he'd have to.

'What do you think of it then, eh? The future?'

Bernice looked about and replied honestly. 'From what I've seen so far, the drink is a little dearer, the music a lot louder, and as for the conversation . . . '

He laughed again, his horrible hot minty breath wafting across the table. 'So you don't plan to stick around, then?'

'I don't think so. As soon as my friend —'

'The Time Lord?'

' — the Time Lord, locates his Fortean flicker, I'll be on my way.'

'I get it. Now I'm supposed to say, What's a Fortean flicker, then?'

She smiled again. 'Believe me, I'd be quite happy if you didn't open your mouth again until the crack of infinity.'

He smiled back. Grief, does he still not get the message, she thought. But then, she reflected, that's always the way with boring people. Having never experienced any other reaction, they assume that being yawned at, insulted and walked away from is the norm for human social interaction.

'A Fortean flicker, Mister Funass,' she said, quoting the Doctor, 'is a metaphysical phenomenon. Left unchecked, it could cause irremediable damage to the web of time.'

'You've lost me, darling,' he confessed. (I wish, she thought.) 'TARDIS I can take, Time Lords I can take, but meta-what-nots don't mean anything to me.'

'I was similarly lost until my friend explained,' she said.

'And what was his explanation?'

'Well,' she began, selecting her words carefully to get through to him, 'have you ever come across a word somewhere, or heard a place name for the first time, and then seen it everywhere? Maybe you've punched the wrong code into your communicator and become connected to an old friend you lost touch with years earlier.'

'No,' he admitted, 'but I've heard about it.'

'Nobody can be quite sure how or why,' Bernice continued, now glad to have the chance to sort the Doctor's explanation out in her own mind, 'but it's those same chaotic forces of coincidence that can snowball unpredictably, breaking the links in the chain of causality. And that's a Fortean flicker. It moves things and people − events, if you like − out of place, out of their natural order. In time as well as in space.'

Funass nodded with his customary scepticism. 'Tell me, darling,' he said, supping from the beaker in his hand, 'your mate, the Time Lord, right?'

'Right.'

'He's trying to find this Fortean flicker, yeah?'

'Yes. He's in the TARDIS right now, building a tracking device for that very purpose. I don't like building tracking devices and he doesen't like crowded bars, so we though it best to diverge.'

'Okay. So he finds his flicker. Then what?'

'I'm sorry?'

'Well, what does he do with it then? Knock it on the head?'

Bernice considered a while. Funass had produced, certainly for the first time that evening and, she suspected, probably for the first time in his life, a valid point. She had grown to trust in the Doctor's abilities so much that this problem had simply not occurred to her.

'Maybe,' she replied. 'He tends to reason with things and then knock them on the head. In a roundabout sort of way.'

'Pardon me, darling,' grinned Funass, 'but I'd like to see anyone, even a "Time Lord", knock a coincidence on the head.'

Bernice decided that she'd had enough. She had been looking for an excuse to return to the TARDIS anyhow.

'Then be thankful it's not your problem,' she said. She made to stand up, but Funass clamped his wrist around her right arm.

'Forget your fantasy world, girl. Come over to the docks with me and I'll give you something that'll propel you two hundred and thirty years into the future.'

Bernice reviewed mentally the options for extrication from scenario seventeen of *The Everywoman Guide* and decided that there was only one left open to her. It gave her enormous pleasure to pull back her left arm, form a fist, and then push it forward into a punch that sent Funass sprawling on to the table, which he brought crashing to the floor.

The neighbouring revellers fell into silence. Bernice became the centre of attention, a position that her exceptional skills had often led her to and which she had never shied from. She collected the Doctor's drawstring purse from the table where it had fallen, turned, and walked calmly for the door.

A thought occurred to her. As alcohol was one of the three luxury items she had been unable to find a supply of in the TARDIS (the others being weaponry and duvets), it would be a good idea to stock up for future journeys.

She strode up to the bar. The barman eyed her warily.

'Do you do carry outs?' she asked.

The answer had been yes. A quarter of an hour later, Bernice entered the TARDIS with two plastic carriers.

'I'm not drunk,' she called. 'I'm ever so slightly sloshed, though.'

'I'm not your mother,' chuckled the Doctor. He was in his shirtsleeves, crouched over his now completed tracking device. It had, just over two hours before, been a heap of components dredged up from the TARDIS's dusty stores.

'How was the spaceport, then?'

'A spaceport is a spaceport is a spaceport, I suppose,' she replied, kicking off her shoes. 'I found quite a good bar, though.'

'And your money worries?' he asked absently, his stare fixed on the device's display screen. His rubbery features, which could run up any expression from simpleton to demigod, were locked into a concentrated frown.

Bernice threw his purse on to the console. 'No problem. Eventually.' She stared at him curiously. 'There's some very strange currency in there.'

'Strange people value strange things.'

She hung up her shoes on the hatstand hook next to the Doctor's outdoor clothes, then crossed over to peer over his shoulder at the tracking device. 'You've been busy.'

'Yes. Very nearly ready. A few small adjustments ... '

Bernice regarded the device, a large yellow piece of technology supported by a couple of rickety stanchions, with the same suspicion she had afforded the Doctor on their first meeting. The Doctor turned and straightened up to his not very full height. He could see the misgivings in her eyes.

'This machine,' he proclaimed proudly, rapping it with his knuckles, 'is one of the most sophisticated applications of science you are ever likely to encounter. Its range is universal, its power cells inexhaustible, and its usefulness in our present plight irrefutable!'

'But does it work?' she asked.

The Doctor flicked a switch on the control panel of the device. A bank of lights lit up and it began to emit a regular, high pitched pulse. 'Yes,' he said.

'Oh, it bleeps,' teased Bernice. 'Wonderful.'

The Doctor smiled back. 'Well, of course it bleeps. You can't build a tracking device that doesn't bleep, can you?'

He walked over to the console and began to ready the TARDIS for dematerialization.

'What's it telling you, then? Has it found the flicker?' She stared into the display screen, which remained resolutely blank.

'Don't linger, Bernice,' he said. 'Watched pots . . . '

She joined him at the console. As he flitted from panel to panel she wondered, not for the first time, if the TARDIS was supposed to have six operators rather than one.

It looked like their trip to meet the three eyed Toad People of Miradilus Four was going to have to wait. The Doctor had brought the TARDIS to the spaceport to ask for directions (the navigation equipment kept dephasing, which was odd), only to have the console alert him to massive temporal fluctuations in this sector of space-time.

'Doctor. When you've found the flicker — .'

'Yes?'

'What exactly are you going to do about it?'

'Build another machine,' he said confidently, 'to nullify it.'

'Another machine. Tch.' Bernice had realized a while ago that the Doctor operated on a different technological plane to the rest of the universe. 'More fiddling about with spare parts?'

'I'm afraid so.'

A worrying thought entered Bernice's mind. It was compounded by the spine of a book that lay opened and face down over a console display: *Displacement Of Theoretical Anomalies*. She picked it up and read:

Ducrov's hypothesis postulated that the centre of such a Fortean disturbance would, paradoxically, be the area least directly affected by random event stimulation. His belief was that, in its earliest stages, the flicker would act somewhat like a magnet, attracting random events towards its point of origin. Suggested methods for obviation of this phenomenon remain understandably vague.

'Have you ever done this before?' she asked him.

There was no reply.

'Doctor –' she began reproachfully. She was interrupted by a sudden increase in the frequency and volume of the bleeping.

'If the theory is sound, its application should be no problem,' he replied. 'Now, if you would?' He indicated the machine.

Bernice crossed over. A string of co-ordinates had appeared on the screen. Surprisingly, the notation was Earth standard decimal. The Doctor usually preferred to work in a meticulous, very alien scrawl.

She read off the numbers. 'Zero nine six two by eight six five five six five.'

The Doctor's face fell. 'Oh dear.' He did some sums on his fingers, nodded, and sighed. 'Oh dear,' he repeated.

'What's up?' asked Bernice. 'Hadn't you better check those co-ordinates on a starchart or something?'

'I've no need,' he said as he completed the dematerialization sequence. The transparent centre column began to rise and fall. 'It's a remote region of your galaxy, out beyond Lasty's Nebula. A dreadful, boring part of the universe.

'Still,' he sighed, consulting the console, 'our journey shouldn't take too long, relatively speaking.' He began to punch in the co-ordinate program.

'Don't be ridiculous,' Bernice chided him, although she had a strange feeling that she had stumbled on another of the Doctor's incredible talents. 'How can you have worked that out from a ten digit series? You must have a memory the size of a red star.'

'Some of us have it, some of us don't,' he replied. He peered into one of her carriers. 'I doubt very much whether I could tell the difference between one bottle of that stuff and the next. Although,' he continued airily, punching a complex sequence into a particular panel of the console, 'it will be as well to check the data bank for further morsels of information.'

The small screen above the panel sprang into life, displaying all the information pertaining to their destination contained in the TARDIS's extensive data core.

The Doctor scanned the screen with an experienced eye. 'It seems I was right,' he said smugly. 'The Fortean flicker is centred on what all the records say is Hogsumm, a rather dull old planet circling a fairly average star.'

He squinted at the foot of the screen. 'That's odd ... '

'What is?'

'How very peculiar ... '

'Grief, just tell me, would you?'

He turned to face her. 'Under the heading of additional information, the TARDIS suggests that we consult the works of Gustaf Urnst.'

'I know the name,' Bernice said, searching her human sized memory. 'Urnst ... Yes, he was a writer. Some sort of occultist, wasn't he? About thirty years ago — sorry, early twenty fifth century — there was some sort of fuss or something, wasn't there?'

'There was indeed,' said the Doctor solemnly. 'He disappeared.'

4:

Urnst

Only seven of the tanks in the First and Third Divisions had been damaged beyond combat worthy standards. One of them had been Jinkwa's own, and a space had now been cleared for him aboard the General's command vehicle. It was a substantially larger craft, and allowed both officers the luxury of padded harness straps.

Half of Jinkwa's left eye was fixed on the large forward screen and its display of their movement through the featureless green rock that was so much a part of this planet's landscape. The other half scanned a smaller screen, where, on Fakrid's orders — 'it'll get their blood up, and by Mif we need it' — one of the many video presentations prepared by the Ministry for Expansion was playing. Scenes of triumphant victories on over a dozen infested worlds were intercut with shots of eggs hatching, mothers cooing over their young, and vast harvests of verdant green stretching out over the cleansed soil. All this was set to a heart swellingly martial rhythm.

Jinkwa's right eye monitored the effect of all this on the command vehicle's two gunners. True to form, they had begun to slaver at the prospect of the forthcoming battle.

'Not very much further now, Kwintas, Obzelid,' Fakrid croaked reassuringly from his now restored harness. 'You shall soon have your vegeance on the scuttling clypes who have dared to challenge the might of Chelonia!'

'Sir, we are now entering the area where the energy surge was registered,' the Environments Officer reported from his position at the rear of the vehicle.

'Excellent,' the General snapped. Jinkwa was pleased to see that his commanding officer's customary resolution, if not his good temper, had returned. 'First Pilot,' he ordered. 'Clear all tertiary vision linkage for my pep.'

Jinkwa toed the relevant control on the panel before him. The propaganda video was replaced immediately by the image of Fakrid, as it would have been in every other tank.

'Warriors!' he began fiercely. 'You are hereby authorized to release seventy quintols of adrenal-amyl into your bloodstreams.'

Every Chelonian in the assult force obeyed, and felt a rush of heightened awareness that enhanced their righteous anger.

'The time is now!' barked Fakrid. 'Make ready your disintegrators! Forward!'

Breathing heavily, Kwintas pumped up the command vehicle's motive power unit. It rumbled forward into what the screen showed to be a wide, flat area between surrounding sides of tall rocky outcrop.

Jinkwa was struck by a feeling of familiarity. An attack on a parasite force trapped in a wide valley such as this was one of their own most established strategies. This strange concept buzzed around his brain, looking for something in his past experience to make a logical connection with. It failed.

The combat grid cobwebbed automatically over the forward screen. For the moment, however, there appeared to be nothing to combat.

The Environments Officer spoke up again. 'Sir, sensornet registers the residual of an enormous clean radiation release in this area. At gridmark four by nine.'

'Magnify,' ordered the General. 'Prepare disintegrators.'

Four of the small areas covered by the grid zoomed up to fill the screen.

'There!' Jinkwa shouted eagerly.

The gunners' front feet hovered centimetres above the firing buttons of their weapons.

'Hold!' Fakrid cried. 'That is —'

He was unable to complete the sentence. When Jinkwa realized exactly what the screen was showing them he could understand why. There were literally no words to describe it and no equivalent concepts in his mind to frame it.

What had been the Second Division was now a scattered pile of metal fragments. The absorption armour plating had not protected the tanks from the weaponry of the eight twelves.

Jagged edged chunks of it formed smoking, pitted peaks that jutted up through the ever swirling mists.

Jinkwa found that the spectacle provoked in him an emotional reaction so strong he was all but overwhelmed by it. He had once seen a tank topple hundreds of feet from the edge of a crumbling cliff, only to bounce comfortably off the rocks below thanks to the wonder of bumper buffers. The supremacy of Chelonian technology was unquestioned on all the worlds, but it had not saved his brave brothers of the Second Division.

He was not alone in these thoughts. Kwintas and Obzelid stared fixedly at the screen, only barely aware of their task in guiding the command vehicle further forward. Their nostrils flared, first with shock, then indignation.

But it was Fakrid who reacted most noticeably.

'Fire,' he whispered.

The command was met with silence.

'Fire,' he repeated.

Kwintas and Obzelid stared at each other and then at Jinkwa in bewilderment.

'There is no target registered on the grid, sir,' said Jinkwa.

The General shook with a spasm of rage. 'Fire!' he bawled. He opened up a voice channel to the entire assault force. 'Fire, fire, fire, fire, fire, fire, FIRE!'

Kwintas, stirred into an ungovernable frenzy by all of this, was the first to obey. He sent a volley of bright pink points off into nowhere in particular. He was soon joined by the majority of the gunners in the other tanks. The green valley was zigzagged by sparkling pink explosions that bounced pointlessly off the rock walls.

The dinning volume of the barrage caused Jinkwa to reset the parameters of his tympanic membranes. Therefore, he didn't quite catch the urgent warning of the Environments Officer.

A bubbling black globule hissed its way across the forward screen. A sharp report came from outside the area covered by the combat grid.

'Vehicle lost, vehicle lost!' cried the Environments Officer.

'Screen!' screamed Fakrid. 'Screen!'

The screen zoomed out as the scanner turret spun around. It displayed the blasted remains of one of the tanks and the confusion of its neighbours.

A second later, another fizzing blob shot over from the rockface to the left, hovered, sizzled ominously, then descended to hang just above another of the nearer tanks. It settled slowly, slicing through the plating. Then it ignited, blasting the machine and those within to pieces in a blaze of colour.

'Fire!' Fakrid fumed once more.

'Sir, there is no —'

'Oh, give me that, you cack footed moron!'

Fakrid swung himself across the command vehicle and into Obzelid. He knocked the young gunner from his position. The left of his front feet hammered on the firing button while his right angled the disintegrator in a wide arc up at the rock face. This succeeded only in dislodging large areas of rock, which came tumbling down onto them.

At least four more globules shot over into the valley, fizzed, then whizzed over to their targets and ignited.

'Scum!' the General snorted. Once again, he opened up his all stations address channel.

'Hear me!' he screamed. 'This is a strategic movement order! Regroup at gridmark,' he glanced at the screen, 'fourteen by three, where we will recommence our attack on the eight twelves.'

Kwintas just stared at the General. 'To it, boy, to it!' The gunner hurried to obey.

The command vehicle turned roughly about on its treads and followed the remaining tanks out of the valley. The black globules continued to fall, dispatching more of the assault force to oblivion.

Jinkwa watched as Fakrid returned to his position and Obzelid clambered back into the straps of his harness. He struggled to work out recent developments once again. Fakrid's movement order would undoubtedly prove to be another brilliant stratagem in the tradition of all his great achievements. For the moment, however, Jinkwa could not help but be reminded of the retreat of parasites when they knew they were going to die.

Sendei returned to the edge of the crater and took another long look out into the mists. His watch had stopped on their transportation here, and his body clock had likewise been rendered useless by lack of sleep, so he had no way of telling exactly how long Rodomonte had been gone. He was quite certain, however, that night could fall again at any moment. Already the chill, still air had dropped in temperature by several degrees.

As was his habit, Sendei attempted to analyze his own reaction to the dilemma. Without Rodomonte, the motorspeeder was useless. Molassi had claimed to be a qualified driver, but if he handled cars the way he handled his guitar, Sendei was in no hurry to put him to the test.

There was also something inexplicably reassuring about Rodomonte: the deluded innocence that had drawn them together in the first place. He'd been the only interesting person in their cohort at the Seminary. Thrown wild parties, knew lots of girls, had lived a nomadic life. He was fun to be with, even if he did surround himself with weird people sometimes. He had reminded Sendei of wild and impressive characters from books. Books that had been burnt by Molassi the night before.

That fire would never see another night. Sendei slid down into the bowl of the crater. Molassi was engaged in a feeble attempt to relight the small, charred pile of paper. In the cold, he could barely hold the matches steady in his hands. Eventually he gave up, and returned to the crevice between two boulders that had become his refuge from the universe.

Sendei walked over to him. 'I'm going out to look for Rodo,' he said, slowly and clearly.

Molassi growled indistinctly back at him. He reached inside his thick skin coat and produced another of the pink cans. He pulled up the ring, took a long swig, and smiled his stupid smile. Sendei had taken a dislike to him from the moment Rodo had introduced them. Instead of bringing them together, the current situation had made their antagonism worse.

Sendei shrugged. He turned and made for the crater's edge. Molassi laughed loudly. It almost coaxed the tears into his eyes again.

He reached the lip of the crater and turned a full circle, intending to select a direction and commence his search. His glance swept over the crater.

Molassi was climbing into the driving position of the motorspeeder.

Sendei ran down into the crater, its steep sides hurling him down the last few feet. He heard the engine roar into ignition and the backfiring belch of the exhaust. The wheels inflated with a hiss of decompression.

Sendei had two and a half seconds before his only means of transport on this planet disappeared forever at a speed of three hundred and fifty miles an hour, taking his food supply with it. The quick wits and resourcefulness he'd had little occasion to call upon in his previous pampered existence sent him flying on to the rear of the 'speeder. His outstretched hands clutched desperately at the rail on the rim of the open topped passenger section.

Molassi glanced back. He laughed manically and pushed his foot down on the power pedal. The motorspeeder began to twist and turn about the crater. The rushing wind pushed the hair back from Molassi's face, revealing an expression of invigorated stupidity.

Sendei screamed as Molassi turned the 'speeder on its side and began to climb the walls of the crater. He was flung almost upside down at one point as they circled about the rim at what felt like top speed.

Molassi turned a sharp corner. Sendei used the momentum released by the manoeuvre to fling himself forward and over into the back of the 'speeder. He was secured immediately by its internal gravity field. He scrabbled about amongst their accumulated junk, searching for something.

He found it behind the drinks dispenser. A large red box covered with poorly copied logos. Sendei flicked up the catches and pulled out a discod at random.

'Pull up, Molassi!' he shouted over the roaring wind.

'Get yours, clever boy,' Molassi shouted back. He threw something over his shoulder. It missed.

'Pull up!' Sendei repeated. 'Or,' he glanced down at the discod, 'Deep Space get theirs!'

Molassi understood immediately, confirming to Sendei that he was not half so far gone as he liked to make out. He brought the 'speeder crashing to a halt within seconds and turned, showing an expression of alarm that Sendei relished.

'Give me that, runt!' he grunted.

'You know what they've always said about the discod format,' Sendei teased, still breathing heavily. 'Perfect digital reproduction of sound. Synchronically aligned holographic vision. Unparallelled in the history of recorded music.'

He held the precious item aloft. 'But they're so fragile . . . ' He let the discod slip from his hand and fielded it neatly with the other.

Molassi cried out as if he had been physically injured. Without really knowing it, Sendei had made a good choice. Deep Space's first discod was one of the rarest recordings in the Inner Planets. It had cost Molassi a month's wages from his job at the fairground.

'Give it to me, boy,' he begged.

Sendei pointed past him to the dashboard. 'Ignition cube,' he said.

Without hesitation, Molassi removed it from the panel and threw it over. Sendei took it, then jumped out backwards from the 'speeder. He held the discod before him.

'Give it to me,' Molassi growled as Sendei walked away. 'Give it to me!'

'We didn't make any deal,' Sendei replied. 'I'm going to look for Rodo.'

As soon as he had left the crater, Molassi grabbed the red box from the rear section of the 'speeder. He clutched it protectively to his chest.

'You're dead, clever boy,' he whispered.

'How pretentious,' Bernice remarked as the Doctor handed her the huge, padlocked leather volume he had unearthed from somewhere deep inside the TARDIS. 'Typical of the man.'

'Ah, no,' countered the Doctor. 'Typical of his publishers.' He passed her a rusty key. 'Look at the date opposite the title page.'

Bernice opened the book, passing hurriedly over the frontispiece. (The author astride another heap of rock, binocs strung over his shoulder, shocked gaze fixed on some distant point.)

'*The Collected Works of Gustaf Heinrich Urnst*. This printing dated June 2503, London.' She raised a surprised eyebrow. 'So

47

Urnst suffered a revival.'

'Yes,' the Doctor confirmed. 'That bombastic style of his struck a chord with the people of the twenty sixth century. Hence gimmicks such as that rather elaborate binding.'

'I can't imagine why,' Bernice said. 'As far as I remember, the man was a laughing stock, a lunatic.'

'Or a visionary,' the Doctor suggested, only half joking. 'He had quite a band of followers, even in your time.'

'Wasters,' Bernice said dismissively. 'Wasters or nutters. Taken in by such an obvious fake.'

'Oh, there was never any question of him being believed,' the Doctor said. 'I believe that this later resurgence of interest was based purely on literary grounds. The children of your generation developed florid tastes.'

He stared at her abstractedly. 'How much of Urnst have you actually read?'

'Not a lot,' Bernice replied proudly. 'People used to swap copies in my archaeology classes. As a joke, I suspect. They were supposed to be frightening, but they were so stodgy and repetitive I gave up after a couple of chapters.'

'And what were your impressions?'

Bernice wracked her memory. 'Long journeys through the infinite, unfathomable depths of uncharted space,' she recited sceptically. 'Equipment failures leading to crash landings on worlds where men were never meant to set foot. Where science demanded rational investigation but every primal instinct screamed "Go back!" The ill advised expedition to the distantly glimpsed ruins. Obelisks, monoliths, etcetera, etcetera.'

'And?' prompted the Doctor.

'Oh,' she sighed. 'The abominable stench, of course. The indescribable creatures, the unnamable secret. The panicked flight back to the hastily repaired spacecraft and back to Earth. Then finally, a dire warning to others, begging them never to go to that evil place lest the secret be uncovered.

'All exactly the same. All complete nonsense,' she concluded brightly.

'He claimed he was telling the truth,' said the Doctor.

'He had to,' Bernice scoffed. 'The only danger he was ever in was from his readers.'

'I'm not so sure,' the Doctor said.

'Don't go enigmatic on me, Doctor,' Bernice laughed. 'A man of your intelligence can't seriously believe any of this stuff.'

'Not all of it, no,' he agreed. 'But I flicked through it on my way back here from the library and there's something very strange about the last entry. It's a short story, written just before his disappearance.'

Bernice found the place. 'Being An Account Of My Discovery Of The Unnamable Secret Of Sakkrat,' she read. 'I presume this is the connection with our destination?'

'Just read it,' said the Doctor. He turned away and tensed suddenly.

'What's up, Doctor?'

'Where is it?' he thundered, strangely, as if there was somebody else beside them in the control room.

'Where is what?' she asked, reasonably enough.

'The hatstand!' he stormed, and disappeared angrily through the inner door.

Bernice thought for a moment. She could have sworn the hatstand had been standing in its usual position next to the door on her return from the spaceport.

She shrugged and sat herself down on the Doctor's uncomfortable armchair. She opened the book and began to read.

Never shall I, in the days left before me, dare to venture again beyond the fulminating spiral that is Lasty's Nebula . . .

Bernice sighed and continued.

It had become customary for space travellers to joke about the unreliability of sleep suspension systems. Horrific tales, inspired in the earliest days of speculative fiction, circulated, of people who had never woken, or who had become trapped and were discovered centuries later as dusty skeletons clawing at unyielding doors. If the truth were known, such incidents were uncommon, particularly as by the twenty-fourth century this method of travel had been all but superseded by the advent of ever faster super light drives.

As Rosheen pushed up the lid of the third cabinet, memories of all those half heard stories returned to trouble her.

It was obvious that there had been a severe disruption of the sleep process at the moment of Postine's revival. The huge woman lay flat on her back, her eyes and mouth wide open. She appeared to be dead. A closer examination revealed that she was still breathing, shallowly.

'You only half made it, my girl,' Rosheen muttered. 'If the choice was mine, I'd let you die.'

It was apparent that this was not Postine's first brush with death. Her large bald head was scarred and lumpy. Her right forearm was a badly matched graft, tacked on by a barely qualified surgeon in a dimly lit trench on Regurel. That had happened during the skirmish between the Skaas and the Vetrux, two obscure races who had had the misfortune to be fighting right on top of a rich seam of the mineral Postine's then employers had called her team in to protect.

Rosheen reached inside the recess at the foot of the cabinet. She pulled out the manual and flicked through to the trouble-shooting guide.

In the event of an emergency, please don't hesitate to call Dozing Decades on New Oslo 7271 9116 8643 4AP1, it read. *One of our staff will be pleased to assist you with any difficulties involving non user serviceable parts. If you're unable to reach us, please refer to the emergency procedures outlined in the easy to follow diagrams on Page 84.*

As Dozing Decades had probably gone into liquidation centuries ago, Rosheen turned to page 84. The diagram showed a sleeper in his cabinet as a smiling colleague prepared to connect two large black pads to his chest.

You'll find emergency convulsers in the small recess at the end of the cabinet, read the notation.

Rosheen could tell before she checked that the recess was empty, another fault of the second rate system purchased by Sheldukher. She considered returning to the flight deck, but knew that Sheldukher would only force her back to complete the task. Without the convulsers, there was only one way to do that.

Rosheen disconnected the power line on the side of the cabinet. She unscrewed the safety coil. The bared end of the line buzzed with electricity.

She weighed the line in her hand, took a deep breath, and then plunged it down on to Postine's chest.

Postine screamed a low pitched, passionless scream.

Rosheen kept the line down for three seconds. She hauled it back. There was silence.

She forced herself to look over into the cabinet.

The moment their eyes met, Rosheen knew that Postine was going to try to kill her. She rose from the cabinet with a snarl of rage and launched herself at Rosheen.

Rosheen felt Postine's huge hands close around her windpipe. She was forced to her knees. Her attempts to push back were thwarted by the phenomenal strength of her opponent. Areas of her body started to go numb.

Postine gave a sudden cry and fell backwards. The impact of the fall shook the cabin.

Rosheen's senses started slowly to realign, aided by the rushing intake of air returning to her deflating lungs. The power line fell from her grasp. The attack had been so sudden that she had forgotten about it. Ironically, the charge had saved her life.

Rosheen felt reluctantly for Postine's life signs. She was just on the other side of consciousness. Rosheen backed hurriedly from the cabin and secured the door behind her. It appeared that at least two of Sheldukher's reluctant accomplices were unlikely to be of much use to him in his moment of glory.

I plead with you, my friends, to cast aside my catalogue of deceits and heed my words. All travellers, beware! Never must you venture into those murkiest of zones! For, beyond Lasty's Nebula, there it remains! Out there, on that emerald giant of a world! My very eyes did see the sacred stones and the wonders of the null space! These very hands, oh foolish hands of mine, they did work on the translation of the ancient hieroglyphs! I have heard the baying of the Monumental Guardian! I have stood but metres from the doorway to the abominable, unnamable secret of Sakkrat — the Highest Science!

Bernice closed the heavy leather covers of the book. Urnst's final work had been nothing more or less than she'd expected. After his trusty explorer ship blew a gasket in orbit, she had groaned with boredom and flicked through to the end, skimming over all the usual melodramatic discoveries and ghastly warnings.

She glanced up at the Doctor, who had returned to the control room carrying the hatstand with him. He had changed into his outdoor clothes; checked trousers and a well cut dark brown jacket that struggled to conceal a garish yellow sweater peppered with red question marks. The latter going to show that his bizarre and deprecatory sense of humour could extend even to his own personality and its pretentions. It also served as a reminder of all his recent chatter about patterns and coincidences, because surely it could only have been knitted by accident.

He offered her her shoes from the hatstand. She took them and stood up. 'I'll get my coat —'

'One moment.' He stayed her. 'What did you think?'

She weighed the book in her hand. 'Pretty much what I'd expected, to be frank.'

He looked at her curiously. She resented that penetrating stare. 'And you weren't left wondering?'

'Wondering what?'

'Wondering if Urnst really had discovered the lost cities of Sakkrat.'

Again, Bernice made for the inner door. 'No,' she replied, gripping the handle. 'As he'd already notched up most of the other lost civilizations in the galaxy, it was surely only a matter of time.'

'Ah, but Sakkrat was always rather a special myth, a cut above the rest,' he reminded her. Despite herself, Bernice had found that there was something strangely troubling about Urnst's last work, although she doubted whether even the Doctor could persuade her to believe it.

'The last paragraph,' he said. 'Read it again.'

Bernice found the place and read aloud. 'I plead with you, my friends, to cast aside my catalogue of deceits . . . '

'That's it,' interrupted the Doctor. ' "My catalogue of deceits." It was the last thing he wrote, remember, before his disappearance. He admitted all his previous lies. It sounds like he felt he had to.'

The Doctor crossed over to the console and began to fiddle idly with the controls. His gaze fixed on the rise and fall of the centre column, into the very heart of the TARDIS. Bernice had the impression that, despite his evident concern, the Doctor was not really concentrating fully on their conversation.

A little of his concern had begun to contaminate her also. She struggled to muster her response.

'You're suggesting that after years of falsely claiming to have discovered the lost secrets of space, Urnst accidentally stumbles on the ruins of the biggest of them all. That's what I'd call a coincidence.'

The Doctor turned to face her. She flinched from his piercing stare. 'Exactly,' he said.

Bernice felt like kicking herself. 'The Fortean flicker,' she sighed. Her mind boggled at her inability to see such an obvious connection, and from the possibility of what they might find waiting for them if they really were going to Sakkrat.

The Doctor took down his short, paisley patterned scarf from the hatstand and arranged it neatly under his lapels.

'A metaphysical disturbance that nobody understands,' he said, 'and the final discovery on the scale of scientific advancement. They could well be connected.'

'What's so special about the Sakkrat legend, anyway? It always sounded rather average to me.'

The Doctor rolled his straw hat onto his head. 'In itself, yes,' he agreed. 'About as relevant and original as last week's chip paper. But it wasn't the legend itself that was particularly inspiring. The galaxies are cluttered with similar stories, of mighty civilizations brought down by some terrible discovery.'

He considered a second. 'In fact, the galaxies *are* cluttered with mighty civilizations brought down by terrible discoveries.'

'No,' he continued, unhooking his umbrella, 'what makes the legend of Sakkrat so special is its sources.'

Bernice was pleased to find herself on more familiar ground. 'It's mentioned in ancient Martian mythology. The fall of Sakkrat, City of the Wise.'

'Oh yes,' the Doctor confirmed. 'But that isn't all. The Draconian myths speak of Ssaa Kraat and the High Knowledge. The children of Mulkos learn of King Sacrat and his unspeakable discovery. Even the Eternals know of the story. Worlds immeasurably distant from each other, and yet the culture of each has somehow been imbued by this myth.'

Something else occurred to Bernice. 'Didn't anybody think

to check up on Urnst?'

The Doctor smiled and put his arm around her shoulder. 'I think your reaction said it all,' he said. 'As you said, virtually nobody took him seriously. Certainly, his followers wouldn't have been able to finance another expedition to substantiate any of his claims. It was part of the man's technique to work so far out from the spaceways.'

'But if it's mentioned in the TARDIS data bank —'

'Oh, the Time Lords are a thorough lot,' chuckled the Doctor. 'Throughly boring. I imagine some junior clerk in the Archive Tower made the connection, but I can't see the High Council authorizing the use of a TARDIS to investigate something so spurious.

'Particularly,' he added wickedly, 'when they could be watching paint dry on the Panopticon walls.'

Bernice was pleased to see that the intensity of the grey fire in the Doctor's eyes had faded, at least for the moment.

'I can't help but think,' she confided, 'that it would be best to leave well alone. I don't fancy learning about the Highest Science, considering what it was supposed to have done to its creators and their civilization.'

'Neither do I,' the Doctor said, tapping at his chin with the red handle of his umbrella. 'Secrets are best kept secret. But we appear to have been painted into a corner. I'm afraid I can't just ignore a Fortean flicker.'

'I suppose so,' she nodded. 'Although sometimes, Doctor, I wish you wouldn't treat the universe like it was your own personal responsibility.'

She walked through the inner door, and had gone halfway down the connecting corridor before she noticed something very strange indeed.

The hatstand was in front of her.

Sheldukher munched contentedly on the cream cheese sandwich he had unpacked from the freezer. Now food was something you really could rely on. Unlike people.

Klift was behind him. He was hunched over in the far corner of the flight deck, hands pressed over his aged face. He moaned quietly. The psychic shock of ageing forty years in a second had been too much for his already weakened system.

Sheldukher had toyed with the idea of killing him, but his continued existence at least secured the co-operation of Rosheen. He would need her if the secrets of Sakkrat were protected in any way by computer technology. Klift's whimpers and groans had been irritating earlier, although a couple of knocks about the head had quietened him down a little.

The Cell coughed to gain Sheldukher's attention. He smiled.

'Just talk to me, my little one,' he said. 'Don't waste time on social niceties. Bad manners have never offended me.'

'This ship's sensor pods are next . . . to useless,' the Cell complained. Sheldukher noted with satisfaction that after only a few hours in human company, it had mastered a more complex speech pattern.

'They can't penetrate . . . the electric storms . . . that make up most of the planet's atmosphere . . . All I've been able to . . . pick up are . . . vague details of tectonic outlines, areas . . . at the extremes of the temperature range . . . and the like . . . '

'That's still not bad for an F61 that's survived nearly three hundred years of interstellar travel,' Sheldukher commented.

'But it's not good enough,' he whispered to himself. 'That planet is huge — ten times the size of Big J. It could take years to find the city on foot.' He relished a challenge, and this was one of the few occasions life had provided something difficult enough to be classified as one.

An idea. 'Any life signs?'

The Cell sloshed to one side of the bubble. 'Well . . . ' it sighed, 'there was some indication . . . of activity . . . in the southern hemisphere earlier . . . but I can't be more specific . . . '

They were interrupted by the arrival of Rosheen. The black square appeared immediately in Sheldukher's hand. He waved it almost playfully at her. 'Where is Postine?'

'She's lying unconscious in her cabin. And when she comes to, she's all yours. I'm out of it.'

Sheldukher noticed the red weals on her neck. 'Oh dear, don't tell me she was too much for you?'

'You're an arrogant swine,' Rosheen said evenly.

He shook his head. 'No. I'm very, very intelligent. You can't imagine how much more distressing that is for me than for you.'

'You really think we're at Sakkrat?'

'I know it,' he said confidently. 'The Cell's one purpose in life was to locate it.' He tapped the computer next to the bubble. 'Every detail from all of the legends has been cross checked on every planet we passed in our long sleep.'

He indicated the screen. The huge green planet now filled the plate. 'That is Sakkrat. Its size, age, atmospheric envelope; everything tallies.'

'You're a fool. There are ten times five to the eleventh power planets in the galaxy. There was bound to be one that matched the legends.' She crouched down and began to lever Klift into a more comfortable position.

Sheldukher crossed over, and offered her a water pouch from his food pack. She pressed it to Klift's lips.

'I'm disappointed, you know,' Sheldukher said. Rosheen caught a note of what might almost have been regret in his usual even tones. He is confiding in me, she thought with a shiver. I wish I was a criminologist. I'd make a fortune out of this.

'People said you'd done something with your life. I admired your achievements, even looked forward to meeting you. Oh, you're talented, yes, but what did you make of those talents?'

He leant forward. 'Cringing in a no place like the North Gate, surrounded by fawning cronies, luxuriating on padded bidets. And I'd thought perhaps I'd find somebody worth talking to at last.'

He stood up and returned to the console.

'I wish you were insane,' said Rosheen. 'Insane as in all rolling eyes and gnashing teeth. I think I could handle you better then.'

He smiled. 'I think perhaps I could handle me a little better too.'

'No doubt about it, sir,' the Environments Officer insisted. 'It came in on the sensornet at gridmark nine four by eight three. Exactly two minutes ago.'

'Excellent,' said Jinkwa. He broke the connection and scuttled over to the General.

Fakrid had been unable to watch the camp being made up on the other side of the valley from where they had been attacked. The sight of Chelonian soldiers cowering from the enemy had been too much for him to bear. The Third Pilot had been among those lost in the second attack. The only senior officer he had left was Jinkwa. He had found himself a quiet spot away from the action, where he now sat, staring into space.

'Sir,' called Jinkwa. 'Sensornet has picked up another surge, this time some distance away. Your orders?'

Fakrid cocked his head to one side. 'A reconnaissance mission would be best, I think,' he said. 'We will survey the area, consolidate available intelligence on the enemy forces, and then call in the assault force to eradicate them.'

'We, sir?' queried Jinkwa. It was most unusual for officers to lead a scouting party.

'Yes, Jinkwa, you and I,' the General barked impatiently. 'We'll do this well or not at all. Prepare a suitable vehicle.'

'Sir!' Jinkwa turned and motored hurriedly back to the remains of the assault force.

Fakrid stared out into the darkness. Another night was falling already on this dingy, scrub infested planet.

'Soon, eight twelves,' he whispered into the night. 'The hour of your obliteration is at hand.'

The small tank carrying Fakrid and Jinkwa trundled away from the camp to begin its reconnaissance mission. As he viewed its departure, the Environments Officer puzzled over the nature of the second energy surge which the officers had gone to investigate. Whereas the first had been a straightforward enough increase in the aura of background electricity, the second had registered, for just a second, *on every waveband of the sensornet at once*.

Still shaking his head in bewilderment, the Environments Officer shuffled off to help with the wounded.

But then, he had never encountered a Time Lord before. If he had, perhaps he would have recognized the massive displacement of artron energy caused by the materialization of a TARDIS.

5:

The Freaks

A blue beacon flashed through the night mists. Seconds later, the police box shell of the TARDIS had solidified from transparency.

The door opened, to reveal the tip of the Doctor's umbrella. It was followed by Bernice, who was holding it outstretched at arm's length. A large torch was clasped in her other hand.

'I think I was right. It is a bomb,' she called back into the TARDIS over her shoulder.

She reached out cautiously with the umbrella to the oddly shaped object before her.

She felt the Doctor's eyes on her back and whirled about. He stepped from the TARDIS, recovered the umbrella − 'Allow me' − with a self-contented tip of the hat, and strode confidently over to the bomb.

He knelt down and twisted a control on its side. A static blur formed on its triangular frontplate.

'The universe isn't entirely littered with explosives, Professor Summerfield,' he smiled.

'Littered is the word,' she said, for now the object seemed to resemble less a bomb, more an archaic two dimensional video unit.

'This proves we're on the right track,' said the Doctor. 'It must have been brought here by the Fortean flicker. I don't think anybody on Sakkrat watches television, do you?'

Bernice crouched down and fiddled with the tuning controls. All the screen could provide was a hiss of static.

'Just like Earth,' the Doctor said. 'BBC2 on a foggy night.'

Bernice stood up, glanced about, and shivered. 'These weather conditions aren't exactly ideal for atmospheric broadcasts. Rarefied atmosphere, yes?'

The Doctor nodded. 'Hmm, oxygen a little thin on the ground.

But nothing worth worrying about.'

A distant storm rumbled. 'Not the best of times to arrive. What a pea souper.'

He returned to the TARDIS, shaking his head.

Bernice turned the eye of an experienced explorer over her immediate surroundings. She recalled the words of Urnst: *the crawling emerald mist froze the skin, horny branches reached out as skeletal digits, to rip open the weighted floss.*

She knelt down and crunched thin green silt between her fingers. Surely this could never have supported life?

The Doctor returned from the TARDIS, now wearing his duffel coat, and snapped his tracking device neatly into place just outside. Bernice watched with amusement as he played at the controls. He always seems so much more relaxed outside the TARDIS, she thought. As if something about his beloved ship made him nervous.

The machine began to bleep again. Bernice stuck her fingers in her ears. 'Do you have to do that?'

'We're close to the centre of Fortean activity,' he said. 'But it's a very large centre. When the flicker starts up again, the exact source should register here.'

'What's to stop it affecting us?' she asked.

'Absolutely nothing,' he replied. 'So I'd better hurry up and find it.'

'Good. Then all the bleeping can stop and we can do something interesting. When do I get to meet some monsters?'

'Never, hopefully,' he replied grimly. 'Ah.'

The bleeping rate had increased a little. His brow furrowed over, his face lit by the display screen.

Bernice turned the torch over in her hands. 'I'd like to take some soil samples to analyze in the TARDIS.'

There was no reaction from the Doctor.

'I said, I'd like to take some soil samples.'

'How extraordinary,' the Doctor enthused. 'A reflective bounceback on the magnetronic spectometer index.'

At moments like these, Bernice felt like an accidental addendum to the Doctor's life, somebody for him to talk to on the rare occasions he got bored by the sound of his own voice.

'Doctor.'

He glanced up. She threw him the torch and walked briskly away, hands thrust deep into the pockets of the frock coat she had found in the TARDIS.

'Er, don't go wandering too far,' the Doctor called half-heartedly after her. He shrugged his shoulders and stared into the middle distance for a few seconds.

'Ah, well,' he said finally. He returned to the machine.

Ten minutes later, the Doctor rose from the device with a sigh of resignation. His efforts to track the flicker had come to nought. Even the reflective bounceback on the magnetronic spectometer index had turned out to have been caused by a misphasing of the proton links.

He yawned and stretched. 'Time for breakfast I think, Bernice,' he said, then remembered the parting of their ways.

He snapped on the torch and followed the trail of her foot-prints. A short distance away, they were swallowed up by a smattering of weed like undergrowth. There was no other sign of Bernice.

'She can look after herself,' the Doctor said, with almost total confidence.

The average star that Sakkrat circled had returned for its daily attempt to pierce the dense cloud cover and failed. The Doctor appreciated the dawn. It was, he decided, probably his favourite time of day on any planet. A time of optimism before things got under way and everyone realized it was going to be just the same as yesterday.

He walked back over to the TARDIS and perched himself comfortably on a rock. He slipped the torch into one pocket of his duffel and produced a small, tartan effect Thermos flask from the other.

After he had drained a couple of lidfuls of winter vegetable soup, the Doctor decided it would be polite to save some for Bernice. He returned the flask to his pocket and set off in the direction she had taken.

His shoe struck something in the ground. He nipped back hurriedly and extended the tip of the umbrella just as Bernice had done earlier. He tapped the object gently. It was a small metal triangle.

He smiled. 'Ah,' he said, picking it up. 'Perhaps this will prove stimulating to my critical faculties.'

He returned to the oddly shaped video unit and popped the triangle into a slot beneath the tuning controls. The static cleared instantly and was substituted by a beautifully resolved colour picture.

A voluptuously attractive woman wrapped in white feathers sat on a huge shell throne. Before her stood an improbably square jawed young man in gold braided uniform. He carried a large laser pistol.

'Ah, Captain Millenium,' the woman's lips drawled wetly. 'I've been expecting you. Your young friend has told me so much about you.'

The young man strutted boldly forward. 'What have you done with her? If she's dead . . . '

'Fool!' the woman sneered, striking a melodramatic pose. 'Do you think you can threaten Libida, Queen of the Virenies, with a puny laser pistol? Guards — seize him!'

The picture cut to show three young women in revealing one piece catsuits. They leapt from behind the throne and knocked the weapon from the young man's grasp. He was led away by the guards, struggling furiously.

'Idiot!' the woman spat contemptuously, her face now filling the screen. 'Do you think we have not learnt patience in a hundred million years?'

The Doctor's critical faculties had indeed been stimulated. 'Oh, this is appalling,' he chortled happily to himself. 'What nonsense.'

Fifteen minutes later, the Doctor was still absorbed in the intergalactic adventures of Captain Millenium. The episode ended with the Captain's lovely young assistant trapped at the mercy of a giant robot. The Doctor decided that it was almost like real life, in a glamorized sort of way. He stuck out his jaw experimentally.

He toddled off to look for another triangle so he could find out what happened next. There would be no harm done while he waited for Bernice and/or the flicker to show themselves.

Suddenly, the Doctor tensed. At the edge of his hearing he had detected an irregular, metallic jangling sound. It was coming

61

closer.

He scurried back to the big rock he had been sitting on earlier and crouched down behind it. That metallic jangling noise brought back unpleasant memories of nasty metallic things. He half expected the robot from Captain Millenium to appear.

What eventually emerged was considerably less alarming. A youth of about twenty stumbled into view. He was dressed in a torn leather jacket and ripped black jeans. Both garments had been customized with rattling bells and chains. He was covered in green dust and the Doctor could see a nasty cut on the side of his forehead not covered by a cowlick of shiny black hair.

Estimating that the chances of this figure constituting a serious threat to his safety were nil, the Doctor appeared from behind the rock. He raised his hat and extended a hand to the youth.

'How do you do? I'm the Doc —'

'The weirdo in the hat!' the youth exclaimed and collapsed.

'Charming,' said the Doctor and leant over to examine his new charge.

Bernice stopped to rest beneath the branches of a tall tree. The flat area where the TARDIS had materialized had given way gradually to a steeper, winding rock formation. More objects of uncertain origin and purpose were scattered here and there; an unsettling reminder that destabilized reality could strike at any moment.

A small, four legged mammal broke from the safety of its burrow under the tree and darted off.

'I'm sorry,' Bernice called. 'I didn't mean to evict you.'

She snapped off a twig from the nearest branch. Marks had been left by tiny incisors.

'There must be something nutritious in the wood,' she surmised. She squeezed the twig. A trickle of viscous fluid squirted on to her glove. She dabbed at it with her tongue. 'Not bad,' she decided.

A couple more of the little mammals scurried past her. 'You seem to do well on it, anyway.'

She set off up the slope again. 'The Sakkratian squirrel,' she began, 'was discovered by Professor Bernice Summerfield on her expedition of 2680. These small, burrowing creatures have

62

adapted themselves to live on the sap of the leafless trees of the planet ... '

Her dreams of academic glory were interrupted by a distant sound. She glanced up at the clouds, but their continual rumble was unconnected to this deeper, throbbing note.

'That is a combat vehicle,' she whispered. 'It grinds and clanks. Only combat vehicles grind and clank. It's supposed to be frightening.' She considered a moment. 'It *is* frightening.'

She flung herself flat on her face. She heard the gear of the machine switch its pitch and looked up tentatively.

A large black tank trundled nonchalantly down, its treads moulding to firm up their grip on the almost vertical slope. There were scars and stains of battle on every surface. A long, thick disintegrator attachment swept arrogantly from side to side at the front.

'The Sakkratian Megablaster,' Bernice whispered, 'was discovered by Professor Bernice Summerfield on her expedition of 2680. Designed not only for maximum murderous efficiency, but also to create an almost theatrical effect of shock on first sighting.'

The machine continued towards her.

'It is to be hoped,' Bernice continued, 'that this is not Professor Summerfield's final discovery.'

She leapt up and ran in a zigzag down the rocky track.

'Parasite!' shouted Jinkwa.

At last, something to shoot at!

Two pink explosions went off over Bernice's shoulder.

'Pathetic!' she shouted. She steadied herself and ran on.

'Look at the stupid creature,' said Jinkwa.

'It is a female,' Fakrid said. 'The most dangerous. We must kill it before it breeds any more.'

Bernice was thrown over a small drop by the third blast. It was her salvation.

'We've lost it, sir,' said Jinkwa.

'No. We must have hit it,' Fakrid countered. 'That's the trouble with disintegrators.'

'What's that, sir?'

'They disintegrate. Totally. Nothing left to make sure about.'

Bernice felt liquid tipping from one side of her head to the other as she lifted it. There was an awful taste on her tongue, as if she had been licking batteries.

She pulled off a glove. Her nails were cracked, damn! And her palms were grazed.

'I must have a double,' she said, 'who really deserves to get shot. And people keep mistaking me for her. I bet she's lying on a beach somewhere, surrounded by admirers, being mistaken for me.'

Then she heard more movement, and a voice.

'Doctor,' she said and popped her head over the ridge.

Two giant tortoises had emerged from the tank.

She pulled her head down.

'Not the Doctor.'

Jinkwa motored furiously about, startling more of the little mammals from their burrows. There were no signs of any other parasites.

'Ah!' Fakrid indicated a line of tracks that travelled up the rise. 'The female parasite came from down there. We will pursue and destroy any others.'

Jinkwa followed the General eagerly back into the tank. It felt good to have the half formed doubts fall down about him. They had an enemy. The enemy were parasites. Parasites are easily disposed of.

Bernice watched from hiding as the tank rolled off down the slope. She had to reach the Doctor before the aliens. Fortunately, the mist would form an effective cover. Likewise, the tank would be slowed down by the uneven surface of the planet. She stood a chance.

Bernice ran on.

The Doctor looked into the open eyes of the youth and shook

his head sadly.

'Malnutrition. Exhaustion,' he diagnosed. 'And some sort of chemical poisoning, perhaps self induced.'

He pulled out the Thermos from his pocket, unscrewed the lid and wafted the aroma of warm winter vegetables under the youth's nose.

'Now, tell me, my friend,' the Doctor began, 'exactly how do you come to be here?'

'You look like ... '

'Yes?'

'This guy ... my Ma used to bring home ... '

'Er, no,' the Doctor said hurriedly. The conversation was not likely to go anywhere with the newcomer's neurotransmitters in such a confused condition. He weighed up the factors in his mind. Perhaps there was a way.

He pushed the boy up into a sitting position. His posture was firm but flexible in a doll like way. Then he switched on the triangular screen directly opposite.

'Yes!' the Doctor congratulated himself. 'The addict will react to a repeated visual stimulus.' For the youth's eyes were now fixed on the static storm.

The Doctor coughed and straightened his tie. 'Son?' he said in a voice completely different to his own. He suddenly looked taller.

'Pa!' the boy cried deliriously.

The Doctor cursed himself inwardly. The replacement of one delusion with another was a cruel and primitive method of treatment. But he needed to know and it was his only recourse in these circumstances.

'Listen, son. You're in a safe place.' He leant forward anxiously. He would have to handle this part very delicately.

'Tell me your name, son. Tell me your name.'

'Rodo. Rodomonte Van Charles.'

The Doctor breathed a sigh of relief. His mesmeric skills were in good working order after some disuse. 'I've been looking for you, Rodo. Where've you been?'

'I've been running, Pa.'

'All alone?'

'No. Me and Sendei, Molassi. We were going to the

Ragasteen Festival. On Evertrin.'

'Who was playing, son?' the Doctor asked, searching for clues to place the boy. It looked as if the TARDIS was going to be leaving with at least three extra passengers and it would be as well for him to know as soon as possible when and where he would be returning them to.

He noted the badge on the youth's jacket. 'Was it M'Troth? Were M'Troth appearing?'

'Yeah, M'Troth. The Great Mothers of Matra, Is Your Baby a God,Televised Instant Death, all the big names.'

The Doctor struggled to place these names. Unfortunately, the popular culture of the third millenium was not one of his strong points. His occasional visits to the period had been spent mostly in battling monstrous invaders and he'd had neither the time nor the inclination to indulge in what he considered to be a rather synthetic, packaged form of entertainment. Now, if he'd been asked about Charlie Parker . . .

'But Pa, we never made the Festival.'

Obviously not, thought the Doctor. And I can guess why.

'No, son? What happened? Tell me.'

Rodomonte frowned. 'Blue lights. Then we hit this weird place. Like a kind of a — crazy planet.'

The Doctor could stand it no longer. He placed his fingers around Rodomonte's temples and squeezed gently.

'Sleep. Sleep and forget.'

For the first time in five days, Rodomonte's eyes closed.

Bernice pushed her aching legs even faster. She could just glimpse the blue of the TARDIS through the mist. The Doctor was standing over what looked like a dead body. Still, there would be time enough for questions later. Hopefully.

'Doctor! she shouted, waving her arms in a scissor like motion.

He looked up and smiled. 'Bernice!' he shouted back, waving his arms similarly.

Grief, she thought, he thinks I'm mucking about.

'Doctor, get into the TARDIS!'

He frowned. 'It's all right,' he called. 'I'll let you in in a moment.'

Groaning with panic and frustration, Bernice stumbled forward.

A pink thunderbolt shot out from the mists behind her. It exploded only feet away, showering her with fragments of rock.

'Bernice, someone's shooting at you!' shouted the Doctor.

'Oh, *really*?' she screamed back.

The Doctor came rushing forward to meet her. 'I'm so sorry,' he said, dabbing at her dust besmirched features with the wettened tip of his handkerchief.

'Forget it. Let's get into the TARDIS. There are some very big and very angry tortoises after me.'

The Doctor's face twisted into a knot that combined alarm, outrage, surprise, fear and disappointment. 'Oh, no!' he cried, stamping his foot.

'What?'

'Oh, of all the planets in all the galaxies, they had to walk into this one!'

'Who?'

Another burst of pink sparkles detonated about them. The Doctor and Bernice ran for the TARDIS.

'Chelonians,' the Doctor said bitterly.

'Another three of them, sir,' Jinkwa reported. 'They're moving too fast for me to get a clear shot. They seem to be heading for that blue wooden object.'

'Destroy it,' Fakrid ordered.

It had been a good few years since Jinkwa had been a gunner. He was soothed by a nostalgic warmth as he hammered on the firing button.

The disintegrator bolt ricocheted off the door of the TARDIS. The police box toppled over slowly on its side. The Doctor and Bernice were thrown back by the blast.

'I thought it was supposed to be indestructible!'

'It is!'

Rodomonte had been woken by the din. He lurched towards them confusedly.

'Hey, what gives, man?'

Another bolt shot past them and struck the prone TARDIS.

67

The Doctor hooked the handle of his umbrella around Rodomonte's arm and dragged him off into a stumbling run. Bernice followed.

'Who's your friend?'

'Later!'

'We've lost them, sir,' said Jinkwa. The tank had stalled on a jagged edge of rock, allowing the parasites to flee into the concealing mists. The electrical disturbance had blanked out the full range of sensornet functions, so they could not be traced that way.

'No matter. They are but three,' the General said with satisfaction. 'I wish to examine the blue wooden object.' He gibbered with anger and curiosity. 'It has shown formidable resistance to our firepower.'

Jinkwa brought the tank to a halt just outside the TARDIS.

The Doctor pulled Rodomonte and Bernice into a small depression in the rock.

'Don't tell me,' Bernice gasped, catching her breath. 'They're between us and the TARDIS.

'Yes,' the Doctor scowled. 'And they've got access to the tracking device.'

'Well, I hope they enjoy it.'

'No, this is serious.' He paced angrily about the little dip. 'There's no telling what havoc the Chelonians could wreak with such advanced technology at their disposal.'

Bernice indicated Rodomonte, who had collapsed in a corner. 'The flicker, I presume?'

The Doctor grunted his assent.

Bernice sat next to the youth. His eyes stared emptily into hers.

'Drugs,' she said.

Jinkwa approached the glass fronted object gingerly. 'I think I was right, sir,' he called over his shoulder. 'It is a bomb.'

'Nonsense,' Fakrid cackled disdainfully. 'By Nim, use your brain.' He pushed Jinkwa aside rudely and tapped the machine.

'Listen to that bleeping,' he said. 'It's some sort of environment tracker. You can't build an environment tracker that doesn't bleep.'

Jinkwa wondered at the General's brilliance. 'So that is how they located the Second Division!'

Fakrid kicked the blue wooden object angrily. 'If only it were that simple,' he said.

'General?' Jinkwa was more confused than ever.

'Think, First Pilot,' Fakrid said. 'What was the reaction of these parasites when we attacked?'

Jinkwa blinked. 'Why, they ran, sir. That is the way of parasites.'

'Exactly. If they were in any way connected with the eight twelves they would have attacked us.'

'Then these are not eight twelves?'

'No,' Fakrid confirmed. 'I believe this to be the work of freaks, parasites advanced to an unthinkable level.'

Jinkwa nodded. Logic supported the General's words.

Fakrid frowned. 'The smaller of the males,' he said. 'It wore a disc on its head and carried some sort of silly stick.'

'Yes sir, I recall it.'

'I believe it to be the leader of the freaks. Remember how it directed their flight.'

'Indeed.'

'I care not for the others, but that one must be taken alive. If it can construct objects such as these, it could destroy the eight twelves.'

'A parasite, sir!' Jinkwa gasped. 'To aid the Chelonians!'

Fakrid turned away from him. 'Desperate times . . . ' he croaked resentfully.

'Hermaphrodites!' Bernice exclaimed. 'Hang about, an old flame of mine kept tortoises, and he definitely had one of each.'

'Oh really, how fascinating,' remarked the Doctor. 'He was a hermaphrodite too?'

'No!' Bernice spluttered. 'I mean he had a boy tortoise and a girl tortoise!'

'Well, these aren't just tortoises,' the Doctor explained. 'For one thing, they're considerably larger —'

'I *had* noticed.'

'— and for another, they're considerably more intelligent. They've a powerful, though sterile, technology behind them.'

Bernice nodded. 'In common parlance, they don't half move.'

'Cybernetics,' the Doctor informed her. 'The blind alley of the organic sciences. Crude, hydraulic units implanted on reaching maturity. Add a little genetic recoding to incorporate sexual characteristics for improved reproductive efficiency, and you have a typical Chelonian; broody, hungry, and bad tempered.'

'You seem to know an awful lot about them,' Bernice pointed out.

He smiled. 'I know an awful lot about an awful lot of things.'

'But you have met them before?'

The Doctor nodded. 'Yes, I've had the pleasure of their company. Their conversation is so extraordinarily dull. They're always ranting and raving about some military accomplishment or other.'

'And who are they fighting? Anyone in particular?'

'Anybody or anything that gets in the way of feeding or breeding,' he said grimly. 'They call it war. You'd call it genocide.' He shook his head sadly. 'The Chelonians have wiped out entire populations the way that humans weed out an allotment.'

An amplified voice assailed their ears. 'Parasites!' it stormed. 'You are ordered to present yourselves. Come forward and your lives will be spared.'

'Surely nobody still says that,' Bernice laughed.

'I told you they were boring conversationalists.'

Rodomonte jumped up, alarmed. They had all but forgotten him.

'What's that?' he cried. 'What's that?' He made to leap out from their hiding place.

They pulled him down together, Bernice clamping her hand over his mouth.

'What are we going to do with him?' she whispered to the Doctor as the Chelonians' stentorian ultimatum repeated itself.

The Doctor looked into her eyes. 'What do *you* think?' he asked slowly.

Bernice sighed. 'I think I know what *you* think.'

The Doctor smiled and tapped her proudly on the shoulders.

'Give me two hours. There may be a way.'

'You'll find it.'

She removed her hand from the boy's mouth and offered it to him. 'Professor Bernice Summerfield. You call me Benny, okay?'

'The pretty woman,' he said. 'You call me Rodo.'

'Your perception can't be all *that* blurred. Let's go.' She led him up the far side of the dip.

'Up and at 'em, Doctor,' she whispered down encouragingly.

'Take care,' he whispered up. 'Two hours.'

Alone again, he produced the fobwatch from the top pocket of his jacket and flipped it open. It might just work.

The Chelonian voice blared out a third time.

'Oh, stuff a sock in it,' he muttered, and continued his deliberations.

They had run for about half an hour before Bernice decided it was safe to stop. Despite his desperate condition, Rodomonte had kept up a good pace.

Bernice recognized the feverish, hyperactive look in his eyes from her expedition to the quagmire planet of Mordala. One of the team, a young biologist, hadn't turned up for breakfast one morning. Old Dr Cartwright had found him in his tent, brain blown out by an overdose of quarkdust. She had never been close to him, but Bernice had cried with the others as they had buried him on that armpit of a world. And then there were the Travellers and their puterdeck. Safer, Jan had always claimed. Well, at least until the Hoothi turned up.

'I've got to find my mates,' Rodo said.

'We'll search for them later,' she said, and put her arm around his shoulder. Someday, she thought, this protective instinct will be the death of me. 'It's dangerous with the Chelonians about.'

He grinned inanely. 'No, the rocks will fall.'

'Sorry?'

'The rocks will fall. Down below.'

'Sure.' His words were filled with the strange conviction of the addict.

She looked for a landmark that would guide them back to the Doctor. Her nostrils were twitching.

Surely that couldn't be strawberry trifle?

'No!' Rodo yelled suddenly. 'No!' He scrambled away even faster than before, back in the direction they had come from.

'Oi!' Bernice shouted, following after him.

She surprised herself when she gave up halfheartedly and turned back.

'Shot away,' she said to herself. 'Completely shot away.'

What do I care? she thought. There's some strawberry trifle about here and my stomach is rumbling.

An internal voice told Bernice that these were most unusual thoughts for her to be having. It was soon subdued by her longing for a helping of trifle.

He nose led her forward.

6:

Dinnertime

Think worm, thought the Doctor as he inched himself along horizontally. The Chelonians were only metres away. Their gruff mutterings cut through the thick vapours.

'Atom blaster assembled, sir,' said the first.

'Activate!' ordered the second.

Understandably eager to discover exactly which atoms his reptilian enemies intended to blast, the Doctor crept on. Spying missions had never numbered among his favourite activities and this clandestine crawl was particularly irritating because his hat kept slipping over his eyes.

'Ha!' he snorted smugly as the scene finally came into view before him. The Chelonians had pointed the snout of a crude molecular dissociater at the TARDIS. 'Oh, give it up,' he mumbled into his shirt collar. 'Many have gone before you . . . '

Then a terrible fear overcame him.

Despite the jangling which announced his arrival, Sendei almost failed to recognize Rodomonte as he crashed into visibility, covered as he was in dried blood and dust.

'Rodo!' he cried. He ran forward and kissed him, so great was his relief. 'I'd given up on you! I thought —'

His friend pushed past him fearfully. 'We've got to get away!' he yelled. 'It's back there, the . . . ' His face crumpled into a mockery of its usual bravado and he burst into tears.

Sendei understood at once. 'It's okay,' he said and put an arm around his friend's shoulders. 'You're okay. It can't leave the swamp, can it?'

'The pretty lady —'

'What?' More hallucinations. The block of A Rodo had taken days ago on Exalfa was taking its time to pass through his

73

system. They didn't have time for this. 'Let's get back to the 'speeder, right? We must move on.'

'I've seen her! The pretty lady from Molassi's prophecy,' he gabbled. 'And the weirdo in the hat, I've seen him, too.'

'Yeah, sure. We'll go and tell Molassi, yeah?' He led Rodomonte gently away. How the hell was he supposed to deal with them both?

Rodomonte held up his hand and opened it. His whitened palm revealed its secret, a small silver ear ring. 'The pretty lady,' he repeated.

Sendei took it. 'Oh God,' he said with a reluctant certainty. 'It's true, isn't it?'

'I've seen her,' Rodomonte said. 'And the weirdo in the hat.'

'We've got to find them,' Sendei said. 'They may know what's going on here.' He strode off hurriedly in the direction Rodomonte had come.

'No!' shouted Rodomonte. '*It's* there! Another one!'

'Wait here,' Sendei ordered with his recently acquired confidence. 'I got you out. I'll get her out.'

Bernice looked around and smiled. Good. The planet wasn't green anymore. It had transformed itself into a happier, yellower world with a dusky blue sun. She drew in deep lungfuls of unpolluted air, scented only by that hint of strawberry.

She felt sure that she had some friends here, just out of sight. They were probably saving some trifle for her. If not, there was no hassle, because Mummy could easily make some more. As long as there was a nice big helping on her plate. And maybe some protein jellies. And real chocolate instead of the ration card stuff.

'Oh, my tummy's rumbling,' she shouted. She began to sing. 'Dinnertime, dinnertime, la la la ... '

Not far away, something big and nasty was having similar thoughts.

The Doctor heaved one of the heaviest sighs of relief he would ever heave in his long life. The Chelonians' atom blaster had not even scratched the surface of the TARDIS.

Well my little friend, he thought, at least you know better than to muck around with the force field prisms.

'Shall I activate again, General?' the first, slightly smaller and less wrinkled Chelonian enquired.

'Leave it, Jinkwa,' his superior sighed. 'Sooner or later, the freaks will return to claim this device. And we shall be expecting them.'

'Freak, indeed!' mouthed the Doctor. Well, you won't be expecting this.

He shuffled back into the dip they had concealed themselves in earlier and began to turn out his pockets.

There it was, just as she'd expected! A big long table draped with a gingham cloth. And sat around it were her friends! There was Malver, and Tomm, and Marie. And what a lovely big bowl of trifle! She ran down to say hello to all of them.

'Hello!' she cried.

'Hello, Bernice!' her friends replied.

'Trifle please, Mummy!' she shouted. Where was she?

That was funny. The ground felt all sort of runny, like she was sinking into the sea. There was water in her mouth. But she couldn't see it.

What a horrible looking thing there was in front of her. It was a bit like one of those creatures that you see on zoo discs, or what boys say the inside of a Dalek looks like when they're trying to scare you.

A long curly bit of it wrapped itself around her neck.

'Hello, Mister Sea Monster,' she tried to say, but there was too much water in her mouth. She looked around, but all her friends had gone.

She began to feel a teensy bit frightened.

'Mummy!'

Muscular pangs and that pain round the back of his neck had returned to trouble Sendei. He was tempted to turn round, grab Rodomonte and head back to the 'speeder to get a can from the dispenser. But the cold metal of the ear ring in his hand reminded him that this was his first chance to make some sense of what had happened him in the past few days, so he went on.

The sickly fumes curled up his nostrils. The pain twinkled away instantly. What a nice smell, he thought. Sort of like fruit custards.

Sendei shook himself. No way was one of those things going to claim him. He pulled out a torn and dirty piece of gauze from his jerkin pocket and clamped it over his mouth. It was better than nothing and although he was alone, at least this time he knew what to expect.

The gulping of the mud led him to the thick, steaming swamp. Carefree thoughts fermented in the bog slipped wispily up to ensnare his mind.

At the edge, a huge slimy tentacle had risen from the creature's mercifully mud concealed body. It was curled around a tall, attractive woman dressed in old fashioned clothes. Denims were concealed under a long woollen coat. She was murmuring to the creature in a silly, high-pitched voice, obviously well under the influence of the fumes. Her head tried to bob up now and again in an automatic defensive reaction. It was countered by the languidly drooling tentacle that pulled her down to its puckered ingestion orifice. Sendei was again struck by the perverse slowness of the creature. Somehow it made the spectacle of its feasting all the more horrifying.

He gathered his spirits and ran down to the banks of the swamp. His free hand reached tentatively over. There was no Molassi to help him this time and if he were to fall into the sticky, belching waters he would stand no chance of getting out again.

Fortunately, nature had not equipped the monster with more than a minimum of tensile strength. The ease with which it attracted its diet and the smaller nature of the items on its usual menu made it no match for the force of an almost fully aware human.

Sendei pulled the tentacle from around its victim. It flopped backwards limply with a squelch and the woman bobbed up from the mud, gasping at the tainted air. Sendei grabbed her around the waist and lifted her from the swamp. He stared into her dazed eyes as she collapsed on the bank. They were cool, intelligent and blue, but clouded with childish incomprehension.

'You're not my Mummy,' she said.

He hauled her up on to his shoulder and carried her away. The swamp creature squealed angrily behind him.

'What a clever little Doctor you are,' the Doctor congratulated himself. He was desperately proud of his latest achievement and slightly miffed that there was no Bernice about for him to boast to.

In just over fifteen minutes he had built what she would have dismissed as another gimcrack contraption from various items selected from his capacious pockets. The torch rested on the Thermos. The catapult and a chain of safety pins connected them up to his radiation detector, which in turn was balanced improbably on a tin opener. The bizarre assembly was topped off by two dark green objects that resembled spoons but weren't.

'Molecular resonance,' he quoted, from a textbook that had yet to be written. 'The inherent anomaly of disparate atomic structures in an induced state of symmetric inversion.'

He settled his umbrella gently on top of the spoon-like objects. It teetered unsteadily.

'Don't let me down,' he whispered. 'After all, you are supposed to acquire a certain sympathy with the individual who carries you!'

The umbrella began to turn slowly about. The entire creation hummed and rattled with a life of its own.

'What genius,' the Doctor laughed and doffed his hat to an imaginary audience. 'Now, for my next trick . . . '

He flipped open his fobwatch again and fiddled with the minute controls inside. 'I must get the exact frequency.'

It began to ping.

The umbrella speeded up its crazy spin instantly and became a black blur with a flash of red at either end. The Doctor threw off his duffel coat and picked up the unlikely contraption, cradling it like a baby in his arms.

He hauled himself out of his hideout, noting the resistance to the movement with pleasure. The air wobbled around him unsettlingly. With the Chelonians out of the way, he could get on with the task of locating the Fortean flicker. And if he happened across the secrets of the Highest Science along the way, so be it.

Every telepathic race vivisected by Earth biologists on their characteristically bloody quest through the galaxy had shown an enlarged cranium and the development of an extra ganglion or two. It had been easy enough for the scientists at the gene labs on Checkley's World to engineer the replication of such organs in the Cell. Its rudimentary extra sensory ability had been employed along with all other means at its disposal to detect signs of life on Sakkrat. Now it had detected something well worth reporting.

'Sheldukher,' it groaned.

He turned from the star maps he had been consulting. 'What have you found for me?'

'There is ... somebody down there ... a sharp mind ... '

Rosheen started forward. Sheldukher flashed her a superior grin.

'It can read our minds?' she asked.

'If there's anything worth reading. I imagine it can decipher the thoughts of another telepathic creature easily.' He grasped the Cell's containment bubble excitedly. 'Tell me. What is this mind? Where is this mind?'

The Cell crackled quietly as it weighed up its response. 'It wants to be rid of ... the ... Chel ... onians?' it said confusedly.

'What are Chelonians?' Rosheen asked.

'I've no idea,' Sheldukher replied, shushing her. He turned back to the Cell. 'Go on.'

'And if ... I should stumble ... across the secrets ... '

'Yes?' Sheldukher queried furiously.

' ... of the Highest Science ... along the way ... '

It's true, Rosheen thought. She looked out at the huge green world. It is Sakkrat.

' ... so be ... it ...'

Sheldukher leant forward over the bubble and said urgently, 'Locate it. Find that mind. I don't care what you have to do.'

Molassi lay stretched out like a cat in the back of the motor-speeder. He was flicking through the Ragasteen Festival programme. Most of the bands billed to play were freaksters, the kind of useless Brugg guano that Rodo and the clever boy

78

had chummed up with him to see. Wimpy offworlders who couldn't even program their synths properly. It was way past time that the riggers allowed real groups like Zagrat back into the charts.

What a snorter of a still. Bezzli bent double over his strings, Matyre wailing his heart out on lead vocals. The caption beneath read, *Slon Matyre of Zagrat: 'It's up to the individual cat to interpret our lyrics. Sometimes I feel like I'm an agent for a higher power, dig? Like the music and the words are coming through to me from some far-out dimension. It's an epic whizz.'*

He looked up. The two weazels he was lumbered with were staggering up. Slung over their shoulders were the arms of a well made chiclet. Only — no. More of a well made grown up woman. A pretty woman. A pretty lady.

Sendei held out the ignition cube. 'Get us started.'

He snatched it. 'I want Deep Space 'fore I budge one cent.'

'Look what we've brought you back, Jab,' Rodo interjected. 'It's your crazy prophecy coming true.'

Molassi shrugged. 'It's the work of a higher power, yeah? All coming together.' He turned back to Sendei. 'Give me the discod, clever boy!'

'Get us started,' Sendei replied. He tapped the discod-shaped bulge in his jerkin threateningly. Molassi growled and slipped over into the driver's position.

The pretty lady was lowered gently into the back of the vehicle. She was all but ignored as Sendei and Rodo reached thirstily for cans from the dispenser.

'What's that?' Fakrid said.

Jinkwa turned from dismantling the atom blaster. 'Sir?'

'Don't you feel that? A faint vibration.'

'Seismic activity, sir.'

Fakrid shook his head slowly. 'It isn't the ground that's moving — it's us!'

Jinkwa felt his protected organs churning inside his shell. It was a most unpleasant sensation.

'Sir, the eight twelves!' he cried, in the nearest a Cheloniaan officer had ever got to panic. The words came slowly through his vibrating lips.

The General roared 'No!' as the leader of the freaks ran into the open, carrying what appeared to be a revolving collection of parasite junk. The hum that had incapacitated them seemed to come from it, twisting the air itself against them.

Jinkwa attempted to raise the snout of the atom blaster. Despite the General's earlier orders he was quite prepared to shoot down the parasite. It had shamed them so embarrassingly. But the sheer force of the vibration held the weapon locked tight in the hydraulic grasp of his foot. As events turned out he would not have needed it anyway.

The freak had now reached the blue wooden object. It turned its small pink head and laughed. 'For a race of ruthless warriors,' it jeered, in the typically squeaky voice of a parasite, 'you seem remarkably prone to shell shock!'

Fakrid shook a little more at this. 'I'll see you splattered in red pieces —' he began, but a second later the bluster was no longer necessary.

The freak collapsed, somersaulting forwards as if somebody had kicked its posterior. The strange pile of humming rubbish fell into its constituent pieces around it. Jinkwa and Fakrid were instantly freed from the trap.

Jinkwa raised the atom blaster and gurgled, savouring the moment, 'Die, parasite!'

Fakrid knocked the blaster from his foot. 'No, First Pilot! We will learn much from this creature.' He kicked it. 'And then we will kill it.'

7:

Mind Like a Sieve

Bernice woke from a strange dream in which the Doctor was mashing potatoes before a crowd of derisively laughing robots.

An unfamiliar face appeared before her. Something was pressed into her hand. 'I think this is yours,' said a voice she didn't recognize.

Her hand reached automatically for her left ear. 'I didn't even notice it was gone,' she said.

'That's Rodo for you,' said the voice. 'He used to steal Twikka bars from the hypermall and the surveillance cameras didn't see a thing.'

Rodo. The name meant something but she didn't know what.

'Very interesting, I'm sure. But I'd much rather be given useful, relevant information like where I am.' Even to herself she sounded much less convincing than usual. Evidently this was the case. Somebody laughed nearby. Something told her that turning her head to locate the source of that laugh would be a really bad idea from the pain side of things.

She coughed. The roof of her mouth was coated with something disgusting. She attempted to laugh. 'What have I been eating?'

Something warm and metallic was pressed to her lips. An over-sweet, over-carbonated liquid slipped over them. 'Thank you very much,' she said, genuinely grateful. 'Have you got anything to eat?'

A small, dry fibreburger was provided. Bernice propped herself up and took a bite. Although she was hungry she wanted to throw up, which made swallowing difficult. Nevertheless she managed to eat it all up. She took the can in her gloved hand, which was caked in black mud.

A series of images passed before her mind's eye. An ugly, leering man in a bar. A mahogany hatstand in a mile long white corridor. The wrinkled face of a gigantic tortoise. She couldn't yet decide which bits were real and which were dreams. Life had often treated her like that since she had met the Doctor. The Doctor!

'My friend — I have a friend with me —' Damn, she had moved her head! Her brain had obviously decided to mount a break out attempt on her skull. She let out a cry. Grief, I hate people seeing me like this, she thought.

'The weirdo in the hat, we know,' said her rescuer. She examined him more closely. He too was covered in mud and green dirt, but the features that they almost concealed were boyishly pleasant. The kind of guy, thought Bernice, who had probably made a lovely baby but would be an embarrassing boyfriend. He had a few days growth of stubble but something about him was fundamentally clean cut. His hair was dark, thin and wispy. He wore a tattered leather jerkin and denims.

'You only just made it,' he told her. 'A couple of minutes more and you'd have been somebody's dinner.'

She sipped at the can. 'I'm terribly sorry, but I really have no idea what you're talking about.'

Another face presented itself to her and this time she remembered it. 'Rodo.'

He grinned. The other youngster said, 'I'm afraid he's forgotten your name.'

'Benny. Look, about my friend, I must get back.'

'Yeah,' he said guiltily. 'Let's hope he doesn't get too close to the swamp.'

Bernice had had enough of this. 'What swamp?'

Rodo replied, 'The swamp you near enough got yourself eaten in.'

More memories bounced back to crowd her perception. A tentacle . . . Wasn't that another dream? She felt for her throat and touched tender tissue. Obviously not. She turned to the younger stranger. 'Thank you, Mister?'

'Just Sendei,' he replied. Bernice was disappointed to see the deadened look in his eyes as well.

'I still can't recall exactly what happened,' she confessed.

'It's not surprising,' Sendei explained. 'The gas from the swamp induces a dream state. I reckon it must draw the little squirrely things to the monster. It works on people, too. One of them nearly got Rodo when we first arrived here.'

He seemed intelligent. 'Thank you again,' she said and handed back the now empty can, 'but I've got to find my friend, the weirdo in the hat. He's in a spot of bother with some big tortoises.'

Rodo started. 'There, I told you! A can't give you that sort of mind bust!'

Sendei shrugged. 'Okay, okay.'

Bernice attempted to rise. 'I left him behind a ridge of small hills, in a very flat area —'

'Try telling that to our pilot,' said Sendei. He cocked his thumb over his shoulder. 'You've just come along to fulfil his prophecy.'

Bernice had just enough strength to raise her head and see past him. Awareness of the exact nature of her surroundings was alarming. She was in the passenger section of a large, open topped vehicle. It was moving at an incredible speed through the green desert. A dirty looking young man was at the wheel.

'Turn this thing around!' she shouted. 'Where the hell do you think you're going? The Doctor's back there!'

'We're going forward,' said Sendei. 'What other way is there?'

Jinkwa and Fakrid hoisted the freak into the tank between them.

'Careful,' the General warned. 'The flesh of parasites is flimsy. They have no shell to protect them, remember.'

'Their internal organs are particularly susceptible to pain,' Jinkwa said. 'I can hardly wait to begin the interrogation.'

The creature was lowered into the space next to the vacant sensornet console at the rear of the vehicle. Its silly stick, the other items it had used in its contraption, and the environment tracker, had already been loaded aboard by Fakrid. Attempts to move the blue wooden object had proved fruitless.

Jinkwa stared down at the creature's ugly face. It looked like any other parasite. Could it really possess the intelligence to outwit the eight twelves?

Fakrid powered up the traction motor. 'We will now return to the battlezone,' he said. 'To your post, Jinkwa.'

Jinkwa took up his position at the console. He began to compute the orientation vectors for their return.

Klift entered the flight deck. Rosheen immediately waved him to silence. She pointed at the Cell. 'It's made contact with something down there.'

'On Sakkrat?'

'Yes,' replied Rosheen. 'On Sakkrat.'

'What's happening?' Sheldukher quizzed the Cell impatiently. It had been silent for several minutes.

'The mind . . . has shielded itself . . . '

'Then break through the shield!'

The Cell fizzed unhappily. The bubble steamed up. Parts of its head wrinkled up into a half frown. 'I . . . will attempt . . . to communicate . . . but it is . . . very strong . . . '

'I must know,' said Sheldukher. 'The Highest Science. Ask it about the Highest Science.'

The Doctor's mind sensed the return of the invader. This force possessed none of the gentle, coaxing qualities associated with telepathic races. It bludgeoned harshly with its ceaseless questions.

'Tell me,' it sent. 'Tell me about the Highest Science.'

The Doctor knew that it was futile to resist the intruder. It was undisciplined but incredibly powerful and, after all, its initial greeting had all but burnt away the shields around his mind. There was only one strategy left open to him. Counter information.

The Cell groaned and closed its eyes.

'Two ounces of corn . . . flour . . . ' it said. 'Two eggs . . . a glass of medium sweet . . . sherry . . . '

'What?' Klift spluttered.

'The secrets of Sakkrat?' Rosheen laughed.

'It's rambling,' said Sheldukher. 'Force it to speak the truth.'

The Cell spoke again. 'Mix the eggs . . . into the flour . . . not too frothy now . . . sprinkle the nutmeg to taste . . . whisk lightly . . . '

Sheldukher smiled despite himself. 'I am quite looking

forward to meeting the owner of that mind.'

The Doctor's subconscious danced happily along the ethereal plane that carries telepathic communication. Until his body recovered from the effects of the psychic blast this was his only means of defence. He had never favoured telepathy as a means of communication; something about rolling words about on his tongue (particularly ones with lots of rs in) appealed too much to him. But he was confident enough to attempt turning the tables on his inquisitor.

He sent, 'Why should I tell you anything? I don't even know your name.'

Nothing could have prepared him for its response. For a second, it shared with him an existence of utter misery and unbearable agony — the frustration of an active intelligence trapped in a twisted body. Hatred oozed from it. The Doctor recoiled in shock and threw the barriers back up around his mind. For this was not the anger of the cripple, who can never be sure if he has been shaped by some vengeful god or made accidentally by a purposeless universe. It was loathing. For humans. For the beings who had created it and would not let it die.

The Doctor introduced himself tentatively. Surely there was something he could do to alleviate the suffering of this creature?

'Good morning, my friend,' he greeted it. 'I am the Doctor.'

The Cell experienced new emotions as the stranger re-entered its consciousness. Its mouth curled upwards for the first time. It sensed forgiveness and compassion. An almost frightening moral certainty swept over it and began to soothe its pain.

Bernice had attempted, with little success, to explain her presence on the planet. She was irritated with herself. Her normally lucid style had slipped and she had forgotten huge chunks of the recent past. Bits of her story had disappeared as she had told it.

'There's something very important about this planet,' she finished, sipping at another of the pink cans, 'but I can't think what. It's as if I was talking to somebody. About a book or something.'

85

She shrugged her shoulders. A doubt nagged at her. She was almost sure that if somebody had asked her about all this business when she had first woken in the back of the vehicle, she could, despite her pain and discomfort, have replied. Although she now felt a little better physically, her mind had developed a nasty habit of wandering.

'Don't worry yourself, doll,' Rodo said, tapping her reassuringly on the shoulder. 'It looks like you got here pretty much the same way as us.'

Sendei nodded. He reached out a hand to the small metallic dispenser beside them and pressed the sensor plate on its side. Another can shot out with a clunk.

'What is this stuff, anyway?' asked Bernice. She swished the dregs around at the bottom of her can. 'I hate to say it, but it's pretty disgusting. Hardly Solar Cola.'

'We don't know,' Sendei said. He indicated their driver. 'Molassi found the machine along with a heap of other junk just after we got here. It must have been brought here like us.' He swigged again. 'It tastes okay. A bit sweet, I guess.'

I'm missing something here, thought Bernice. Something really obvious is staring at me and I can't see it. It's as if there's a kind of screen before my eyes. I can't even remember the really important thing about this place. And didn't I make some sort of arrangement to meet somebody?

She leant forward and rested on the padded cover of the front seating. 'Hello,' she said, in what she thought was a friendly enough manner. 'Enjoying the ride?'

Molassi took his eyes off the way ahead. His command of the vehicle seemed fairly arbitrary. On a crowded traffic way he'd have been dead in under a minute but the barren landscape of this world offered little in the way of obstacles and the vehicle seemed able to right itself over the irregular peaks that occasionally reared unexpectedly out of the mists.

He simply stared at her. Bernice's instincts remained sharp enough to warn her that here was somebody dangerous in a very unsubtle way. The threat in those pale blue eyes disturbed her. They reflected a kind of profound stupidity in their owner. Like a child sticking out its tongue, they seemed to be saying, *I know something you don't know.*

Rosheen had prepared a simple meal for herself and Klift. He gulped down the spread of cold meats eagerly but chewed slowly, like the old man he had become.

'So we are at Sakkrat,' he said between mouthfuls.

'It looks like it,' she replied. 'At least we'll die knowledgeable.'

She found that he revolted her. You pathetic old fool, a voice inside her head screamed. Their love vows meant nothing now. He was no longer the same man.

'Rosheen,' he began falteringly. 'That time on Ita —.'

'Does it matter?' she snapped. 'You don't understand, do you? Sheldukher controls us. He can make us do anything he wants. We're his puppets. And when he's finished with us we're dead.'

She turned away from him. 'What does it matter about Ita?'

He laid a land on her shoulder. 'We were together. Lying on the banks of the lake. You held my head in your arms.'

She sighed. 'So what about it?'

He smiled. 'It was the best day of my life. Whatever happens now, I want you to know that.'

He wiped his mouth and walked quietly from the cabin.

'Perhaps I should have killed you then,' Rosheen quietly. She followed him in the direction of the flight deck.

Sheldukher considered turning up the voltage on the Cell again. Its eyes had closed, apparently in concentration, some minutes ago. But now an incongruously beatific smile had etched itself across its slit of a mouth.

'What have you got to be happy about?' he wondered.

A chunk of its purple crystal section cracked into pieces. Its roots rustled contentedly and it sighed deeply.

Sheldukher leapt for the computer linkage controls.

Klift entered the flight deck. 'What's going on?'

The Cell was jerked rudely back into life with a massive charge of electricity. Its high pitched screams for mercy were literally unbearable and Klift turned away, sickened.

'I've not finished with you yet,' Sheldukher told it.

It screeched incoherently back at him.

'How can you keep it alive?' Klift asked. 'It should never have been created.'

'You could say the same about anybody,' Sheldukher snapped back.

'I don't agree with that.'

'It's a little too late,' Sheldukher said calmly, 'for you to start moralizing, my friend.' He finally removed his hand from the voltage control.

The Cell groaned. It spoke again. 'Sheldukher,' it roared gutturally. 'I ... will ... destroy you ... '

'You are hardly in a position to try.'

'I was ... close to the ... end ... '

'It was killing you.'

'It felt my ... pain ... It showed me ... peace ... '

Sheldukher turned to Klift. 'Such a useful piece of apparatus. If only it were more reliable.'

'I don't understand.'

'The Sakkratian intelligence was about to grant its death wish.' He slapped the bubble, the interior now spattered with droplets of blood. 'I feel like a general in charge of a suicidal army.'

Rosheen hurried in. 'Postine's woken up,' she reported. 'I can hear her trying to get out of her cabin.'

Sheldukher handed her a cotton disc from his belt pouch. 'Tranquillize her.'

'You've just got to be joking.'

'Don't disappoint me again, Rosheen,' he warned. He pointed to the door. 'Both of you. Out.'

They left without further question. Sheldukher turned back to the Cell. 'Now report,' he ordered simply.

'I have pinpointed the ... exact location ... of the Sakkratian ... ' it gasped, almost with reluctance.

'Excellent,' said Sheldukher. 'We make progress, at last.'

The Doctor's mind slowly reassembled its awareness of itself. 'How can one's unconscious be knocked unconscious?' he wondered curiously. The force of the disconnection had certainly lessened the chances of a swift revival of all physical functions. He could only hope that his Chelonian captors weren't engaged in fiendish torture or hadn't cut off his legs or anything. After all, it would take ages to grow another pair.

Bernice's fingers worked on her coat button. It was a simple task made difficult by something she couldn't name. Her grip slipped helplessly from the enamelled disc.

She had curled herself up in a corner of the motorspeeder to get some rest, but there was too much adrenalin swimming aimlessly about her system and her eyes kept opening themselves. She waited for the unpleasant tingling on the back of her neck to go away and bother somebody else. It didn't.

Rodomonte started to sing. She looked over, and saw him sprawled over the inbuilt mini-heater vent.

'Oh, give it a rest,' she shouted across.

'Don't mind him,' said Sendei. He sat alertly upright next to her. 'It's the prophecy, see.'

'I don't see,' she replied weakly.

He scrabbled in Molassi's red box and handed over a small multicoloured disc, marked ZAGRAT SHEER EVENT SHIFT Patent Licence 110044. An artist with delusions of grandeur and a virtual airbrush to match had provided a holographic picture of a ruined temple on the flipside. Bernice had seen such items in the Cultural Histories Museum on Adorno.

'It's a discod, isn't it?' she said. 'Parallel reproduction.' Astonishing that she should remember that and not what that weird word 'tardis' that kept battering at her brain meant.

'Look at the lyrics, girl,' said Rodomonte.

Bernice squinted into the vinyl effect swirl. The encoded information shot out at her misted but still functional retina to form generic groupings that became words flitting across her mind.

> *Got me out of reality*
> *Hounded by wolves of transcendentality*
> *Sucked out through the door by a flashing blue light*
> *Struck out at the clever boy who said he was right*
>
> *Got me in nowhere the end of the road*
> *Weirdo in the hat speaking secret code*
> *By the roadside at the ruin saw a pretty lady crying*
> *The rocks fall down below hear the cries of the dying*

'Nauseating ninth grade dribble,' was her verdict.

'That doesn't matter now,' enthused Sendei. 'Listen. I'm the clever boy, you're the pretty lady.'

'Don't be ridiculous. It's just a —'

'Coincidence? That everything on Sheer Event Shift is coming true?'

All that was left of Bernice's rational practicality marshalled itself for a final, concerted assault on her bewildered brain. *Coincidence*, it screamed at her, *coincidence!*

'What do these lyrics mean anyway?'

Sendei shrugged. 'Nothing. Or so I'd always thought. Everyone thought that Zagrat were just a bunch of old beardies from the headster time.'

'The what?'

He looked at her curiously. She didn't look old enough not to know of the riggers. 'Every three years,' he explained, 'the riggers on Earth change the music style. To keep things fresh. Zagrat were the most popular band of the headster time, but now they're just embarrassing.'

'But somebody told you to think that?'

He looked confused. 'So?' he asked, as if overt state manipulation of popular entertainment was the most natural, acceptable thing.

'What happens to all the old groups then?' she asked.

'They get an allowance until the riggers bring their cycle back again. For nostalgia value.'

Bernice shook her head. She didn't remember anything like this the last time she'd been on Earth.

'I suppose we're going to these ruins, then,' she said. *Ruins*, part of her brain protested.

She glanced back at the discod. The track listing read: EVENT SHIFT, UNDER THE SWAMP, NO SLEEPING, THE RUINS, GHOSTS AND GUILT TRIPS.

'Five tracks on one discod,' she sneered. 'Hardly what you'd call value for money.'

'Every number is over twenty minutes long,' Sendei told her. 'Nobody ever understood the lyrics until now. Most of their other discods were about elves and warlocks, but this one is just spaced out.'

'Oh. Great. I'd love to experience it,' she said without enthusiasm.

'Not possible. Our system blew after we got here.'

She slapped her thigh and giggled. 'Shame.'

A cramp jabbed her across her middle. She cried out and doubled up then sat up.

During the second that pain lasted, everything was gone. Every memory, every thought, every trace of her identity was wiped from her mind.

Her senses returned. Rodo pressed another pink can into her grasp. She tore off the ring with nimble fingers.

Molassi had listened to the conversation between the clever boy and the pretty lady. Geeks. Still, they were not to know. They were just pieces in Matyre's game. And Matrye was but a tool, too. Of the higher power. The power that had selected him to fulfil the prophecy. Yeah, him. The bastard son of the scuzziest Whirli Go Round operator this side of Alpha Centauri. He was going to change the universe forever.

He was going to be crowned Wizard King.

The motorspeeder journeyed on through the plains of Sakkrat. The tracks it left behind it bisected a faded trail of bootprints. The boots in question had belonged to an explorer called Gustaf Heinrich Urnst.

8:

Deadly Weapons

The Doctor's eyes flickered gingerly open. He had been knocked
unconscious on so many occasions that the process of revival
had become for him little more than the formality of asking three
simple questions as soon as his senses could be trusted to provide
reliable answers.

'Where am I? Who am I? And who are you?' He leapt up
to discover the truth.

This was a bad move. In his confused state the Doctor could
not reasonably have been expected to remember that he had been
captured by Chelonians — creatures whose girth was of a
considerably more impressive span than their height. His head
smacked firmly and noisily on the low metal ceiling of the tank,
threatening to send him spinning back into unconsciousness
almost straight away.

'Foolish parasite,' said a low voice.

The Doctor looked about him. The tank was about ten metres
wide and fifteen metres long. The panels that ran along the walls
were covered with large, functional looking controls that,
thought the Doctor with distaste, had none of the elegant
modernity of the TARDIS console. The two Chelonians he had
seen earlier were strapped into padded harnesses that suspended
their front set of limbs conveniently over the main instrument
panel. Smaller levers had been built flush into the floor for them
to manipulate with their rear feet.

'Nice vehicle you have here,' he said. 'A little spartan,' he
ran his finger along the nearest buttress and examined the dust
it collected, 'probably seen better days, but nothing a good lick
of paint and a few ornaments wouldn't help to brighten up. I
think perhaps a scatter cushion in that corner, maybe some chintz
curtains?'

The Doctor had expected this to provoke some reaction but

the Chelonians remained resolutely silent, their eyes fixed on the big screen that showed a trundling view of their journey through the wastes.

The smaller spoke to the larger. 'Orientation vectors will be aligned in two time units, sir. We're passing close to the battlezone.'

Uncomfortably the Doctor edged himself closer on his knees. He insinuated himself between the shells of his captors and coughed loudly. When this failed to elicit a response he turned directly to the larger. The red stripes across the top half of its shell marked it out as some sort of high ranking officer. He struggled to remember the details of Chelonian military hierarchies.

'Marshal,' he began, 'you look like a man I can do business with − '

The other Chelonian interrupted him. 'The General does not converse with parasite scum!'

The Doctor feigned disappointment. 'Oh dear,' he said. 'And I so wanted to chat with him. Still, he's a busy man, I'm a busy man, maybe some other time . . . ' He edged towards the emergency escape hatch at the rear of the tank.

The smaller Chelonian whirled about and kicked him painfully in the ribs. Winded, the Doctor toppled over on to his side.

'We must kill it, sir,' he heard it say. 'If only to stop the ache of its stupid squeaking on our eardrums. Surely such a creature cannot be of use to us?'

'It is a clever little thing, Jinkwa,' the General replied. 'It fakes the ignorance of the parasite to confuse us.' He turned to meet the Doctor's gaze as he righted himself into an undignified crouch. 'The freak would do well to keep in mind that we have preserved its existence on the grounds of its intelligence alone.'

The Doctor shook his head. 'Oh no,' he contradicted. 'I'm afraid you really have come to the wrong man. I mean,' he gestured expansively about him, 'look at this wonderful craft of yours: a tank that doubles up as part of a spacecraft. You're obviously much cleverer than I am.' He leant forward to confront the General. Suddenly he looked much more like the genius he was. 'What could I, a mere parasite, possibly offer you?'

He was answered in part by a deafening blast from outside the vehicle. The heads of all three of its occupants whipped round to the large screen, where a buzzing black shape hovered expectantly.

'Oh no!' cried the Doctor. 'Why on earth didn't you tell me?'

He leapt for the navigation panel before Jinkwa could stop him and began to manipulate the unfamiliar controls with ease and skill. The tank twisted violently about at its top speed. The harnesses that supported the two Chelonians swung from side to side, knocking them against the sides of the tank.

The black cloud returned to the screen as if it had followed them. The Doctor cursed and spun the tank about again, this time almost tipping it over on to its side.

'Stop him!' shouted the General.

Jinkwa stretched out a foot and cuffed the Doctor about the chin. He was knocked away from the panel.

The black cloud fizzed its way towards them until it almost filled the screen.

The Doctor hauled himself up and reached for the tank's hyper reverse facility. It shot backwards at an incredible velocity, rattling its passengers up and down.

Still the shape pursued them. The Doctor wrestled frantically with the controls.

'Give it more lateral!' the General cried.

'That's exactly what it wants us to do,' the Doctor snapped back. He wheeled the tank ever so slightly to one side. The shape darted forward for the kill.

But the Doctor had already wrenched the tank about and stepped up the output of the traction motor.

As the tank lurched away the shape ignited on a surface of bare rock, blasting it to pieces.

There was silence inside for some seconds. The Doctor mopped his brow with his handkerchief.

'Unthinkable,' the General said at last. 'That black fire has claimed the lives of at least fifty Chelonians. And yet the parasite evaded it.'

'I merely confused it,' said the Doctor. 'You can't just run away from one of those things.'

'You talk of the eight twelves' energy bolts as if they were alive,' remarked Jinkwa.

'In a way,' said the Doctor, 'they are.'

Bernice munched on another fibreburger, wiping away the unpleasantly spicy taste with more of the pink drink. In the first faltering light of the dawn, she mulled over Molassi's headster time discod collection.

'These are probably worth a bomb,' she told Sendei, who had spent the night as sleeplessly as her.

'No probably about it. Maybe we'll find a discod mart about here,' he joked bitterly. 'We could make a fortune.'

'They're in such good condition for antiques,' she continued, examining another.

'What do you mean, girl?' asked Rodo. 'The oldest can only be about ten years old.'

The confusion that had overcome Bernice earlier returned. She stared blankly at the boys for a couple of seconds, then shook her head and tried to ignore the fears that crowded her.

She noticed that Molassi was regularly throwing threatening glances over his shoulder. She replaced the discods hurriedly.

'Don't worry about him,' laughed Sendei.

'Shouldn't somebody else take over at the wheel?' she asked anxiously. 'He must have been driving for hours.'

'Doesn't need to sleep, does Molassi,' Rodo explained. 'The night is his hour, that's what they used to say at the fairground. Just like his old man. Had to sleep with both eyes open in case somebody pulled out a knife on him.'

'There's more to it than that ... ' Bernice began, but the spirit of enquiry was sapped by the deceiver in her brain.

'Anyhow,' Sendei continued, 'while we've got *this* we can make him do pretty much what we want.' He produced another discod from his jacket. Bernice examined it curiously.

She was even less impressed by this lyric scan. 'Liquorice castles in ivory skies, Spinning top girl with whirligig eyes,' she read disparagingly.

A component somewhere deep inside the motorspeeder chose that moment to explode from stress. The vehicle ground to a halt. Evidently it did not share the tireless dedication of its driver.

'Cam lock cellulizer's gone,' Molassi shouted back at them.

'Has he got some sort of fault indicator up there?' asked Bernice.

Rodo shook his head. 'Uh-uh. Guessing.' He leant forward. 'It can't be the cam lock or the internal pressure gauge alarm would be sounding.'

Molassi laughed. 'And how do you know, sir, that the gauge isn't screwed as well?'

Rodo scrambled from the passenger section and joined Molassi at the inspection hatch on the left side of the vehicle.

'Sump channels, must be,' he diagnosed.

'Nah,' scorned Molassi.

Rodo jostled him angrily, 'Who bought the thing?'

'We all did,' Sendei whispered to Bernice.

'You know nothing, funny man,' drawled Molassi. His hand reached for the knife on his belt.

'Liquorice castles . . . ' sang Sendei.

Molassi scowled at all three of them and sheathed the knife. He strutted angrily and aimlessly off. Wizard King had no business to be hanging round freaksters. The Grand Warlock was polishing the crown of ice magic in the ruins and he had to find him.

Bernice noted that the air was clearer here and the mist thinner. The words *Rarefied atmosphere, yes?* spoken in her own voice, returned to bother her. She couldn't remember who she had been talking to.

Rod grabbed a couple of cans from the dispenser and followed him. 'Hey, Molassi!' he called. 'It's got to be the sump channels, I'm telling you — '

Bernice turned to Sendei. 'What now?'

He shrugged. Suddenly he gave a cry and put his hand to the back of his neck.

The attack seemed to pass. Bernice stared curiously at him.

'What stuff do you do?' she asked, hoping that she'd got the correct slang. 'A?' She'd heard of that. Hadn't the source been blocked years ago?

'I don't touch drugs,' Sendei replied. His dilated pupils told one story, the honesty of the eyes that enclosed them another.

Bernice jumped from the 'speeder. 'It's cold.'

'Yeah,' he agreed. 'When the motor stops so does the heater. We'll look for some firewood. That was why we stopped before. Didn't have much luck.'

Bernice peered into the inspection hatch. 'Have you got any idea about this thing?' she called up. 'It must be ancient.'

'It is,' he replied, misunderstanding her. 'And no, I don't. I'm no good with machines.'

Bernice rose to face him. 'I've got an idea what might be wrong —' she began.

Sendei interrupted her. She had been resting against his trunk and now he could see what had happened to it. 'The lock on my trunk's been forced,' he said angrily. 'Molassi's taken my books!'

He leapt from the 'speeder and then halted himself. 'No,' he said, 'I've already ... ' His voice trailed off.

'I know how you feel,' said Bernice. 'I can't remember much. I was on this planet. Heaven. A great place, right out at the edge. I remember waking up in my tent. It seems quite a while ago now, but it's about the last thing I remember. It feels like somebody else's memory.'

She pointed to the inspection hatch. 'There,' she said. 'A faulty connection on the inward combustor.'

'You a driver?' Sendei asked her.

'I can get it going for you, I think,' she replied. 'Girls at school used to say their Professor could fix anything. I remember that at least.'

She reached inside the hatch and began to unscrew the connection. 'There,' she said triumphantly, displaying the frayed ends of the linkage. 'I was right.'

Sendei knelt down beside her as she fiddled about inside the hatch. 'How about the weirdo in the hat?' he asked her.

'Sorry?'

'That guy you were with. Rodo saw him. You were very insistent about going back for him. Giant tortoises, you said. Said he was a doctor or something.'

Her face remained blank. 'No,' she said. 'Maybe I was dreaming it. I don't know any doctors. Or anybody that wears a hat.'

'Sentient defence installations,' the Doctor explained. 'Commonly known as living bullets.'

'You have knowledge of the eight twelves?' asked the General. 'What kind of creatures are they?'

The Doctor chewed over possible responses internally. Knowing too much was an occupational hazard of his travels. On occasions when he knew too little he preferred to keep quiet. Unless, as now, his survival was dependent on the provision of the information available to him.

'I've seen similar systems, yes,' he said eventually. 'They must be an incredibly advanced race. To fashion patterns of light into such weapons. To give those weapons a destructive consciousness all of their own.'

Jinkwa spoke. 'Could you do it,freak?'

The Doctor frowned. 'Doctor, if you wouldn't mind. With the right equipment and several hundred years of practice,' he lied, 'possibly.'

'Yet,' the General remarked, 'you created a debilitating weapon from parasite junk.'

'Oh, that,' the Doctor said dismissively. 'Oh no, it was a miracle that came off at all.'

The General turned his piercing green eyes on the Doctor's face. 'I do not believe you, parasite.'

The Doctor faced him back. 'Believe what you like.'

'You are not of this planet?'

'Correct.'

'Then how do you come to be here?'

The Doctor shrugged. 'Much the same way as you and your eight twelves, I imagine,' he bluffed. 'There I was, merrily going about my own business, when I suddenly disappeared in a puff of metaphysics. To reappear here.'

The General growled disbelievingly. His rejoinder was forestalled by Jinkwa.

'Sir, we have arrived at base camp.'

The vapours cleared from the screen to reveal the remnants of the Chelonian assault force. The Doctor was shocked by the extent of the damage. Logic suggested that the Chelonians had marched themselves into battle with their customary lack of subtlety, only to find that their enemy was of a higher calibre than anticipated.

'My, my,' he remarked. 'What a mess.'

Jinkwa spluttered. 'Show respect for the mightly Chelonian assault force, parasite!'

'Respect?' snorted the Doctor. 'The respect your race displays to the species it murders?'

'Your race is less than life,' Jinkwa snarled.

The Doctor turned to the General. 'Charming. I suggest, General, that if we are to secure a good working relationship, such remarks could be kept to a minimum?'

'You are a parasite, Doctor,' he replied. 'A freak, maybe, but still a parasite. We tolerate you. We do not work with you.'

The Doctor nodded. 'Ah,' he said hurriedly. 'Well, if that's all settled.' He had now firmly ascertained that he was too important to kill. In other words, he had a licence to do virtually anything.

The tank came to a halt in the middle of the camp. The General and Jinkwa were lowered down and out. The Doctor gathered up his hat and umbrella and hopped down after them.

A welcoming party of three juniors awaited them. They bristled at the sight of the Doctor.

'Do not be alarmed,' the General told them. 'We have good reasons for keeping this parasite alive. How goes the campaign?'

'Since you gave the strategic movement order, General Fakrid,' the first replied briskly, 'there have been no further engagements with the enemy and no further casualties.'

'Strategic movement order,' laughed the Doctor. 'That's a good one. Perhaps next time you could surrender and call it a tactical strike without arms.'

'Silence!' Jinkwa ordered.

'The condition of the wounded worsens steadily,' the junior continued. He shuffled uneasily. 'There is one casualty that puzzles us, sir.'

'In what way?' asked the Doctor curiously.

The soldier gaped at him.

Fakrid sighed. 'Answer it.'

'Well,' he said, 'perhaps it would be best for you to take a look for yourself, sir.'

'Excellent,' the Doctor said happily. 'Lead the way.'

He strode confidently towards a nearby tent of clear plastic sheeting, over which the gaudy Chelonian flag fluttered limply at half mast in the moaning wind. The Chelonians bustled after him.

Jinkwa pushed his way to the front of the party and nudged the Doctor none too gently. 'Freak,' he whispered. 'Make no mistake. Whatever the General may consider best, I will destroy you at the first available opportunity.'

'They can't really be friends,' said Bernice as she worked on repairs to the faulty connection.

'What's that?' Sendei asked absently. He was hunched over next to her, clutching at his stomach.

'Rodo and Molassi, I mean. One looks stupid but harmless, the other could be a candidate for the psychiatric adjustment clinic.'

'They aren't really friends, no,' Sendei confirmed. 'Then again, I'm not too sure myself what being a friend is about any-more. Not since Hugo, anyway.'

'Hugo?' she queried.

'Right now,' Sendei continued, 'Hugo's probably languishing in a confinement block on Exalfa. Bread and water notwith-standing, I wish I was with him.'

'I've heard of Exalfa,' said Bernice. 'It's a small trader, one of the Inner Planets.'

'We stopped there,' said Sendei. 'The four of us. We had another week before the Festival and we figured we could hitch ourselves a ride the last leg of the way on a fast freight loader from Exalfa City.'

'What happened?'

'Well,' said Sendei, 'it looked like just about everybody else had had the same idea. Molassi got mad because we weren't going to make the gig, Rodo took some bad A from a backstreet dealer.

'They started a fight in a big bar in the city centre. All kinds of people Molassi had been winding up about their music taste started piling in. Soon it was the four of us against all of them. The manager was okay — all she wanted was to get the the place calmed down — and she showed us out the back way.'

100

'So what happened to Hugo?'

Sendei sighed. 'He found out next day that Molassi had knifed somebody in the confusion. The guy was paralyzed and the doctors couldn't straighten him out. So Hugo went to the police.

'When Molassi found out, he panicked. He bribed an operator at the transmat port to send us over to the space docks. We grabbed the 'speeder from the motor park and amazingly enough got ourselves passage to the Festival on a grain hopper.'

'Why did you run?' asked Bernice. 'You don't owe Molassi any favours, surely?'

He shifted uncomfortably. 'I guess not. And that's what I mean about friends. I stuck with Molassi 'cause he's supposed to be a friend of Rodo's, who's supposed to be a friend of mine. And look where it's got me. Stuck in the middle of some crazy loser's dream that's coming true.'

'At least,' Bernice reminded him, 'you remember who your friends are supposed to be.'

The Doctor's ebullient mood was muted by the sight of the Chelonians' makeshift field hospital. The small, dimly lit plastic tent was crammed with survivors from the eight twelves' second attack: soldiers who had been pulled from the wreckage of their half blasted tanks with feet missing or shells split. Most were connected up to fluid intake tubes. It was immediately evident to the Doctor that, accustomed as they were to successful action, the Chelonians were ill prepared for such a large number of casualties.

The junior led them to a trooper lying plastron up some distance from the others.

'Why is this brave warrior isolated from his brothers in the hour of supreme glory?' Fakrid demanded angrily.

'We feared contamination,' the junior replied. 'As you will see, the lad appears to be suffering from some sort of alien plague.'

The Doctor edged forward to the soldier and began to examine him. The Chelonian's eyes stared vacantly at the roof of the tent.

'He returned from patrol duty shortly after you departed to investigate the second energy trace,' explained the junior. 'We noticed something wrong straight away.'

The young soldier gave a cry as he saw the Doctor. 'Parasite,' he groaned.

'Mumtaz,' the junior ordered a nearby subordinate, 'show the General what the boy brought up.'

Mumtaz shuffled forward bearing a white tray on which a mangled piece of pink metal had been wrapped in plastic.

'What that might be, we don't know. But it certainly isn't a foodstuff, as he obviously believed,' said the junior. 'What we *do* know is that he is delirious but constantly conscious. The alien contamination has poisoned his mind. He seems barely able to recognize us and refers to last year's campaign on Azrad as if it were yesterday.'

'That isn't surprising,' remarked the Doctor, straightening up, 'when you consider that he has ingested bubbleshake.' He took the tray from the orderly's grasp and shook his head sadly.

'What do you know of this, Doctor?' queried Fakrid.

'Bubbleshake,' he replied, 'is very nasty stuff. It was invented by the Joseph-Robinson corporation, a particularly unscrupulous food company that operated for a time amongst the outer colonies of the planet Earth.'

'I see,' said the General. 'The substance from that metal container is suited only for consumption by parasites.'

The Doctor shook his head. 'Oh no. It has a very similar effect on human systems. It was designed for use as an appetite suppressant, to be taken along with a certain pill. When it's taken on its own, the body becomes reliant on further doses of the drink, an addiction that leads to hyperactivity, personality changes, compulsive behaviour, short term memory loss, and eventually the total disintegration of the brain.'

'Why would parasites poison one another in this way?' asked Jinkwa. 'It is illogical.'

'Not from the commercial point of view,' the Doctor pointed out. 'Before the revenue laws were tightened up, the Joseph-Robinson shareholders made a fortune out of this stuff. They argued that people had a choice.' He returned the tray to the orderly and went to stare out through the transparent sheeting.

'The pathetic exploits of parasites,' Jinkwa scowled. 'I remember the many stupid things they have created. Roadways that run through city centres, food refrigerators that destroyed the ecosystem of their homeworld. Why should we allow your destructive race to flourish?' he shouted after the Doctor.

'Is there a cure for this?' Fakrid asked anxiously.

The Doctor was touched by the General's concern for the life of just one of the least important members of his force.

'Bubbleshake contains the extract of the Fabi weed,' he answered. 'Only a massive course of decontaminants can restabilize the brain cells.'

He turned back to the young soldier and patted him affectionately. 'I think forced withdrawal is your only option. As you say, your Chelonian constitutions are much stronger than those of us parasites. He may well pull through.'

He swung his umbrella over his shoulder and made for the exit.

'Where do you think you're going?' Jinkwa demanded.

'Out,' the Doctor replied shortly. 'I need time to think.'

'You are to devise a means to destory the eight twelves,' said Fakrid.

'Exactly,' he replied. 'And I just cannot concentrate with people fussing around me.' He pushed through the tent flap.

'Follow it,' the General commanded Jinkwa.

Jinkwa opened the sheet. The Doctor whirled angrily about.

'If you want me to help you, just leave me alone for a while!'

Jinkwa turned to Fakrid for instructions. 'We'll leave it,' the General decided. 'It isn't foolish enough to attempt escape. And it may yet provide the means of our victory.'

Bernice dusted herself down. Her hands were covered with blue oil. She had thrown away her gloves.

'That's it,' she announced proudly. 'One fully functional motorspeeder.' She flopped down on to the padded driver's seat, planning to catch up on her sleep. She felt desperately tired but couldn't yawn. It was almost as if she had forgotten how to.

She heard the crack of another can opening behind her. She turned to see Sendei gulping down more of the pink drink.

'You!' she called, with uncharacteristic rudeness. 'Chuck me a can!'

Sendei obtained one from the dispenser and tossed it to her. She tapped it with her palm repeatedly to quell its inner fizzing and pulled open the ring. The sweet liquid felt good on her tongue. In her desperate condition, stuck on some rock of a planet without a trace of memory as to how she had got there, the drink felt pretty much like her only reason for living.

She drained the can, crushed it in her hand and was about to throw it away when she realized that Molassi was standing right next to her. His face was curiously calm.

'Where's Rodo?' demanded Sendei.

Molassi took the can roughly from his grasp. 'On a rock.'

'What do you mean?'

'On a big, high rock. Almost as high as he is. Says like he's gonna jump off.'

'Grief!' exclaimed Bernice.

'Where is he, Molassi? I've still got your discod, remember,' Sendei threatened.

Molassi turned from them. 'I'll take you to him, if you like. You can rescue your funny man again.'

Bernice and Sendei left the protection of the motorspeeder and followed him into the mist.

The Doctor strolled in an apparently leisurely manner around the perimeter of the Chelonian camp. Despite his earlier pro-testations to Fakrid, he had begun to feel a little lonely pondering his various dilemmas. A movement in the mist revealed itself as a single patrol guard.

'Hello, soldier,' the Doctor greeted him warmly.

'Hello, sir,' the soldier replied politely.

'Now, isn't that remarkable?' said the Doctor, sitting down next to him. 'The first friendly words I've heard all day. I thought you Chelonians were a taciturn bunch.'

'Depends, sir. On whether we think we've got anything interesting to say.'

The Doctor smiled. 'Unlike parasites, eh?'

'If you wish, sir.'

'I thought you didn't care to converse with the lesser races, anyhow.'

'If the General says we're to let you pass, then I'll let you pass.' The soldier sighed. 'As I see it, sir, this whole operation's washed up. Can't really see the point of hanging on to old grudges at this late stage.'

'Indeed not.'

The two of them stared aimlessly into the distance. For a few seconds there was no sound but the ever present atmospheric rumblings.

'Are you from a military family?' the Doctor asked, more to break the embarrassing silence than out of genuine interest.

'Like my mother before me, and his mother before him,' replied the soldier proudly.

'I suppose you trained at all the military academies?'

'The best, sir.'

'Of course.' The Doctor turned to face him. 'What was their strategy on war priorities?'

'Well,' the other said, 'they always used to say, if you've got an infestation ahead of you and an infestation behind you, always go for the infestation to your side.'

'Wise words,' chuckled the Doctor. 'You see, I find myself in a similar position.'

The soldier was puzzled. 'Sir?'

'Well,' the Doctor began, 'first I've got your General Fakrid barking at me to find a way to polish off these eight twelves. Secondly, a dear friend of mine has gone wandering off with a person I'm fairly sure is addicted to a very nasty personality altering drug. And thirdly, I have certain highly specialized information about this planet, worrying enough in itself, that somebody has been trying to prise from my mind. Which do I attend to first?'

'When I had my first implant, sir,' the soldier confessed, 'my old woman said to me, Frinza, he said, get yourself in the army soon as you can, boy. A life of excitement and a good pension waiting for you at the end of it.'

'And?' the Doctor prompted him, now interested.

'Well, I had considered floral arrangement as a career. So, like you sir, I didn't know which to choose.'

'But you obviously plumped for the army.'

'More for the pay than any other reason,' the soldier admitted. 'Didn't seem much of a life to me. Parading up and down, shouting and hollering, shooting down the occasional little animal.'

He sighed regretfully. 'Looking back on it now, sir, I wish I'd stuck with my flowers. I was happy as Buf positioning my stalks, you know.'

The Doctor smiled. 'Do you know,' he said, 'it's at times like this I think there's hope for the universe yet.'

'Doctor!' a voice called out behind them. 'Doctor! Where are you?'

'Uh-oh,' said the soldier. 'Better look sharp, it's the General.' He straightened himself up, put on an aggressive looking frown and motored off.

'Goodbye, my friend,' the Doctor muttered softly and raised his hat in farewell.

'Parasite scum!' Jinkwa blared as he emerged from the mists. 'We have indulged you long enough!'

'A good twenty minutes, I'd say,' nodded the Doctor. 'You can't bake a potato in twenty minutes, let alone cook up a masterplan to defeat an invincible alien force.'

'Oh, Doctor,' threatened Fakrid, 'you'd better have come up with something. For you own sake.'

'Yes, yes. For my own sake, final chance, etcetera, etcetera,' he said impatiently.

'Do not mock us, Doctor,' warned Jinkwa. 'You will find that our patience is not inexhaustible!'

'Well, then,' he said smugly, 'it's just as well that I *have* worked something out for you, isn't it? I'd hate to have kept you waiting a whole twenty minutes for nothing.'

'You may have the mind of a genius, Doctor,' said Fakrid. 'But you prattle like any other parasite!'

The Doctor drew himself up angrily. His pliant features contorted into an expression of indescribable apoplexy.

'*Me*, prattle?' he screamed. 'As the representative of a species that never ceases its overweening boasts of "military conquest", perhaps you should examine your own conversational short-comings before criticizing mine!'

Fakrid bristled. 'The Chelonian race is rightly proud of its great accomplishments!'

'What accomplishments?' the Doctor jibed. 'A campaign of mindless slaughter here, a consolidation of unjustifiable geno-cide there. A race of bullying cowards, sweeping through the

106

stars on a mission of extermination with no philosophy more inspiring than their own petty arrogance behind it!

'I have encountered many species in my time, Fakrid,' he concluded, 'but never have I been forced to endure such unfounded bombast!'

It is doubtful whether even one of the eight twelves' living bullets could have cut through the atmosphere created by the Doctor's words. The Chelonians appeared stunned by his outburst.

'You will live to regret those words, parasite,' Jinkwa said eventually.

'The weapon, Doctor!' Fakrid stormed. 'Now! Or you die!'

'The weapon?' the Doctor queried absently. 'Oh yes, of course. How silly of me to forget. The deadly weapon that will destroy the eight twelves and restore the mighty Chelonian race to its position at the top of the universal tree!'

Fakrid motioned to Jinkwa. The First Pilot raised the small blaster in his left foot. 'Your last chance, Doctor!'

He beamed back at them. 'Your deadly weapon has been staring you in the face from the moment you first arrived here, Fakrid,' he said.

Fakrid's eyes darted from side to side, 'Where?'

The Doctor smiled. 'It's called diplomacy,' he said.

Bernice and Sendei rounded the outcrop of rock indicated by Molassi. They saw Rodo balanced precariously on the edge of a sheer cliff face about a hundred feet above them.

'What are you up to, you idiot?' shouted Sendei.

'I rather think one is supposed to talk suicides down gently,' Bernice reminded him.

'I've had it,' Rodo cried down to them. 'I've had it with all of you.'

Sendei stepped forward. 'Come back to the 'speeder, Rodo. We're going to the ruins, remember? You've got to come with us.'

'Forget it, shortie,' came the reply. 'When the food runs out, we're finished!'

'Keep him talking.' Bernice whispered to Sendei. 'You,' she pointed to Molassi, 'come with me.'

Molassi shrugged. He had nothing better to do. And hey, the Wizard King could show mercy too.

She led him stealthily up the path Rodomonte had taken to the summit. Climbing to the top of a precipice in the company of a psychopath was not something she would have considered in her normal state of mind, she felt sure. But in the hazy world she had mysteriously entered it seemed as wise a move as any.

She heard Rodo's voice again as they reached the top. He was now seated on the very edge of the drop, swinging his legs childishly down at Sendei.

'When I give the word,' she whispered to Molassi, 'grab him.'

They edged closer to Rodo. He turned, saw them and giggled without any of his old charm.

'Now!' shouted Bernice.

Molassi darted forward. Rodo pushed him back with unexpected strength and stood up arrogantly. He dangled his foot over the drop.

Bernice threw herself recklessly forward, knocking him over and then back. The entire experience was over in seconds, before she had time to panic.

'You fool!' Bernice shouted at the giggling body beneath her. 'You nearly got us both killed!'

Molassi laughed behind her. The Wizard King could sneer at the games of mortals.

Angrily, Bernice picked herself up and went off down the winding path.

'Get yourselves killed, then. I don't care.'

'I still do not trust the parasite, sir,' Jinkwa confided. 'What is this diplomacy it claims to possess? I have never heard of such a thing in all the worlds.'

'Nor I,' said Fakrid. 'But remember, First Pilot, how the eight twelves' attack on our vehicle was beaten off by the Doctor's skills. If we have any chance of defeating them, the freak will provide it.'

'Thank you, General,' said the Doctor, returning from the quiet corner of the camp where he had been working. 'And here it is!'

With a flourish he produced another motley collection of

spinning components, this time cobbled together from the Chelonians' technical stores.

'Ah,' Fakrid grunted appreciatively. 'So that, Doctor, is a diplomacy.'

'Indeed,' he lied happily. 'One of the finest achievements of parasite thought.'

'On what principles does it operate?'

'Ah,' the Doctor said knowingly. 'Well, perhaps it's best to think of it in these terms: the dog kicks the cat, the cat kicks the budgerigar.'

'These terms are unfamiliar to us.'

'It's not complicated,' he continued, 'just a matter of perspective. You quite happily went around killing parasites because they had no way to defend themselves against you. Now the eight twelves are killing you for the same reason.'

'I see,' said Fakrid, not seeing at all. 'And a diplomacy will reverse this situation?'

The Doctor nodded. 'It will restore you to a more tenable position, yes.'

'Then we must apply it immediately,' the General said eagerly. 'Jinkwa, secure the diplomacy to the command vehicle.'

'No no no,' the Doctor flapped. 'I must take it across to the eight twelves.'

'What is the meaning of this?' Jinkwa snarled. 'Do not trust it, General!'

'Don't get yourself excited,' scolded the Doctor. 'That's half your trouble. Hopping about like a cat on hot bricks when a little reasoned thought would serve you better.'

'Why must you go alone, Doctor?' Fakrid enquired suspiciously.

'Because the diplomacy may affect you, too. Remember what happened to you earlier,' he pointed out. 'This time, it could be much worse.'

He hoisted the contraption in his arms and made for the battle-zone. Suddenly, he turned back to them.

'Of course, there is another way to solve the problem,' he said tantalizingly.

'What is that?' growled Fakrid.

'Well you could always just call it quits and head off somewhere else. The eight twelves don't seem particularly bothered about any other area but their valley.'

'That suggestion is truly worthy of a parasite,' Jinkwa replied.

The Doctor shrugged. 'Oh, well,' he sighed. 'It was worth a try.'

He doffed his hat and walked off into the mist. 'Expect me back within the hour,' he called back. 'I shall return!'

From their hiding place on the rim of the wide valley, two of the eight twelves observed the Doctor's approach.

'It *looks* human', said the first.

'*And* unarmed,' said the second.

The Doctor was confident that his scheme would prove successful. The Chelonians were fooled. Now all he had to do was to convince the mysterious eight twelves to negotiate a settlement.

Poor creatures, he though. Transported to this bleak planet only to be confronted by a marauding gang of giant tortoises. No wonder they had opened fire.

That small part of the Doctor's character that allowed for scepticism reminded him of all the times such naivety had landed him in trouble before.

He picked his way around the smoking wreckage of the Chelonian tanks. In the middle of the valley he hastily dismantled his collection of rubbish for fear that the eight twelves might mistake it for a weapon. Then he turned outwards, coughed, straightened his tie, and began the real business of diplomacy.

'I come in peace,' he shouted. His voice echoed around the valley. There was no response.

'Please hear me out. I wish to negotiate a settlement between yourselves and your attackers.'

'It's all right, we understand,' a voice came from above him.

The Doctor blinked in astonishment. On the top of the rockface before him stood two practical looking young women in their early twenties. Although tattered and torn, their clothing revealed them to be citizens of late twentieth century Earth.

'Good grief,' exclaimed the Doctor. 'And who might you be?'

The first introduced herself. 'I'm Vanessa, she's Hazel.'

The Doctor chuckled. 'So you're the eight twelves.'

'Do you know anything about how we got here?' asked Hazel desperately.

He nodded. 'I have a fair idea, yes.'

'See, we were on this train. The eight twelve semi-fast Amersham to Aldgate. Then suddenly,' she concluded helplessly, 'we were here.'

9:

The Sceptic

Bernice's fingers drummed on the plastic of the dashboard. She felt calm.

Just at the moment I'm fine, she thought. I don't need a past. I don't need a future. Just let me sit here on my own at this moment forever.

Molassi and Sendei appeared, carrying the staggering Rodo between them. The spell was broken.

'Help me with him, Benny,' Sendei pleaded pathetically. She replied with a venomous glance.

Molassi almost dropped Rodo into the back of the 'speeder. He climbed into the driving position next to her and jerked his thumb backwards.

'Get back over,' he said.

She almost argued with him, but his hand had slipped meaningfully down to the handle of his knife. She obeyed.

The 'speeder burst into life. It shot forward in erratic leaps before settling back into its usual roaring rhythm.

'See, I told you. It *was* the sump channels,' said Rodo gleefully.

All the suspended pain, anger and confusion of the last day overcame Bernice.

'What's going on here?' she wailed. 'I don't know where I am.' She turned to Sendei. 'I don't know any of you, I don't want to know any of you! I just —'

Rodo smiled. 'Yes?'

'I just want to die!'

Rodo giggled. Sendei said, 'Look, it's all right. We're going to be okay. The ruins —'

'Shut up about your ruins!' She would have cried but her eyeballs were burning, hot and dry.

She sneered at Rodo. 'You think you're so clever. But you're

112

a nothing, nothing but a nothing. You wear those clothes, you behave that stupid, sad, pathetic way, all to express your personality, right? The truth is you haven't got a personality!'

She leapt at him hysterically, tearing at his face. 'What have you done to me?'

She slumped backwards limply, staring in confusion at her hands. Sendei nudged her gently. He offered her a can.

'It's in the cans, isn't it?' she said weakly.

'What is?' he asked stupidly.

'I don't know. Some sort of drug!'

She leapt up suddenly. Her dulled eyes flashed momentarily with renewed alertness. 'Some sort of drug!'

The storm finally broke.

The Doctor wrung out his hat and turned back to Vanessa and Hazel. 'You were saying?'

They had run for shelter in a tiny cave on the side of the valley a second after the storm had begun. The suddenness and ferocity of the downpour had caught all three of them by surprise. Despite having been in the open for only a few seconds, they had been soaked.

Vanessa produced a long black rod with a transparent sphere attached to the end. The business end. There was a small activator stud at the other. 'Yeah,' she said. 'Well, then we found these. Just lying in the open.'

The Doctor took it from her very gently. 'Fascinating,' he said, turning it over in his hands. 'I haven't seen one of these in years. Fortunately.'

'Don't worry, we've got another one,' Hazel said proudly, brandishing it.

The Doctor gave a strangulated squawk. 'Please,' he said, 'would you be extremely careful with that. Strangely enough, something about it makes me feel rather unsafe!'

'So anyway,' Vanessa continued, 'then all those tanks appeared. This voice kept shouting something. I can't really remember what. It didn't sound friendly.'

'Something along the lines of surrender immediately or face total annihilation, I imagine.'

'Yeah, that was about it,' Hazel confirmed.

113

'We shouted back, trying to explain who we were and where we came from. But they kept coming. It was pretty frightening.'

'Basically,' said Hazel, 'we was shitting bricks.'

'What a colourful turn of phrase you have,' the Doctor said.

'So we let rip,' said Vanessa, indicating the black rod in the Doctor's hand. 'I thought they were guns. And I was right.'

'Considerably more than just guns,' said the Doctor. 'Every bullet is itself an artificial intelligence. It works out what the target is, where the target is, and how to get rid of it, all for itself.'

As he spoke, he unscrewed the transparent sphere gently from the rod. 'But not any more,' he said. Removing a tiny red element from inside, he crushed it between his fingers. 'That's fixed it.'

'Here, what have you done?' Hazel cried in alarm. 'What are we gonna do about them aliens now?'

'Oh, you needn't worry about them,' the Doctor reassured her overconfidently. 'I have the whole situation under control.' He gestured to the other rod. 'May I?'

Without really knowing why, Hazel found herself handing it over. There was something about this weird little man that she trusted.

'Weapons,' the Doctor tutted as he disarmed the second rod. 'They're so unsubtle. I've never been one for loud bangs.'

Coincidentally, or maybe not, the storm chose that moment to let off a sheet of dazzling green lightning and an earsplitting crack of thunder. All three of them jumped a foot in the air.

'Who are you, anyway?' asked Vanessa. 'And how did we get here?'

He sighed. 'It's a long story,' he replied, 'that began in the past, or perhaps the future. And who knows where it will end?'

He turned abruptly. 'I'd like to know a little more about you,' he said. 'I've travelled in the rush hour myself, and I must say two passengers in one compartment seems unlikely.'

'Oh, there's plenty more,' said Hazel. 'Back there.' She pointed backwards, away from the valley.

'So why are you two all alone?'

'We got fed up waiting,' explained Vanessa.

'And besides,' Hazel continued, 'there's this prat of a bloke

114

who's made himself our glorious leader.'

The Doctor glanced at his watch and considered. A settlement between the Chelonians and the eight twelves was still his aim, after all. And his hour was not up. He still had a good forty minutes to prove the power of diplomacy.

'Very well,' he said. 'I'd like a word with the rest of your people, if only to explain what's going on. It'll take a few trips, but I should be able to get everybody involved in this mess back home eventually.'

He grinned disarmingly. 'Next stop, Earth.'

'There, we was right!' Hazel shouted excitedly.

'About what?' enquired the Doctor

'Well,' said Vanessa. 'We always thought we were on another planet.'

'Very astute of you,' the Doctor said approvingly.

'But Witcher,' she continued, 'that's the bloke who's put himself in charge. Well, Witcher thinks there's been a nuclear disaster and that we're the only survivors.'

'Never mind,' the Doctor said, stepping bravely from shelter into the rain. 'I'm sure he'll understand when we explain the truth.'

Not for the first time that day, the Doctor was to be proved wrong.

Sheldukher completed checks on the F61. The descent spiral would bring them out from the cloud at almost the exact point where the mysterious Sakkratian doctor had been located by the Cell. The heat shields were still intact and the computer assured him that they would not crack or fall off on the journey through the atmosphere. It would, he thought with a smile, be most unfitting to explode on landing under the circumstances.

Rosheen and Klift had already changed into more sensible clothes for deep space exploration: dark blue atmosphere suits with floppy plastic helmet attachments that folded back hood-like behind their necks.

'Hadn't you better get suited up?' asked Rosheen.

He stood up from the flight deck console and crossed over to where Postine lay, successfully sedated, on a buttress.

'Dear me, no,' he said. 'You don't expect me to discover

115

the secrets of Sakkrat dressed like a rescue ranger, do you?

'Besides,' he continued, 'the atmosphere down there isn't all that thin. The only problem of that nature that we have to worry about is an electrical storm about a thousand kilometres wide.'

'It sounds more like a hurricane,' said Klift stupidly.

Rosheen was alarmed to see Sheldukher prodding at Postine's body experimentally. 'I wouldn't,' she warned him.

He looked up and smiled. 'Such concern.'

'I just don't fancy tackling her a third time.'

'You shouldn't have to,' he replied. 'When Postine next revives, her brain activity should have returned to normal.'

'Which doesn't go far beyond maim, raze, kill at the best of times, if you remember,' Rosheen said.

'Exactly,' said Sheldukher with relish. 'She's so delightfully unsophisticated.'

Klift spoke again. 'I see you finished the machine.'

'What machine?' asked Rosheen.

Klift pointed to the far corner. An oblong box about four feet by two sat on the console, blinking its flashing lights at them.

'He showed me that before we went into sleep,' he told her. 'He took it from the gene labs. Said it was a prototype.'

'It isn't perfect, no,' agreed Sheldukher. 'But it will do.'

Rosheen crossed over. Inside the box, concealed beneath a transparent cover, were a mass of tiny wire filaments.

'It's a carrying case for the Cell,' she guessed.

'Yes,' Sheldukher confirmed.

It was certainly one of the most surreal sights the Doctor had experienced in his many years of travelling. Thankfully, the storm had abated, at least for the moment, and the eight twelves had emerged from the shelter of their dull grey carriage. They were now gathered around a large rock, on which stood a rather ordinary looking, dark haired, middle-aged man. The most striking feature of his appearance was a sheepskin jacket which looked as if it had seen better days, sometime in the late nineteen seventies.

The Doctor, Vanessa and Hazel joined the gathering crowd as unobtrusively as possible. The Doctor had known many of the great leaders in the history of Earth and his instincts told him immediately that Witcher was not one of them.

'Now listen,' Witcher addressed the crowd. 'We all know what's happened. We all know what we've got to do.'

There was silence. It appeared that nobody did.

'That radioactive storm was just the beginning. There's probably nuclear fall-out creeping all over us at this very moment. Yes, my friends, we have one obligation and one, sole obligation alone. We have to survive!'

He obviously expected some sort of reaction. The crowd of commuters stood muttering in bewilderment.

'Our lives in this brave new world will be tough, my friends. Oh yes. We must learn to live without televisions or microwave ovens. The womenfolk will all have to be pregnant all the time, of course, if the community is to survive. It'll be like Raquel Welch in that film with the dinosaurs, except there won't be any dinosaurs.' He licked his lips.

Hazel nudged the Doctor. 'See what I mean? What a git.'

'My Dad bought a car off him once. And he was on the PTA at school,' said Vanessa.

'A second hand car sales man with delusions of grandeur,' mused the Doctor. 'I've faced worse.'

He stepped forward and raised a hand. 'Excuse me?'

Witcher looked at him in amazement. 'Who the hell are you?' he demanded suspiciously.

'I'm the Doctor,' he said, doffing his hat to the crowd. The commuters warmed to the little stranger immediately.

Not so Witcher. 'A scavenger, eh? Come to steal food from our tribe?'

'Er, no,' the Doctor said politely. 'Actually, I've come to take you all back home.'

There was a burble of relief from the crowd. At last, here was somebody who might offer a perfectly sensible explanation for what had happened.

'Home?' scoffed Witcher. 'Home?'

'Yes. Home.'

'You must have flipped, mate. There's been a nuclear accident, savvy? Or maybe the Ivans changed their minds again and opened up. We'll probably never know. You've got to accept it.'

'Well, I could be mad,' the Doctor said. 'Perhaps I'm a lunatic with a fevered imagination.' He smiled. 'It must be very fevered.'

'Listen,' Witcher said firmly. 'Either you join us and help us to survive or we leave you. We can't carry deadweights in our tribe.'

The Doctor had had enough. He shouldered his way through the crowd and joined Witcher on the rock.

'Oi!' Witcher cried, his dreams of empire crumbling.

'Oh, do be quiet, there's a good fellow,' said the Doctor. The crowd roared with laughter. The Doctor remembered why, long ago, he had decided not to go into politics.

'My friends,' he said, 'all I ask of you is a little patience. The truth will be revealed in time. The important thing to do is wait.'

With that, he hopped down from the rock, leaving its previous occupant free rein over the throng.

'Don't listen to him,' Witcher blustered. 'He's mad.'

'Tell him, Doctor,' Hazel shouted encouragingly. 'Tell him we're on another planet.'

'Oh no,' the Doctor mumbled to the ground.

'Did you hear that?' Witcher crowed gleefully. 'He thinks we're on another planet.'

The Doctor chose wisely to ignore him.

'We must move out,' Witcher continued. 'Our food supplies are already depleted. We must go to the ruins of London for food.'

The Doctor imagined the likely result of such an action. The thought of Witcher squaring up to Fakrid was not a comforting one.

He turned back. 'Yes, you are on another planet. But you'll be perfectly safe here until I have time to take you back!'

'Take us back, eh? In your spaceship?'

'Yes. In my spaceship!'

Witcher was uncomfortably aware that nobody was laughing at the Doctor. 'He's a spy,' he ranted. 'Sent to steal away what food we have by another tribe!'

'Don't be such a plonker,' Hazel shouted up at him.

'And you're no better, you two,' he retorted, pointing at the two young women. 'You've about as much sense as that bottle of tomato sauce over there.'

'Everything the Doctor has said is the truth,' Vanessa told the crowd. 'We know, we've actually seen alien beings. Somehow we've been transported to another world.'

Witcher could see the belief in the eyes of the commuters. He made a last desperate attempt to sway them back to him.

'Don't listen to them. They've been reading too much space fiction. It's like something out of that rubbish they used to put on after Grandstand.'

He pointed to the Doctor's umbrella. 'What's that, then? A space gun?'

The Doctor fixed him squarely with a look that had frozen the hearts of evil intelligences the universe over.

'I am presently endeavouring to protect you from a race that considers all human life to be a dangerous, parasitic infection. When I look at you, it is barely within my powers to convince myself that this is not, in fact, the case!'

He stormed off, the tails of his jacket flapping behind him.

He felt a presence at his elbow. Vanessa and Hazel had followed him.

'We believe you, Doctor.'

'I know.' He smiled and took both of their hands. 'I'm relying on you now, both of you. You must keep Witcher and your people back, out of sight behind the valley. It's very important.'

With that he relaxed his grasp and set off alone in the direction of the Chelonians.

A few minutes later the Doctor had reached the valley. Suddenly he threw himself down on the ground and rolled over and over in the dust. He hated getting his clothes dirty, but the effect had to be convincing. Then he walked over to the assemblage of components he had constructed earlier and tore it to pieces systematically.

Fakrid and Jinkwa had spent an anxious hour waiting for the Doctor. The rain had done nothing to improve their tempers.

'Where is the freak?' Jinkwa demanded. 'The hour is almost up.'

One of the surrounding officers spoke up. 'There it is, sir!'

They motored forward to greet him as he appeared from the mists. He staggered forward, covered in dirt, his clothing ripped and ragged. In his hands were clutched his umbrella and all that was left of the diplomacy.

'Doctor,' Fakrid croaked angrily. 'What happened to you?'

He collapsed at their feet. (I hope I'm not overdoing this, he thought.)

The Doctor raised his head. 'They're ... gone ... '

'The eight twelves?' Jinkwa queried anxiously.

He nodded. 'The dip ... the diplomacy ... It was too much for them.'

Jinkwa smiled. 'Another Chelonian victory!'

The Doctor grunted indignantly, 'Hardly.'

'That is how it will be written in the history books, Doctor,' Jinkwa sneered.

'Don't I get a medal? A certificate?' He looked up at the circle of menacing faces surrounding him. 'A glass of water would be nice.'

'Your only reward will be annihilation, parasite,' Jinkwa continued, 'after we have drained the knowledge from your brain.'

A trooper appeared with a message for Fakrid. He snatched it away anxiously.

The Doctor stood up, swayed and reeled about. 'I won't deny it was tough,' he continued. 'You've never seen such creatures. Huge green blobs seven feet across. With one glowing eye. Urrgh.'

He shuddered. 'Thankfully, the diplomacy destroyed them all. Now you can all go home to Chelonia.'

'Not yet, Doctor,' Fakrid said menacingly. He limped forward, waving the message angrily about in his front right foot. 'This report has just come in from the Environments Officer. Did you really think a Chelonian officer would trust your word? I ordered listening posts to be established as soon as you were gone.'

'Why's that?' the Doctor asked guilelessly. A rising tide of panic was creeping up on him. 'Nothing left here for you to shoot at. There's certainly nothing worth eating.'

Fakrid read from the golden sheet. 'Listening station five

reports: The parasite known as Doctor was then heard to say "Not any more. That's fixed it. I have the whole situation under control." Inference is that Doctor disarmed the weaponry of the eight twelves.'

Fakrid looked up from the paper and screamed:

'*And the eight twelves are* **parasites**!'

Jinkwa raised his blaster. 'Die, Doctor! Die!'

Yet again, Fakrid stayed him. 'Oh no, First Pilot,' he said. 'Before the Doctor dies, let it witness the destruction of the other parasites it was foolish enough to disarm!'

'No, Fakrid,' the Doctor pleaded. 'You cannot do this, I beg of you!'

'I do not listen to the words of parasites,' Fakrid replied. 'Jinkwa, make preparations to clear infestation!'

Bernice threw five of the pink cans over the side of the motorspeeder. They exploded in fizzy blasts against the rocks.

'What are you doing?' Sendei asked. 'That's our only supply of water!'

'After that storm?' she exclaimed. 'Oh no, I think we've all had a bit too much of this stuff.'

Rodo leaned over and put his arm around her shoulder. 'Come on, girl, take it easy.'

She shrugged him off angrily. 'It's a drug, you idiot! We don't know what it is or where it came from, but there's obviously something in it!'

'Correction,' said Rodo with sudden menace. 'We don't known what *you* are and where *you* come from. All's I see is a crazy woman throwing away our supplies.'

'Listen,' she said impatiently. 'Sendei, you said you don't touch drugs.'

'Right.'

'Well, neither do I. At least, as far as I remember, I don't. Another thing. I don't suffer from constant around the clock insomnia. I'm not given to panic. I have a good memory.'

Sendei sighed. 'Look, we don't know if it's got anything to do with the drink.'

'Of course it has!' she shouted. 'We don't know what it could be doing to us. We'd be the last people to see what it's doing to us. It could be killing us!'

'It must be something in the atmosphere,' said Sendei. 'That's what I reckon. Something in the atmosphere of this planet.'

Bernice grabbed more of the cans and began to hurl them overboard. 'It isn't you, Sendei, it's the drug talking!' she cried. 'It's been staring us in the face all this time. We've got to destroy this stuff before it destroys us!'

The others hauled her back from the edge. She struggled furiously for a few seconds but her former strength was lost to her. She flopped backwards suddenly like a broken doll.

'Crazy,' Rodo said calmly.

Sendei nodded. 'Yeah.'

'There can't be anything in this stuff,' Rodo continued as he broke open another can. 'I could tell if there was.'

'Yeah,' Sendei said again. But something deep inside told him that Bernice had been right.

She sat up weakly. 'I was probably just dreaming,' she told them unsteadily, her words slurred and slow.

'Sure,' Rodo said. He passed her the can.

'I mustn't drink it,' she said as she did. 'It's addictive.'

She smiled as the familiar sweetness passed over her tongue.

'I think it's going to kill me.'

The motorspeeder came to a sudden halt. They looked forward to see if another component had malfunctioned. But Molassi had stopped the vehicle himself.

He stood upright on the driver's seat, staring up into the clouds. Here it was. Another sign for the Wizard King.

At the edge of her hearing, Bernice picked up the sound of a roaring furnace engine, overlaid with the high pitched whine of cooling heat shields. She knew that sound well from her days as an explorer.

'It's a ship!' she cried.

'They've come to get us, boy!' Rodo screamed illogically at Sendei.

They scrambled from the 'speeder on to the hard rocky ground. A huge black shape moved between the clouds, which rumbled and spurted unhappily at its passing.

'It's a freight vessel,' said Bernice. 'Old fashioned transporter carrier. A Kezzivot, I think.'

The ship disappeared into the distance, taking their hopes of rescue with it.

'Just passing by,' Molassi grunted. He slid down into the seat again.

Bernice shook her head. 'No. It was on a descent pattern. Coming in to land somewhere near here.'

Sendei panicked. 'We've got to find it before it takes off again!'

'We don't need to,' Bernice replied happily. 'It's a freighter. It must have somebody to trade with. Perhaps this place isn't as empty as we thought.'

Rodo jumped with glee. He pointed to a small ridge of higher land before them. 'There's probably a city just over those hills!'

Molassi had already started the ignition sequence. The 'speeder set off again with a renewed sense of purpose. Bernice felt a lot happier. If there were space travellers on this planet, and it seemed that there were, their forward flight through the wastes took on a more logical purpose than the pursuance of a prophecy from a discod sleeve. Rodo might even be right. There could be a city over the hills!

Although only twenty eight tanks — just over half the original number — remained, the amassed Chelonian assault force made a terrifying spectacle. The sweeping of the disintegrator ports, the rumbling of the traction units as they powered up, the distant crackle of internal radio communication: all conspired to create the impression of one vast, murderous, destructive creature.

The Doctor stood outside the command vehicle under heavy guard. Fakrid and Jinkwa ambled smugly up, having completed their preparations for battle.

'The time draws near, Doctor,' Jinkwa sneered. 'The parasites will be swept from the surface of this planet!'

'Fakrid, once again I beg of you, stop this senseless slaughter,' the Doctor pleaded. 'Those people pose absolutely no threat to you. Just go! Leave this planet alone!'

The General sidled up to him. 'You never understood us, Doctor. It is not the Chelonian way to turn away from an enemy. It is not in the Chelonian nature to deceive. It is not part of our code to stand helpless and alone and wait for death. All these things you have done. Because you are a parasite.'

'And all parasites must be destroyed,' Jinkwa concluded.

The Doctor thought of Vanessa, Hazel and the other humans from the train. He could not bear the thought that his own under-estimation of the Chelonians would be responsible for their deaths.

He stepped forward. 'I cannot allow you to do this, Fakrid!'

Fakrid smiled mockingly. 'You *cannot* allow . . . And what exactly to you propose to do to stop me?'

That, thought the Doctor, was a very good question. He simply hadn't had time to lay one of his spectacular contingency plans or clever traps. It was just like the bad old days again.

And just like in the bad old days, it was coincidence rather than cleverness that saved the Doctor.

Every head turned up automatically at the sound of the furnace engine. A huge black shadow passed over the area.

Grit stung the Doctor's eyes. A powerful backblast blew one coating of dust from his clothes and replaced it with another that was tinged with soot.

The Chelonians milled about confusedly in the sudden darkness, their optical aids realigning frantically to provide them with a coherent picture of their environment.

The Doctor wiped his bleary eyes with his scarf and doffed his hat to the landing spacecraft.

'I think my luck has finally changed,' he said happily.

10:

Death Of A Salesman

The motorspeeder had entered a canyon at least a mile wide. For ten minutes now, the roar of the engines had been overlaid by a scraping, spluttering sound. A bank of purple neons had begun to flash on the dashboard. Molassi didn't know or care what that meant. But it was soon to become apparent.

He wrenched the wheel around to negotiate a treacherous curve. The chassis lurched forward and then back sharply, knocking the four passengers off balance. The engine gasped and died.

Sendei sighed. 'Another fault.'

Bernice shook her head. 'I don't think so.'

They jumped as a cheery metallic voice rasped tinnily from a concealed speaker. Bernice almost laughed at the comical expression of shock that passed momentarily over Molassi's normally impassive features.

> *We fuel cells have done our best*
> *You really put us to the test*
> *Exhausted now the charge is done*
> *Replace it with another one*

Rodo smiled. 'Auto messages. For kids.'

'Very funny,' Bernice said tersely. 'Do we have another charge for the fuel cells?'

Sendei shrugged. 'Didn't know we needed any,' he said pathetically. 'The guy that sold us the 'speeder said it was good for another million miles.'

'And you believed him?' she said incredulously.

He leaned forward aggressively. 'Look, we hardly expected to wind up here, did we?'

'I suppose not.'

She climbed out of the 'speeder and gazed up at the darkening sky. 'But here we are. For better or for worse.'

Rodo joined her. 'Where's my city now?'

'We all saw that ship,' said Sendei. 'There's got to be poeple around here. There must be.'

Bernice moved purposefully over to the corner of the passenger section where their meagre supplies were stored. She began to pack them together in a pile.

'We'll just have to continue on foot,' she said briskly.

Sendei smiled and helped her. 'You're some lady,' he said. She smiled automatically. 'Thank you.'

For a moment there, she had almost felt like her old self again, or at least glimpsed the idea of what her old self had been. What she should be were it not for the constant muscular spasming and the recurrent confusion of her senses. Could those senses be trusted? Had the ship been real?

And what about those eight dark shapes on the horizon?

'My God.'

'What is it?'

She pointed.

On the other side of the gorge stood a line of eight irregularly shaped monoliths. They were barely visible against the shifting darkness of the clouds.

Bernice blinked and squinted. The objects remained, in all their unlikeliness. It was impossible to believe that they had fallen so mathematically into place by themselves. The jagged outline of ageless stone suggested the lost, the ancient. Rodo's gleaming, futuristic metropolis was not in evidence.

Molasssi screamed with delight. 'This is it, boys!'

He scrambled down into the cold, howling plain that separated them from the stones. Bernice calculated that it would take the best part of an hour to reach them on foot. In the perilously low night temperatures of this planet, it was a foolish journey to make.

Sendei and Rodo were already scrambling over the side of the 'speeder.

'I wouldn't,' she called. 'You could die of exposure.'

Sendei turned. 'Don't you remember? The prophecy.'

Bernice leaned over the 'speeder and pulled out the Zagrat discod. In the dim light it was difficult to make out the illustration. But there, behind that gaudy, fantastical temple stood a line of monoliths. Eight in all. Of irregular height.

So, she thought, I am the pretty lady. Sendei is the clever boy. The weirdo in the hat, whoever he might be, is the weirdo in the hat. And the explanation for all of this lies in those stones.

She slipped the discod into her coat pocket, collected some cans from the dispenser, and made to follow the others. Behind her a bleeper sounded. The word EMPTY lit up on the dispenser.

The Doctor had been all but forgotten by the Chelonians, which suited him perfectly. He scuttled behind the nearest tank and watched Fakrid and Jinkwa's predictable reaction to the latest development with amusement.

'A parasite spacecraft!' exclaimed the General. 'I have seen similar. Look at it. Unsightly and inefficient.'

The Doctor was forced to agree. The ship, large and grey, sat only a few hundred metres from the assault force. Weld scars confirmed his suspicion that a hefty furnace engine had been appended to its original short hop retro reaction coil system. The roomy silos of the hull flanks gave it a bulbous appearance that defied approval by any aesthetic but the purely functional. Nearly all of the Chelonian tanks could have fitted inside.

'I hazard that it is constructed of reinforced megalanium,' Jinkwa said. 'We can easily destroy it.'

'And by Mif, we will!' Fakrid shouted. 'Order all stations to open fire in thirty seconds. We'll blast the wretched parasites half way across the universe!'

The Doctor was less worried than he might have been. Nobody would be foolish enough to land an old ship like that in the middle of a war zone without a very good idea of how to defend it.

'We're in the middle of a battle!' cried Klift. The tanks edged forward on the big screen.

'I am well aware of that,' Sheldukher said calmly. He leant over the Cell, which had now been transferred, painfully, to its carrying case. 'Suggestions, please.'

'Taking off would be a good idea, I think,'said Rosheen.

The ship's aged sensor pods had provided the computer, and

thus the Cell, with a swift approximation of the state of play outside the ship.

'The creatures ... outside would ... appear to be ... reptilians with bionic ... rebuild,' it reported. 'Suggest adoption of ... McArty technique ... '

'What's that?' asked Klift.

Sheldukher replied while fiddling furiously with the communications panel. 'Don't you remember your military history? McArty led the third campaign against the Iguanoids in the Koftan war.'

'I remember,' said Rosheen. 'But he had months of planning and an intelligence network the size of a planet behind him. How are you going to find the right frequency before they blow us to pieces?'

'*I* don't need to,' said Sheldukher. He stepped back from the console and whispered to the Cell. 'It's all yours now.'

Rosheen and Klift looked on. Neither had confidence in Sheldukher's plan.

'Five ... four ... three ... two ... '

Jinkwa's foot hovered eagerly over the firing button.

Fakrid prepared to give the order.

'One ... fi —'

Jinkwa's eyes swept crazily from left to right. His limbs pulled themselves up at ridiculous angles. His heart pumped faster and then slower. His ears popped and fluid seeped from his nose.

The world had turned upside down again.

The Doctor jammed his fingers in his ears. The ultrasonic whine had created a pressure of its own, threatening to compress his brain. His hat flew off.

'The McArty technique,' he said. 'Very clever. But not nearly refined enough!'

He collapsed, rolling about in agony, teeth gritted.

'Turn down the power! Turn it down!'

Sheldukher reached out for the modulator control.

'What are you doing?' asked Rosheen. 'Turn it up. Destroy them!'

128

'Certainly not,' he said, reducing the power of the emission. 'What do you take me for?'

'A lunatic who wouldn't let a bunch of bionic reptiles loose unless he had a good reason.'

He pointed to the screen. 'Out there is a very clever being. A telepath with knowledge of the Highest Science. I can't risk destroying it.'

He crossed over to a concealed hatch on the wall, punched in a complex security code, and withdrew a fearsome looking, three foot long rifle. It was time for Postine to play her part.

The Doctor pulled himself up and dusted himself down. The disabling whine had lessened to an irritating tinnitus.

'My own way was much better,' he said, jamming his recalcitrant hat back on his head. 'Subtler, even.'

The hatch at the base of the command vehicle swung open and Fakrid lurched out. To the Doctor's amusement he was cross eyed. His limbs flailed impotently, pulling him helplessly in four different directions at once. His injured rear left leg wheeled over and over in a frantic bowling motion.

'Doc . . . tor . . . ' he croaked, his mouth seizing up as he tried to speak.

'Yes?' he replied politely.

'If this is your doing . . . '

Fakrid's mouth clamped shut with a snap and he was reduced to making mumbled threats, none of which sounded very pleasant for the Doctor.

'Cybernetics,' the Doctor sniffed judgementally. 'So very useful. Until somebody throws a spanner in the works.'

He turned to face the ship. 'I think it's time I made the acquaintance,' he said, and strode confidently over to the entry hatch on the side, umbrella readied for knocking.

Before he could reach the hatch, there was a sharp crack and it slid slowly open.

The Doctor raised his hat. 'Hello, I'm the Doc −' he began.

An enormous bald headed woman dressed in battle fatigues emerged. She carried an enormous weapon.

The Doctor turned. 'Not today, thank you.'

The woman sprang forward. She turned the rifle on its side and clubbed him down brutally with the butt.

Rosheen watched as Postine came into view on the big screen, her massive frame picked out in infra-red against the night. She marched over to the nearest tank. One of the reptiles crawled aggressively towards her, its limbs flailing helplessly. Postine subdued it with a single blow to its long wrinkled neck.

'They look like tortoises,' said Klift. 'Giant tortoises.'

Rosheen turned from him dismissively. Was he going senile?

'I've never seen that species before,' Sheldukher confessed. More of the confused reptiles emerged from their tanks. 'They're rather sweet, aren't they?'

'Oh yes,' said Rosheen sarcastically. 'We could take them home and sell them as pets. Psychotic tortoises would have gone down well on the North Gate.'

'I don't think they're locals,' Sheldukher surmised. 'This is hardly the environment for reptilian life. There can be only one explanation.'

'And what's that?'

'They've come to steal the secrets of Sakkrat,' he said.

The Cell spoke up, 'Sheldukher ... '

'Yes?'

'The sensor pods ... have completed their search ... of the area ... '

'Good. Anything of interest?'

The Cell squirmed. 'Massive amounts of ... clean rad energy have been ... released here ... recently. There is a ... a group of humanoids ... on the other ... side of ... the westward valley ... '

Sheldukher sighed with satisfaction. 'Is that so? Somehow, I didn't think this Doctor was a tortoise.'

He snapped open a direct link to Postine. 'Postine, this is Sheldukher.'

The only reply was a guttural grunt. In the background they heard the sound of brittle necks breaking.

'I told you to assemble them, not disassemble them,' he chided her.

'Some have weapons, master,' Postine's flat, low pitched

voice filtered back.

'Well, do your best. Anyway, prepare to receive secondary instructions.'

'Shall I kill them, master?' she enquired eagerly.

'No no no,' he replied, irritated. 'Just listen. When you've finished with the reptiles, I want you to round up a group of humans. They are on the other side of the valley.'

'Instructions accepted, master.'

Rosheen asked, 'Do you really think she's stable enough? She might well turn around and kill us all.'

Sheldukher turned to her. He produced the black square. Rosheen had almost forgotten about it. She took a step backwards.

'At the first sign,' he said calmly. 'At the very first sign of such an act . . . ' The threat was obvious.

Rosheen considered. That was the trouble with Sheldukher, she decided. He seemed so ordinary, so harmless. He was almost fun to be with at times. Doubtless many of his victims had believed the same.

But she had recognized faint glimmerings of fanaticism in his recent actions. Fanaticism was a flaw. A flaw which could lead to him making mistakes. She would be waiting for that moment. Waiting to take her chance.

The cold could have killed them. Bernice shivered inside her coat as she ran the last few feet to the stones. Only the promise of an answer to the mystery of her blanked out past kept her going. She had stopped to drink from a can on the way up, caring little now for what it might be doing to her. All that she knew was that she needed it.

She found the three others standing disconsolately between the jagged stones. For that was what they were. Nothing more than blank, toppled chunks of rock. There were no inscriptions or markings. Only the precision of their linear positioning suggested that they had any significance at all.

They crowded forward silently. In response to the unasked question she handed them the last cans.

'That's it. There's no more,' she told them.

'We'll survive,' said Sendei, with an optimism she could tell he didn't feel. 'There's water here.'

She laughed and pointed to the can in his hand. 'That isn't water.'

She looked around. A huge dark rock, at least two hundred feet high, reared up a short distance away. It was hard to make out its shape in the darkness. It was bulky and rotund at the base and tapered into slender points at the top.

Slender points. Or could they be slender spires?

She ran over to the rock and touched it. Its surface was worn and rough, but her fingers could make out irregular indentations and shallow groove markings.

She stepped back and looked up again. This was the temple.

'Sendei!' she called. 'Sendei, come over here! Look!'

All three youths ran over.

'What gives?' Rodo asked, confused.

'This,'she said, patting the stone. 'This is the temple.'

'The Temple of the Event Shift,' Molassi said slowly. 'Here the Wizard King meets the Lady of the Moonlight.'

He ran wildly around the temple, his boots crunching in the thin soil. They heard him give a cry of wonder from the other side and followed him.

Molassi had passed through a tiny opening that could just be made out in the dim light. It had obviously once been a door. but the stone lintel above had given way centuries before. Whatever decorative covering had concealed the entrance had likewise rotted into dust.

Rodo made to follow Molassi. Bernice halted him. 'Do you think that's wise?'

He shook her off aggressively. 'This is *it*, girl!' he snarled. 'The Temple of the Event Shift! Molassi was right, Zagrat was right!'

He slipped himself through the gap. The jangling of his chains and bells was swallowed up by the blackness.

Sendei wasn't ashamed to show his fear. 'I suppose we'd better go in,' he said with trepidation.

'At least wait until it's light,' Bernice advised him. She spoke with sudden authority. 'One doesn't go blundering into unsound structures without a light source at the best of times. Would you go potholing without a rope?'

Sendei licked his lips. 'I owe it to them,' he said. 'We were brought here together. There must be a reason.'

Bernice frowned. 'You told me you didn't owe them anything.'

He smiled. 'I don't remember.'

She took his hand and squeezed it. She knew that nothing she could say would change his mind. She also knew there was a possibility that she would never see him alive again.

'Take care,' she said. 'I'll be waiting here, just outside.'

He nodded awkwardly and followed the others through the gap.

Bernice shivered again. She walked back over to the standing stones and leant her forehead against one of them. The irritating clarity which her dissolving mind afforded long gone events brought back memories of an archaeological expedition to classify similar megaliths on Sensuron. The team had chosen one stone each, the stone that most resembled them, and given them nicknames. Hers had been called, affectionately, Snooty Cow.

She prayed to the spirits of the long dead gods to whom the stones had been erected. If I'm going to die, she pleaded with them, kill me now. If I'm going to live, give me a future to live in and a present to build from.

Long sleepless hours passed. Bernice's spinning head finally turned from the stone. Why hadn't the temperature killed her? Perhaps it wasn't as cold as it seemed to her distorted senses. She gasped.

An old and deserted city had been revealed by the daylight. It sprawled, as cities will, on a hillside some distance away.

Rosheen stepped on to the surface of Sakkrat. Sheldukher walked ahead of her, hands clasped behind his back.

The atmosphere was fuller than she'd anticipated. The low pressure was uncomfortable, however. It gave the misty, miserable planet an added aura of gloom.

Postine's task had been completed. She stood proud and upright next to an ill-matched circle composed of frightened humans dressed in most unsuitable clothing and whirring, clattering, helpless tortoises.

'Excellent, Postine,' Sheldukher congratulated her.

She inclined her head. 'Master.'

He swept the crowd with a brief glance. 'What a bizarre collection we have here.'

Only a few yards away, the Doctor stood with Vanessa and Hazel. He had sneaked himself into the crowd of humans as the huge woman had herded them over from the train. Her rifle butt had given him a nasty knock, but there would be no lasting damage. Still, he had been knocked out twice in a short space of time and would appreciate some rest. He thought longingly of returning for a cup of cocoa and a slice of toast to the TARDIS. He had a feeling that precious moment would be some time away.

'What's going on here then, Doctor?' asked Vanessa. 'I thought you said all we had to do was wait and you'd get us home.'

'I'm afraid you may have to wait a little longer,' he replied apologetically.

'And what are those horrible Ninja Turtle things?' asked Hazel, indicating the Chelonians.

'Please indulge me just a moment,' he said. 'To be honest, I'm not quite sure myself what's going on. It makes a change, I suppose. Although,' he added ruefully, 'I much prefer it the usual way.'

He tried to keep his eyes off the little man who had emerged from the ship. He was of average enough appearance: smooth skinned, dark haired, in his early fifties. He wore a neat, unremarkable dark blue suit with a fashionably wide collar. He strutted about with the woman at his side, looking the picture of a freighter captain. But there was something worrying about that deceptively bland face. The Doctor's well honed instincts warned him. *Watch out. Shifty. Intelligent. Probably dangerous. Definitely mad*. In fact, the kind of person who could easily keep a deformed monster alive in eternal agony.

His thoughts were interrupted by an irritating tap on the shoulder. He turned to confront Witcher. 'Oh no, not you again.'

'Listen, Doctor Spock,' Witcher blustered. 'I've had just about enough of this.'

The Doctor tried to shake him off. 'Please go away,' he said through gritted teeth.

'This is all some sort of joke, isn't it?' Witcher shouted. Everybody turned to look at him.

'Well go on, then. You've had your laugh,' he continued hysterically. 'Wheel on Jeremy Beadle and get it over with.'

To the Doctor's chagrin, Witcher's outbursts had attracted the attention of the little man and his two female aides. He had hoped to remain out of their way and gain some thinking time.

'What is going on here?' the little man said smoothly.

Witcher strode forward. 'I'll tell you what's going on, mate,' he said, slapping a none too friendly arm around the other's shoulders. 'You've gone too far this time. Digging molehills in somebody's garden, maybe. Smashing up somebody's car, maybe. But this . . . '

He gestured inarticulately around at the spaceship and the Chelonians.

'I'll have the law on you for this, mate, I tell you,' he finished helplessly.

The Doctor watched all this in horrified fascination. He had no choice but to intervene.

Before he could, the little man brought out a small laser pistol from a pouch at his belt. He pulled the trigger. A bright yellow beam shot from the tip.

Witcher gaped down at the smoking hole in his chest. 'You *are* a spaceman,' he gasped, and died.

His killer sighed and pocketed the pistol. He turned to address the crowd, who were now, understandably, bunched together in alarm.

'The same for anybody that gets out of line,' he said calmly. There was almost, thought the Doctor, a trace of boredom in those measured tones.

He returned his glance to the area around the body. His eyes swept over Vanessa and Hazel uninterestedly, then settled on the Doctor. 'Who are you?'

'Beg pardon?' the Doctor said stupidly. Vanessa and Hazel were astonished by his sudden adoption of a broad West Country accent.

'I said, who are you? What is your name?'

135

'Ah well, seeing as you ask, I'm Norman. Norman Brown. But what's it to you mister?'

'And what are you doing here, Mister Brown?'

The Doctor sucked at his teeth. 'Well there I was, clearing out my hamster's cage, when all of a sudden, whoosh, off I goes to another planet. I'm a bit worried 'bout my Elsie. See, it's gone five and she'll be creatin' if I'm not back for my tea.'

Sheldukher raised a hand to silence him, a pained expression on his face. What a grubbing non-entity. Probably a remedial. He turned dismissively and moved off with his entourage.

'What was all that about, Doctor?' Vanessa asked.

'It's very simple,' he said lightly, but his eyes betrayed the seriousness of his thoughts. 'And from now on, it's Norman, please.'

11:
Death By Trivia

The exploration of the temple was an unsettling experience, for Sendei at least. Its ancient architect had cut large openings in the outer walls to allow light to filter through, but the planet's night, moonless and starless, offered no illumination.

They seemed to have been stumbling through pitch blackness for hours now. Molassi led them silently onwards and downwards. He did not stop to warn them of any of the unseen hazards he was first to discover. Sendei and Rodomonte were forced to navigate the tiny passages for themselves, and had narrowly avoided falling into open pits at least twice.

'Rodo,' Sendei called. The jangling of his friend's bells and chains, which he had been using as an aid for navigation, had ceased abruptly. 'Rodo!'

He sensed Rodo's presence a few metres ahead of him. 'Rodo, speak to me!'

Rodo's voice came back. 'He's gone.'

'Molassi?'

'Who else?' There was panic in his voice.

Sendei licked his lips nervously. 'Let's turn back. Let's go back for Benny.'

He heard Rodo slide to the ground defeatedly. 'You lead the way, then.'

Pointlessly, Sendei looked around. His eyes were wide open but he could see nothing. They were trapped.

'We've got to go on,' he said.

Rodo pulled himself up. Sendei felt his friend's hand brush his cheek.

'Not just the clever boy, are you?' he said admiringly.

Sendei smiled. 'Come on.'

He pushed Rodo aside and took the lead, his hands outstretched. The rough rock walls had already scraped a layer of skin from the palms.

A few minutes of silent shuffling brought them to a junction. The passage was narrower here, tapering off into three turnings. None of them offered any distinction from its neighbour.

Then a voice echoed tunelessly from the passage directly opposite. 'Source of the Light, Wizard of the Night, Wild Lady of the Ruins ... '

Both Sendei and Rodomonte recognized the opening lines of another of Zagrat's interminable anthems.

Rodo sighed with relief. 'Molassi.'

Sendei remained still and silent, ignoring Rodo's push at his shoulder. 'There's something wrong.'

'Get mobile,' Rodo urged impatiently.

'Light,' said Sendei. The outline of the junction was just visible. The light was coming from straight ahead, the same passage that Molassi's voice echoed back from.

'Move,' Rodo said. 'Come on!'

Sendei walked on reluctantly. Now that the answer to the mystery seemed so close, why did every instinct warn him to turn away from it?

The passage continued for another few metres. As he edged forward, Sendei glanced up occasionally at the far end. The light was brighter now. Details of decorative paintwork were visible on his left side although only the lower portion of the work could be seen clearly. It depicted what he took to be some sort of religious ritual. Most of the figures involved were obscured by the slanting roof. The passage had obviously once been a high ceilinged corridor.

Sendei turned the final corner and emerged into a small circular space. The walls were covered with a riot of colourful designs, patterns that swirled like those on a headster-time blouson. Molassi sat cross legged next to a thin column of bright white light, which stood like a radiant strut at the centre of the chamber. His mantra like repetition of the lyrics continued as the others emerged wide eyed into the light.

Such power. All there in the light, waiting to be claimed by the Wizard King. He was protected now. It was time he started getting mad with the freakster and the clever boy.

'This place is,' Rodo shrugged his shoulders. 'Cosmic.' That word was so uncool, so headster-time, but there was no other way to describe the sight.

Sendei looked into the pillar of light. Its core was unbearably bright, but the outer edges were tinged a paler green. A low buzz of power warned him away from touching it.

He turned to examine the walls. The people of the planet could be seen more clearly here. They were humanoids: short, Caucasian but hairless, with thin lips and bulging black eyes. Most were naked, indicating a profound environmental change at some point in their planet's history, although some of the women wore simple, collarless robes of deep purple. Some were eating, drinking or making love; others spun cloth on machine looms or baked bread in silvery stoves. Another group, exclusively male, was gathered around what Sendei guessed was a highly advanced piece of technology. Two of them were making adjustments with hand tools. Two others stood watching over them with plans clasped in their hands.

There was evidently more to this alien antiquity than he had first supposed. Perhaps it had been an oligarchy, in which scientifically aware elders kept the mass of the populace in a state of ordered ignorance. It was a sociological model established on many worlds, arguably on old Earth itself.

He turned back to the pillar of light, into which Rodomonte was now staring gormlessly. Might it have been placed here in the temple by the rulers to inspire the religion of the herd?

Molassi sang on. 'Wizard King, shine the light on your servant, Wild Lady of the Ruins, protect us from the moonlight's scars —'

'Moonlight's *stars*,' Rodomonte corrected automatically. He hated Zagrat, but Molassi had spun the discod so many times on their journey to Evertrin that he could have recited all their lyrics backwards.

Molassi turned and looked at him. 'Give me a can,' he said.

Rodo laughed nervously. 'You heard what the pretty lady said. None left.'

Molassi leapt up. He grabbed Rodomonte by the scruff of the neck and pushed him towards the light, holding his nose inches away from the crackling fluorescence.

'Give. Me. A. Can!' Molassi repeated, tightening his grip.

139

'There's none left,' Rodo gasped. 'There's none left!'

'Put him down!' shouted Sendei. He took the Deep Space discod from his jerkin and held it meaningfully towards the light source.

Molassi relaxed his grip. Rodo collapsed, choking. The bastard had gone too far this time. Well over the limit.

Sendei backed off, alarmed by the ferocity in Molassi's eyes.

Molassi growled, sprang forward, and shoulder-butted Sendei to the ground. His hand clamped around the clever boy's neck.

Sendei raised the discod again. 'Drop it!' Molassi screamed. He bashed Sendei's head against the wall. 'Drop it!'

Rodo pulled himself up, rubbing at his throat. He hooked an arm around Molassi's spitting, jerking body and pulled him off.

'There's no more stuff, Molassi. No more stuff!' he said again.

Sendei got up, bruised and angry. He had tolerated Jab Molassi for too long. The crazy headster needed teaching a lesson. He looked down at the discod still clenched in his hand and threw it impulsively into the pillar of light.

It glittered eerily for a second and exploded, forming a cloud of tinsel.

Sendei realized immediately that from every possible viewpoint, the destruction of the discod had been a bad move. But his mind had clouded over again at the wrong moment and now it was too late.

There was silence. Molassi pushed Rodomonte away and strutted forward. His expression was unreadable beneath what was now almost a full beard. His pale blue eyes were fixed on Sendei's own. His hand slipped down to his belt.

His knife struck upward and punctured the area below Sendei's ribcage.

Sendei watched it happen. He saw the blade go in and then come out gleaming red with his blood. He sank to his knees, more from shock than pain. He couldn't die. Not now, not when there was so much left to discover.

'It was only a discod,' he whispered weakly. The answer had been so close.

'It was my life, clever boy,' said Molassi. He wiped the blade clean on his skin coat and walked out.

Rodomonte hovered nervously on the other side of the chamber. He tried to think of something to do or say, but it was too late. Sendei's kneeling body twitched and then was still.

Sheldukher panned the scanner camera slowly over his captives. He slammed his fist down angrily on the console and turned to the twinkling carrying case.

'You are certain there is no other life in this area?'

The Cell groaned an attempted response.

'Well?'

'I have ... located no other ... life signs ... '

Sheldukher sighed. He returned the scan to the small group of humans, watched over by the formidable figure of Postine and the less formidable figure of Klift. They really were a most peculiar bunch. What were they doing here?'

Rosheen entered the flight deck. Her left hand was concealed behind her back. 'I interrogated a sample, as you ordered.'

He swivelled his chair to face her. 'And?'

'Well,' she said, 'I'd say they were remedials of some sort. They say they come from Earth, and that they were transported here by some means they cannot understand.'

Sheldukher nodded. 'Many remedials call their worlds Earth,' he said. 'The low quotient members of society have never been noted for their imagination.'

'I assume they were brought here in a spacecraft,' Rosheen continued. 'They have no conception of any technology beyond level three, so we can take their account of a magical transposition less than literally. They are obviously very primitive.'

She glanced out at the humans. 'I've no idea why they are here, though.'

'And the tortoises?' Sheldukher asked.

'I can't get very much out of them,' Rosheen admitted. 'They're called Chelonians. As we know, they're cyborgs. Their tanks seem to be part of the framework of a ship; there are meteorite impact scars on some of the surfaces. From the angle at which their vehicles were pointing, I'd say they were getting ready to blast those remedials.'

'Chelonians,' Sheldukher muttered. 'Indeed.'

'So what's your next move?'

'I have to find this doctor.'

'Use the Cell.'

He shook his head. 'I can't risk losing it. It was almost destroyed the last time.'

He leant forward suddenly. A detail on the screen had caught his eye. He selected the relevant area and magnified it.

One of the humans, the short man in the hat, was talking animatedly to two young women. His face achieved several improbable expressions as his arms flew wildly about, like an epileptic conducting a symphony orchestra.

'Norman Brown,' Sheldukher mused. 'I wonder.' He opened a communications channel. 'Postine?'

'Master?'

'Postine, when you assembled your human prisoners, exactly where did you find that short man with the umbrella?'

'Master?' she grunted uncomprehendingly.

Sheldukher rolled his eyes up to heaven. He flicked open another line. 'Show her, Klift.'

A few seconds passed. 'You're right,' said Rosheen, her attention held by the screen. 'There is something odd about him. And he dresses slightly differently from the rest.'

Klift's voice filtered back to the ship. 'Sheldukher?'

'Yes?'

'She says she found him just outside the ship.'

'Did she indeed?' Sheldukher said. 'Behind the Chelonian lines . . . Thank her for straining her brain cells for us.' He broke the connection.

He stood up and moved towards the door. 'I think we've got him.'

Rosheen saw her chance. She raised the oddly shaped blaster she had taken from one of the Chelonians and fired.

The bolt shot past him and blasted a hole in the wall next to his head. His instinct for self preservation had warned him of her move long before she had made it.

He extended a leg and kicked the weapon from her hand. They both dived for it. He reached it first, typically.

'Kill me,' she taunted him. 'Pull the trigger.'

He smiled.

'You still need me,' she gloated. 'You need all of us.'

142

He removed the charge from the blaster and tossed it aside. There was no need for such a weapon. His hand went into his pocket. The black square appeared.

A rush of blood went to Rosheen's head as the infection he had implanted did its work. Her heart palpitated. She felt her spine curving and keeled over on to her front.

'Expect me back in a few minutes,' she heard him say distantly. He left the flight deck.

She raised a hand to her hair. It was thinner. Her fingernails were flecked with white spots.

Bernice lay face upwards on the rock. Her ambitious trek to the distant city had been curtailed by protests from her over-worked nervous system, crying for more of whatever the pink cans contained. Her mouth was filled with bilious acids that her stomach had sent up in sympathy.

Footsteps crunched past nearby. She propped herself unsteadily up on her elbow. Molassi appeared from the mist. It was much thinner here. His breath formed green clouds in the clear air.

'Molassi!' she cried out. 'Where are the others?'

He stared at her for several seconds as if he could not remember who she was. Then he strode forward and shook her roughly by the shoulders. She tried to resist but hadn't the strength.

'You've got stuff,' he slurred in her ear. 'Where is it? Tell me!'

She shook her head. 'It's all gone,' she said weakly. 'The dispenser is empty.'

'Where is it?' he screamed. 'I'm the Wizard King. You must tell me. Where?'

Bernice pushed him away. 'I don't know, I ... ' she began confusedly.

She registered the bloodstains, dark red on the dirty white skin of his coat. 'Where are the others? What have you done with them?'

He took her roughly by the hair and pushed her face down into the ground. He kicked her savagely. Then he walked away.

Bernice fought back a wave of panic. She got to her feet and started to run back down to the temple. She collapsed twice, but pulled herself back up angrily and went on.

The temple came back into sight at last. In the daylight, it resembled a gigantic anthill. Small holes dotted its rough green bulk.

She walked around the building, trying to find the entrance. Two bodies were sprawled outside it.

Rodo lay face downward, his arm draped protectively over Sendei's shoulder. Bernice saw that he was sobbing silently.

'Rodo,' she called.

He looked up, his eyes small red weals. His jacket was covered in blood.

Bernice prodded Sendei's body gently. His head flopped back pathetically. She winced and turned away.

'It was Molassi,' Rodo stammered. 'Molassi killed him.'

He staggered into her arms. 'Sendei was all right,' he said. 'He was my mate.'

Suddenly he broke free from her grasp. 'Where's Molassi?' he shouted. 'You've seen him, haven't you?'

Bernice nodded. Her head turned automatically over to the city on the horizon.

Rodomonte grunted and stumbled off.

'He'll kill you,' Bernice shouted after him. 'He's insane.' Rodo did not reply.

She turned back to the body. It wasn't right that Sendei should just be left here. She peered cautiously inside the temple. Daylight showed a rough-walled stone entranceway and several small tunnels leading off from it. A trail of blood had been left by Sendei's body, dragged up from below by Rodomonte.

She went back out into the daylight and began to gather together some of the larger rocks that were scattered about.

The Wizard King knew that his coronation was near. The ice crown was waiting for him in the city, protected only by the ghosts. Still, something was wrong. He recalled the lyrics of the final track of Sheer Event Shift, the mournful Ghosts And Guilt Trips.

> *Don't meet your masters unprepared*
> *The dragon is stirring in its lair*

>*Hyper destiny is a kinetic philosophy*
>*Got to open your mind and stare*

Yeah, Matyre was a poet. A dark poet that sang about dark things. And old geek critics had laughed at him. Well, the laugh was on them now.

The higher power that gave Zagrat their music was warning the Wizard King in those words. He had to open his mind or the dragon would destroy him.

He took a small cube of A resin from the pouch next to his knife. There was no pipe to hit, so he'd have to swallow it.

Jinkwa had stopped trying to break free from the trap. His spirit had not been broken; rather he was afraid of tearing himself apart with the involuntary jerking of one side of his limbs in the opposite direction to the other. He had managed to find the General, but with one eye pointing up at the sky and the other angled down at his nose, there was little scope for effective communication.

'Gen ... eral,' he stammered, 'we must ... be free ... of this ... '

'Do you ... think I ... did not know ... that?' Fakrid retorted.

'We must ... override the ... parasites' ... signal ... '

'Fear not ... Jinkwa ... ' the General stormed through his vibrating lips. 'The Doc ... tor has ... deceived us ... for the ... last time ... '

'Sir?'

Jinkwa's peripheral facets caught a glimpse of Fakrid's twisted features. His mouth was contorted in a grotesque snarl, pulling back his lips to reveal yellow teeth dripping with misdirected digestive enzyme fluids.

'When the ... time ... comes ... the Doctor ... will be ... immersed in ... boiling mercury ... ' he threatened with relish. 'And I ... will make ... a nosebag of ... its skin ... '

The Doctor had decided to share as many of his various dilemmas with Vanessa and Hazel as time, and their limited comprehension, would allow. He needed allies, and with

Bernice hopefully safely out of harm's way with Rodomonte and his friends, these two young women were fine substitutes.

'My main worry,' he concluded, 'is that the Fortean flicker may start up again at any moment. It would be just my luck to get myself knee deep in even worse trouble.'

'I hope your friend's all right, Doctor,' said Hazel. 'What with that funny drink and all that.'

He sighed. 'She's very capable,' he said. 'I'm sure she'll be all right. Almost sure, anyway.'

Vanessa dug him in the ribs. 'Watch it. Here comes trouble.'

Witcher's murderer had emerged from the spaceship and was walking towards them. He signalled to the enormous woman to join him.

'Good morning, Norman Brown,' he said sceptically.

The Doctor returned his menacing glare with an expression of vacuous innocence. 'Ah. Morning, sir.'

'Morning, Mr Sheldukher,' the other corrected.

The Doctor struggled hard to retain his composure after this revelation. Never would he have expected encounters with an assault force of Chelonians *and* the galaxy's most notorious criminal in the space of a day. One problem at a time was more than enough. But that was a Fortean flicker for you.

'Morning, Mr Sheldukher,' he replied.

Sheldukher pointed to a nearby mound of rock. 'What is that?'

Vanessa spoke up. 'It's where we buried the man you killed,' she said bravely.

'How touching,' he said flatly. He turned back to the Doctor, and looked disdainfully at his attire. 'Why do you wear that?' he asked, indicating the sweater.

'Why?' repeated the Doctor. He pointed to each of the question marks in turn, answering in his village idiot voice. 'Why. What. Where. How.'

Sheldukher smiled and stared into those innocent eyes again. 'Who.'

'And who, of course.'

'Of course.' Sheldukher turned around and walked over to where another of the eight twelves, a woman in her late twenties, sat on a rock. A baby was cradled in her arms. It could not have been more than six months old.

'If I may?' He plucked the child from its mother's arms before she could protest. It started to cry.

Vanessa and Hazel turned in agitation to the Doctor. He stood frozen, his face a mask of indecision.

Sheldukher held the baby up with one hand. 'I'm looking for somebody,' he drawled casually. 'And they know who they are. Unless that person steps forward immediately, this child will die.'

There was a long pause. 'Very well,' Sheldukher said eventually. He glanced over at the huge woman. 'Kill it,' he said simply. 'And mind my arm. I'm rather attached to it.'

Postine, unquestioning as ever, raised her weapon.

'No!'

The Doctor leapt forward. He snatched the baby from Sheldukher's grasp. It stopped crying.

Sheldukher smiled and produced his laser pistol.

12:

Guilt Trips

Bernice heaved the final stone into place on top of the makeshift burial mound. Sendei's accusing face was at last concealed from her.

She sank down to the ground, hugging her knees and rocking herself back and forth to keep warm. The craving for the cans had returned, this time coupled with a dull, burning pain that seared along her arms and legs. Withdrawal symptoms, she knew. Without any information as to the nature of the chemical that had poisoned her system she had no way of telling if she would come out alive at the other end of the process. Even if she did, she might end up a helpless vegetable.

Sendei, despite his faults, had been her last link with a sane, reasonable universe. More than that, he'd been a friend, in a funny sort of way. Now he was gone and she was alone again.

'It's way past time,' she thought aloud, 'you started thinking for yourself.'

She forced a grim grin. 'Smile, and the galaxy smiles with you,' she said, and clambered to her feet. She set her sights on the city and pushed herself painfully on.

'Forward!' she cried halfheartedly. 'What other way is there?'

The still atmosphere of this area had protected the city well. Rodomonte hardly noticed the magnificent, unearthly architecture preserved so beautifully away from the squalls of the less temperate zones. He stumbled with vengeful intent through wide, open-topped courtyards and along covered, low-ceilinged walkways. The toppled heads of long forgotten deities and dignitaries observed his passing, the silence they had enjoyed for centuries broken by the rattling of his chains and bells.

It was easy enough for Rodomonte to follow the path taken by Molassi. Recent bootprints were marked in the thin coating of green sandy soil that had been blown by gentle breezes over the buildings.

Molassi seemed to be heading for a large structure. It was a cone, similar in shape to the temple, that dwarfed the other buildings in this quarter of the city. That made sense. There was something in the last track of Sheer Event Shift about the Wizard King being crowned in a towering castle.

Rodomonte came crashing to a halt as withdrawal pains shot through his arms and legs. He cried out and grabbed at a nearby wall to steady himself. The nausea threatened to overcome him, but his determination to avenge the death of his friend was too strong. The pain subsided. He pulled himself up and went on.

Minutes later, he stood outside the cone shaped building. Its sides were moulded in a swirling, perfectly symmetrical design. A small flight of steps led up to its entrance: a low, doughnut shaped arch through which Molassi had recently passed.

Rodomonte picked up a football sized rock that lay close to the entrance, and passed through.

Unlike the temple, this building was illuminated. The entrance hall was lit by three light pillars. Rodomonte picked his way around them cautiously.

'Molassi!' he called. 'Molassi!' His shouts echoed around the cylinder formed by the walls. Unsurprisingly, there was no reply.

He walked on further into the building and through into a vault at the end. It seemed to be empty. He glanced upwards. At the very top of the structure, at the point of the cone, a space had been left open to let in the light. Murky clouds passed over, mocking its long-dead designers' memory of the now obscured sun.

There was another source of light. Rodomonte saw where a large stone had been lifted, presumably by Molassi, to reveal a wide hole through which shone an upward rushing beam of soft yellow light.

He ran over and peered down. Rungs had been moulded into the stone on either side. With the rock still grasped firmly in his left hand, he began to negotiate the glowing gap. He was going to kill the evil headster whatever he did.

Only nuttos take resin straight, his Pa used to say. If you're gonna drop A, hit the pipe.

Now the Wizard King understood why people said that. It was a conspiracy, see. Only special people, chosen ones like him and Matyre, could see it. All the stiffs, straights and squares, hippies, heavies and hardcases, they were all in it together, trying to stop the headster-time ever coming round again. And when you took A resin straight, well then, yeah, then you could see it, see what they were up to, bribing riggers, faking reports.

You could see a lot on A, more than usual. So while his real eyes glanced round at another vault of blank green rock, his A eyes saw the first of the ghosts sliding out of the stone to say hi.

It felt inside his head. It wanted to know all about him. Well, that was cool. It had to be sure he was the Wizard King, after all.

So he thought up lots of cool things he had done, to impress it, to show it how much he deserved the ice crown. Like when he'd pushed that mouthy girl under the Whirli Go Round. Like when he'd poured acid into Hugo's water carrier. Like when he'd killed the clever boy, who had blasphemed the headstar time.

But the ghost wasn't interested. It kept asking him something different, something weird he didn't understand. This wasn't right.

Now it was showing him something back. It was vaguely familiar. Yeah, it was the opening credits of that cruddy freakster holo show Rodo used to record sometimes.

And then he saw a face he recognized. It was Matyre. This was more like it. But no, it couldn't be Matyre. His hair was cut short with a cowlick dropping over at the front, like a freakster. He was wearing chains and bells like a freakster.

'Great. So, Slon, how do you feel about Zagrat, looking back from the freak time?' asked the bimbo interviewer.

'Zagrat was sad music, Erada,' he replied primly. 'My new discod *Style Over Substance* couldn't be further away from it.'

'Yeah it's like, well,' Erada remarked, head tilted nervously towards an unseen floor manager, 'the lyrics, well, yeah, the lyrics are very different to those on Zagrat's final discod, *Sheer*

Event Shift.'

'Now they were appalling,' laughed Matyre. 'The music company wanted new product fast before the headster time ended so I dashed it off one afternoon after I'd dropped some A. Goodness, some of the interpretations people came up with! And it was all rubbish!'

'Yeah. Great. Well. So you've no A influenced numbers on *Style Over Substance*, yeah, no?'

'Certainly not,' he replied firmly. He turned to face the camera lens. 'Listen, I love my fans. So listen, kids. Don't touch dumb hallucinogens like A. Listen to your Ma and Pa, and forget the headster time ever happened. It's fun to be a freakster!'

Molassi reeled. He couldn't believe it. Matyre had *sold out.* Sold out to the freaksters. And Zagrat didn't mean anything. It had never meant anything. The freaksters had taken over. It was like the headster time had never happened.

He reached for his knife.

The Doctor was marched on to the flight deck of the F61 at pistol point. He looked about at the patchwork of technologies.

'Oh dear,' he said flippantly as he caught sight of the Cell, floundering helplessly in the carrying case. 'Not another one.'

He addressed Sheldukher. 'Call me old fashioned, but I think brains belong in heads, not in tanks.'

'It's not a brain, and that's not a tank,' Sheldukher replied evenly.

'Same difference,' the Doctor said casually, and slipped into the command chair as if he had been the ship's pilot for years.

'Get up,' Sheldukher said smoothly.

'Shan't,' said the Doctor with infinite menace.

The tension of the moment was broken by a groan from the corner. Rosheen crawled limply into view.

The Doctor leapt instinctively to her side. Surely this couldn't be the woman he had seen earlier? She appeared to be at least twenty years older. He felt for her life signs, then looked angrily up at Sheldukher. 'You had no right to do this,' he blustered.

Sheldukher slipped the laser pistol back into his pocket and substituted the black square. 'Nothing irritates me more than righteous indignation,' he said lightly. 'And I'll do it again if you refuse to co-operate.'

The Doctor settled Rosheen as comfortably as possible in a chair. 'What is it you want from me?'

'The Highest Science.'

The Doctor shrugged. 'I'm as much in the dark as you are.'

'You didn't arrive with those remedials. You must be a Sakkratian,' Sheldukher continued with cool logic.

'Really,' the Doctor snorted. 'Do I look like the kind of person that would make his home on a ball of rock like this?'

'Then you've come to steal it.'

'I have come on a scientific investigation to rectify the freak effect which brought those poor unfortunates,' he waved at the screen, 'to this forsaken place. I'm afraid that the commercial appeal of this planet is entirely lost on me.'

'I'm not speaking of money,' Sheldukher continued. 'I'm talking about knowledge. Ancient secrets. A lost power. Perhaps we have something in common.'

The Doctor shook his head. 'I doubt it. Absolute power never appealed to me either. Fine for the first couple of weeks, but then there's all that tedious paperwork.'

Sheldukher smiled approvingly at the Doctor's witticisms. 'You're a scientist, I'm a scientist.'

The Doctor snarled. This was all wrong. People weren't supposed to react like this. 'You, a scientist?' he scoffed. 'I suppose you're kind to dogs and small children as well?'

Sheldukher leaned forward with interest. 'So, I am remembered?'

The Doctor sighed. 'Remembered and reviled,' he said bravely. 'People always wondered what had happened to you. In the end, they were just thankful that you'd gone.'

He turned back to Rosheen. The Doctor recognized the signs of an unstable metabolism that had been forced into accelerated decay.

'You must have been asleep for a very long time,' he said. 'She's pumped full of preservative.'

'A long journey. Three hundred years, near enough.'

'To get here? In a ship like this, it shouldn't have taken you more than eight from the central hub.'

Sheldukher indicated the Cell. 'It took that long for the Cell

152

to find this planet.' He drew a circle in the air with his free hand. 'We took a circuitous route.'

The Doctor glanced at the Cell. Its appearance was shocking, even to a traveller accustomed to many different varieties of life.

'It's fascinating,' he admitted. 'It should never have been created, but it is fascinating.'

'It is thought, Doctor,' said Sheldukher excitedly. 'It thinks for itself. Its potential is infinite. Think about it. A living creature that can solve every riddle in the universe.'

'You created it?'

Sheldukher shook his head. 'It wasn't me. Doctor. Tell me, did the great galactic public ever find out what was going on on Checkley's World?'

The Doctor sighed. 'The Horror Planet. I might have guessed,' he said sadly.

'All that costly security for nothing. I took it from under their noses. An entire fleet of the most advanced ships was sent to get it back. They didn't expect this old transporter carrier to be fitted with cellular disrupters.'

'I only hope the poor creature's effort was worth it.'

'Oh yes. Now tell me where to find the Highest Science,' he said. He indicated Rosheen. 'Or I'll kill her and every one of those remedials.'

The Doctor looked at the screen on which the eight twelves and the Chelonians could be seen, still under the watchful glare of Postine. He knew that Sheldukher would not hesitate to carry out his threat, and also that he was far too intelligent to risk attempting to deceive him as he had Fakrid. He would just have to play along for a while and wait for an opportunity.

'Very well,' he said at last. ' ''Where the gas seeped weakly over the rock, ten thousand or so miles from the blasted pits of volcanic ore that blazed with the light of a thousand suns, there I made my abhorred discovery ... '' '

'What are you talking about?' Sheldukher demanded angrily.

The Doctor shrugged. 'Those are the only directions I have. From the account of another ''scientist'' who once passed this way.'

Sheldukher turned eagerly to the Cell. 'Well?'

'There are ... active volcanos ... in only ... one area ...

of the planet . . . near to the northern . . . pole . . . '

The Doctor winced at the sound of the creature's voice. He recalled the agony it had shared with him.

'Excellent,' Sheldukher said tersely. 'Set a course. Program the sensor pods to seach for any sign of ancient habitations within a twelve thousand mile radius of the pole.' He turned his attention back to the screen. 'Time to recall the rest of my gallant crew, I think.'

Postine was bored. She had taken to growling menacingly at the more impressionable of the remedials to keep herself occupied. How she longed for the excitement of blasting away slimy aliens. Guard duty was not her strong suit.

Her communicator buzzed. 'Postine, return to the ship,' Sheldukher ordered. 'Bring Klift with you.'

'Master.' She grunted her assent and shuffled off to collect Klift.

Jinkwa overheard the exchange. 'They are . . . leaving . . . '

'Good . . . ' Fakrid growled. 'As soon as . . . the signal . . . is out of range . . . we shall . . . follow and . . . destroy them . . . '

Rodomonte emerged from the glowing tunnel into a dimly lit passageway. The source of the light was a tiny phosphorescent ball, hot to the touch, that lay at the foot of the rungs. Absently, he picked up a blackened spacesuit glove that lay next to it. Its significance was lost on him and he let it drop, confused.

He continued down the passage. Every step he took seemed to be resented by the stonework, which creaked and rumbled ominously about him. Such was his sense of purpose that he didn't notice.

The passageway ended in another small, circular chamber. The light was much dimmer here, but he could see something, a shape, at its centre. He edged forward nervously, the rock raised in his hand.

He came closer and recognized the shape as Molassi. He was sprawled at an unusual angle, arms and legs stuck out in all directions. Rodomonte leant closer and dropped the rock in shock.

The haft of Molassi's own knife was embedded in his throat.

A rumbling sound was coming from somewhere near. Rodo glanced confusedly up at the ceiling, half expecting the roof to collapse in on him. But the sound was coming from behind him.

He turned his head wildly about from side to side. The light was getting brighter. The rumbling had become a steady, low roar, that seemed to be coming as much from inside his head as from all about him.

The cavern was illuminated fully for a second. Molassi, with his long blond hair and still expression, was made to look strangely angelic.

Rodo screamed as the light surged up to a brilliance that stung his eyes. He screwed them up and sank to the floor.

The noise stopped. The light faded. Rodomonte opened his streaming eyes tentatively.

A transparent humanoid figure hovered a few feet away. A tiny point of light shone from the centre of its forehead. He felt like it was asking him a question or searching for something in his mind. He couldn't answer.

Rodomonte saw his father beating his mother. He heard himself telling a girl that if he hadn't made it in the music business by his twentieth birthday, he would kill himself. He saw Sendei laughing and joking about an acquaintance one night in the Seminary bar.

He picked up the rock. There were tears in his eyes.

The Doctor broke open a water pouch. He sniffed disapprovingly at the scent, and brought it to Rosheen's lips. She sipped at it gratefully.

They examined each other and drew the conclusions people will on first acquaintance.

'Relax,' the Doctor suggested.

Rosheen sprung up from her couch in panic as she remembered what Sheldukher had done to her. She put a hand to her face. 'No!'

The Doctor put an arm around her shoulder. 'Please, rest,' he urged her.

She shook him off. 'You can't know what this is like.' She

looked about, confused. 'Where is this?'

'Your cabin,' he replied. 'Sheldukher allowed me to bring you here.'

'I'm surprised,' she said. 'He seemed to consider you quite a threat. You are the Doctor?'

'When it suits me.' He leant forward. 'Sheldukher has the means to kill every one of those people out there if I move against him.'

'Believe me,' she said grimly, 'he'd do it. He once destroyed an entire constellation just for the sake of it. The deaths of a few remedials won't shake him.'

She struggled to rise from the couch. The Doctor pushed her down gently and tried to make her comfortable. 'Just lie back and relax,' he said.

He turned to the food container. 'I'll make you something. You'll need protein.'

He riffled through the box, selecting and discarding various items. She asked, 'Anyway, just who exactly are you?'

'Never mind about that now,' he said. He set one of the packets to boil and walked back to her. She looked up at him trustingly.

'Just the Doctor, then?'

'Just the Doctor, yes.'

She extended a hand weakly. 'Rosheen.'

An alarm bell rang somewhere in the Doctor's memory. 'As in Rosheen and Klift?'

She took back her hand. 'I'm surprised people remember us.'

The Doctor turned his back on her. 'I've seen entire worlds in ruins because of what you did,' he said. 'People starved. Wars were fought. Millions of innocent lives . . . ' He trailed off, lost in appalled thought.

Rosheen seemed to be revived by his words. Her face hardened. 'Those things happen every day. They would have happened had we withdrawn that credit or not. You obviously don't understand economics, Doctor.'

He stared at her. 'I understand morality.'

'It's easy to talk,' Rosheen replied. 'We were accused of all those things. Maybe we were "responsible". People seemed to forget that the entire fourth zone was in a perpetual state of

156

starvation anyway.'

She leant forward angrily. 'The money we lifted was hardly intended for them in the first place, was it?'

The Doctor gave a deep sigh. It was easy to forget sometimes that the rest of the universe, particularly the human part of it, did not operate on the basis of his own clear-cut standards.

'I suppose not. We none of us are innocent.'

She swung herself off the couch. 'If you're looking for somebody to blame for needless deaths, look no further than Sheldukher.'

'That does puzzle me,' he confessed. 'Why you took up with him on this unlikely enterprise.'

She held up her wrinkled arm. 'Do you think this was through choice?'

Before he could reply, the cabin started to vibrate. They clung to each other for support.

'Pre-ignition warm up sequence,' said Rosheen. 'Where can we be heading?'

'The lost city of Sakkrat,' said the Doctor.

'You told him?'

'Yes,' he replied despondently. 'I'm afraid I did.'

Vanessa and Hazel watched the ignition of the F61's mighty furnace engines with a mixture of relief and trepidation.

Hazel cheered. 'Good riddance!'

Vanessa sighed. 'But the Doctor's in there.'

There came a sudden metallic commotion. The Chelonians, inspired by the signs of the F61's imminent departure, were struggling furiously to free themselves. The rasping and clanking was most unpleasant to the ears of the humans. Vanessa was reminded of her father sharpening blades over Sunday roast.

'I think we ought to get out of here,' she said.

Hazel nodded. 'Oi!' she shouted to the crowd of eight twelves. 'Follow us, come on!' They stared blankly at her, like a flock of sheep startled by a tractor. She set off, away from the Chelonians and the spaceship.

Vanessa hung back to count off heads as they followed Hazel. When the last of the humans had gone, she dashed nimbly over to the nearest Chelonian and swiped the strangely shaped gun

157

from its unresisting grip.

There would be time to work out the exact nature of its functioning later. She hurried off after the others.

'. . . power indices at factor eight . . . impulse clamps at vector strength minus four . . . anchor/ballast ratio nine point four to the . . . seventh and rising . . . '

Sheldukher leant lazily back in his chair as the Cell droned on. A hard copy map of their course was spread out over the console before him. The sensor pods had succeeded in pinpointing an area of the planet's surface that correlated exactly with the Doctor's mysterious directions. About eleven thousand miles north north west of the volcanic pits, the atmospheric envelope thickened considerably. It was a logical place to build a city.

Klift tapped him on the shoulder. 'Yes?'

She pointed to the screen. 'It's the Chelonians.'

Sheldukher noted the reptiles' struggles. 'What about them?'

'They might follow us,' said Klift. Sheldukher stared at him approvingly. So, a streak of his practical talents remained.

His hands flickered over the console and brought up the weapons display. Most of the systems, including the spectronic destabilizer (handy for blasting planets), were too large scale in their effects to be of any use in this situation. Only the hull mounted cellular disrupter was flexible enough in its calibration response for what he had in mind.

A small panel on the hull slid smoothly back. A slender pointed cellular disrupter swung out on skeletal brackets.

Sheldukher angled the disrupter vaguely in the direction of the huddled mass of Chelonians and fired indiscriminately.

A stream of invisible particles shot from the barrel of the disrupter. Four Chelonians bubbled inside their shells and then exploded loudly.

Sheldukher returned the console to navigation functions. He had considered destroying the Chelonians completely, but the ship was now ready to take off and he didn't want to waste time. The deaths of a small number should serve well enough as a warning.

'That was unnecessary,' said a voice from behind him. He turned to see that the Doctor had entered the flight deck with Rosheen.

'You really are beginning to bore me, Doctor,' he said in disappointment.

The Doctor's reply was forestalled by Klift. He rushed over to Rosheen in concern. 'Rosheen . . . '

She brushed him off impatiently. 'I'm all right. Just leave me alone, okay?'

He unsettled her even more than before. She still felt the same inside. Why should he be so changed?

Postine's rifle had turned automatically to cover the Doctor. He edged around the snout nervously. 'Would you mind pointing that the other way?'

Sheldukher gestured to Postine to comply. She lowered the weapon reluctantly.

The Doctor peered at her. 'I hear you had trouble with her earlier?' he said airily. 'She seems sharp enough now.'

'She's one of life's fighters, Doctor,' said Sheldukher. He offered the seat next to him on the console. The Doctor sat.

'We don't have to be enemies,' Sheldukher continued. 'We can help each other. After all, we are looking for the same thing.'

The Doctor raised an eyebrow. 'We are?'

'Answers.'

The Doctor frowned. 'No. I'm looking for a way out. I have enough dark secrets of my own. I'm not particularly interested in anybody else's,' he lied. 'Particularly when there are other matters pressing heavily on my mind.'

'Which are?'

The Doctor consulted his fobwatch. 'A previous engagement of long standing. Of *very* long standing.'

'You're not alone here?'

The Doctor shook his head. 'A friend. She may have wandered off into some terrible danger or other.'

'Doctor, you're neurotic.'

159

The Doctor looked over at him. 'A neurotic,' he said, 'is a man who's just worked out what's going on.'

Sheldukher laughed heartily for the first time since his destruction of the Krondel constellation. He slapped the Doctor playfully across the shoulders. 'We are going to have fun together, I can see.'

The Doctor shrank back from the chill of his touch.

The Cell wheezed into life. 'Systems fully ... aligned ... Ignition sequence complete ... '

'Launch,' ordered Sheldukher.

As the whine of the furnace engines disappeared into the crackling clouds, so the debilitating signal faded slowly away. Jinkwa extended his front left foot forward experimentally. He stretched it and then curled it in and out. Implants locked themselves painfully back into place. A hinge that had been digging into his stomach freed itself. His eyes swivelled crazily about one last time before settling back into place. Facet augmentation returned a few seconds later.

The sudden release after tortured hours of imprisonment was almost too much. Jinkwa let his mid-plastron sink feebly to the ground in the manner of the aged and infertile. Restorative chemicals flooded through his system, soothing his aching muscles. How nice it would be, he thought, to sit collapsed like this forever. With a line of shrubs before you and a sandy bank behind. Cool blue water to swim through ...

No! That was not the Chelonian way! He released a hundred quintols of amyl to remind him of that.

'First Pilot!' the General bellowed from behind him.

He turned about. 'Sir!'

Fakrid's eyes had turned a livid yellow. 'Reassemble the force!' he barked. 'Close down the hospital station! Our strength must be total. We will pursue and destroy! Destroy! Destroy! Destroy!'

'But sir,' Jinkwa protested. 'The parasites' weapon —'

Fakrid kicked his shell. 'Idiot!' he roared. 'Technical stores will set up a cancelling wave. The parasites will be blasted a hundred times for the indignities they have inflicted on us!'

He pointed to the mangled remains of the four Chelonians

160

destroyed by the matter disrupter. 'Their deaths shall be avenged a thousand times!'

'And the eight twelves?' Jinkwa queried.

'We will return for those puny creatures later! I will supervise the sprinkling of zarathion myself. They will die in excruciating pain!'

Jinkwa was stirred by the General's words. But there was something disturbing about the sheer unreasoning rage behind them. He seemed to have exceeded his own limits.

'At this moment,' he continued, 'I can think of only one thing, picture only that thought in my mind. I see the Doctor screaming for mercy as I inflict upon it every agony in the infinite skies!'

'Rodo!' cried Bernice. 'Rodomonte!'

There was no reply from the eerily glowing hole at her feet. She sighed. She had followed the tracks of Rodomonte and Molassi through the city and into the cone shaped building, her poor physical condition blinding her archaeological curiosity. The only way forward seemed to be down. For all she knew, Molassi could be waiting for her at the bottom, his knife drawn, standing over the body of Rodomonte.

She shrugged. Her head pounded, forcing her to come to some decision.

At last she started to descend the rungs into the hole. She had no way of telling how deep it was, but it was narrow enough to support her easily if she slipped or lost her hold.

Only ten feet later she touched firm ground again. As she jumped from the final rung, the structure of the stonework around her seemed to judder. She decided that it was probably just another disorientating effect of withdrawal.

She looked around. At her feet was a glowing ball, the source of the light. It looked hot.

The tunnel she had emerged into led to a circular chamber. In the light from the ball she could see two shapes inside — the bodies of Rodomonte and Molassi. It seemed logical to suppose they had killed one another. But when she looked again, she realized that they were too far away from each other for that to have been possible.

She had seen enough. She turned back to the space through

which she had entered, all the while trying to calm herself. So she was alone? She would have to survive.

The exit was gone. The stonework covered it completely, as if it had never existed.

It was an optical illusion, obviously, probably connected with that deep rushing noise coming from behind her. She'd read about such things. She closed her eyes and took a step forward, into solid rock.

She turned about in unashamed panic. The light was increasing now, blinding her. The rush became a deep howl, inside and outside her head.

The light faded away. A ghostly figure hovered at the end of the tunnel. A point of light shone from the centre of its forehead. She felt it probing her mind, as if it was asking her a question, searching for something in her mind.

Bernice tore her gaze from the creature. She turned and pummelled furiously at the rock wall with her fists.

Something brushed her shoulder. It was a three fingered hand that became more solid and substantial second by second.

13:

Burn Up

Rosheen and Klift ate silently. The throb of the ship's engines vibrated the cabin.

Rosheen pushed away her empty plate and wiped her fingers absently on a sheet of tissue. 'The Doctor told me something amusing earlier,' she said.

Klift looked up, surprised. This was the first time she had addressed him directly since take off. She had spent most of the first hour of the journey deep in conversation with the Doctor, who had gone to the flight deck to check up on Sheldukher.

'Yes?' Klift prompted her.

'Apparently they made holovids about us,' she laughed. 'You were played by Arrad Swanson.'

He smiled. 'What about you?'

'Lithola Baxter, believe it or not.'

His face fell. 'Not very flattering.'

'Oh, I don't know,' said Rosheen. She turned to catch her fifty year old reflection in the metallic wall of the cabin. 'I've started to look a bit like her now.'

She stood and crossed over to the food box, searching for something sweet. 'I must be going senile, you know,' she said.

'What do you mean?'

'This lost civilization business,' she said, turning to face him. 'This exploring. I'm beginning to look forward to it.'

The Doctor shuffled the cards and cut the deck. He would have preferred chess, but Sheldukher could not provide a board, and they both disliked playing on computer grids. Besides, the card game reflected his present situation well. Instead of his usual behind the scenes stage management of pawns and other pieces, he was confronted by an array of unpredictable variables. What was worse, he could not be sure of his opponent's moves or what their outcome might be. His only choice at present was to wait for the right moment to play his hand. The game continued.

'I still don't know who you are,' said Sheldukher.

'It's not worth worrying about,' the Doctor replied. 'My past is so complicated even I get confused occasionally.'

Sheldukher grinned and laid down his suit. 'First round to me, I think.'

The Doctor grimaced and threw his cards on to the console. 'I was never very good at this.'

He gathered the cards together again. 'Just the two of us to play again?' he asked, indicating Postine and the Cell.

Sheldukher nodded. 'One of them has no brain at all, the other is all brain.'

'Ah yes,' agreed the Doctor. 'First precept of a successful card game; do not mix guests of uneven ability. It can be most embarrassing.' He showed off several clever shuffles from his extensive repertoire of parlour tricks.

The Cell spoke. 'Sheldukher ... The sensor pods ... register electrical surge ... at destination point ... '

'Really?' he said, reaching for the map. 'Now that is interesting.'

'But hardly surprising,' said the Doctor. 'We are obviously heading right into the centre of the Fortean flicker.'

Sheldukher looked up. 'Your freak effect?'

The Doctor nodded. He stood up and crossed to the Cell. 'If I may?'

Sheldukher waved a hand in assent. 'Please, go ahead. But don't get any funny ideas, will you?' He winked at Postine. 'I believed that's what one is supposed to say in these situations.'

The Doctor coughed and addressed the Cell. 'Excuse me ... '

'Speak ... Doctor ... '

The Doctor was touched to hear a note of affection in its voice. It obviously recognized him as the only being that had ever showed it kindness.

'I was wondering,' he said. 'Have your sensors picked up any similar surges in other areas recently?'

The Cell consulted the computer. 'No other ... traces ... Doctor ... '

He sighed. 'Good. The flicker seems to be dormant, at least for the moment.'

'We picked up another surge in orbit, Doctor,' Sheldukher informed him. 'Very close to where we picked you up.'

He nodded. 'Indeed,' he said. 'That would have been the arrival of those humans. It was what brought the Chelonians to their valley. I do hope they're all right.'

'There is ... ' said the Cell, 'constant background ... electricity ... on this side ... of the planet ... '

Sheldukher nodded. 'All that is left of the Sakkratians' science,' he said. 'Think of it, Doctor. From what you say, a science that can bend reality any way it wants.'

The Doctor frowned. 'Reality is bendy enough as it stands,' he said. 'At least for me.'

'Two hours ... until touchdown ... ' the Cell reported dutifully. The Doctor looked at it curiously. Sheldukher, absorbed in his map, seemed not to have noticed its newly acquired air of placid servitude. What was really going on inside its mutated mind?

Bernice woke to find herself lying outside the temple. She searched her mind for vague traces of memory. She remembered the touch of a ghostly hand on her shoulder. Now suddenly she was back here. Had she somehow walked here in her sleep? That she had slept at all was an encouraging sign that the contamination was fading.

Night was falling again. She stood up. Across the way she could just glimpse the motorspeeder. Was there any kind of material around here suitable for fuel conversion?

Her head felt much clearer. There was a new sense of purpose in her step as she set off for the 'speeder. She tried to push the painful memories of her young companions' deaths to the back of her mind.

She had not walked a hundred metres before she tripped over a loose stone and went crashing over a steep overhang. Her head was dashed on the rock below and she blacked out.

The night returned. A luminous shape appeared. It stood over

165

her body protectively for several hours, unmoving.

The roar of a furnace engine broke the silence. The ghost flitted soundlessly away.

'Clamps down,' reported the Cell. 'Anchor/ballast symmetry achieved ... anti-grav wave at sine ... '

'All right, all right,' Sheldukher snapped. 'Why can it not just say we've landed?'

Rosheen and Klift had been summoned to the flight deck for touchdown. Rosheen caught the Doctor's arm. 'Look.'

The scanner camera had picked out what was almost a straight line of four unusual things. A mud spattered yellow buggy, beyond it a line of standing stones, an anthill shaped building, and some distance beyond them, the ruins of a huge city, at least two miles wide.

Sheldukher rose to his feet. 'Yes,' he said simply.

'I'm impressed,' the Doctor was forced to admit. 'I'd go so far as to say I was very impressed. Very very impressed.'

'What's that yellow thing?' puzzled Klift.

The Doctor frowned. 'I think it may have something to do with my friend. I hope she hasn't gone into the city.' He sighed, knowing full well that she would have done.

'Think of it, Doctor,' said Sheldukher suddenly. 'In that city, the ultimate secrets of scientific advancement are to be found. The product of millions of years of progress: the wheel, the combustion engine, the stellar drive ... '

'The fruit corner yoghurt,' the Doctor murmured disrespectfully.

Sheldukher turned to them briskly. 'Let's go,' he said. 'Remember, you take your orders from me.'

He gestured to Postine to lead the way from the flight deck. She turned and moved off. Just as she reached the door, it slid shut in her face.

'What is this?' stormed Sheldukher. He moved over to the door control panel, which now glowed red for locked. His touch had no effect.

The Doctor glanced over at the carrying case. 'I think ... ' he began, pointing to it with the point of his umbrella.

Sheldukher dashed over to it. 'Open this door or I'll destroy you,' he stormed. It gurgled smugly up at him.

'You're forgetting something,' Rosheen said. 'That's what it wants you to do.'

'There's something else,' said Klift. 'Haven't any of you noticed? Listen.'

A moaning noise, rising steadily in pitch, was overlaid on the steady background hum of the life support systems.

The Doctor nodded. 'Yes, we've landed. But the furnace reaction has not been damped out. It's building up to critical.'

In the silence that followed his grim pronouncement, all five of them felt the temperature rise by at least ten degrees.

Sheldukher leapt for the control point attached to the carrying case. 'Reverse this!' he yelled. 'I will not be cheated of my prize!'

'Die ... Sheldukher ... ' it rasped. 'Know my ... agony ... as you ... boil away ... in tempering ... megalanium ... '

Sheldukher's hand went for the voltage control.

The Doctor pulled him away. 'That's not the way,' he growled. 'Watch.'

He stood over the Cell. 'Please,' he said politely. 'There is still time to reverse the reaction.'

It stared up at him, smiling. 'All must ... die ... Doctor ... '

'But I was your friend,' he pointed out, a little desperately. 'I have interesting plans for the next few centuries. I want to live!'

'We will be ... united in ... peace ... Doctor ... ' it groaned.

The moan had by now become a furious screech. Rosheen and Klift covered their ears. Even Postine winced. She raised her weapon to fire at the door.

The Doctor knocked it from her hand. 'No!' he yelled. 'This space is too small for a thing like that, you'd kill us all!'

Sheldukher fumbled for his laser pistol. Its thin beam barely scratched the surface of the door. 'Another fifteen years and maybe,' the Doctor snorted.

'I don't understand this,' Sheldukher cried. He put away the pistol and ran to the controls, none of which responded. 'There are failsafes which should have stopped it from doing this!'

'It's had nearly three hundred years to work out how to override them!' the Doctor shouted back. 'I'd say we have three minutes left to do the same!'

Sheldukher turned to Rosheen. 'Do something!' he pleaded.

'It's over!' she sneered back at him. 'Can't you see!'

The Doctor crossed to the control panel and knelt to examine the inspection hatch. He yowled as he touched one of the plates, which took away a layer of his skin. 'It's white hot!'

Thick, greasy black smoke began to pour from loosened fittings around the flight deck. The humans doubled up coughing as it invaded their lungs. The Doctor hooked the handle of his umbrella over his top pocket and pulled his paisley scarf from around his neck. He used one end to shield his mouth from the smoke and wrapped the other around the fingers of his free hand. Why had he never got round to building another sonic screwdriver?

The whine of the furnace reaction stepped up yet again. The knees of the Doctor's trousers were scorched off in an instant. He gripped the edge of the nearest inspection plate and ripped a quarter of it away. His eyes were streaming. He wiped them clear and peered inside the smoking gap. Two wires were visible. The heat had burnt away the coloured insulation so he had no way of telling what functions they governed.

'Sheldukher!' he called. There was no reply. He turned to see that all four of the others had collapsed helplessly on the floor. Sheldukher raised his head. 'What system?' the Doctor mouthed, pointing frantically at the opened panel. There was no longer any point in even trying to shout.

Sheldukher just shrugged. 'There must be a way!' he attempted to shout back. Flames burst from the panel on which he was resting and he leapt up.

The Doctor turned back to the wires. 'Eeny, meeny,' he muttered to himself. 'After all, I've nothing to lose.'

He reached forward and snapped one of the wires clean through between his fingers. Nothing happened.

'Eeny, then,' he said crossly and broke the other. The door hissed asthmatically open. He leapt to his feet. 'Come on, all of you! Move!'

He pulled Rosheen and Klift to their feet and shoved them through the door. Sheldukher grabbed the carrying case and followed with Postine. The Doctor took a last look around. With his usual presence of mind he nipped back and picked up Sheldukher's hard copy map of the planet.

He ran out into the companionway. The heat and the smoke were almost too much for him. He stumbled through, his mouth still covered by the scarf, using his hat to cover his face. At last he came to the exit. His sabotage had opened all the doors around the ship, and the ramp waited for him invitingly. He threw himself almost sideways through the gap, rolling across the ground as much to put out the fire that was burning him as to lessen the momentum of the fall.

He picked himself up. Rosheen, Klift and Postine were still dangerously close to the ship. He caught a glimpse of Sheldukher who, with his usual instinct for self preservation, was scurrying off with the Cell case tucked under his arm.

'Come on, move!' cried the Doctor, racing towards the others. 'We must get out of range!' He led them off, setting a furious pace.

'It's too late, Doctor!' he heard Rosheen say as she slumped to the ground. 'She's going to blow!'

The Doctor turned back to see the ship glowing bright red. 'Down!' he yelled, throwing himself face down. 'Cover your ears! Close your eyes!'

He jammed a finger in each ear. The furnace reaction gave one last bellow.

The ship's middle crumpled inwards. The infection spread, eating up the hull in a wave of fire. A second later, the ship imploded with a deafening blast.

The shockwave passed over them, rattling their bones. The Doctor pressed his nose into the ground and waited for salvation or destruction.

His head popped up a second later. His ears were ringing. He brushed molten fragments from his charred coat. Only a few hundred metres away, the ship was now just a bubbling silver pool. The heat from the wreck straightened the curls of his hair.

He gave a sigh and let his head fall backwards.

Bernice turned uneasily. She wasn't sure if the explosion had taken place in the real world or inside her head. She lifted a hand to her forehead and felt blood and grit.

A dark shape stood silhouetted against the bright morning sky. As it came nearer she saw that it was a little man in his mid-forties. His peculiar clothes were covered in green dust and black soot. Sharp grey eyes peered out from his blackened face. Standing there with his upturned collar and downturned straw hat, from which wisps of smoke still issued, he looked like a garden gnome that somebody had thrown accidentally on to the barbecue.

He smiled. 'I've come to take you away from all this.'

'I'm sorry. I don't know who you are,' she said anxiously.

From his position, the Doctor was equally concerned. Bernice had obviously fallen from the ledge above her. Unlike some of his old friends, she was not the sort of person to go stumbling helplessly into holes. The knock on the head alone could not account for the glazed look in her eyes.

The mind was a delicate mechanism that he disliked inter-fering with at the best of times. He realized that what he was about to attempt was fraught with dangers, for Bernice and for himself. In this situation, however, he could see no alternative.

He held out his hand and angled the blue gemstone of his ring to her face. It caught the smudgy Sakkratian sunlight and refracted it, forming a sparkling glint. 'Look,' he said. 'Look into the blue light.'

Her eyes were drawn by the stone immediately. It seemed to be the only real thing in the universe; the temple, the city, the motorspeeder, all of these were illusions devised to distract her from the important issues, the real business of life.

No, that wasn't entirely true. There was something else, something that stood, like her, four square and solid on both sides of the shutter. It was the dirty stranger in the straw hat. The stranger? No.

The Doctor.

The Doctor was spring cleaning her mind, dusting the mantel-piece of her memory and righting the cracked ornaments that had fallen from it. Every one of them sprang back, mended, into its rightful place in the line. It was a line that began with the excavation work at the Heavenite observatory and her first trip in the the TARDIS (how could you forget the TARDIS?), continued with a confused recollection of pointing a gun at the Doctor in a tunnel somewhere, and ended on Sakkrat (Sakkrat? Zagrat?) with an all too tangible ghost.

The blue glow faded from the ring and it was an ordinary looking gem once again. Bernice's aura had been restored. The Doctor breathed a sigh of relief.

'Listen,' he told her. 'You are Professor Bernice Summerfield.'

'Of course I am,' she mumbled drowsily. 'I'm not that far gone.'

He sighed affectionately. That was more like it. 'Your brain has been poisoned. You must ignore the effects of the toxin. It cannot harm you.'

'I haven't got the faith required for faith healing, Doctor,' she replied.

'You have faith in yourself. Use it. On the count of three, you will awake from the trance feeling rested and refreshed. One, two, three.'

Bernice yawned and stretched. When next she looked up, her eyes were clear, if a little confused.

'I'm starving,' she said innocently.

'Er, well ... ' The Doctor fished inside his pocket and produced a fluff covered dog biscuit. 'There is this.' He regarded it with suspicion, as if afraid that it might suddenly sprout legs and run off. 'Do you know, I thought I'd finished these.'

She sighed, took it from him and took a bite. He waited for the inevitable question. 'What have you been doing? You look as if you've been bickering with a volcano.' She winced and put a hand to her head.

The Doctor wet his grimy hanky and fussed over the wound. 'Don't worry, it's not very deep.'

She pushed his hand away. 'I don't remember how I got it. What's happened?'

The Doctor fiddled nervously with the handle of his umbrella. 'You've got rather a lot to catch up on,' he said.

'Hold it,' Bernice interrupted him. 'You've put the 'fluence on me, haven't you? I feel fine and I'm sure I shouldn't.'

He tapped her on the shoulder and walked away. 'It's for the best.'

She got up and swung him around. 'Doctor, what has been going on?'

'You're ill,' he said evenly. 'Very ill. You may not feel it at the moment because I've blocked your mind from the pain. The important thing now is to clear all this business up before you get any iller.'

'What business?' she demanded angrily. 'I won't be much use to you if you won't tell me.'

He sighed and took her by the arm. 'Come with me. I'll explain on the way.'

'The way to where?'

'The city of Sakkrat,' he said guiltily, pointing to the ruins on the hillside above them.

Sheldukher sat huddled over the Cell case, some distance away from any of the others. His index finger rested on the inbuilt voltage control. The creature inside writhed and squirmed.

'You could have killed me any time you wanted to,' Sheldukher sneered sadistically down at it, 'just by shutting down life support. But no, you really wanted to put me through it, didn't you?'

'Please, Sheldukher ... stop this ... You must stop ... '

'I'll keep you alive forever for this,' he continued. 'An amusement for my old age.'

'The ship is ... gone now ... How can I ... be of use ... to you ... ?' it gasped.

Sheldukher took his finger from the control. 'You have a complete copy of the ship's data core stored in your brain.'

'No, Sheldukher, I ... will not ... '

He picked up the case and cast his eyes about. He could see Rosheen, Klift and Postine examining that curious yellow buggy.

The Doctor turned sadly from his examination of the Zagrat discod. Bernice had been through a lot in the days they had been separated and he was proud of her. She deserved an explanation. 'Another example of Fortean distortion.'

172

Bernice took it from him and shook her head in amazement. 'The entire prophecy, a coincidence. Still, that doesn't stop it from being an accurate prophecy, does it?'

'No, indeed,' the Doctor agreed. ' "Down below the rocks fall, hear the sound of the dying". '

'And the Wizard King?'

The Doctor shrugged. 'Crowned with ice. Death.'

'You'd have liked Sendei,' she told him. 'His death seemed so pointless.'

He nodded and put a consoling arm around her shoulder. 'Every violent death is a pointless death.'

They had stopped on a small rise, at Bernice's insistence, to compare stories and devise plans. The Doctor had wanted to run straight back into danger, as was his wont, but she had persuaded him that on this occasion at least, some forethought and preparation would be a better idea than just leaving everything to chance and inspiration, particularly as the former seemed hell bent on giving them a hard time of things. She still found it hard to believe the Doctor's explanation.

'It doesn't end properly. The discod, I mean. It's Molassi's story. We don't really come into it.'

'At least we know something of what we're getting into,' the Doctor said, optimistic as ever. 'We have Urnst's account and now this to guide us.'

Bernice stood up. 'Let's get on with it, then.'

'If you're feeling up to it.'

'Watch it, Doctor,' she joked. 'It takes more than a poisonous soda to subdue me.'

She walked off. The Doctor stared after her anxiously. 'I hope so,' he said.

Rosheen gave the motorspeeder's controls one last thump and gave up. 'It's packed up. No fuel charge.'

'It's an antique. Shouldn't work at all,' agreed Klift. 'We're stuck here.'

'We must find Sheldukher,' said Rosheen. 'He's got the Cell, it could still help us.'

'Help us?' Klift exclaimed. 'It wants to kill us!'

Postine nudged him with the butt of her rifle. 'He is back,' she said.

They looked up to see Sheldukher coming towards them, the Cell case under one arm. He held the black square in his other hand.

'Postine,' he said. Her gun raised automatically to cover Rosheen and Klift.

'You can't be serious about going on with this,' Rosheen protested.

'As far as I'm concerned, nothing has changed,' he said.

'There is the small matter of a splattered ship,' she reminded him.

He came towards her. 'There is the Doctor's ship.'

'Sorry, but it's a two seater,' said a familiar voice. They turned to see the Doctor and Bernice approaching.

'That's all right,' said Sheldukher. 'I only have one bottom.'

'There's gratitude,' said the Doctor. 'I'm sorry, but this is where we get off.'

Sheldukher raised the black square again. 'I'll kill them, Doctor.'

'You've persuaded me,' he said lightly. 'Besides, my young friend here is intrigued by the archaeological implications of our situation.'

Sheldukher strode over to her. 'Another expert?'

She eyed him coolly. It was an odd sensation, coming face to face with the bogeyman of her childhood. 'You are Sheldukher, then.'

'Yes.'

'My mother used to say you had scaly green skin and terrible halitosis.'

'Really,' he chuckled. 'It seems that reports of my breath have been greatly exaggerated.'

'This is all very pleasant,' said the Doctor. 'But I suggest we move on.'

Sheldukher turned to him. 'You seem remarkably keen all of a sudden, Doctor.'

He shrugged. 'Well, I'm curious, you know,' he said. 'And there are those, of course.' He pointed with his umbrella in the direction of the destroyed ship.

The remains of the Chelonian assault force trundled aggres-

174

sively into view across the plain.

The Cell laughed wickedly. 'Nothing to save you ... now, Sheldukher.'

'It's true what they say about pets taking after their owners,' the Doctor whispered to Bernice.

'We've no defence against them,' said Klift in alarm.

'Indeed not,' said the Doctor. 'It's budgerigar time again.'

'I should have destroyed them,' said Sheldukher. 'But the science of Sakkrat will help us.'

'Then I suggest we find it quickly,' Bernice urged. 'They're closing in fast.'

She and the Doctor broke into a stumbling run. Rosheen and Klift followed. Sheldukher turned to Postine. 'Hold them off for as long as you can.'

'Master.' She straightened her weapon and turned to stand her ground. Sheldukher scurried after the others.

Up ahead, Bernice paused to take a deep breath. 'Are you all right?' asked the Doctor.

'Well, I feel fine up here,' she tapped her head. 'It's my body that seems sluggish.'

'You've been through a lot,' nodded the Doctor. 'I wish I could say take it easy.'

Rosheen and Klift had caught up with them. 'Come on, Doctor,' urged Rosheen.

Bernice glanced back down at Postine. 'She'll be blasted to pieces,' she said.

'You haven't seen her in action,' said Rosheen. 'Now move!'

The Environments Officer turned from his console at the rear of the command vehicle. 'Sensornet confirms that that is the wreckage of the parasites' spaceship.'

Jinkwa turned to Fakrid. 'It appears that they have somehow been destroyed, sir.'

The General's stare remained fixed on the forward screen. 'No, I do not believe it.'

Jinkwa sighed. The General's behaviour was becoming ever more illogical. 'But the sensornet, sir —.'

'To Gaf with the sensornet!' screamed Fakrid. 'I sometimes wonder what you'd do without the stupid machine. You believe

175

everything it tells you!'

Jinkwa pointed to the screen. 'My own eyes tell me that their ship is gone, sir.'

'And my own instincts tell me that they escaped!' fumed Fakrid. 'When you've been a soldier as long as I have, I tell you, you can smell a parasite from the other side of a black hole! We go on.'

'First Pilot,' the Environments Officer called urgently.

'Report.'

'Sensornet confirms visual sighting of infestation in this area. Massive electrical energy releases underground have reduced the accuracy of our equipment by seventy one per cent.'

'There!' jeered Fakrid. 'Even your precious sensors, Jinkwa, concur with me! Forward! Maximum power!'

Jinkwa shuffled himself about to face the Environments Officer. 'The detection of the parasites is good news,' he whispered. 'We shall crush the spineless fleshies in our mighty claws.' He glanced about cautiously and lowered his voice even further. 'But I am concerned for the General. His shame at the hands of the Doctor parasite seems to have unhinged him. Never before has he dared to question the sensornet or insult another officer so openly.'

The Environments Officer glanced over at Fakrid's shaking shell. 'Have you not realized, sir?'

'What are you speaking of?' Jinkwa asked.

'The time is day twenty of the occupation schedule,' the Environments Officer continued. 'We were supposed to have returned to Chelonia by now. The occupation force would have come in to settle Vaagon.'

'So?'

'The General should have received another dose of fertizol to stimulate his brood cycle for his next assignment. He has not. Neither has his brood cycle been deactivated, like yours or mine, or any other serving soldier's.'

Jinkwa turned with horror to the General. The unthinkable had happened. Fakrid had entered the Time of Blood.

14:

City of Ghosts

The Doctor and Bernice had reached the boundary of the city some distance ahead of the others, after a long and exhausting run. They collapsed gasping to the ground.

The Doctor wiped his brow with his handerchief. 'We've put quite a distance between us and them.'

Bernice looked around at the city. Her mind was free to appreciate it properly for the first time. 'I can't believe this place. It's ... ' She shrugged. 'Well, it's one of the best I've seen.'

The Doctor followed her gaze. 'Ironic, isn't it? The Chelonians will probably blast it to pieces.'

'That side looks older,' remarked Bernice, pointing out a further quarter of the city. 'The spires resemble those of the temple.'

The Doctor peered in the direction she had indicated. 'Yes. There seem to be a lot of triumphal arches, which would suggest regular ceremonial occasions, possibly victory parades.'

'And yet,' Bernice continued, 'the nearer sections seem much less ordered: the rational street-grid replaced by narrow alleys between various tacked on blocks.'

The Doctor nodded, intrigued. 'You're suggesting a slow social reversal rather than the legendary toppled empire?'

Bernice shrugged. 'Could be. War, disease or climatic change could account for such a throwback. Although the additional buildings would suggest population growth rather than loss, which argues against those possiblities.'

The Doctor stared at her silently for a few seconds. 'Bernice, you're a pleasure to know,' he said finally.

She smiled. 'Oh,' she said, rather surprised. 'Thank you, Doctor.'

Rosheen and Klift staggered into view, followed by Sheldukher. 'Those things are still coming after us,' said Rosheen.

'Good as she is, Postine won't hold them off for long,' said Klift.

'You're finished. Finished,' the Cell cackled.

'There's no alternative,' said Sheldukher, ignoring it. 'We must enter the city, find some way to destroy them.'

'You're presuming rather a lot,' the Doctor pointed out, 'from a heap of crumbled ruins.'

'This is Sakkrat, Doctor,' he replied. 'Who can tell what's in there?'

The Doctor raised his eyebrows to Bernice. Her story of the fate which had overtaken Rodomonte and Molassi had intrigued and alarmed him. Whatever terrors awaited them in the city, it would be better to take a chance than simply wait for death at the hands of the Chelonians. 'Very well,' he said. 'Professor Summerfield, would you lead the way?'

She looked back at him. 'You really want me to take you there, Doctor?'

He nodded. 'Down there seems a better bet than up here at the moment. As the man said, we may find something useful. It's our only hope.'

'Provided we can ever get out again,' she reminded him.

A loud explosion echoed up the hillside. 'Let's get moving,' ordered Sheldukher.

Postine had loved guns from the moment her mother had passed a toy replica through the bars of her playpen. Other children had developed similar fondnesses for teddy bears or dolls or even blankets. 'Look at little Marjorie,' her mother's friends had laughed as she fired aggressively at them during boring plastiware parties. 'She's going to be a proper little madam when she grows up!'

Parents of other children in their block had dispatched their reluctant offspring to the door of number nine to enquire if Marjorie was coming out to play. 'But she's creepy,' they had protested. 'She's a shy little girl who needs friends to bring her out of herself!' their elders had protested, shaking their heads in exasperation at the thoughtlessness of the younger generation.

Such charitable gestures had proved fruitless. Little Marjorie Postine had refused all offers, and seemed content to remain up in her room all day, with the curtains drawn. Nobody knew that she really was playing with the local children, in her own way. She would lift a corner of curtain up now and again, imagine she had a blaster with sights attachment, and use her would be playmates for target practice as they leapfrogged and hopscotched around the courtyard below.

School had simply made matters worse. Slow to make friends and disappointing academically, Marjorie had developed a perverse popularity by dint of an enterprise nichnamed 'rent-a-beating' by her classmates. For a small fee, usually a week's tuck allowance, she would duff up any victim selected.

The electroshock therapy that followed her hospitalization of one unfortunate schoolboy left Marjorie a dull husk of her former self. Despairing of ever finding any use for her, her parents sold her to the military, a callous practice common in the commercially minded years of the mid-twenty-fourth century.

And so Postine became a mercenary, developing a reputation second to none. Sheldukher's choice of bodyguard had been a good one. But the reason she obeyed him so readily was not financial. She had no need of money. She was fond of Sheldukher because he had given her her dream weapon. A Moosehead repeater. It could blast a hole in a neutron star and it was all hers.

Now it was time to use it.

The forward screen zeroed in on the figure of a parasite. Although most parasites looked exactly the same, Jinkwa recognized it as the large female who had snapped the bones of several of his division.

'There is but one!' screamed Fakrid to his gunners. 'Destroy it!'

The gunners aligned the disintegrator with practised ease. 'Target aligned, gridmark nine by one.'

'Fire!' ordered Fakrid frenziedly.

Jinkwa thought he saw the parasite raise its weapon in a puny gesture of defiance. Much good would it do against a disintegrator!

The command vehicle rocked from side to side. The crew righted themselves to find that the forward screen had blanked out.

'Fire!' Fakrid shouted again.

The gunners hammered at the controls. 'Disintegrator will not respond, sir,' cried the first.

Jinkwa snarled. 'What parasite trickery is being played on us now?'

The Environments Officer swung about. 'Our disintegrator cannon has been blasted off!' he cried incredulously.

'What?' spluttered Fakrid. 'What?'

'It must have been blasted off at the weak point of the stalk,' the Environments Officer continued. He shook his head in reluctant admiration. 'Amazing marksmanship for a parasite.'

'And forward vision?' asked Jinkwa.

The Environments Officer shrugged. 'The scanner turret must have caught the blast, sir,' he said meekly.

Another blast rocked the command vehicle. 'We're running blind, General,' Jinkwa called over to Fakrid. 'We must pull back. We cannot co-ordinate an assault from such a position!'

The second blast had done more damage. The lights began to flicker on and off. Reports began to come in of successful strikes on other vehicles. One had been destroyed.

Fakrid reached for the emergency stop control and pressed it. The command vehicle ground to a halt. He began to shake loose from his harness.

'Sir, what are you doing?' cried Jinkwa in astonishment. 'We must turn back!'

Fakrid grabbed a footgun from a nearby wall rack and primed it. 'The parasite is but one,' he said. 'I am but one.' He operated the exit control.

Jinkwa straightened himself. 'General Fakrid, I cannot allow you to leave the command vehicle,' he stuttered reluctantly.

'You're a good man, Jinkwa,' said Fakrid. 'But hear this. You'll have to kill me to stop me going out there. And if you try, I'll make sure I kill you first!'

He disappeared down the exit hatch. Jinkwa shook his head in bewilderment. 'Orders, sir?' prompted the second gunner.

Jinkwa turned to him. 'Pull back. All units are to pull back. The attack will resume shortly.'

He swivelled round to the Environments Officer. The scientist shook his head ruefully. 'The old fool may be the death of us all,' he said. 'If the parasites don't get him first.'

Jinkwa nodded. 'The Time of Blood,' he sighed, remembering the legends of his people, 'it was always so.'

Postine watched suspiciously as the Chelonian forces retreated. Her grip tightened on the butt of her rifle. The loss of one vehicle and the leading tank's offensive capability was not enough to cause a full scale withdrawal. She suspected trickery and stood her ground.

She glimpsed the shell of one of the creatures scurrying behind a line of rocks. It was obviously a scout of some sort. She aligned the sights of her rifle and loosed a fusillade of bolts that split the rocks apart.

The creature came into vision. It was a little larger than any of the others and a red stripe had been painted across the length of its shell. It limped forward unevenly; one of its back legs had been damaged.

One of its front limbs came up. A pink sparkle shot through the air. She did not have time to dodge it. It caught her on the elbow of her right arm and sliced right through the botched teflon sutures that held the forearm below it in place.

She roared with pain and anger, and used her good arm to send a volley of shots in the direction of the Chelonian. The rockdust prevented her from seeing if she had been successful in her kill. She grunted fiercely and set off up the slope. A higher vantage point would give her the advantage in battle if the creatures returned.

Bernice led the way through the ruins. She stopped for a second to point something out to the Doctor.

'That artwork suggests a two tiered society,' she said. 'The workers toil in the beautiful city that their masters have provided for them.'

'We've seen no evidence of high technology,' pointed out Rosheen.

'Not so,' the Doctor said. 'Technologies can develop along very different lines.'

Bernice nodded. 'Many of the first colonies were built at the expense of societies the settlers didn't understand because their cultures varied from Earth basic,' she said.

'This is all very interesting, I'm sure,' Sheldukher interrupted. 'If I'd thought we were going on a lecture tour, I'd have brought a notepad and a lunchbox. Can we please move on?' He gestured the way forward with his laser pistol.

They turned a corner and found themselves outside the cone shaped building. 'That's it,' said Bernice. 'There's an entrance inside that leads underground.'

The Doctor whispered to her, 'And that's where you saw this ghost of yours?'

She nodded. 'I think so. It could have been the drug making me hallucinate.'

'I doubt it,' he replied. 'Bubbleshake is an extremely harmful substance, but it's —'

The following words never came. The whole world seemed to twist and shake about Bernice. She feared that the contamination had broken through the Doctor's makeshift hypnotic conditioning, but she blinked a couple of times and felt fine again.

The Doctor, however, lay crumpled over the steps outside the building. She hurried over to him and loosened his collar. His eyes opened woozily.

'Is he all right?' Sheldukher asked.

Bernice felt the Doctor grip her arm urgently. 'Did you feel that?'

She nodded. 'Obviously not as badly as you did.'

'It's not how much it affected you, it's the fact that you were affected at all,' he said, straightening himself up.

'What's the matter, Doctor?' sighed Sheldukher. 'I'm anxious to continue.'

'Nothing, nothing, just a sudden dizzy spell. All this excitement's bad for the liver,' he said cheerily and got to his feet. 'On we go, then.' He strode briskly into the building as if nothing had happened.

Klift spoke for all of them as they looked around the sloping entranceway. 'It's amazing.'

Rosheen went over to one of the light pillars. 'This looks more like it,' she said.

'Don't get too close,' warned Bernice.

The Doctor was examining a carving on the far side of the chamber. 'Come and look at this, Bernice,' he called.

Sheldukher set the Cell case down and walked slowly about. 'Yes,' he breathed contentedly to himself. 'Yes.'

'I gave you this ... Sheldukher ... don't forget the Cell ... '

He ignored it.

'What was all that palaver about outside?' Bernice whispered to the Doctor out of the corner of her mouth.

'I'm a Time Lord, remember?' he whispered back, keen to make sure none of the others overheard him.

She sighed. 'How could I ever forget? Well?'

'I've crossed the time lines so many times in the TARDIS that I'm extremely sensitive to temporal disturbances. My head fuzzes up and I want to be sick.'

'That's what I felt,' said Bernice.

He nodded. 'Exactly. Although you've made far fewer trips, so the effect is not as strong.'

'So there's some sort of kink in time about here?' she said. She snapped her fingers. 'The Fortean flicker!'

'Well done,' the Doctor congratulated her. 'Throwing out the occasional tendril of unlikeliness. Somebody, somewhere, has probably just telephoned an old friend by mistake. The trouble is, we're walking right into the heart of it.'

'It could knock us flying at any moment,' she said grimly.

'Indeed,' he nodded. 'Although we can use our reaction to lead us to it.'

'Great,' sighed Bernice. 'I feel like one of those canaries they used to send into mines.'

'Doctor!' called Sheldukher. They hurried over to where he had found a previously unseen exit between two large boulders.

'That isn't the way you went down,' the Doctor asked Bernice, 'is it?'

'No,' she replied, pointing through to the space at the far end of the entranceway. 'There's a tunnel through there.'

'Rosheen, Klift, you go through,' Sheldukher ordered. 'We need to cover as much ground as possible.' He waved the black square at them. 'Remember, the range on this thing is quite long enough for me to dispose of you at any moment should you try to desert me or plot against me.'

Rosheen smiled acidly. 'Would we?'

He indicated the passage. 'In you go. We will follow the route taken by Miss Summerfield.'

The Doctor took Rosheen by the hand. 'Be careful.'

She smiled and turned to Klift. 'Come on.' To Sheldukher she said, 'We'll report back in an hour, yes?'

He nodded. Rosheen and Klift passed through the small gap without a backward glance.

Sheldukher levelled his laser pistol at Bernice. 'Lead the way.'

'After what happened last time,' she replied. 'I've no desire to go back. There's something very unpleasant down there, and it kills.'

'I have a weapon,' he pointed out. 'Now move.'

'Do you know,' she said coolly. 'I've always thought there was something a bit sad about grown men waving guns about like that. It makes me wonder if they aren't deficient in some other aspect of their lives.'

The Doctor winced. Bernice's bluntness had got her into trouble before.

'Do you?' Sheldukher replied calmly. 'Do you indeed?' His finger tightened on the trigger.

He moved with his usual lightning speed, slapping her brutally across the face. She reeled back. 'I should keep your opinions to yourself.'

He waited for them to pass through into the central chamber. The Doctor picked up the Cell case. It had quietened itself down to a low, continuous burble. 'I assume we'll be taking him along?'

'Just do it, Doctor,' Sheldukher said impatiently. He waited for the Doctor to pass in front of him and followed.

'Don't antagonize him,' the Doctor warned Bernice.

'We could jump him,' she whispered. 'That thing down there could kill us. So he's got a gun. There are two of us.'

'Don't even consider it,' the Doctor chided her. 'It isn't for nothing that he was called the most dangerous man in the galaxy.'

Postine waited on the far side of the temple building, her teeth gritted. She was accustomed to pain, but had never yet let an opponent strike her and survive. She smiled as the Chelonian appeared in the valley below her. Good. It was right that she should make it suffer for what it had done.

She lined up the sights on her rifle on its empty front foot and fired twice. Let the contest be equalled!

Fakrid screamed as his right front foot was blown off. 'No,' he whispered through gritted teeth. 'I will not allow one puny parasite to better me!'

He scanned the area above him and caught sight of the parasite. It had reappeared around the side of some crumbling, unimportant rock structure. He swiftly adjusted the setting of his footgun. It began to glow red for overload. This would be his finest moment. He brought back his foot as far as it would go and channelled all its hydraulic power into a forceful throw. The grenade left his grip at almost the same moment as another beam struck him full across the carapace, cracking it. No matter. The parasite would not live to see its success. All the indignities he had suffered since their abduction to this rock of a planet would be avenged.

'Die!' he screamed up the hillside. He saw the footgun, now glowing white hot, head straight for its target in a graceful curve. 'Die in the name of Nazmir and for the glory of the mighty Chelonian race!'

The temple was blown to pieces, showering the helpless Postine with enormous chunks of rock. She held the Moosehead repeater to her chest and died with a sentimental smile on her face.

Bernice was blown off her feet by the shockwave from the explosion. The Doctor struggled to keep himself from slipping down the glowing tunnel, which he had entered first.

'Are you all right, Doctor?' Bernice called down after him.

'Just about,' he called up. 'Let's get on.' He gripped the Cell case tightly in his hands and continued the climb down.

Bernice turned to Sheldukher. 'What do you think it was?'

'It sounded like Postine at work,' he said. He gestured to the tunnel with the pistol. 'Follow him down.'

Bernice lowered herself into the hole. Whatever it was down there, the Doctor should be able to find a way round it. She heard the stonework about her creaking and shifting.

'I don't like the sound of that at all,' she whispered to herself.

Klift cocked his head at the distant rumble. 'What's that?'

Rosheen sighed. 'Probably nothing. Go on.'

The route they had taken into the underground passages had led them along a wide, high-ceilinged passageway that was easy to negotiate. Light pillars were spaced at regular intervals.

They reached what appeared to be the end of the tunnel. Klift stretched out a hand to the blank wall before them. 'This is it, then.'

'Looks like it,' agreed Rosheen. 'We'd better get back to the Doctor.'

'You trust him, don't you?' he asked curiously.

'He isn't stupid,' she replied. 'He knows how to survive.' She turned her back on him and walked away.

'Rosheen,' she heard him call embarrassingly. 'Was I stupid? Stupid to love you?'

She turned. He stood in the light from the nearest pillar. Traces of his old personality remained in the lined face. She was shocked by how much she didn't care.

'Probably,' she admitted. She just didn't understand some people.

The rumbling and creaking returned, much louder this time. Rosheen looked up automatically. She saw the stones above her crack across. Fine powder rained down on her.

'What's happening?' asked Klift.

'What do you think?' she yelled. 'Get down!'

She made to run across and pull him away but was knocked down by chunks of falling masonry. She rolled herself up in a ball and covered her head. She heard Klift cry out under the shattering din of the falling rock.

The rockfall lasted at least a minute. When she was confident it was safe to do so, Rosheen pulled up her head. She could see nothing through the thick clouds of dust that choked her. She attempted to stand. To her horror, her left leg was trapped beneath a lump of rock. She pulled it frantically to no avail, then forced herself to remain calm and sat up. She wiggled her toes and gave a sigh of relief. With care she manoeuvred her upper leg from the rock. Her foot then slipped through easily.

She stood up and clambered clumsily over the fallen rocks towards where Klift had been standing. He was trapped, face up, under a thick stone slab.

'Rosheen . . . don't leave me . . . Rosheen . . . ' he moaned. She could see that he was concussed.

'I'll go and get help,' she said. 'The Doctor will help you get out.' She turned and retraced her steps back along the tunnel.

'Rosheen, don't leave me on my own . . . ' she heard him cry pathetically.

'Just wait a moment,' she called back angrily and walked on. That despairing bleat touched a heart she hadn't been sure still existed.

Klift lay beneath the fallen slab, broken in body and mind. Pain prevented him from thinking clearly. Under the rock, he could feel himself losing a lot of blood.

The light in the passageway suddenly brightened into a blazing radiance. So he was going to die again.

A translucent figure appeared before him, its three fingered hand outstretched as if to claim him for death. Strange thoughts about his recent past were torn from his subconscious mind, as if the thing was asking him questions. He tried to shield his past from its probing.

He screamed again and again as it came closer, certain that it had been sent to judge him. The screaming stopped. His eyes closed.

The ghost sensed the emptiness that follows the death of a mind. The subject had been responsive and his death unnecessary.

At the foot of the laddered tunnel, the Doctor bent over curiously to examine the glowing ball. 'Different again,' he mused, 'from those pillars. Could be amplified phosphor emission, I suppose.'

'Don't touch it, Doctor,' warned Bernice. She was now burdened with the unpleasant task of carrying the Cell.

'Do I look like a half wit?' he snapped, pulling his hand back hastily. Something else caught his eye. 'Hello, what's all this then ... '

'What is it, Doctor?' asked Sheldukher anxiously.

The Doctor held up his find. It was a tattered blue spacesuit glove, charred at the fingertips. 'Not a Sakkratian artefact.'

'Urnst,' said Bernice. 'He must have passed this way.'

The Doctor nodded. 'And he obviously *was* stupid enough to touch that thing. Didn't mention that in his account, did he?'

Bernice grinned. 'He probably thought such rash actions would tarnish his reputation as a scholar.'

Sheldukher sighed. 'Enlighten me, please.'

The Doctor waved the glove at him. 'This belonged to the gentleman explorer who happened upon this city many years ago,' he explained. 'A man whose footsteps we are now re-tracing.'

'He came here? Without finding the secrets?' Sheldukher demanded.

'He ran away from them,' Bernice informed him. 'Easily intimidated. Not a hardened pioneer like us, you see. A novice.'

'The question remains,' the Doctor continued, 'what exactly scared him off? He gave only vague hints in his account.'

'That we are about to discover,' said Sheldukher. 'Let's move on.'

Bernice looked with dread at the far end of the passage. She could see the bodies of Molassi and Rodomonte.

The Doctor noted her anxiety. He tapped her reassuringly on the arm. 'Whatever happened to them,' he said, 'remember, you survived it.'

They walked through into the chamber. The Doctor looked sadly down at the bodies. 'Senseless waste of life ... '

Bernice pointed to Molassi. 'He was completely screwed up. But Rodo was okay. A bit wild, but okay.'

The Doctor nodded. 'If only I'd recognized the signs of Bubbleshake contamination when I met him. I think his system had already been weakened by some other compound, anyway.'

Sheldukher looked about angrily. 'What is this? There's no way out!'

The Cell spoke. Bernice was so shocked she nearly dropped the case. 'Can't you feel it ... Sheldukher ... ' it gasped. 'Can't you ... feel it?'

'What do you mean?' he snapped at it. 'Tell me!'

It laughed up at them. 'It's telepathic, remember,' said the Doctor. 'It can sense something here. Some sort of presence.'

He concentrated hard but could detect nothing.

'Doctor!' cried Bernice. She pointed to the far side of the chamber. Three ghostly shapes were forming gradually out of nothingness.

15:

Exits and Entrances

Jinkwa had left the command vehicle under the control of the Environments Officer and ventured forth in a scouting party with two of his troopers.

'Now remember, lads,' he briefed them as they scuttled purposefully over the rough rocky ground, 'this isn't some parasite we're searching for, it's a Chelonian officer. A highly respected officer, at that.'

He spoke these words with a heavy heart. The General had been the emblem of the service, his name synonymous with all that was glorious, right and true. His eggs had been the first to hatch on many worlds. His reduction to insanity would have been unthinkable before the events of this most peculiar of missions.

'Strikes me, sir,' said Ozaran, first of the troopers, 'that although it's a terrible shame and all, we're only risking our own necks going after him. I didn't like the sound of that big bang earlier. I mean to say, what with him having gone twisty, like, and those freaky parasites probably still hanging around ... ' He trailed off uneasily, having noted Jinkwa's pernicious stare.

'Never in my career,' said the First Pilot, 'have I heard such insolence. There can be no excuse for such remarks. Three stars are hereby deducted from your promotion chart!'

There you go, thought Ozaran mutinously. Typical officer class. Old Fakrid's hardly been gone two time units and already our clever First Pilot has begun to sound exactly like him.

Linta, second of the troopers, started anxiously. 'Look, sir,' he said, pointing ahead with his left front foot.

Only a few hundred metres from them lay Fakrid. He was slouched pathetically against a boulder, his face turned shamefully to be the ground. One of his feet had been blown away and he had lost a lot of blood from a wide crack in his shell.

'Stay here,' Jinkwa ordered Ozaran and Linta. He motored off alone. He didn't want any of the riff-raff polluting the moment.

'Look at him,' Ozaran muttered disrespectfully to Linta. 'Jumped up little strawberry sucker. Looking back on it, I think I'd prefer to take my chances with the General.'

Linta averted his gaze. 'I'd keep such thoughts to yourself, if I were you,' he said haughtily.

Jinkwa stopped before the General. 'Sir,' he said awkwardly.

Fakrid's neck rose just a little. His eyes turned to Jinkwa. 'Ah, Jinkwa, my boy ... ' he cooed weakly.

'Sir, your injuries are severe, but the efforts of our best cybersurgeons could replace your foot ... '

Fakrid shook his head. 'Don't humour me, boy. I destroyed the parasite but it wounded me badly. I know my time has come.'

'There may still be hope −'

'There is no hope,' interrupted Fakrid. 'All that I command is yours now. But ... ' A wistful look filled his eyes.

'Yes, General?'

'There is something,' he said falteringly. 'Something ... I'd like you to know.'

Jinkwa nodded. 'I'm listening, sir.'

'It's about your mother, Jinkwa,' he said.

Jinkwa frowned, puzzled. 'My mother died when I was very small, in transit to the colony on Mantikroz. His ship was caught in a rockstorm.'

'That is not so,' Fakrid said. 'That was your adopted mother. Your real mother was a soldier in the Chelonian army. Promotion to officer class meant that he no longer had time to care for his own litters. As you know, the state places such eggs in the care of foster mothers.'

A burning sensation crept across the back of Jinkwa's neck. He could not believe what he was hearing, but he knew that the General would not deceive him in these, or any other, circumstances. 'And?' he prompted.

'That officer went on to great deeds. His children were

hatched and grew on many different worlds. Many years later, he found himself assigned a new First Pilot. A lad with a name that was somehow familiar.

'You see, Jinkwa,' he concluded inevitably, 'I was that soldier.'

'No General, it cannot be,' protested Jinkwa. 'The state computer does not allow related officers to serve in the same force. And besides,' he indicated his shell, 'my colours . . . '

'Oh, Jinkwa,' breathed Fakrid heavily, 'if only you'd inherited my common sense. Computers have been known to make mistakes. Shells are easily painted. You really are my daughter. And all this time, I've known and had to keep it from you.'

A tear fell from the corner of Jinkwa's eye. 'Mother . . . ' he croaked in a broken voice.

'There must be no tears now,' said Fakrid bravely. 'But before I join our ancestors on the banks of the sea of the dead, promise me two things.'

Jinkwa leaned forward eagerly. 'Anything, mother. Name them.'

Fakrid's heavy eyelids were closing for the last time. His voice was now barely a whisper. It seemed that his final revelation had soothed him, prepared him for death. But there were obviously still more things he had to say.

'My ashes,' he wheezed, 'scatter them over the plains of Narazel, where I was born, and frolicked through the blackberry fields . . . '

'And?' Jinkwa said anxiously. 'There was something else.'

'Something else?' queried Fakrid. 'Oh, yes . . . ' His wizened features twisted back into the snarl that had so characterized his time as General. 'Just one more thing. You must see to it . . . that the Doctor . . . dies . . . '

He exhaled his terminal breath and his neck flopped down limply. Jinkwa stifled a sob. He rested his own head against his mother's shell.

Ozaran and Linta looked on. They had overheard nothing of their superiors' conversation.

'A scene that will be immortalized in our history,' said Linta and began to hum the opening bars of the Chelonian anthem.

192

'If you ask me, that's going a bit far,' said Ozaran as he watched Jinkwa snuggling up to the dead body of the General. 'I mean, let's face it, he was a good leader, but a right miserable old prune when it took him.'

Linta did not have the chance to reply. Jinkwa had wheeled about and was now coming back over to them. 'You will carry the General's body back to the command vehicle,' he ordered. 'We will then return to the attack. It would appear that the parasites have fled underground — their traditional defence. We will destroy the aged structure on the hill and trap them.' He shuffled off.

'Come on, then,' Ozaran urged Linta. 'Let's shift the dead-weight.' They crossed over to the General's body.

The Doctor and his party watched warily as the three ghostly figures beckoned with one digit of their three fingered hands. An exit had appeared magically behind them.

'What are they?' Sheldukher whispered in the Doctor's ear. His fingers tightened around the trigger of his laser pistol.

'I'm not entirely sure,' replied the Doctor. He stepped forward hesitantly. The wraiths did not react.

'The one I saw earlier,' recalled Bernice. 'Its head lit up, like it was probing my mind for something. If felt like somebody's hand inside my head.'

The Doctor nodded. 'They're not substantial, remember,' he said. 'It's probably how they communicate.' He walked bravely over to the nearest of the shapes. Even at close hand it remained ill formed and shadowy, rather as a cloud of mist apparently disappears on examination. The Doctor's hand passed through it. 'There, you see. Just like faery gold.'

'No,' said Bernice. 'I remember it touched me on the shoulder.'

The Doctor smiled. 'I didn't say it couldn't touch you. I said that you can't touch it.'

She frowned. 'That's ridiculous.'

His grin spread even further. 'Isn't it?'

Sheldukher moved to join the Doctor. 'Then these are pro-grammed projections of some sort?'

'Nothing so elementary,' he replied. 'They have a life of their own, limited as it may be. They can open and close doorways. They also have the power to kill.' He gestured at the bodies of Rodomonte and Molassi.

'Surely they killed themselves,' reasoned Sheldukher.

'Yes, but why?' puzzled the Doctor. 'Those things must have implanted some sort of image in their mind, stimulated the right emotions to make them do it.'

'Ghosts and guilt trips,' said Bernice, almost to herself.

'Exactly,' said the Doctor. 'So why did it kill them, but leave all of us, and Urnst presumably, alive?'

'Intelligence,' said Sheldukher.

The Doctor pondered a moment. 'It could be.' He looked from the beckoning figures over to the smooth blank walls and tapped the handle of his umbrella against his chin. 'Yes, it could be,' he muttered quietly, thinking otherwise. 'Yes, yes . . . '

Sheldukher pointed to the still beckoning figures. 'I suggest we go on. They seem anxious that we should.'

The Doctor snapped out of his reverie and peered down at the Cell, still clasped in Bernice's grip. 'What do you think?' he asked it.

It remained silent, unused as it was to being asked for its opinions.

'Come on,' said Sheldukher, gesturing with the pistol.

The Doctor shrugged and was about to lead the way from the chamber when they heard footsteps from behind. Rosheen stumbled in, coughing. The Doctor rushed to her side. 'What happened?'

'It's Klift,' she gasped. 'There's been a rockfall. He's trapped.' She started as she caught sight of the ghost shapes. 'What are they?'

'We must go on,' insisted Sheldukher. 'There's no time for this.'

'I can save him,' said the Doctor.

'He doesn't matter,' replied Sheldukher. 'You're to go on with me.'

The Doctor sighed. 'I'll be as quick as I can,' he said to Bernice and set off back down the passageway with Rosheen.

'Doctor,' shouted Sheldukher. 'Come back here!' He let off a warning shot.

The Doctor turned to face him. 'I've no time to argue,' he snapped. 'Watch him,' he said to Bernice, 'and watch yourself.' He hurried off.

Sheldukher raised the weapon and then lowered it with a sigh. 'No, Doctor. I've got other plans for you.'

The junior's reedy bugles sounded, as Jinkwa had ordered. The body of General Fakrid was lowered slowly into the cremation unit. All the remaining soldiers were gathered in silence. When the last notes of the anthem had faded away on the moaning wind, Jinkwa shuffled forward.

'General Fakrid was an officer of unparalleled repute. He led successful campaigns to clear infestation on over forty worlds and was respected and admired by all of his colleagues in the forces. More than that, I think I can say he was loved by the public. Many of you younger boys, I know, were inspired into military life by his example.

'That his distinguished career should have ended in such tragic and unforseen circumstances is regrettable. But let us not forget that he gave his life in an act of selfless devotion to the race. He would not rest until every last parasite was cleared from this ball of rock, and,' his voice began to rise, 'neither will we. Our mission is simple. We shall destroy the parasites that remain as the General would have wished!'

There were cheers and throatily enthusiastic cries for retribution from the crowd. Even the less bellicose members of the force, Ozaran included, had been stirred by Jinkwa's words and were ready to attack. This was not surprising. Jinkwa had used cremation ceremony speech number 401 from the officers' manual to stimulate just that effect.

'Now,' Jinkwa shushed them. 'Now, go back to your vehicles and prepare for the attack.'

Bernice lowered the Cell case gently down and sat next to it. Her vision seemed clouded and her arms weak and stringy. It seemed that the Doctor's hypnotic conditioning was wearing off. She took a few deep breaths to calm her nerves. The presence of the bodies of Rodo and Molassi did nothing to reassure her. Sheldukher was hardly the most comforting companion either. Secretly, she resented the Doctor leaving her with him.

'I see you're ill,' he said, in a voice totally empty of expression. He could have been giving a traffic broadcast.

She looked up. 'Health is a state of mind. Or so I've recently been led to believe.'

He circled the chamber slowly, stopping occasionally to examine the never changing activities of the ghostly figures. 'They must get frightfully bored, standing there beckoning all day,' mused Bernice. 'I wonder if they have a union? It certainly doesn't need three people to do a job like that.'

Sheldukher stared down at her suddenly, as if registering her presence for the first time. 'I should like to discover your limits,' he said suddenly. He spoke so casually that it took Bernice five seconds to realize the implications of what he had said and another five to fear it.

'My limits?' she replied, equally casually. I have to get out of here, she thought.

'Yes,' he said. He crouched down in front of her. 'You see, I get bored too, sometimes. I like to amuse myself.'

'That's nice,' she said and tried to stand.

He prevented her, laying a firm hand on her shoulder. 'You're very cool, very confident. I should like to see what I would have to do to expose other aspects of your personality.'

Bernice launched herself at him, using all of her weight to throw him off her. He clung to her like a clammy spider, pulling her down beside him with unexpected strength. She tried to use aikido moves against him, but he blocked every one with the expertise of a master. They scrabbled furiously about on the floor. Several times, Bernice thought she was getting the better of him, only to realise that he was toying with her expectatons and reactions.

He pushed her down beneath him finally, holding her down with a hand around her throat. Every time she tried to move he squeezed his grip and she felt herself begin to black out. What made it worse was that his face remained so still, as expressionless as it had been earlier when discussing trivia with the Doctor.

There must be a weakness, Bernice thought frantically. Every

196

opponent must have a weakness. It was one of the Doctor's basic philosophies and had always served him well enough.

'You've got such beautiful hands,' she gasped, as calmly as she could.

'What?' he said without relaxing his grip.

'Beautiful hands. A real man's hands.'

She saw a flicker of expression in his blank eyes. Confusion? Anger? She wasn't waiting to find out. She brought her arms up and pulled his hands from her throat. For one terrifying moment she thought he was going to subdue her again but she threw him off with a shove.

His laser pistol clattered from its holster. She dived for it and levelled it at him. 'I have no qualms whatever about firing this,' she warned him. Her finger tightened on the trigger almost by itself. How easy it would be to destroy him.

She backed hurriedly from the chamber and along the passageway. Sheldukher stared after her.

'Not taken by your ... obvious charms eh ... Sheldukher ... '

'Be silent,' he ordered the wretched beast. Its suffering would be as nothing compared to what he had in mind for Bernice. She really should have shot him.

Rosheen led the Doctor over the fallen rocks. A surfeit of rock dust blocked their vision and irritated their throats. In the light from the glowing pillars they could see it twist and settle slowly as they disturbed it.

'He's through here,' said Rosheen, pointing to the end of the tunnel. The Doctor hopped nimbly forward, careful not to disturb the fragile balance of what remained of the structure.

He stopped suddenly. Klift's head was plainly visible. It poked out from the edge of the fallen slab. His eyes were closed and his expression blank.

The Doctor turned to Rosheen. 'I'm afraid he's dead.'

She shook her head. 'That's not possible, he was talking to me ... '

The Doctor clambered over the slab. He prised Klift's eyes open gently and winced. He had seen that look so many times. It never failed to chill him. 'Something odd is happening here.'

Rosheen remained silent. The Doctor looked up. She was staring into nowhere, her face set. 'I'm sorry,' he said.

'Don't be. Sheldukher killed him a long time ago.'

The Doctor stood up and sighed. 'You must have had some feeling for him,' he said a little crossly.

'He was quite something when he was young,' she replied. There was a hollowness in her voice that disturbed the Doctor. He just didn't understand some people.

'He wasn't killed by the rockfall,' the Doctor continued.

'One of those ghost things?' Rosheen asked.

The Doctor sat down on a nearby rock. 'No. Well yes, probably, though indirectly. You see, he died of terror. Something he saw.'

Before Rosheen could react Bernice came blundering in. The Doctor could see she was not in the best of moods.

'The little runt tried to kill me!' she shouted accusingly at him. 'He's insane.'

The Doctor jumped up and took her by the hand. She calmed herself down immediately. There was something about the look in his eyes that told her this was a time to listen and not argue.

'Bernice,' he began, 'and you, Rosheen. This is your chance and you must take it. Get up to the surface.'

'I'm not about to argue with that,' said Rosheen and started to move off.

Bernice frowned. 'What about you, Doctor?'

He sighed. When he spoke again, Bernice recognized the staccato growl that meant business. 'Somebody's got to stop Sheldukher. He's meddling with things he doesn't understand. Things the universe isn't ready for yet and perhaps never will be. If he can take control of the Highest Science, the consequences could be cataclysmic.'

'I want to help you,' Bernice said loyally.

He shook his head in irritation. 'There isn't time for a debate.' He squeezed her hand even tighter. 'You must go. Believe me, I have very good reasons.'

He passed her the TARDIS key from his pocket. 'Wait for me back at the TARDIS.'

She gulped. 'The TARDIS is thousands of miles away.'

'You'll find a way,' he said steadily. 'Have confidence.'

'That's just it,' she said. 'I think the conditioning may be slipping. Can't you give me another shot?'

'It doesn't work like that,' he snapped. 'Now please, just go.'

She smiled bravely. She could see Klift's body from the corner of her eye. 'Down below the rocks fall, hear the sound of the dying,' she quoted.

'Sorry?' enquired the Doctor, worried that her condition had worsened suddenly.

'Nothing,' she said. 'More coincidences. Goodbye.' She kissed him affectionately on the cheek and dashed off before she could persuade herself not to listen to him.

Left alone, the Doctor dabbed at the wet patch on his cheek with a corner of his handkerchief. 'Really,' he sniffed, embarrassed. Then he straightened up, reminded himself of the import of his task, and set off to find Sheldukher.

Instead of retracing his steps back along the tunnel he walked forwards. As he expected, this path, newly uncovered by the rockfall, led him impossibly back to the tunnel where Urnst had dropped the glove. 'All roads,' he mused, 'lead to Rome.'

Sheldukher did not believe in wasting time. He knew the Doctor would return and he made an amusing and, more importantly, an informed companion on his explorations. He had taken the knife from Molassi's body and was studying its bloody tip with interest when the Doctor entered.

'Why didn't you leave with your friend? You didn't have to come back,' he told the Doctor.

'That's just it,' he replied, picking up the Cell case. 'I did. I couldn't leave you here with only misery guts for company, could I?'

Sheldukher sneered. 'We're so alike, Doctor.'

'I sincerely hope not.'

'Curious to the last,' he continued. 'You can't bear the thought of not knowing, can you? You have to know.'

The Doctor crossed over to the ghosts. His face was still but Sheldukher could see that he had been troubled by these words. 'We could both leave now. Come back with me to my ship and I'll drop you off somewhere. We can forget we ever met, that this ever happened, leave this place as it should be.'

Sheldukher chuckled. 'You know what my answer would be. And I know you're only offering to make yourself feel better.'

The Doctor scowled. 'Let's not prolong this.' He walked right through the ghosts and through the entrance they had opened. Sheldukher followed.

The ghosts and the entrance disappeared immediately.

Bernice had caught up with Rosheen as she left the city. They could both tell that in normal social circumstances they would have disliked each other. In their present situation there was no time to worry about such things. Survival was all that mattered.

'Your ship,' enquired Rosheen as they walked down the hill. 'What principles does it operate on?'

Bernice smiled. 'Guesswork, from what I can tell.'

Rosheen stopped. 'You mean to say you can't pilot it?'

'Only the Doctor can,' Bernice explained. 'And even he has problems. It's an erratic vessel, to say the least. Still, it usually gets us where we want to go, near enough.'

'The Doctor's as good as dead,' Rosheen said dismissively.

They had now reached the ruins of the temple. It had collapsed in on itself and only the partially covered base remained to show a glimpse of its former beauty. The two women walked slowly around it. Bernice's glance flickered briefly over to Sendei's grave.

'Bernice,' said Rosheen. A patch of blue coverall showed in the rubble. It looked like Postine had been crushed instantly by the collapsing temple. 'I think the Chelonians have called.'

Bernice cast her eyes about. 'She had a gun, didn't she? We need it.'

Rosheen bent down and pushed aside the rocks that covered Postine's horribly crushed body. She rescued the rifle from the grip of her one remaining hand and grasped it firmly. It made her feel a lot better. 'A Moosehead repeater. Thank God Sheldukher didn't skimp on this. It has a constantly recharging fuel source.'

'I think we're going to need it,' Bernice said. 'The Chelonians are back.'

Rosheen looked up. The few remaining tanks of the Chelonian

assault force were moving rapidly over the rock towards them.

'We don't stand a chance,' Rosheen cried despairingly.

Bernice took the repeater from Rosheen and tossed her the laser pistol in exchange. 'There's always a chance,' she told Rosheen. 'Now get under cover.'

They ran for the shelter of a large chunk of dislodged temple that had fallen a few metres away. Loud blasts echoed up from the valley below.

'They can't have seen us already,' said Rosheen.

Bernice popped her head over the rock. Pink bolts were rattling randomly about the area. 'I don't think they did,' she called down to Rosheen. 'The idea seems to be to blast everything in sight.'

Rosheen slumped down helplessly. 'This is it, then,' she said. 'We might as well face it.'

'No way,' Bernice shouted bitterly. 'I've lived too much to die like this. Even if they get me, I'll go down fighting.'

'What's the point?' screamed Rosheen.

'A good question,' shouted Bernice as she examined the firing systems. 'Philosophers have been pondering it for thousands of years.' She leapt over the rock with one smooth movement and landed in a cat like crouch, weapon raised.

'Hanging about waiting to die is not my idea of a good answer!'

'Visual sighting of parasite at grid mark four by five,' called the Environments Officer from his new position in the tank designated as the replacement command vehicle.

'Destroy it!' ordered Jinkwa. The forward screen zoomed in on the slight figure of the target. Jinkwa noted with pleasure that it was the female he and the General had encountered near that strange blue object. He really was getting better at telling the difference between the ridiculous creatures.

16:

Strategy Z

'I don't like the look of this at all,' said the Doctor. Without
knowing how or why, he, Sheldukher and the Cell had appeared
inside a huge and completely empty white room. 'First law of
space-time travel: avoid voids.'

It was only as he looked around with a keener eye that he
realized they were not quite inside a room at all. Rooms have
walls and doors. This had none. It was a space, borderless and
blank.

'This must be the centre of power,' said Sheldukher. 'The
concealed base from which the elders of Sakkrat governed.'

'You'd expect at least some seats of government,' the Doctor
observed, less reverently. His voice echoed strangely around
them. 'Mind you, all powerful figures aren't the type for sitting
down. Ruins their dignity.' He put down the Cell case on the
invisible floor, which they floated rather than stood on, and
extended an arm experimentally.

'What are you doing?' asked Sheldukher. The Doctor had
struck a number of apparently meaningless poses with arms and
legs outstretched in peculiar directions.

'Testing a theory. Hold your arm out,' he suggested. Sheldukher eyed him suspiciously. 'Go on.'

Without removing his gaze from the Doctor, Sheldukher did
as instructed. 'So?'

The Doctor leaned forward and whispered conspiratorially,
'Doesn't your hand seem further away than usual?'

'No,' Sheldukher replied quickly. He took another look down
the length of his arm and blinked in surprise. 'Yes.'

The Doctor nodded. 'Dimensional distortion. A hall of
mirrors with no mirrors.'

'This is a process room?'

The Doctor hesitated about this. 'No,' he said eventually. 'The

202

distortion is a side-effect of passing through a slow time conversion unit.'

'Slow time!' exclaimed Sheldukher. 'It was just being hypothesized when I entered sleep.'

The Cell picked up its cue. 'Slow time compression . . . was first theorized in 2386 . . . It involves the lengthening of temporal flow in . . . one area . . . '

The Doctor nodded grimly. 'So whatever's down here is still almost exactly how it was however many millions of years ago it was constructed. And we are being slowed down to match it.'

Sheldukher looked about, alarmed. 'There's no door.'

The Doctor looked him over. Sheldukher's normally blank and unreadable features were flushed with excitement. 'There'll be a door,' he replied. 'When the time is right.'

A ghost eased itself from a block of stone at the edge of the ruined city. It had sensed more disturbance and come to investigate. Anything contrary to its purpose would be eradicated, as instructed.

It had no eyes. It saw the way ahead by touching the minds of the living beings that surrounded it. It drew on their experiences, usually without them realizing it, to form an impression of events. It knew that the human that called itself Professor Bernice Summerfield and the human that called itself Rosheen had responded and were thus entitled to proceed, along with the three men they associated with. It sensed fear from their minds and turned its attention to the Chelonians.

It probed the minds of several of the creatures and sensed only confusion and anger. Moreover, they did not respond to the program stimulus. They were supernumeraries and random actions could endanger the city and its secrets. Eradication might prove necessary. For the moment, it would watch and wait.

Rosheen kept her head down. A salvo from the Chelonian convoy blasted away the rock she had been using for shelter. Without looking up she scurried desperately away. Any second she expected to be struck by one of the disintegrator beams.

She heard four shots from the Moosehead repeater and looked up to see Bernice struggling to keep the mighty weapon upright.

Sheldukher had chosen it for Postine, after all. Its new operator could barely keep it steady and fire it at the same time. Her aim was lousy, but several of her shots struck Chelonian vessels out of pure luck. Two were blown to pieces.

The disintegrator cannons began to sweep from side to side in an obviously well practised routine. Huge clouds of dust blew up all around her but, incredibly, she was not hit. She shuffled on. Maybe she was going to make it, after all.

The next blast blew her legs away. The second killed her.

The ghost was overwhelmed by a series of unrelated images. A young male human; a string of digits connected to an even longer string of noughts flashing up on a screen; a large pool of clear green water; another male with a flat, square object in his hands. There was pain and then the link was severed. The mind of the human called Rosheen was beyond its reach now. Perhaps one day, like the ghost, it might be called back to perform tasks for cruel, unthinking masters.

It searched for the mind of Professor Bernice Summerfield. There was an odd psychic reverberation whenever that name was used. Something about it was false and assumed. No matter. It was important that Professor Bernice Summerfield lived. Two responsive subjects could not be lost.

Direct action was not advisable. Unfortunately, it was necessary. The ghost called on the mysterious energy beneath the city that animated it. It grew stronger and more solid.

Bernice's luck had finally run out. The heavy rifle slipped from her grasp and clattered to the ground. The little protection it had given her was gone. She watched as a glowing pink ball of disintegrator energy sped towards her. She had no time to think of any decent last words. Anyway, who was around to appreciate them?

She yelped as a white wing embraced her from behind. It expanded to become a shroud that enveloped her. The soles of her feet were tickled by the molecular excitation that precedes transmat transmissions.

'Rescue, eh?' she said to the warm, pillowy cloud. 'Smart.'

The Environments Officer shook his head in disbelief. 'Not

again.'

'What has happened now?' demanded Jinkwa. 'Continue the advance!' he yelled at the nervously distracted gunner.

'The parasite has disappeared,' said the Environments Officer. 'Telemetric flaring suggests use of short range teleporter.'

Jinkwa cursed. Teleportation was a technique Chelonian scientists had yet to perfect. Certainly no parasite had mastered it before. 'Trace the flaring.'

'Impossible, sir,' the Environments Officer admitted. 'No such signal can be traced through the electrical disturbance in this area.'

Jinkwa slammed a limb in frustration onto his control panel. 'Useless garbage!'

'I'm doing my best, sir,' the Environments Officer pointed out resentfully.

Jinkwa sat in simmering silence for a few seconds. He seemed to come to a decision. 'Halt the advance,' he ordered. 'Then get out of here, both of you.'

The gunner looked up, surprised. 'You cannot be serious . . . '

'Do it!' shouted Jinkwa.

'This is the command vehicle. Hold your fire and stop motors. Orders of First Pilot Jinkwa.' The gunner gave the last three words of his announcement a grudging emphasis that did not go unnoticed by his superior.

The motors cut out. The gunner slid silently from his position and left through the hatch. The Environments Officer followed. Just as he was about to climb on to the platform, he turned to Jinkwa.

'Sir,' he pleaded, 'this is a bad move. We must press home the attack. Maybe drop plague pellets. The men don't like this. Just because the parasites can teleport short distances —'

Jinkwa snarled. 'Do you know why we have officers and why we have soldiers? And why some people will never be officers no matter how long they serve?' He sighed. 'So we go blazing in again or drop pellets. They will simply teleport away and survive to trouble us further.

'No, there is another way to ensure total destruction. We shall have to creep up on them and destroy them before they realize what is happening. We must have the advantage of surprise.'

The Environments Officer gulped. 'You can't mean . . . Strategy Z?'

'I mean precisely that,' Jinkwa said briskly. 'Now obey your orders and leave me.'

The Environments Officer shuffled anxiously off. Jinkwa stared bitterly at his departing shell. 'Yellow shelled nothing,' he whispered.

When the vehicle was empty, he took a deep breath. He was not used to having his orders questioned. His first command should have been on a glorious campaign, purging a world of its mammalian infections. Instead he was here, surrounded by fools and incompetents. Well, no more. Strategy Z would silence the doubters. Literally. The glory days were not over yet.

He punched a complex code into the panel before him. Command systems options appeared on a small screen. He selected Strategy Z.

OPTION CLOSED the screen failsafed. He entered more codes. STRATEGY Z: CONFIRMATION OF IDENTITY REQUIRED.

Jinkwa laid his left front foot on an adjacent sensor plate. REQUEST DENIED said the screen. OPTION AVAILABLE TO COMMANDING OFFICER ONLY.

Jinkwa informed the screen that Fakrid was dead. It cross referenced this claim with the environment systems, which confirmed that the General's heart tracer had ceased transmission. COMMANDING OFFICER NOW FIRST PILOT JINKWA OF RALZAR the screen reported and flashed up the Strategy Z options.

Three should be enough, thought Jinkwa. But which of his brave troops should he choose? His new gunner? Yes, there was poetry in that. The boy obviously needed stiffening of the moral fibre. The insolent Ozaran, too. As for the third . . . an insignificant trooper. It was with genuine regret that he punched in the last name. How much more satisfying it would have been to dispatch the quibbling, but still unfortunately useful, Environments Officer.

STRATEGY Z IMPLEMENTATION DELAY? queried the screen.

Immediate, Jinkwa ordered. After all, what was the point in

waiting? The screen confirmed that the sequence was now in operation.

Before he closed down the screen, Jinkwa accessed the crew registration codes. As commanding officer he now had the authorization to alter them. He found his own entry, deleted RALZAR and hammered in NAZMIR. His mother's name would continue.

Then he opened the all stations address network. 'Troopers Izta, Ozaran and Nefril. I have urgent information for you. You are about to perform the ultimate sacrifice.'

As he spoke these words, Jinkwa congratulated himself on his problem solving capabilities. He was reminded of the old adage about killing two parasites with one disintegrator.

Sheldukher prowled the white room, searching for any signs of change. A fuzzy outline was forming in one particular area.

'Doctor,' he called, reaching nervously for his knife. 'I think our door has arrived.'

'I don't think so,' the Doctor observed. The hazy shape was resolving into a figure. 'Looks more like a materialization of some sort.'

Bernice appeared before them. She reeled about groggily, then collapsed.

The Doctor raced over to examine her. He slapped her a couple of times around the face and checked her eyes as they opened. The anti-bubbleshake conditioning was holding up well, but not as well as he would have hoped. 'Wake up, sleepy head.'

'Weird,' Bernice replied as she revived.

The Doctor looked about. 'I've seen weirder.'

'No, not this place,' she corrected him. 'I got rescued from the Chelonians by some sort of transmat process. I thought the angel of death had got me at one point.'

'What happened to Rosheen?'

'I didn't see,' she replied. 'I think they must have got her.'

The Doctor cursed. He turned back angrily to Sheldukher. 'This is all your fault.'

He tutted. 'Forget all that, it isn't important,' he said. 'Don't you realize what's happening here? We are standing on the threshold of ultimate knowledge, ultimate power.'

'I keep telling you,' the Doctor stormed, 'I am not interested. Power holds absolutely no attraction for me. I ran Taunton for two weeks in the eighteenth century and I've never been so bored.'

'I offer you the universe and you blither of Taunton!' cried Sheldukher. Bernice noted the change in his manner. Perhaps that was why he rarely lost his temper, she thought. He looks much less impressive like this.

'Doctor,' he ranted on, 'whether you like it or not, my genius gave you this opportunity.'

'Genius?' the Doctor sneered. 'Your talents are reserved for death and destruction. Your obsession with this planet has revealed only the paranoid basis of your twisted philosophy.'

Sheldukher was unmoved by this onslaught. Indeed, it seemed to inspire him. When next he spoke, it was with his customary casual manner. 'Not so. A sensualist cannot be judged. It is his task merely to gratify himself wherever his instincts lead him.'

'A sensualist?' scoffed the Doctor. 'A slaughterer, a destroyer of life, must be accountable.'

'Accountable to whom?' he replied. 'Another group of destroyers or their representatives?'

'There are higher powers, higher constants,' the Doctor blurted reluctantly.

'Higher powers!' crowed Sheldukher gleefully. 'You've said it yourself. Those powers shall be mine.' He stalked off to look for a way from the arena.

The Doctor shook himself down, trying to get rid of his anger in the same way a dog shakes itself dry. Bernice laid a hand on his arm. 'So what happens now?' she asked. 'I warn you, don't even consider going back to the surface. The Chelonians are very angry.'

'No, you're right,' he said. 'We must go on.' He seemed preoccupied, as if there was something one half of him desperately wanted to tell her but the other half wouldn't allow it.

'What's up, Doctor?' she enquired gently. He really looked shaken.

'I didn't want to involve you in this,' he said at last. 'You should have gone back to the TARDIS.'

'Now, come on,' she exclaimed. 'There was an army trying to stop me.'

The Doctor was now literally hopping up and down in an agony of indecision and frustration. 'That's not what I meant!' he blustered. 'This is a tremendously difficult situation.'

Bernice had caught a glimpse of something in his grey eyes. It was the squint that appeared whenever a particular subject was raised. 'Doctor,' she said calmly. 'You've seen something here. There's something you don't want me to know, isn't there? Why can't you trust me to keep your secrets?'

He scowled horribly. Bernice had never seen that look before and she hated it. 'I don't want to talk about it!' he snarled emphatically and walked away.

Bernice sighed. She was too tired to be angry with him. Besides, he seemed more frustrated with himself than with her.

A cry from Sheldukher alerted her. A metal door had appeared from nowhere.

The ghosts had left the visitors to their city safely gathered in the conversion unit and returned to guard duty outside. All the responsive subjects were now within. Only the supernumeraries, the Chelonians, remained. Three of them were moving towards the city.

At first, the ghosts had discounted them. Three could not cause sufficient disruption to warrant intervention. If they attempted to gain entry then they, as non-responsives, would be eradicated according to procedure.

It was only when they entered the minds of the creatures to examine their motives that they discovered the alarming truth. Each of them had been made into a living bomb. Their purpose was to enter the city and explode. Such action might endanger the lives of the remaining responsives and could not be tolerated. They would have to intervene again.

Ozaran made his decision and came to a halt halfway up the hillside. He shouted across to the other soldiers recruited to implement Strategy Z. 'Izta, Nefril, listen to me!'

They did not reply. Their measured tread up the hill towards the city continued in stoic silence.

'Can't you see, we're being used!' yelled Ozaran desperately. 'That high and mighty First Pilot of ours wants us out of the way!'

'You profane the Chelonian cause,' Nefril called back. 'Such an accusation is treasonable. It is the greatest honour to die for the race.'

Izta, the gunner who had served on Jinkwa's tank, seemed less sure. He glanced anxiously back at Ozaran but continued up the hill. 'What you suggest is unthinkable, Ozaran,' he replied. 'Chelonian does not kill Chelonian. That is the parasite way.'

'You know that isn't true,' Ozaran pleaded desperately. But his two brothers were now out of earshot.

Unthinkable. Ozaran turned the word over and over in his mind. It was a favourite of the officer class. Many of their unthinkables had been challenged on this most peculiar of missions. It had been unthinkable that parasites could triumph over Chelonians. Unthinkable that Chelonian technology could be bettered. Unthinkable that Chelonian could kill Chelonian.

He had the chance to reverse another of those unthinkables. He gave a wry smile. 'It is unthinkable,' he chortled happily to himself, 'that a soldier could disobey the orders of an officer.'

He turned himself about and started to retrace his steps.

The ghosts, almost invisible in daylight, appeared before Nefril and Izta. They had rescanned the mind of the third Chelonian and discovered that it meant the city no harm and was unimportant. These others, though, would have to be dealt with.

The ghosts reformed themselves into two ectoplasmic globules and surrounded the Chelonians.

Seconds later, Nefril and Izta were startled to find themselves miles away, on the far side of the city.

Jinkwa swivelled his harness so that he could face the Environments Officer. 'How is Strategy Z proceeding?'

The Environments Officer, who still nursed unspoken doubts as to Jinkwa's intentions, replied smoothly, 'All is well, sir.'

'Good.' A neon flashed on the panel before Jinkwa. He answered the call. The face of the Stores Officer appeared on the communications panel.

'First Pilot Jinkwa,' he said brusquely, without waiting for the formality of being invited to speak by his superior. 'I must protest at your decision to reduce the troopers' chlorophyll rations.'

'Has it escaped your notice, Hanfra,' Jinkwa retorted snidely, 'that there is a certain lack of greenery on this rockworld?'

'And has it escaped yours,' the Stores Officer continued, 'that your own ration has been increased in these trying times? An error, surely?'

'No error has been made,' Jinkwa replied. An undertone of menace had crept into his voice. 'Surely you would agree that the commanding officer of any mission requires sufficient sustenance to remain active?'

The Stores Officer's temper boiled over. 'By Mif, we have wounded men aboard, Jinkwa! They need chlorophyll. You cannot allow them to die while you feast!'

There was silence for some seconds. 'I wonder if our raid on the city will be successful?' Jinkwa said finally. 'Perhaps some tenacious parasites will survive. More volunteers may be needed for further Strategy Z operations.

'And I'm sure you'll agree,' he went on threateningly, 'we officers cannot expect troopers to carry out such tasks without complaint. Perhaps one of us should set an example?'

The Stores Officer muttered resentfully and broke the connection. That was what made the Chelonian race strong, reflected Jinkwa. A readiness to obey the orders of superiors.

'Sir!' cried the Environments Officer. 'Something is wrong!'

Jinkwa sighed and put down the leaf he had been about to munch. 'What now?'

'One of the boys on Strategy Z, Trooper Ozaran, has doubled back,' came the report. 'He's almost right outside this vehicle!'

'This cannot be!' cried Jinkwa. 'Nim! Why was this not registered before?'

'Surprise is the idea of Strategy Z,' replied the Environments Officer simply.

'Stop the explosion,' Jinkwa ordered. 'Halt the timing sequence.'

'It cannot be altered,' the other replied helplessly. 'Sir, we must do something!'

Jinkwa went through the options in his mind. To move back would not take them out of range with the detonation point so close. He scanned the combat chart before him, noting the numbers of nearby tanks. There was but one course of action left open to him.

He opened up a communications channel. 'Units Nineteen and Forty,' he ordered, 'regroup at grid mark one by one.'

'Sir!' The Environments Officer was outraged.

'You will carry out your orders immediately,' Jinkwa finished. He broke the connection and relaxed.

The Environments Officer stared incredulously at him. 'You cannot do this, sir. Chelonian cannot kill Chelonian!'

Jinkwa stared at him. 'Subordinates will obey superiors.'

The Environments Officer turned to the sensornet. Tracers showed the approach of Trooper Ozaran, now only metres away. Units Nineteen and Forty were trundling towards him unquestioningly.

Ozaran could see Jinkwa's command vehicle, only metres from him now. This would be the end for him, but a glorious beginning for his fellow troopers. With Jinkwa gone, they would be free to take control. Work would be needed to build a home on this world but it could be done. He pushed himself on. Already he could feel some of his internal components heating up.

He was astonished to see two other tanks, manned by troopers like himself, trundling forwards to shield Jinkwa. No! This could not be!

Trooper Ozaran exploded. The charge of heated mitrine he carried within him took Units Nineteen and Forty along with him.

The Environments Officer stared, horrified, at his screen. He could not believe what had happened.

'Chelonian has killed Chelonian,' he said despairingly. 'We are no better than parasites now.'

'Nonsense,' snorted Jinkwa. 'We had no choice but to act as we did.'

The Environments Officer rounded on him. 'This would not have happened if General Fakrid had lived. You are as nothing compared to him.'

Jinkwa gibbered with rage. 'How dare you say this! Fakrid was my own mother!'

'You are not the man he was,' the Environments Officer continued. 'You are unfit for command. Nothing can excuse what you have done today.' He pulled himself up. 'I hereby depose you. I will lead this mission.'

Jinkwa laughed derisively. 'You! The son of a petalpainter, lead an assault force!'

'Face it, Jinkwa,' said the Environments Officer, refusing to respond to the slur on his family. 'You're finished when the other men hear about this.'

'They will never hear of it,' said Jinkwa. He pulled out a gun from a wall rack and shot the Environments Officer. Once. It was a very clean shot, to the head.

A moment later, the console on to which the Environments Officer had collapsed confirmed that the other two units in the Strategy Z operation had completed their task.

Excellent, thought Jinkwa. The Doctor and its freaky parasite friends are finished. Only one task remained before they could depart this world. Only one shame remained to be avenged.

'Troopers,' he announced over the all stations address channel. 'Strategy Z has been a complete success. We will now return to the eight twelves and destroy them. Zarathion will be used.'

A cheer went up. Zarathion was always popular with the ranks. Surely, Jinkwa thought, I am a great leader.

'There is some sad news,' he added. 'Units Nineteen and Forty have been destroyed in a freak electrical accident. Sadly, the Senior Environments Officer was also killed while trying to repair a faulty circuit. We mourn their loss.'

The Doctor continued his examination of the metal door that offered the only way out from the white room. He had taken to scratching at it with a bent spatula. Finally, he gave up in disgust.

'Well, Doctor?' asked Sheldukher.

'I can't do it, I'm afraid,' he replied. 'It's one of those doors that will open only if somebody on the other side wants it to.'

Sheldukher smiled. 'Oddly enough, it was for a contingency such as this that I recruited the others in the first place. No doors were locked to Rosheen and Klift. And Postine could have shouldered it down.'

'What foresight,' the Doctor said disparagingly.

'Perhaps your friend the Professor can help us?' Sheldukher indicated Bernice. He checked himself. 'If she is feeling healthy enough.'

'Your concern is very touching,' the Doctor observed drily, 'for somebody who tried to kill her earlier.'

Sheldukher raised an eyebrow. 'Oh, nothing so pedestrian. I have so many plans for the Professor before I allow her the luxury of death.'

'You're a depraved abomination,' the Doctor said lightly and walked away. He stared out at the never ending blankness of the conversion unit, as if contemplating infinity and his part in it.

'Of course,' said Sheldukher. 'There is one small remaining component of my winning team. We've rather forgotten him in all the excitement.' He crossed over to where the Cell sat abandoned on the floor.

Bernice, now feeling a little better about things, crossed over to the Doctor. 'One question.'

'I'll do my best.'

'Do we get out of this alive?'

He continued to look upwards, as if waiting for something. The answer came back abstractedly. 'If we're lucky.'

'Lucky.' Bernice seized on the word. 'Luck got us into this.'

'A Fortean flicker got us into this.'

'Same thing, surely?'

The Doctor shook his head. 'We'll deal with that question as and when,' he said mysteriously. 'We could do with a coincidence now. I don't fancy starving to death in here. White is such a boring colour.'

'It isn't a colour.'

'Pedant.'

'Did Urnst come this way?' Bernice tried to remember. She had skim read his account only once, after all. So had the Doctor, but there was that memory of his.

'It's impossible not to come this way. Every possible entrance leads down to that cavern where the ghosts appeared.'

'Only one way in.'

The Doctor nodded. 'And only one way out.'

'How did Urnst get through here?'

'He rushed this section. There wasn't much detail,' said the Doctor. 'There was one thing that did stick out, though —'

He was interrupted by Sheldukher. 'Doctor, Professor!'

They joined him at the metal door. He held the Cell case in his hands. 'Listen to this.'

'I can open this . . . door it has a . . . telepathic lock tuned to . . . my own frequency . . . '

Bernice smiled at the Doctor. 'There's your coincidence. With knobs on.'

'And extra topping,' he enthused. Bernice was glad that his mood seemed to have lifted again. She loved unpredictable people and the Doctor beat the rest of the universe hands down at being that. Just to see him smile was worth all the frowns, fascinating though they were.

They watched as the Cell grunted and groaned, straining to complete its task. The door opened soundlessly.

Sheldukher patted the Cell case. 'Well done.' He set off into the blackness it had revealed.

'That door would have opened anyway,' the Doctor said confidently. 'Urnst must have got through, mustn't he?'

'That isn't totally logical,' said Bernice.

'Yes it is,' he insisted. 'He definitely came down this far. We haven't met the Monumental Guardian yet, have we?'

'Bugger,' exclaimed Bernice. 'I completely forgot about that.'

'Language,' the Doctor reproached her.

A roar came from the blackness Sheldukher had entered. 'I have heard the baying of the Monumental Guardian,' the Doctor quoted.

'I have heard enough,' said Bernice. 'Let's leave it to him, eh?'

The Doctor shook his head in mock outrage. 'Of course not. That would mean leaving *him* to *it*.'

'That doesn't sound unreasonable to me,' Bernice remarked. But the Doctor had already gone through the door.

17:

The Monumental Guardian

The ghosts observed the retreat of the Chelonian assault force.
The reptiles were now of no importance and could be ignored.

The four remaining responsives had now entered the central
area of the city. The final phase of their induction would begin.
That task was for another to perform.

The operation would soon be completed. The ghosts wondered
if perhaps they might then be freed, and allowed to return to
the mysterious point of destiny from which they had been taken
and pressed into action.

They slipped back into the stone and waited, as they had for
centuries.

The familiar stonework of the upper city greeted the Doctor's
party as they passed through the metal door. It formed a hallway
as wide as it was high. On this, the far side of the slow time
pocket, the air was clearer, as if the city had been built the day
before yesterday. At the far end was a wall into which three
well spaced rows of symbols had been carved.

'This is it, isn't it?' Sheldukher said excitedly. 'At last, my
final obstacle.' He seemed almost physically overwhelmed by
his own words.

Another roar came from nearby. Bernice turned her head.
A row of yellow lights — eyes? — was advancing towards them
from the distant darkness of a side tunnel. 'That looks more
like a final obstacle. If those are eyes, it could be forty foot
across. And then some.'

The Doctor was apparently oblivious to all this. He had raced
forward to the far wall and stood staring in horror at the glyphs.
'No, it can't be ... '

The creature roared again. 'Doctor,' Bernice called, 'whatever you've discovered, I think it can wait until —'

She was cut off by the bellow of the Monumental Guardian as it sped angrily into the hall. As a whole, it resembled nothing Bernice had ever seen, although several of its features were present in the anatomy of other creatures. The designers of the monster had fused them together to create a terrifying metallic insectoid. For it was immediately evident that it was a robot of some kind.

The central bulk was a squared off silver thorax from which extended a variety of clamps and probes. Seven yellow beams shone from a rectangular head that twisted about on a flexible black stalk. A swishing, segmented tail balanced it at the rear. Its most surprising feature was its method of movement. It slithered along on several rows of tentacles. Every electronic howl it gave was accompanied by clouds of greasy black smoke that issued from its unseen underside.

'Open the door, Doctor!' cried Sheldukher. 'Open the door!'

The creature swooped down towards him. Bernice found herself enjoying the look of fear that crossed his face. She was human, after all. Which was more than could be said for the Doctor, who was still staring gormlessly at the far wall as if nothing was happening.

One of the Guardian's buzzing probes twitched open to reveal a claw. It gripped Sheldukher and the Cell almost tenderly and brought them up to its eye. For a long moment they just stared at each other. Then it lowered them down and relaxed its grip.

'Great,' sighed Bernice. 'It likes him.' She attempted to avoid the needle thin probe that chased after her and, predictably, failed. A powerful suction pulled at her coat and it lifted her up to meet the creature's glare.

Despite all of this, she wasn't really alarmed. After all, the Guardian could easily have killed them straight away if it had wished. What was more irritating was the Doctor's behaviour. He had left her to deal with this rampaging monster while he pored over those symbols. Surely it should have been the other way round?

She was lowered to the ground. Sheldukher moved to help her up and she kicked him viciously away. She had no doubts as to which was the deadlier creature.

The monster turned its attentions to the Doctor, still engrossed

217

in his wall. Bernice felt it only right to warn him. 'Doctor!' she called. 'Behind you!'

He sighed as another metal claw closed around him and levered him slowly up. 'I really haven't the time for all these theatrics!' he shouted.

The monster growled back at him, its eyes flaring up as if it had somehow understood. 'Don't antagonize it, Doctor,' Bernice called up sweetly.

He snorted. 'You needn't worry, it's just a sort of celestial doorman.'

'That has to be the ugliest bouncer in the galaxy.'

'I imagine its function is to scare off the riff-raff,' he continued. 'We should be all right.'

The Doctor, it seemed, had tempted fate once too often. The claw started to close about him.

'It's going to crush him,' said Sheldukher, fascinated. He hadn't seen somebody crushed in years. The way everything sort of congealed was most interesting.

'Unhand me!' the Doctor demanded, outraged.

Bernice looked around for something to attack the beast. There was nothing. 'It doesn't like you, Doctor.'

'This is ridiculous!' He struggled furiously, his arms, legs and umbrella kicking in all directions. 'I'm the only one wearing a tie!'

What Bernice saw next increased her admiration for the Doctor even further. The struggling ceased. He held himself perfectly still, drew a deep breath and, when the angle suited him, he shot from the grip of the claw and sailed through the air like a human cannonball. He even landed on his feet.

Bernice ran over to him. 'You must teach me to do that.' It was the only thing she could think of to say. 'Amazing. How did you land like that?'

The Doctor frowned. 'Well, I had to, hadn't I?' he said, as if it were the most obvious thing. 'I wasn't wearing a crash helmet.'

Bernice decided to file that one away in the think-about-it-later pile and just get on with things. The Guardian seemed to have lost all interest in them. It turned itself about and sped back down the tunnel it had emerged from still hissing and roaring doomily.

Bernice cocked her head. 'Not very persistent, is he?'

The Doctor nodded. 'I told you, its sole purpose is to induce fear.'

'It tried to kill you!'

'Only to scare you!' he snapped and returned to his deliberations at the wall.

Sheldukher stepped forward. 'The Cell could translate those words, I'm sure.'

The Doctor paid no attention

'I take it that's machine code, yes?' Sheldukher chattered on. His face was flushed, his breathing fast. His goal was but inches away from him. 'To open the door to the final chamber? We solve the puzzle and proceed. Really, you mustn't worry yourself, Doctor. The Cell can open that door as it did the last, I'm sure.'

There was still no reply from the ashen faced Doctor. Bernice joined the men. 'Urnst claimed to have translated those symbols, but the man had no genuine academic standing whatever, and was probably lying. Besides which, there are far too few characters either to create a logical pattern for a machine code, or to form the basis for a translation — at least one based on alphabetical rather than pictorial assumptions.'

The Doctor reacted this time. He turned his head a fraction towards her and glared as he had never glared before.

'There must be a way forward,' said Sheldukher. He put the Cell case down carefully and then lunged forward and grabbed the Doctor by the shoulders. He was shaking. 'Open that door!'

'Do what you like,' the Doctor said. 'That door stays closed. Indeed, it must never be opened.'

Sheldukher gasped. 'You know what's in there?'

'I do,' the Doctor confirmed. 'I wasn't sure about it earlier. Now I am. And I'm telling you, Sheldukher, *you must not let it get out!*'

Sheldukher released him and sprang for Bernice. His knife hand slipped around her neck as the other kept both her hands twisted helplessly behind her back. She realized how easily he could have killed her earlier if he had wanted.

'The slightest movement of my hand,' he threatened, tightening his grip, 'I can slit her throat clean across.' His voice was cracking with hysteria.

'If you harm her ... '

'Open the door, Doctor.'

The Doctor stared horrified at Bernice. He shuddered and turned back to the wall.

'Here,' he translated, 'Libida, Queen of the Virenies, laid her empire of a hundred million years to rest.' It seemed to Bernice that every word was wrenched unwilling from his lips.

'The elders sealed up the secrets of Zagg à Raath and prepared for death. The barbarous hordes were consumed by the great cold. By Mthuluhu, let the terrible science of Kllatun the Wise rest here.'

He turned back to Sheldukher. 'That's what it says.'

Sheldukher released Bernice. She raised an arm to strike him. The Doctor raised a finger and said, 'No.'

Sheldukher hammered at the wall hysterically. Tears streamed down his cheeks. 'Open!' he cried. 'Open! All my life I've waited ... I must see it! I must see it!'

The moment he touched it the wall began to dissolve, crumbling away as if centuries of decay were catching up with it. A shrieking vortex of blue light burst from the debris. The Doctor and Bernice winced and put their hands to their temples.

'You are looking at the residue of an unshielded Fortean flicker,' the Doctor whispered to Bernice through gritted teeth.

She was barely aware of him, or anything else. A spinning hole seemed to have opened up around her. She caught glimpses of herself with layered blonde hair; the Doctor dressed in a stiff creased corduroy suit with a placard that read EAT MORE PROTEIN around his neck; her mother and Sendei, both aged seventy, sipping tea over the TARDIS console. Impossible, stupid, unbelievable things. Things that had never happened. Things that would never happen.

'Explain this!' she hollered. 'Now!'

The Doctor's voice floated back to her, filled with an odd calm. 'Don't worry, they're only time images. An inevitable side-effect of slow time conversion spillage.'

'I want that in English!'

'Later!'

Not being sensitive to temporal fluctuations, Sheldukher saw none of this. Now overcome by uncontrollable ecstasy, he raced through the gap left by the fallen wall.

He emerged in a cold, dark, ancient and empty place.

Two figures stood before him. He raised his knife to challenge them. It was blown out of his concrete grip by a rushing gust of something more than wind.

He was lifted off his feet and drawn up by the invisible force, then pinioned flat against a downwards sloping board on the ceiling. He struggled furiously with no result.

The figures turned to each other.

'The identity of this responsive has been confirmed by the outer monitor. He is Sheldukher,' the first said knowingly.

'Then our task is almost over,' said the second.

Bernice woke from a very Fortean dream about a budgerigar that could predict the outcome of horse races a day in advance. Or was that something she had actually seen in the light of the flicker?

She was lying on something wet, squelchy and smelly. She sat up to find herself covered in fish. The Doctor was next to her, rubbing his head, sore from the impact of a shower of Argentinian telephone books.

The air was filled with tiny blue sparkles. Bernice reached instinctively to touch them but her hand passed straight through. It was impossible to actually look at one of them. She was reminded of the dead cells that float down the eye on their way to watery oblivion in the tear duct.

The Doctor shook his head. 'What a mess.'

Bernice looked about. 'Where's Sheldukher?'

The answer came from a most unexpected quarter. 'He has passed ... through into ... the centre ... '

Bernice caught a note of malicious satisfaction in the Cell's voice. The Doctor was looking less agitated, although still tense. 'The level of Fortean activity is increasing, seeping out uncontrolled through the slow time filter into time-space,' he said worriedly, glancing at the dancing lights.

'At least before,' he went on grimly, 'it was contained down here. Our top priority is to stop it.'

'You're three steps ahead of me,' said Bernice. She stood up and reached for the Cell case.

'About seventeen, actually,' he said brightly and extended a hand to the doorway through which Sheldukher had passed. 'Shall we go in?'

'You sound suspiciously pleased with yourself,' Bernice said resentfully.

'If we sort this out, I'll be even worse,' he said playfully. 'Insufferable.' He picked up one of the 'phone books and flicked through it without interest. 'I can't wait to tell you how clever I've been.'

'Let's just see what's in there,' said Bernice. She moved for the exit.

'I feel obliged to warn you, however,' the Doctor continued as he followed her, and she could tell he meant this seriously. 'Whatever we've been through so far, this is going to be far, far more challenging and dangerous.'

18:

Devious Minds

Two identical, naked bald men waited for the Doctor, Bernice and the Cell. They had no body hair or sexual characteristics. The space between their mouths and eyes was a flat blank.

'The other reponsives have now arrived,' said the first.

'They will be dealt with according to our instructions,' said the second. 'Project FXX Q84 will be retrieved and we shall conclude operations here and proceed to the ship.'

Bernice turned to the Doctor as they entered the cold, empty room. Through the ever present Fortean distortion she could see that it was dimly lit and dingy, like an abandoned warehouse. Two doors at either side led off to other areas. She indicated the two men. 'Genetic constructs,' she said.

The Doctor nodded. 'Yes.'

'Someone forgot to give them noses.'

'With any luck,' said the Doctor, 'someone forgot to give them the power to think for themselves to any great degree.'

Bernice was more confused than ever. She had not expected to find the Highest Science guarded in a dingy basement by elementary clones. Irritatingly, the Doctor, despite his portentous preamble with the translations, was taking it all in his stride.

He pulled himself up and strutted forward grandly. 'Hello, I am the Doctor, and this is my friend Bernice.'

'Silence,' said one of the contructs. Bernice decided to think of him as Construct One. 'You will not speak until interrogation phase begins.'

The Doctor raised an eyebrow. 'Interrogation?' he said in mock outrage. 'Did you hear that, Professor Summerfield? What impertinence.'

'You will give us Project FXX Q84,' said Construct Two.

The Doctor's brow creased in feigned puzzlement. 'I'm sorry, I really have no idea what you are talking about.' He congratulated himself inwardly as his secret theories about the city were finally confirmed.

'You will give us Project FXX Q84,' the Constructs demanded. They raised their hands threateningly.

The Doctor sighed. 'Honestly.' He passed Construct One the 'phone book he had picked up in the hallway outside. 'Here is your new instruction code.'

The Constructs looked quizzically at the book and began to study it. 'Why are these instructions not computer encoded?' asked Construct Two.

The Doctor tapped his nose with the handle of his umbrella in a gesture Bernice was sure they wouldn't understand. 'Security,' he said cryptically.

'You will remain silent while we examine these codes,' said Construct One.

'We certainly will not!' the Doctor retorted angrily. 'Professor Summerfield and I have urgent work to attend to here. Repairs.'

Bernice was bursting with questions and had only the vaguest notion of what was going on. She did, however, have a good idea of what the Doctor was trying to do and decided to back him up. 'We cannot delay,' she said. 'You will allow us to pass.'

'Such action would conflict with our program code,' said Construct One.

The Doctor sighed. 'Which is?'

'The safe retrieval of Project FXX Q84,' said Construct Two.

'Those instructions are hereby superseded,' the Doctor said. He nodded to the Constructs and linked his arm with Bernice's. 'Come along, Professor Summerfield.'

They walked away, Bernice still carrying the Cell case. She half expected the Constructs to gun them down there and then, but they held back.

'These are new instructions,' said Construct One, weighing the 'phone book in its hand.

'Our current instructions order the detention of all responsives,' said Construct Two.

'Our current instructions have been superseded,' said Construct One. 'We will act on this situation when we have fully received our new instructions. I will take them first.' He held up the book, opened its cover, and began to read.

224

'That was smart, Doctor,' Bernice congratulated him as they hurried down an adjacent corridor. 'I thought artificial intelligences only behaved that way in old celluloid. All that cannot compute stuff.'

'It's actually quite easy to fox logical minds,' the Doctor said breezily. 'Illogical minds are another matter entirely, of course.'

'But still,' Bernice enthused, 'for sheer nerve, I'm impressed.'

'It was nothing,' the Doctor said modestly. 'I've had a lot of experience in the field. I once had to convince a deranged dishwasher that it didn't really want to take over the universe.'

'Did you succeed?'

'Of course. A lot of plates got cracked along the way, admittedly. Still, nobody's perfect ... ah!' His attention had been taken by a door in the corridor.

'I still have a lot of questions,' said Bernice.

The Doctor waved his hand over a panel next to the door. It sparked briefly and the door slid open. He poked his nose in and then waved her forward. 'And here you'll find a lot of answers. Data stores, back-up programs. Yes, there had to be. Very thorough.'

Bernice looked in. The room was bare but for an ordinary looking – indeed somewhat archaic by her reckoning – computer, and a chair before it. 'That's Earth technology. It's an old Phipps mark three data store.'

'The most advanced model at the time all this was built,' said the Doctor. He was edging towards the door with a strange look on his face.

Bernice collapsed in the chair. She put the Cell case down next to the computer. 'If I'm laying my life on the line, I like to know what I'm fighting for.' She glared angrily up at the Doctor. 'None of this makes any sense.'

He gestured to the computer. 'Read on,' he said and disappeared through the door. It closed behind him.

Bernice jumped up. She ran to the door and thumbed its release panel. Nothing happened.

'Doctor!' she shouted. 'You've locked me in!'

'I know,' he shouted back. 'It's the best place for you at the moment.'

'It is not!' she cried hotly. 'Sheldukher must be prowling about here somewhere. And what about all that curse of Mthuluhu business outside?'

'I made it up.'

'You made it up?' Bernice called incredulously.

'All it takes is a devious mind and a talent for improvisation. And there's a lot of that sort of thing going on here.' She heard his footsteps padding away. 'Ask your friend in there. He's the key to all this.' His voice trailed off as he continued down the corridor.

Bernice tried to quell her anger. She knew that the Doctor meant well and that he only withheld information for the best of reasons. When the time was right, he would explain. Still, it was easy to resent being locked up like this, as if she were some hapless incompetent best kept out of things. Could that really be the Doctor's opinion of her?

No, it was not, a reassuring inner voice told her. He had put her here for a reason. She decided to take his advice and consult the Cell.

'Would you answer some questions for me, please?'

'I do not speak to . . . humans if I can possibly . . . help it . . . ' it said importantly.

Bernice sighed. 'All right. Just one, then. What is Project FXX Q84?'

'Stupid human,' it cackled. 'That is my name.'

Construct One frowned as he closed the cover of the book. 'These are not instructions for such as we.'

'What, then, are they?' asked Construct Two.

'They are instructions of a completely different nature, intended for less sophisticated systems,' said Construct One. 'They bear no relation to any of our functions.'

'We must, therefore, continue to obey our original instructions. Project FXX Q84 must be retrieved,' Construct Two said, with a hint of reproach.

'The ones known as the Doctor and Professor Bernice Summerfield must be interrogated,' added Construct One. 'They cannot leave. We must find them.' He led the way from the central area.

The Doctor sneaked down the corridor, poking his head around various doors and coming no closer to his goal. 'Come out, come out, wherever you are,' he muttered, wiggling his fingers anxiously. 'How can you hide a Fortean flicker?'

Unlike Bernice, the Doctor did not see the omnipresent temporal disturbance as a dance of twinkling blue lights. To his eyes, the Fortean flicker appeared as a dense web of thick, sparkling blue lines that frayed as they linked or turned corners. He was trying hard to ignore the nauseous feeling that overcame him as he came closer to the source of the disruption, and pushed fears of its effect on him if it became active again to the back of his mind. There really had been too much temporal distortion in his life of late. He found himself longing for a good old-fashioned alien invasion.

Thus preoccupied, he was unprepared for the appearance of the Constructs from behind a pillar.

Construct One held up the 'phone book. 'These instructions are unsuited to us.'

'They do not contain relevant information,' added Construct Two.

The Doctor sighed. 'Of course they do,' he snapped.

'You are wrong,' said Construct One.

Thinking faster than ever, the Doctor reached forward for the book. 'If I may?' He flicked through it. 'What are you talking about? The instructions are absolutely clear.'

'This information is irrelevant,' insisted Construct Two.

The Doctor turned the book upside down and passed it back. 'Perhaps this time you could try reading it the right way up?' he suggested. 'Now let me through, please, I have urgent work to attend to.' He barged past them with a huff.

'What is implied here?' puzzled Construct One. 'There is only one way to encode information.'

'Not in these obsolete systems,' Construct Two corrected smoothly. He took the book from the hands of his twin. 'You are holding this book upside down,' he said, priding himself on the use of the authentic phraseology. 'I will read this time.'

The Phipps mark three data store proved no challenge to Bernice. She gained access to the classified files on Project FXX

Q84 after only a few minutes at the keyboard. The information contained numerous scientific terms she was unfamiliar with. To save time, she opened up a direct response link. She needed to clear up the mystery of the city before she could think straight about herself, the Doctor, or anything. Her head had begun to swim and the figures on the screen had blurred several times. The combination of bubbleshake poisoning, temporal ague and sheer exhaustion was starting to tell on her.

'State your request,' the computer said tinnily, rousing her from introspection.

'Information on Project FXX Q84 is required,' she replied in perfect computer speak.

'Gene codes $zq - f - df$ correlated to the px factor have assimilated $-$'

'No no no,' she interrupted hurriedly. 'Basic level data required only.'

The computer hummed and clicked, selecting the elementary vocabulary of its domestic use facility. 'Project FXX Q84 is the ultimate development of the gene laboratories on Checkley's World. It has the potential to grow to out-think all other forms of life.'

Bernice frowned. 'Refer: Checkley's World.' She had never heard of it.

'Checkley's World,' replied the computer, 'was settled in the Earth calendar year 2290. It was selected as the optimum site for the proposed scientific frontiers base. The laboratories were released from state control in 2300. The source of funding became a consortium of planetary empires and corporations, including Riftok, Masel and Arcturus. The major partner remained Earth Government.'

Bernice sighed and sat back. She glanced across at the bloated, blackened Cell and shuddered. 'The Horror Planet,' she breathed. 'So it really did exist.'

She had heard rumours of the secret experimental centre where some of the more revolting defence systems — Freire's gas, compression grenades — were said to have been created: weapons that turned up mysteriously on all sides at once. The Cell was the end product of their genetic research, something so valuable that the resourceful and wealthy consortium would

228

stop at nothing to retrieve it. She was beginning to see a pattern in all of this.

'Refer: Sakkrat, Sheldukher,' she said. She needed her suspicions confirmed.

'In 2389 Sheldukher removed Project FXX Q84 from the gene laboratories and destroyed its creators and their records. It was necessary to retrieve Project FXX Q84.

'Strategy computers assimilated all available information on the human Sheldukher. It was predicted that he would use Project FXX Q84 to attempt to find the location of planet Sakkrat.'

'And?' prompted Bernice, her mind racing.

'Specific request required,' said the computer.

'Refer: retrieval of Project FXX Q84.'

'Planet Hogsumm was selected as Sakkrat. It corresponded almost exactly to the Sakkrat myths and was reformed climatically to reinforce credibility. This base was then established.'

'And you sat here for nearly three hundred years waiting for the Cell to find this planet and Sheldukher to arrive?'

'Strategy predicted that Sheldukher would be taken only at the moment of supreme vulnerability. He might otherwise escape and destroy Project FXX Q84. A ruined city was created above the base to reinforce the illusion. Sheldukher was to be lured down to the base. Supernumeraries unconnected to the plan would be eradicated by city guardians.'

'Refer: city guardians,' Bernice requested.

'A robot was placed at the centre of the city,' the computer told her. 'Its function was to reinforce credibility of the Sakkrat illusion. Also, Ethers were harnessed to guard the city. Their task was to establish telepathic response to a key stimulus and to eradicate non-responsives as necessary.'

She hunched forward in the chair. 'What was the key stimulus?'

'The word Sheldukher,' it replied.

Bernice sat back, stunned. So Rodomonte had died because of a word he did not know, the name of a man not even born in his time period. She and Urnst, familiar with stories of the infamous master criminal, had been allowed to enter.

The Sakkrat illusion had convinced her totally. Never for a moment had she doubted the city and its strange powers and inhabitants, all of which, from the light pillars to the native paintwork, had been designed as the final trap for Sheldukher. So many little things began to add up in her mind. Her rescue from the Chelonians; the Doctor's wonderfully convincing reluctance to proceed, just what was needed to goad Sheldukher on to his doom; the Cell's lock picking, which wasn't a coincidence after all. The door had been created by its own makers.

There were still many questions left unanswered. How long had the Doctor known about all this? Where did the Fortean flicker come into it? What was the function of the Constructs?

She turned back to the computer. The last question it could answer, at least. Before she could continue, the Cell launched into one of its rare bursts of activity.

'It's me . . . ' it said proudly. 'I'm the important one round here . . . this was all for my benefit . . . '

'Don't get too carried away,' she told it. 'You don't know what they're going to do to you yet.'

Her ears pricked up. Voices came from the corridor outside.

Construct Two threw the 'phone book to the ground. 'This makes no sense whatever way one looks at it.'

'We have, then, been the victims of an enormous deception,' said Construct One. 'The one called the Doctor has lied to us.'

'He is a random element and must be eradicated before we activate the ship,' seethed Construct Two. 'He has endangered the plan.' He strode off down the corridor.

'Wait,' said Construct One. He was standing at the door to the data store. 'My ears detect movement in the room on the other side of this door.'

'We must, then, open the door,' suggested Construct Two.

Construct One waved a hand over the release panel. The door remained closed. 'The mechanism is faulty.'

'The one called the Doctor may have interfered with the systems,' said Construct Two. 'We must, then, gain entry by other means.'

The Constructs raised their left hands and extended their nailless index fingers. Waves of red light appeared from the tips and converged on the door. It began to melt away slowly.

'We will soon gain entry,' said Construct One. 'All random elements must be eradicated.'

The Doctor's search had been unproductive. He turned a corner and found himself back in the central area.

'This is ridiculous, more confusing than the TARDIS,' he said to himself. 'Where is it?'

A cry came from above him. The Doctor looked up. Sheldukher was pinned to a panel on the ceiling by a powerful force field. His hair was pulled back from his face by the matter suction. He fought desperately against the power that held him.

'I wondered where you'd got to.'

'Doctor,' he called down, in a drained, hollow voice. 'Help me, please, I beg you ... '

The Doctor stared up at him, his expression set. 'I cannot do that, Sheldukher.'

'Doctor, please ... ' he called. 'I'm in agony ... '

The Doctor turned his head away. 'This would have happened to you had I been here or not. I cannot interfere. I have no wish to.'

'You're part of this!' Sheldukher shouted manically. 'You were part of this from the start!'

The Doctor shook his head. 'For once, that isn't the case,' he explained. 'It was only when we met those ghosts that I began to work out what was really happening here. They are Ethers, spirits brought into semi-corporeal form to perform simple tasks in war. They're very difficult to kill. As far as I know, they were harnessed on only one world. Checkley's World. It wasn't too difficult to work out what their masters were after.'

Sheldukher was startled. 'This is not the work of the Intergalactic Taskforce?'

The Doctor shook his head. 'The state had neither the resources nor the interest, Sheldukher. You weren't important enough for them to bother about.'

'The Cell?' he cried incredulously. 'All this ... for the Cell?'

'Exactly.'

'But the slow time conversion unit ... '

'I think,' explained the Doctor, 'it was to keep the Constructs nice and fresh until you turned up. Dying on the job would have been rather embarrassing in the circumstances. It is also the most likely source of all the Fortean distortion.'

There was silence as Sheldukher thought over the situation. He seemed drained of all of the sinister life that had animated him. 'What now?' he said finally.

'Well, I have to be off,' said the Doctor, already heading for the door. 'Bernice is waiting and I've a temporal fluctuation to deal with.' He slipped out.

Sheldukher struggled against his invisible bonds. One of his hands succeeded in entering his pocket. 'No,' he whispered. 'Nobody's going to take me alive ... '

Bernice searched the data room for something to use as a weapon. The door was almost burnt through and she could see the Constructs through the red haze of the hole they were creating.

'There's nothing,' she said anxiously. 'There must be something!'

'They have to come to ... claim me for ... their own ... ' grated the Cell.

'There *is* something.' She grabbed the Cell case and waited for the confrontation. Their work completed, the Constructs walked casually through the smoking gap. Pain was obviously another missing part of their design.

'Give us Project FXX Q84,' demanded Construct One.

'Project FXX Q84 is not important now,' said Bernice. 'Have you not received your new instructions?'

'Do not attempt to deceive us again,' threatened Construct Two. 'You will give us Project FXX Q84'.

Bernice shrugged. 'Oh well, it was worth a try,' she said, and made for the door.

'Stop!' the Constructs ordered. Their fingertips sent a flaming spiral over her shoulder as a warning.

Bernice whipped round. She held the Cell case up before her. 'Kill me and you will destroy Project FXX Q84.'

The Constructs stepped forward interestedly. Bernice realized that they had not expected the Cell to have mutated so strangely.

'You will give us Project FXX Q84,' ordered Construct One.

'Stay here,' Bernice said. 'Come after me and I'll destroy it.' She backed away slowly from them.

When she had turned the corner, Construct One turned to Construct Two. 'We will follow and eradicate Professor Bernice Summerfield.'

'She intends to destroy Project FXX Q84 if we do so,' pointed out Construct Two. 'Such an action would endanger the entire plan.'

'That is what she expects us to think,' said Construct One with a superior smile. 'I think I am beginning to see the way the human minds operate.'

The Doctor hurried on through sections of corridor he was almost sure he hadn't passed through before. His footsteps clanked hollowly on a small section of flooring. He stooped, brushed a layer of dust from the panel, and slid it away.

He popped his head down and caught a glimpse of a small entrance hatch with an airlock gauge control. A small spaceship was buried beneath the city. 'The way back,' he mused.

A distant crash returned him to his senses. 'Bernice,' he said worriedly. He was about to return to her when something else caught his attention.

The end of the corridor was a sheet of pure blue light. He had found the source of the Fortean flicker at last. All that remained was to neutralize it.

'If the theory is sound,' he mimicked himself, 'its application should be no problem.' He tutted. 'Silly old fool.'

He patted his pockets, but his copy of *Theoretical Anomalies* was back in the TARDIS. Its suggested design for a nullifying machine would have come in handy. He would just have to go ahead and hope for the best.

Without waiting to consider the consequences, he walked confidently into the light. Ripples of time parted around him. Blood flowed backwards around his body. He considered turning back. 'No,' he told himself, 'it's too late for that ... '

He gritted his teeth as the vortex surrounded him. All sense of space and time was lost to him. His hat was blown off into nowhere. His eyes saw nothing but confusion, half formed images that were impossible to identify. A glittery nimbus formed about him, the normally invisible shield of his Time Lord otherness.

His outstretched hands connected with something that felt as solid and real as himself. It was a silver globe about the size of a football that sat on a slender dais. The image of it flickered like a glitch on primitive videotape. The Doctor moved his head up and down to keep the ball in focus. He identified it easily as a slow time convertor.

He knelt down. The upper half of the globe was transparent. Thousands of tiny components glistened in the blue. His experienced eye selected just one.

'As I suspected,' he said, his voice coming out slurred like a slowed-down record. 'A faulty kronos element . . . '

He flicked up the cover and placed his finger over the offending article. Reality tweaked around him but the vortex returned stronger than ever.

'Only one thing for it.' He raised his umbrella and brought it down on the globe in one blow. Sparks flew from the casing. He was flung to the floor. Rushing winds threatened to pull him apart.

It was with considerable relief that he sat up seconds later to find himself still in that same, reassuringly ordinary corridor. The vortex had disappeared. All that remained of the experience was the inactive globe, a peripheral smattering of blue lights and a horrible lurching in his stomach as a long forgotten breakfast of winter vegetable soup decided it wanted out.

He gave a long, deep sigh. The immediate danger from the Fortean flicker was at last over. He took the globe from the dais and set off back along the corridor. There was still much to be done.

Bernice collapsed. The Cell case clattered down in front of her. When she looked up a man she didn't recognize was standing over her. He carried an umbrella and a silver globe. Strangely, he was surrounded by a kind of halo effect.

'I don't remember you again,' she blurted helplessly.

'I'm the Doctor,' he said urgently.

'Doctor, of course,' she snarled, angry at her failing faculties.

'It's happening again, the sickness . . . '

He pulled her to her feet and helped her to regain her balance. 'Don't worry. The important thing is to get out of here.'

'Well bluffed, by the way,' she congratulated him. 'But Doctor, there's something wrong.'

'There always is. Be more specific.'

'You're glowing,' she told him.

'Thank you,' he said graciously. 'You don't look too bad yourself.'

'No,' she said angrily. 'I mean you really are glowing.'

He looked down at himself. 'Am I? I don't think that can be right.'

'That's what I just said.'

He shook his head dismissively and held up the globe. 'It must be the effect of this.'

'What is it? A ballbearing from a battlecruiser?'

'No,' he tutted. 'How can you be flippant at a time like this? This is the source of the Fortean flicker.'

She stared at it incredulously. '*That?*'

'Small things can be impressive in their own way, you know,' he said with feeling. 'It's a slow time convertor, more commonly known as a temporal telescope. Shuts up the centuries in a little box, which can be very handy in bus queues, or if you're waiting for the arrival of a frozen criminal mastermind. Unfortunately, this one developed a faulty kronos element.'

'A faulty what?' scoffed Bernice.

'Don't blame me, I didn't design the thing,' blustered the Doctor. 'Anyway, that's how the flicker came into being.'

'But now you've dealt with it, right?'

'Not quite,' he admitted sheepishly. 'As with a lot of Checkley's World technology, it's difficult to switch off.'

'So what did you do to it?'

He brandished his umbrella proudly. 'I knocked it on the head.'

Bernice groaned. 'I should have seen that one coming.'

Their conversation was interrupted by a blast of flame that shot around the corner. 'Surrender yourselves and hand over Project FXX Q84,' a voice demanded.

'Bernice, you've riled them,' the Doctor chided her.

She picked up the Cell case. 'Let's just get out of here,' she said briskly and ran off. The Doctor followed, the halo shifting oddly about him.

Sheldukher had managed to free his left arm from the matter suction plate. The object he had removed from his pocket filled him with contentment. If those scientists had thought they could second guess him so completely, they had been wrong. A movement down below caught his eye. The Doctor and Bernice had returned with the Cell.

The Doctor stopped before the exit. 'We can't leave yet.'

'Why not?' she said in exasperation. 'Come on.'

He looked at her seriously. 'Out there is a city full of traps. If we leave now, we won't stand a chance against them. The Guardian, the Ethers, they will not permit us to leave with the Cell.'

'Then let's leave without it.'

'No,' he said quickly. 'We cannot give them the Cell, it mustn't get into the wrong hands.'

'I'm impressed, Doctor,' said Sheldukher. They looked up at him. 'I'm impressed. You are intelligent, genuinely intelligent.'

Both the Doctor and Bernice noticed the return of his calm composure. 'What are they going to do with him?' Bernice whispered.

'Something long and unpleasant, I imagine,' the Doctor replied.

'I can't say I'm sorry.'

'I don't expect you to be.'

'But you see,' Sheldukher continued, 'although I must admit I hadn't anticipated these events, the possibility of capture has never been far from my mind.' He uncurled the fingers of his left hand to reveal the black square. 'I have prepared for this eventuality. So I didn't find Sakkrat? At least I had the ambition to try. My only regret is that I won't be here to see the look on your faces when the full implications of my preparations become apparent.'

He turned the black square to face himself and pressed the activator.

236

The Doctor leapt forward. 'No, you mustn't . . . '

It was too late. Sheldukher dissolved into dust in a second. His empty suit fell to the floor.

The Doctor walked slowly over to it. 'That's one less bad loser in the galaxy,' Bernice observed.

'Listen,' said the Doctor grimly. He pointed to the empty suit of clothes.

Bernice cocked an ear. 'It's a bleep.'

The Doctor shook his head. 'It's a tick. And that's a very important difference.'

'A time bomb?'

He pulled open the lapel of the jacket. A small red box winked evilly up at them. 'A Hercules Devastator on a timed fuse, primed to activate on his death. A range of a thousand miles. I'd say we have fifteen minutes.'

'Go on, then,' Bernice prompted. 'Defuse it.'

'I can't,' the Doctor replied. 'Nobody can. Ironically enough, I think they were designed on Checkley's World.'

Bernice pointed. 'So were they.'

The Constructs had entered the entranceway. 'Give us Project FXX Q84.'

The Doctor snatched the Cell case from Bernice before she could react to the request. In return he passed her the globe and his umbrella. A strange, fluttery feeling came over her as the halo formed.

Construct One blasted more warning shots at the Doctor's feet. 'You will obey us. You must obey us.'

'Evasion is futile,' added Construct Two.

'We're all about to be blown sky high away, so it doesn't really make much difference, does it?' Bernice asked them.

'What are you talking about?' Construct One demanded suspiciously. 'Be warned. There will be no more deceptions.'

She pointed to the bomb. 'Argue with that.'

They turned to examine the device and seemed to recognize it instantly. 'What are we to do now?' asked Construct Two. 'Our instructions do not cover such a situation.'

'We must, then, ignore this,' reasoned Construct One. 'Our priority is the recovery of Project FXX Q84.'

The Doctor had used the time wasted by this conversation

to slip out into the corridors again. Bernice dashed after him.

'Return!' Construct One demanded. 'We must pursue them.'

'Why?' asked Construct Two. 'Our function will soon be ended anyway.'

Construct One looked at him in amazement. 'It is wrong to question instructions. Follow.' He strode off after the Doctor and Bernice.

His brother hesitated a moment, then followed.

Bernice caught up with the Doctor. He was sat hunched over the Cell, for all the world as if there was nothing going on around him at all.

'There's a chance,' he told her. 'We can still get out of this, I can see a way. First we must get rid of the Constructs.'

'Show me.'

He pointed to the Cell. 'The Constructs' instructions are very specific. But the over riding principle is the redemption of this. Without it, their precious program means nothing. With luck, they may even deactivate.'

She nodded. 'Do it.'

His hand reached for the voltage control. His fingers curled around the grips.

'No,' he said and withdrew his hand. He recalled the agonies it had shared with him. 'No, I can't do it. Not like this, not in cold blood.'

The action had brought the Cell out of its contemplation. At last somebody was prepared to grant its wish for death. 'Kill me, Doctor . . . please, put an end to my . . . existence, I beg you . . .'

The Constructs arrived in the corridor. Bernice jumped back as a well aimed heat beam scorched her face. The Doctor leapt up carrying the Cell case before him as a warning against attack.

'This is where I come in!' Bernice yelled over the roar of the spitting fire rays. She leapt over to the Doctor, wrenched the case from his protesting grip, and turned the voltage control up to maximum.

The Cell screamed one last time and fried away.

19:

Way Out Theories

Unlike the Constructs, which had been cobbled together from blank genes, the Ethers had minds of their own. Long ago, somewhere, they had lived as people. Summoned halfway back into existence by the powers of numinous science, they retained vestiges of instinct and intellect. They knew something had gone wrong with the final phase of the operation.

They turned their minds to those of the Constructs. Such useless beings. They had been designed only to retrieve Project FXX Q84, supposedly the simplest of tasks. Their rudimentary, blank gene brains had failed to perform even that function correctly. What was worse, Project FXX Q84 had been destroyed and the slow time convertor had been tampered with.

The architects of the trap had not allowed for the presence of random responsives such as the artful, steel minded Doctor and the sharp witted Professor Summerfield. The plan had failed. The Ethers were angry about that. Anger was another advantage they possessed over the Constructs. They decided to indulge that anger.

The random responsives would be eradicated. They probed the tiny sliver of organic material that animated the Monumental Guardian and suggested that response. It agreed readily. Like them it had, a long time ago, been a part of something else. A thing that enjoyed killing other things.

Construct One looked down at the smoking remains of the Cell. Its central brain had deflated into a flat, black lump of dead tissue. Its crystal half had become a trickle of fine purple dust. The roots at its base had carbonized completely.

He turned to Construct Two. 'We have no purpose now.'

The other nodded. 'We have, then, failed.'

Construct One pronounced, 'We are fit only for withering.'

The Doctor, who had gathered back together his umbrella and the temporal telescope, pulled Bernice back from them. 'Watch,' he said.

The Constructs looked down at their feet. Their toes had gone soggy, melting together to form shapeless, lard coloured clumps. The infection spread swiftly up their featureless white bodies.

Bernice was horrified. 'Can't we do anything to save them?'

The Doctor shook his head. 'For them, it's the only way out.'

The Constructs' legs crumbled like tofu beneath them. Two white pools formed, oozing wider as more of the bodies above — thighs, torso, shoulders — were eaten up.

Bernice and the Doctor turned their eyes away in disgust at the final stage of the process. Two shrivelling heads remained at the centre of the puddles.

'We have, then, withered,' said Head Two sadly.

'Let us hope we are granted better fortune in our next form,' said Head One.

Those were his last words. Both heads slopped slowly down into the whiteness. Chins, mouths and eyes sunk to the floor, until all that was left were two bald pates, swimming on top of the congealing stickiness like eggs frying in a greasy saucepan. Finally even those were liquified.

'That was revolting,' said Bernice. 'What a way to go.'

The Doctor peered down at the ooze. 'They haven't really gone.'

'Sorry?'

'They've withered back into their raw state. It's what Constructs are programmed to do if they fail.'

Bernice turned away from the pool. 'Even if it isn't a nasty way to die, it's a horrible way to live.'

'Better than being blown apart by a Hercules devastator,' the Doctor reminded her. He scurried off down the corridor.

Bernice trudged after him. Despite the urgency of the situation, she was getting back to the point where collapsing and dying seemed a more agreeable option than fighting against the odds. 'You said there was a way out,' she called. 'Or was that just to make me feel better?'

She turned a corner and found herself at the tattered door of the data room. She popped through the jagged edged hole. The

Doctor was hunched over the Phipps, his fingers working at stupendous speed on the keyboard.

'There!' he stated proudly. She peered over his shoulder at the screen and tried to focus on the swimming image.

'It's a map of this base.'

'Exactly. What do you see?'

She squinted. 'Not very much.'

He pointed. 'Look.'

A large oblong was appended to the map. The fin-like shape of the rear meant something to Bernice but she couldn't work out what. She shrugged.

The Doctor examined her worriedly. 'It's a ship,' he said. 'The one that was supposed to take them back to Checkley's World with the Cell.'

Bernice sighed. 'Doctor, it will take hours to power it up. We only have ten minutes left.'

'Exactly,' he said enthusiastically. 'And it's for exactly this sort of emergency that those clever old scientists installed *that*.' He pointed to another section of the map, a small label on one wall of the central hall.

'Sorry, Doctor,' Bernice said weakly. 'I can't remember how to read, so you're going to have to tell me.'

He stood up, gathered his effects, and put a protective arm around her shoulder. 'It says *Emergency Transmat Exit*.'

She gave a whoop of joy. 'That is the best news I've had since we arrived on this bloody planet.'

'Come on, then,' said the Doctor. He led her out into the corridor at a brisk pace. They skirted the remnants of the Constructs carefully.

As they entered the entrance hall, a great bellow came from nearby. The Doctor patted Bernice's arm. 'Don't worry, it's only that Guardian thing going for its daily lurch.'

He turned to the section of wall indicated on the map and ran his fingers along the blank surface, seeking a hidden catch. His sensitive fingertips found a tiny indentation. He pressed at the concealed panel. It sprang open, revealing a conventional transmat booth and control panel.

Bernice looked anxiously down at the ticking Hercules devastator. Another, louder bellow came from the Guardian.

'It sounds as if it's right outside.'

'Just ignore it,' he said. He was engrossed in the co-ordinate panel of the transmat controls. 'The system's simple enough, comparative settings should be easy,' he muttered. 'But where . . . ah, yes!'

He delved into his inside pocket and produced Sheldukher's map of the planet. With a tiny stub of pencil he marked WE ARE HERE in one corner, FAKRID AND EIGHT TWELVES HERE in another, and TARDIS HERE close to it. He tucked the globe under his arm, held the map at arm's length and punched in co-ordinates with his free hand.

The Guardian roared again. The walls shook. 'Doctor, it's trying to get in!' cried Bernice.

'Nonsense,' he said. 'As I keep telling you, its function is only to scare people.'

'It's succeeded!' she shouted back at him. The ticking seemed to be getting faster. The red light on the devastator had increased the frequency of its winking. 'Come on, Doctor!'

'There, get in!' he shouted, standing back from the panel. She ran into the booth. He pressed the flickering globe into her hands.

She glanced nervously over at the co-ordinate display. 'Are you sure you've got this right, Doctor?'

'Of course I have,' he reassured her. 'We'll come out just outside the TARDIS. Now, close your eyes!'

He set the automatic timer and jumped up next to her.

Ten seconds went by. Nothing happened. 'Come on, come on,' he growled angrily.

'Something's gone wrong,' Bernice said, stating the obvious. Her eyes were still closed but she could feel herself starting to cry. How pathetic, how unlike her. That stupid drug.

'Oh well, Doctor,' she said, 'it's been nice knowing you. Hope to see you on the other side. Just think, we'll be able to meet each other's parents. I hope mine will approve of you.'

The Doctor was not listening. He had leapt from the booth and was punching furiously at the program panel. There was no trace of a fault. 'This is ridiculous!' he cried in frustration. He ripped open the adjacent panels. A maze of wiring confronted him.

Bernice opened her eyes. The thump of the Guardian on the far wall was louder now. She reminded herself that it was a poor, harmless creature just going about its duty.

The wall smashed inwards, scattering breezeblocks. The Monumental Guardian swooped in, twisting its flexible thorax to get itself through the gap it had created. Its headstalk swivelled about. Seven eyes, now glowing a fiery red, picked out its victims. Its array of spiny protruberances quivered and buzzed with anticipation. Huge clouds of smoke belched out from below.

Bernice felt something else being pressed into her hand. The Doctor had found a small handgun in the emergency stores besides the transmat booth. 'Try and hold it off!' he shouted.

'I can barely stand up!' she shouted back. He had turned back to the panel and wasn't listening.

She aimed the gun at the headstalk and fired. The force bolts shot off in completely the wrong direction. Angered by her attack, the creature swooped down. A claw plucked her from the transmat booth and lifted her up. It tightened around her, threatening to crush the life from her body. The gun nearly slipped between her fingers.

'Bernice!' the Doctor roared from below.

His cry stirred her to action. She raised the gun. The Guardian had brought her right up to its headstalk. More of its buzzing probes and blades were extending to begin what she guessed would be a long and intimately biological death. She pulled the trigger, this time aiming for the point where the head section joined the stalk.

The bolts tore right through the neck. The head was blasted off over her shoulder. The claw drooped down and opened automatically. She fell ten feet to the floor.

The Doctor ran forward. The creature was thrashing about wildly. Only its eyesight had been destroyed and the controlling intelligence was obviously still active. Somehow it sensed what he was trying to do. It let off a stream of hot steam right into his face and proceeded to lower itself over him.

Blinded, the Doctor pushed through its forest of tentacles. It had electrified them and each time bare skin touched one he jumped with shock. The enormous weight of the creature's bulk hovered over him. Low pitched screams of pain and anger tortured his ears.

He found Bernice, heaved up her unconscious body in his arms and pushed himself backwards through the stinging tentacles.

The Guardian readied itself to crush him. It sank down slowly, coiling its tentacles to cushion its body.

The Doctor squeezed through a tiny gap at the edge nearest the transmat, Bernice still clutched in his arms. He ran for the booth and let her down gently, then darted back to the panel.

The Ethers were waiting for him. He blinked to clear his bleary eyes. The centre of each ghosts' forehead was glowing.

Confused, distressing images of his past were dredged from the depths of his mind to distract him.

He tore himself away from them and returned to work on the panel. 'Yes!' he cried suddenly. 'Of course . . . ' He slipped the blue gemstone ring from his finger and placed it between two sections of the tiny console. The system had been designed for use with an operator's key. There was no time to find it and the ring would make a good substitute. He set the automatic timer and returned to the booth.

The Ethers watched as the Doctor and Bernice disappeared. The ring vanished with them.

The Hercules devastator stopped ticking.

The heatwave boiled the Guardian's outer shell away. Its robotic skeleton was visible for a second, then that too was blasted to ashes.

The data store, the transmat, the Cell case and the pool of slime that had once been the Constructs, evaporated.

The devastation raged through the city. The bodies of Rodomonte, Molassi and Klift, the towers and courtyards and walkways, Urnst's spacesuit glove, all were effaced from the planet.

Postine and the temple ruins, Sendei's grave and the sad remains of Trooper Ozaran and Rosheen, were reduced to flatness by the expanding wave of destruction.

A thousand mile square of the planet was atomized.

20:

Just A Moment

Dawn was breaking. The first light of day revealed a figure. It darted between pockets of mist, keeping low to maintain its cover.

Vanessa had woken an hour before, surrounded by the thirty or so souls that made up the eight twelve community. Hazel, practical as ever, had found a large, warm cave for them to sleep in, not too far from the carriage. A stream of clear water ran through it. Vanessa, a vegetarian of some years standing, had been among the first to enjoy the delights of roasted squirrel. Witcher, she had thought, would have been proud of her.

Since the Doctor's abduction she had taken to rising early in the morning for a good recce of the area. The other eight twelves had taken to her as leader and she felt she had a reputation to live up to. There was also the possibility of more trouble or, if they were lucky, the return of the Doctor and a journey back to Earth.

She heard guttural voices through the mist and flung herself down. Mum, if only you could see me now, she thought. And you told me the girl's brigade had been a waste of time.

Two Chelonians shuffled into view. Each carried something that she couldn't make out in the darkness.

'Position it here, Mubzza,' the first said.

The other dropped the object it was carrying and chuckled throatily. 'How I love the smell of zarathion in the morning. Truly, the parasite scum will be wiped from this rockball before they know what is happening!'

The first Chelonian burst into laughter. 'Their death screams will make music sweeter than the cacophonies of Traal!'

They motored off into the mists, their laughter echoing back at Vanessa as she pulled herself up. 'What are you on?' she whispered to their departing shells.

She knelt to examine the object they had dropped. She had expected some kind of time bomb, but it didn't look like one. It was brown and lozenge shaped, about half a metre across, and reminded her of the worming pills she had used to crunch up in her dog Barney's bowl back on Earth.

She looked closer. The object was covered in a thin, transparent film. Four oriental style characters were embossed in yellow on one side. Handle with care she told herself gloomily.

Her hand went inside her dirty coat and emerged with the Chelonian footgun she had confiscated earlier. She was torn between returning to the cave to warn the others or going to see if she could nobble the Chelonians.

Still, if they were back, maybe the Doctor would come back too. Reassured by that thought, she went on.

Jinkwa surveyed his empire. The zarathion pellets were piled in the centre of the ring of remaining vehicles. Troopers queued up to take one each and spread them over the area according to a well prepared drill. As each soldier filed past with his pellet, Jinkwa swelled a little further with self importance.

An irritating tickle brushed his posterior. He cuffed the trooper responsible with his rear right foot. 'Mind where you put that brush, you oaf!'

'Sorry, sir,' replied the hapless youngster. 'If you keep still instead of shuffling about I'll have the job done much quicker.'

Jinkwa turned his head to meet the gaze of the impetuous one. The boy sat there fecklessly, red paint dripping from his brush. 'By Nim, I'll have you so far down the promotion chart you'll be at the top again if you're not careful!' he threatened.

The trooper gulped and returned to the job in hand. His training in official decoration had taken place in warm, comfortable, well lit barracks on Chelonia. Each session had taken about ten minutes. Jinkwa was such a jumpy subject that he had been working half an hour and had got no further than a few wonky dabs and splashes. The Goddess help him if the new commander ever saw himself in a mirror.

Jinkwa reached for another leaf from his personal ration. He watched as the last of the pellets was taken up. 'Spread them well, my friends,' he crowed. 'In another hour, the eight twelves will be begging for mercy!'

He brushed a set of toes over the controls of the sprinkler system by his side. A large red button sat temptingly at the centre. He fought hard to stop himself from pressing it. No. He would wait until the pellets were spread widely enough to ensure total destruction of all parasites.

The last pellet-carrying trooper left the encampment. A cheer went up from the amassed crowd. Jinkwa smiled proudly. It had been such a good idea of his to use zarathion for the final stages of the operation.

Vanessa rounded a corner. She was hurrying after another Chelonian in the hope that she could either disable or interrogate it when she caught a glimpse of something lying in a ditch nearby. She peered over the rim cautiously and was astonished to see the Doctor.

'Doctor!' she called joyously. 'Doctor!'

He lay unmoving at the bottom of the pit. Vanessa picked her way carefully down its steep sides. Small stones were sent skittering down on to his prostrate form.

She crouched over him and shook him. His eyes opened. 'Who are you?' he said weakly.

'Vanessa,' she said eagerly.

'Look, Vanessa.' He pointed over her shoulder.

She whipped round, expecting a Chelonian at least. There was nothing there. The poor man was hallucinating.

'There's nothing there.'

'Look again,' he said patiently. 'Look and listen.'

She turned her head back up to the sky and gasped in shock. The clouds had stopped moving and their constant rumble had been compressed into a low, unchanging note. 'That's impossible.'

The Doctor sat up. 'Haven't you ever heard of time standing still?'

'Of course,' she said. 'Every morning at work I look at the clock and think bloody hell, it can't only be half past ten.'

The Doctor smiled and got to his feet. 'This is a different matter altogether,' he said. 'We're inside a small pocket of slow time.' He cast his eyes about anxiously.

Vanessa saw what he was looking for. 'Doctor.' She pointed to Bernice, who lay sprawled on the other side of the crater. The silver globe lay at her feet.

The Doctor raced over and took her pulse. He gave a sigh of relief. 'Is she all right?' asked Vanessa. The woman looked in a bad way. She was covered in dirt and there was an unpleasant looking cut on her head.

Bernice opened her eyes and closed them again immediately. 'I've made such a fool of myself,' she moaned.

'Of course you haven't,' the Doctor reassured her gently. 'You've done very well.'

She smiled weakly. 'Where's the TARDIS?'

The Doctor sucked his teeth embarrassedly. 'Er, well, I'm afraid my calculations weren't entirely . . . '

She sat bolt upright. The Doctor prepared himself for her invective, but she just said, 'You did your best.'

'Can you walk?'

She got to her feet. 'Walking's fine. It's running, jumping and blasting monsters I'm not up to.'

'Then you might have problems,' put in Vanessa. 'The Chelonians are back and they're up to something.'

The Doctor sighed. 'Will they never learn?' He picked up the globe, flicked up the cover, and fiddled briefly with its innards. The clouds started moving again. 'There we are. Let's go and see what we can do.'

Vanessa clambered eagerly from the ditch. The Doctor gave Bernice a leg up. As she hauled herself up, something occurred to her. 'The Chelonians should be dust by now,' she pointed out. 'If we were in a slow time pocket, hundreds of years should have gone by up here.'

'We were never deprocessed,' the Doctor explained. 'In fact you were never properly processed at all. So that doesn't apply.'

'That is ridiculous,' she said as she reached the top.

'That is transtemporal differential regression,' he said. 'Now please, no more awkward questions.'

'This way, Doctor.' Vanessa indicated the direction she had come from.

In just a few minutes, they had reached the site of the lozenge shaped object. The Doctor stooped to examine it.

'It looks like some sort of chemical compound,' Bernice observed.

The Doctor rolled the thing over gently. A small catch was revealed, imbedded in the film on the underside.

'Is it a bomb, Doctor?' Vanessa enquired nervously.

He straightened up. 'Sort of,' he said. 'A signal will be sent. The film will break, releasing the substance inside.'

'Gas?'

He shook his head. 'Worse than that. I think it carries a virus, similar in its effects to slow acting napalm. The Chelonians will be immune to it.'

Vanessa backed away from the pellet. 'What can we do?'

'Let me think. We may have very little time.' He closed his eyes and began to reel off possible strategies under his breath.

Vanessa turned to Bernice. 'What's the matter with him? Is he meditating or something?'

'He's weighing up the odds,' Bernice explained. The Doctor chattered on. 'It's very irritating, isn't it?'

The Doctor's eyes snapped open. 'Right,' he said briskly. 'Vanessa, return to your people. Tell them to stay there until I come to fetch them.' She nodded and scurried off.

He turned to Bernice. 'Bernice?'

'Yes?'

'Follow me.'

A message came through on Jinkwa's personal channel. 'Commander Jinkwa speaking. Report.'

'Unit Four here, sir. We have sighted a large group of parasites at grid mark two by nine.' Jinkwa heard the soldier lick his lips. 'May we destroy them, sir?' he pleaded eagerly.

Jinkwa smiled. 'Yes,' he said and reached out his foot to break the connection. Then he was struck by inspiration.

'No,' he said. 'I countermand that order. Round up the parasites, and then bring them here, to the camp.'

'Yes, sir,' Unit Four leader replied.

'I think,' Jinkwa told his surrounding men with relish, 'we all deserve a chance to view the slow death agonies of the parasites.'

Vanessa clambered up the rocks that surrounded the entrance to the eight twelves' cave. Strangely, the look out had gone.

'Hazel?' she called. 'Hazel!'

She entered the cave. It was empty but for a few discarded hats and briefcases.

Something caught her eye. A sheet of photocopying paper had been post-it noted to the far wall. A message was scrawled across it in pink highlighter pen.

It said, GONE A FORAGING SEE YOU LATER and was signed HAZE

'Shit!' exclaimed Vanessa and doubled back out of the cave.

The Doctor and Bernice had had little difficulty locating the Chelonians' new base. Ironically, the reptiles had established themselves in the same valley where many of them had been blown apart by the eight twelves. The Doctor noted that all evidence of that attack had been removed.

He crouched on the rim of the valley with Bernice, looking down on the massed military operations. She had assured him that she felt better, not least because the TARDIS was comparatively near at hand.

'So what's the plan, Doctor?' she asked confidently.

'I'm surprised you haven't guessed,' he teased her.

'Go on.'

He produced the silver globe. 'This can be very useful to us.'

'That?' She had almost forgotten about it, although whenever she closed her eyes she could still just about glimpse signs of Fortean distortion. 'Explain.'

He indicated the valley. 'When that little lot are all back at barracks, all I have to do is point it in the right direction . . . '

'And freeze them in slow time,' Bernice completed. 'That's very clever. Except if we get caught in it too, then it won't make the slightest difference.'

'Don't fret,' he said, already working at the globe's internal circuitry. 'A directional effect should be easy to arrange.'

'You're forgetting, it's faulty. You could start the Fortean flicker up again.'

'You're forgetting, I've cross hatched the kronos element to the dimensional rectifier, so that won't happen.'

She smiled. 'Well done, Doctor. You've got it licked.'

She looked back into the valley and froze. 'Doctor.'

He continued his work. 'Not now.'

'Problem,' she said simply.

He stopped working but did not raise his head. 'Big or small?'

'Big.'

He sighed and looked up. A small group of Chelonians were escorting the eight twelves, none too gently, into the valley. Cries of retribution were hurled at the terrified humans from the vengeful crowd.

The Doctor straightened up. A steely look came into his eye. He made a final adjustment and handed Bernice the globe. 'Wait here,' he said and started for the Chelonian camp.

'Don't be stupid!' she called after him.

'Trust me!' he shouted back.

Jinkwa shuffled forward to assess his catch. The filthy vermin were huddled in a group. Some of the more pathetic specimens were weeping.

'Look at you,' he spat. 'Unprotected flesh creatures will always be inferior. Your existence is forfeit.'

He snapped open his all stations address channel. 'Hear me, troopers. I, First Pilot Jinkwa of the noble lineage of Nazmir, offer you, my loyal troops, the deaths of these parasites. What say you?'

'Yes, yes, yes!' roared the crowd, memories of reduced rations and wastefully sacrificed brothers obscured for the moment by their bloodlust.

A soldier motored up, carrying the sprinkler activator on a padded cushion. 'I offer you the spectacle of death by zarathion,' Jinkwa's amplified voice boomed around the valley. 'What say you?'

'Yes, yes, yes!' the mob replied.

'Then I will proceed,' said Jinkwa. His front left foot reached for the blood red button.

'No!' came a voice which, although not amplified, seemed to resound even more than Jinkwa's. The Doctor had returned.

Jinkwa stared at the puny little parasite as it slid down the last few metres into the valley. 'No,' he muttered, forgetting that his voice was still carrying throughout the camp. 'No, this cannot be!'

'Tell me, what happened to General Fakrid?' the Doctor enquired politely.

'My mother is dead,' Jinkwa snapped back hotly.

The Doctor raised his eyebrows. 'And you have taken his place, eh?' He gestured with the point of his umbrella to Jinkwa's red spotted shell. 'Oh dear. You seem to have contracted some sort of tropical disease.'

Jinkwa snarled. 'It is the custom of our race to stripe the shells of noble leaders.'

'Then I'd suggest the use of paint stripper, Jinkwa,' the Doctor continued, 'because a noble leader is one thing you can never be. A bloodthirsty little tyrant, maybe. But you'll never be the man your mother was.'

From her vantage point, Bernice had a clear picture of the Doctor's plan. Enraged by his words, the Chelonians guarding the eight twelves — and most of the others too — were massing about him angrily. She cursed as the humans remained standing stupidly in the valley. Typical twentieth century behaviour. Her instinct was to leap up and warn them away but she knew that would be fatal.

'The Chelonian shell has cracked wide across,' the Doctor ranted on. 'Your first encounter with technology superior to your own, and your military nobility is shown for what it really is, a ... '

It was not often that the Doctor could be silenced in the middle of one of his pleonastic tirades. This time, however, he had an uncomfortable feeling that he had miscalculated. Badly. A circle of heavy breathing Chelonians, led by Jinkwa, was closing in around him.

'Doctor,' said Jinkwa, 'I promised my mother on his death that I would kill you. His soul will not rest until I do.' He bared his teeth, gave a deep throated, feral roar, pulled himself up on his rear feet and prepared to spring.

A pink beam struck Jinkwa across the shell and cracked it wide open. He gave a cry and toppled backwards on his carapace.

The Chelonians' heads turned as one to the far side of the

valley where Vanessa stood, footgun clasped awkwardly in her hands. She fired again, indiscriminately. More Chelonians fell dead. Others returned fire.

Bernice leapt up. 'Run!' she shouted at the startled eight twelves. 'Move! Get out of there!' The commuters milled helplessly about in the confusion. Bernice saw another young woman trying to organize their flight without success.

The Doctor took advantage of the diversion to slip between his Chelonian attackers. He ran frantically back towards Bernice.

Jinkwa's bloodshot eyes opened. He used all the hydraulic power left in his body to push himself over to where the spinkler activator still sat on its ceremonial cushion. He knew he would soon be dead, but here was a chance for glory. He felt the edges of the activator, straight planes reassuring in his grip. Chelonian technology would triumph again.

He struck the red button. 'Goodbye, Doctor,' he wheezed terminally. 'Goodbye, parasites ... You are doomed ... Doomed ... '

The Doctor saw what Jinkwa had done out of the corner of his eye. He raced up the side of the valley. Bernice handed him the globe without having to be asked. He whirled about and pressed down a particular component.

Brown powder began to seep through the dissolving film of the zarathion pellets. A pink volley was fired directly at Vanessa as she emerged from cover.

The powder hung suspended in a graceful upward curl. The disintegrator energy bolts halted inches from Vanessa's terrified face. The confused movement of Chelonians and humans alike was frozen.

The Doctor and Bernice watched as a sparkling cobweb of the deepest blue span itself over the valley and through to the land beyond, where the other pellets had been set. The sudden silence was astonishing.

'Well, it nearly worked,' the Doctor said breathlessly.

'We can't leave them like that!' Bernice protested.

The Doctor set the globe gently down. 'What else can we do? If we tamper with the stasis field in any way, we're dead. That poison would kill us in seconds. No, I daren't go down there. Entering such an unstable field would be fatal, even for a Time Lord.'

Bernice looked down at the amazing scene. 'So they've just got to stay there. Forever.'

'Not necessarily,' said the Doctor. 'I may think up a way around the problem one day.'

He looked about anxiously, as if expecting another problem to leap out at him. 'Now then ... '

'Now then, what?'

He stared aimlessly into the middle distance. 'It's over, isn't it? This whole disagreeable business.'

She coughed. 'My dissolving brain.'

'Good grief, yes,' the Doctor exclaimed. 'Let's go.'

They found an empty Chelonian vehicle nearby, abandoned after being attacked in the eight twelves' original assault. Some inspired tinkering on the part of the Doctor soon had it working again. Several hours later, the tank trundled into view of the plain where they had left the TARDIS.

Bernice emerged first. The Doctor had taken the opportunity of the long drive to answer some of her questions.

'And so,' he concluded, 'what we saw here was a fascinating microcosm of what happened to the entire Chelonian empire in the end. The fight against more advanced humanoid races demoralized them and they started on each other. Finally, they capitulated and became co-operative members of interplanetary society.'

'A co-operative Chelonian,' Bernice sniffed. 'I can't imagine it.'

'They became renowned as the greatest florists in the galaxy,' he reflected. 'Very modest about it, too.'

They trudged silently towards the TARDIS. Bernice found herself longing for its comforting whiteness. Despite its odd behaviour, it felt like home to her now. A wonderful blue door that could take you anywhere.

Suddenly, the Doctor whirled about. He ferreted in his pockets and then bit his tongue in frustration. 'Oh no!'

'What's wrong?'

'How could I have forgotten?'

254

'What?' she screamed.

'That time warp,' he said. 'I left my spoons in there.'

Bernice giggled. 'What a calamity.'

'*And* my tin opener!'

'Now there's a disaster.'

They linked arms. The Doctor still wore a troubled frown. 'Don't worry, we'll go and get you some more,' she told him. 'I know a good kitchen reject shop on Atvares Minor.'

'You don't understand,' he said morosely. 'Tin openers are very important things.' They had arrived back at the lopsided TARDIS.

He patted his pockets again. 'The key!' he exclaimed, even more alarmed.

Bernice handed it to him. 'Oh. Thank you,' he said.

'Don't mention it.'

'I remember once,' he continued, 'the TARDIS took me to an alternate Earth where the tin opener had never been invented.'

He inserted the key in the lock. 'So?' Bernice asked.

'The entire population died of starvation. They just couldn't get their tins open.'

Bernice smiled. She turned the key in the lock and swung open the door. 'Inside,' she said. 'Before I kick you in.'

He flicked her on the nose. 'Just testing your mental resources.'

'It's you that needs your head examining,' she joked as they clambered through the horizontal doors.

A few minutes later, to the accompaniment of a raucous bellowing and chuffing sound, the TARDIS dematerialized.

Epilogue:

Bernice had collapsed shortly after the TARDIS's departure from Sakkrat. The Doctor had proved to be the perfect doctor, administering the course of decontaminant drugs skilfully and without complaint. Her admiration for him grew even more.

The treatment lasted several nasty days, during which her perceptions played dirty tricks. At one point, she saw the ceiling of her room doing a Mexican wave down at her.

The Doctor had got himself cleaned up and entered her room on the third day of treatment in his usual spotless outfit, complete with hat. Either he had a whole rack of identical clothes somewhere aboard, or he knew the best dry cleaner in space.

As her senses returned, he lent her a long and depressing book about Checkley's World. It had been destroyed in a misdirected missile attack in some skirmish or other, long before its optimisitic controllers anticipated its end.

She spent the next few days updating her neglected diary.

A week after leaving Sakkrat, Bernice returned to the control room with a new spring in her step and a clear head. A chessboard was set up in one corner. The Doctor congratulated her and suggested that she wrap up warmly because he was going to treat her to a special trip.

The TARDIS materialized a few hours later and the Doctor and Bernice disembarked. Behind them, the ceiling did another Mexican wave.

The Doctor threw another stone up at the window of 52 Tavistock Square. 'Out,' he sighed. 'Typical.'

He turned to Bernice, who had gone to buy a newspaper from a nearby stand. 'I was sure she'd be in.'

Bernice smiled forgivingly. 'Never mind,' she said and waved the paper at him. 'Anyway, I'm not surprised. You got the year right, 1935, but it's August.' She shook off her heavy coat. 'The Woolfs will be at Monk's House.'

'Sometimes I wish I'd had a classical education,' said the Doctor as they walked back to the TARDIS. 'You seem to have the poor woman's movements completely catalogued.'

'It was my year twelve assignment, I had to learn it.'

'How about,' the Doctor began as they reached the TARDIS, 'a trip to theatreland?' He pointed south.

Bernice smiled. 'Why not?'

Bernice stifled a yawn. The play the Doctor had chosen was a light romantic comedy packed with colloquialisms that were completely beyond her. The acting was stilted and the situation banal and predictable.

She glanced over at the Doctor. He had chuckled politely at the first few witticisms but had withdrawn slowly into his private universe as the evening wore on.

He tipped out on to his lap the bag of wine gums he had purchased in the foyer, held each one up to the light from the stage to determine its appearance, and then arranged them into ranks — depending on colour and shape — on his knee. Only the Doctor, thought Bernice, could treat the opening of a bag of sweets like a military exercise. Irritatingly, he showed no sign of eating them.

Her mind wandered back to their experiences on Sakkrat, or Hogsumm, or whatever it was called. Sendei's face was the memory that would remain with her the longest. As the band struck up a jaunty, trite theme to announce the interval, she thought of Zagrat, Saccrat, Ssaa Kraat and coincidence, the phenomenon that had seeded the meaningless legend of Sakkrat halfway across the galaxy and brought Sheldukher to his doom. Maybe, she thought, if you could connect up all of the trivial, meaningless coincidences in the universe like that, they might form some kind of logical pattern.

She had to dig her fingers into the red velvet of her arm rest to remind herself she was still in the same universe as Sakkrat. Time travel could get to you like that. It might even send her as loopy as the Doctor, one day.

The interval saw them in the crowded, smokey bar adjacent

to the auditorium. Bernice knocked back a white wine while the Doctor sipped at a glass of water.

'I'm bored,' she said at last.

'Are you? Oh good,' said the Doctor, sliding from his bar-stool. 'Let's go and meet the three-eyed Toad People of Miradilus Four.'

They pushed their way through the crowd and out into the street. A musical instrument Bernice could not identify was playing somewhere near, but out of sight. It was a quarter to nine, and the early evening sunlight had given way to a warm, welcoming dusk.

They turned the corner into Tavistock Square. The TARDIS had disappeared, to the Doctor's irritation and Bernice's alarm. She found it outside the British Museum half an hour later.

'This thing needs a service,' she told the Doctor as they entered.

'It is in perfect working order,' the Doctor replied testily.

'Sure,' said Bernice. 'Sure.'

The play ended. Gustaf Urnst, possessor (or so he thought) of the most terrible secret in the galaxy, clapped heartily along with the rest of the audience, although as a citizen of the early twenty-fifth century, many of the jokes had meant little to him.

It had been six months since those strange blue lights had transported him back in time. He was fitting in well (or so he thought).

He looked around the audience for that peculiar couple he'd glimpsed in the bar during the interval. They had the look of travellers about them. He could have sworn he'd heard the man mention the three-eyed Toad People of Miradilus Four. No, of course not. Even if he had, it must have just been coincidence. Nobody in 1935 could know that there really were such creatures.

He slipped out into the night and set off for his lodgings. The stars were out. He gazed up at a particular cluster. 'Miradilus Four . . . '

A clock struck ten. Well, he thought, they looked harmless enough and he wished them well. Wherever they were going.

THE DOCTOR'S ADVENTURES CONTINUE IN DOCTOR WHO MAGAZINE

Every issue of *Doctor Who Magazine* is packed with new stories, archives, news and features about the world's longest running SF television programme. Special reports cover subjects such as new books — including the New Adventures — visual effects, design, writers and new merchandise.

For full details of the latest subscription details and other Marvel *Doctor Who* products, write to: *Doctor Who Magazine* Subscriptions, PO Box 500, Leicester, Great Britian LE99 0AA.